SOMETHING ON YOUR MIND

George Morris De'Ath

This book is a work of fiction. Any references to historical events, real people, or real places are used fictitiously. Other names, characters, places, and events are products of the author's imagination, and any resemblance to actual events, places, names, or persons, is entirely coincidental.

Interior Graphic Novel illustration by Tiffany Baxter
www.tiffanybaxter.com

Distributed by Simon & Schuster

ISBN: 978-1-998672-18-9
Ebook: 978-1-998672-19-6

FIC031080 - Thrillers/Psychological
FIC015050 - Horror/Psychological
FIC071000 - Friendship

#SomethingOnYourMind

Follow Rising Action on our socials!
Twitter: @RAPubCollective
Instagram: @risingactionpublishingco
Tiktok: @risingactionpublishingco

SOMETHING ON YOUR MIND

PROLOGUE

Panic-stricken, the girl inhaled the thick, suffocating air, her breath ragged. She glanced around. She was alone. She'd escaped death before, relying on luck and the misfortune of others. This time, the monster was closing in. Every second felt like her last.

From the bathroom she stood in, a crash echoed from another room, sending cockroaches scurrying up dirtied white tiles. Heart racing, she crept toward the door. Her path was clear, but as she neared, doors slammed shut, one after another, snuffing out her only hope. Desperation fuelled her as she spotted a distant door glowing faintly—a glimmer of escape.

But as she ran toward it, the house trembled, and the air grew thick with dread. She risked a look over her shoulder—a shadow darkened the floor behind her. The Hollow Man had arrived. His ghoulish silhouette emerged, a grotesque grin, eyes hollow, teeth jagged. He was closing in with every thunderclap, each flash of lightning.

The girl sprinted for the last door. Inches from safety, she leaped through, slamming it shut just as the Hollow Man reached her. Silence fell, but the peace was short-lived. The door began to rumble, glowing crimson. The trumpet-like sound of the Hollow Man's presence filled the room. With a crash, the door flew open, and the monster emerged, unblinking.

She scooped a rusty pipe from the floor. She swung at him, but he vanished. Cold dread crawled up her spine. From behind, the gnashing of his teeth chattered, and she turned to face her doom. Clawed hands reached for her.

Then, an abrupt squeal. The scene froze.

Theo, a small boy, curled up on the couch, his blue eyes wide with fear as the Hollow Man loomed on screen. Carl, his father, sat beside him. He put his bottled beer down on the side table, using a vintage record, *Rhythm of Life*, as a coaster. He didn't want to leave any marks to upset his wife when she returned from her much-needed night out. Carl put his arm around Theo's shaking shoulders.

"Hey, T-Man, calm down," Carl said, ruffling Theo's hair. "Is it the bad writing or the monster that's got you spooked?"

Theo pointed at the screen. "The Hollow Man."

"Ah, he's not real," Carl chuckled. "But if I were your age, he'd scare me too. Those teeth? He definitely needs a dentist."

Theo hesitated. "He … he just scares me."

Carl's face softened. "I get it. But you know what? The girl on screen—she didn't run away. She fought back. Never run from fear, kiddo. You face it head-on. My mom always said, 'You fight with everything you've got.'"

Theo nodded slowly, still unsure. "I understand."

Carl smiled and squeezed his son's shoulder. "That's my boy. And remember—never run away. Kick fear's ass."

Theo grinned. "Kick its ass."

"Exactly!" Carl laughed. "Now, if your mom asks, this was educational. And don't you dare let your mom know I let you swear!"

Theo let out a mischievous laugh. "I won't."

"That's my boy." Carl smiled as he ruffled his son's golden hair. He looked down at his son. "My beautiful boy," he said.

Later that evening, Theo climbed into his pirate-themed bed and cuddled up with his stuffed toy rabbit, Binky, as his father turned on the starry, rotating night light. The dim glow reached the towering stacks of comics piled high around the room. Theo never liked bedtime; he had an unquiet mind with far too active an imagination, as proved by the doodles and drawings dotted around his room. Carl began to tuck his son into bed.

"Can I stay up a little longer? Can you read *Alice in Wonderland?*" he asked.

Carl chuckled. "It's too late already. If Mommy finds out I let you stay up this late, she's gonna kill me. That's if the Hollow Man doesn't get me first," he said with a macabre grin.

"Really?" Theo said, furrowing his brows.

Carl shook with laughter. "No! Not really. Come on. I'm only joking. I promise you no Hollow Man will kill me tonight … or ever! But Mommy might if you don't go to sleep."

The boy sighed.

"Now get some rest." Carl kissed his son's head. "You're not gonna make me check under your bed or in the closet to make sure there's no Hollow Men waiting to get you?"

"Nah. I'm good," Theo said bravely. "I've got Binky and, like you said, Dad, the Hollow Man's not real." He squeezed his stuffed toy.

Carl smiled. "Damn right. And I won't let anything happen to my right-hand man, and neither will Binky. Now rest up. We gotta be up early tomorrow to get to your Little League game. Night, T-Man."

"Night, Dad. Love you."

"You too, Theo." Carl turned out the light and shut the door.

Golden stars spun around the room in time with the lamp's squeaky rotations. Shadows of claw-like branches encroached from outdoors, moving the breeze. The branches grew closer and closer to Theo, who had wrapped himself up in his blankets for protection. Theo finally shut his eyes, beginning to drift, until he heard a knock. His heart raced and his eyes popped open. Another knock. From the closet.

The door trembled, and a red glow seeped out from below. The Hollow Man's trumpet echoed, and Theo froze. The trumpet calls beckoned louder and louder, along with the knocks. The red glow increased along with the noise. And then it all stopped. The red neon flickered back to darkness, to normal.

Unfamiliar noises emerged, each with a different tone.

Cartoonish. *ZAP! POW! SPLAT! BANG! CRACK! KAPOW! WHAM! CLANG! KA-BOOM! SMASH! CRASH!* Then, silence.

The closet door creaked open. A red ball rolled out. Then, two glowing yellow eyes appeared, locking onto Theo. He screamed, retreating under the covers.

"Hiya, kiddo," a playful voice called.

Theo lowered his covers to see a strange boy on a small bike, his limbs looking slightly longer than they should. His eyes, initially demonic yellow, changed to vibrant green as he stepped into the light. The boy smiled mischievously. "I'm Frank. Your imaginary friend."

Theo cocked his head. "You're my … imaginary friend?"

"Yep! And I just kicked that Hollow Man's ugly butt out of your closet. You're safe now."

Theo, still uneasy, asked, "Can't my dad protect me?"

Frank grinned. "Not always. But I'm here when he's not. To protect you, help you, guide you."

Theo, cautiously, shook Frank's hand. "Help me with what?"

Frank winked. "With whatever you need, kid. Together, we're gonna be unstoppable."

The boy led Theo to the mirror. "What do you see?" Frank asked.

"Me," Theo said.

"Exactly. A blank slate. You and me, kid—we're gonna do great things. We're gonna give this world what it deserves. It's our playground. I tell ya, we are gonna have so much fun together."

Theo looked around for his missing stuffed rabbit, Binky. Frank snapped his fingers and produced it.

"There it is! There's that smile"," Frank said, handing it over. "You're destined for greatness, Theo. I'll help you get there."

He pinched Theo's plump cheeks. This 'friend' seemed to know how to hum the right tune, much like the Pied Piper's; it was catchy and somewhat melodic. "You're destined for great things. I can tell; I can always tell!" Frank continued. "I can feel the potential bubbling inside of you. Oh, you are to be a vital part of the grand puzzle, methinks. A future big player in the game of life, and I'm gonna help you get there." His fingers danced with excitement.

Theo sighed. "But I don't understand. None of this makes any sense."

"Nothing makes sense until it does."

"What do you mean?"

Frank tucked Theo back into bed. "Sleep now. I'll protect you. No monsters tonight."

As Theo closed his eyes, the last thing he heard was Frank's voice. "Nothing's gonna harm you, not while I'm around," he said, stroking the innocent boy's hair until he fell asleep.

Frank watched until Theo snored softly, a mischievous grin on his face. "Now … what should I do with you?" he said.

CHAPTER ONE

OLD FRIENDS NOT FORGOTTEN

Seventeen Years Later

Time trickles by, slipping through fingers like sand. An hourglass. Inevitable. Everything has a time to live and a time to die for Theo Gray, and time ticked by faster than he realized. The years had rolled by, and the trips he had travelled around the sun were many. At the young age of twenty-three, having lived through a childhood of mischief and fun, an education of struggle and hard work, and now working at a local bar, he realized life could be very disappointing and repetitive. Full of heartbreak. As he gazed down at his father's coffin, a sense of futility came over him. A heart attack took Carl, the doctors said. But, truthfully, it was time that was responsible.

Theo regretted wasting the time he had with his father. All the arguments, the petty squabbles over the dishwasher or his teenage curfews, he now realized were so insignificant. Because, at the end, it wasn't the bad times Theo thought of, it was the good. The late movie nights, the grilled cheese sandwiches, ball games in the park, long drives to places with the radio blaring. Theo loved the time he had spent with his father, and he always would, and he would always miss it. Now it was the time to let go and move on, but how could he? His grief had swallowed him up whole.

Memories were all he had. As he stared around the dank cemetery, he wiped quickly at his eyes. Theo's Aunt Penny sang a blissful rendition of "Amazing Grace" in tribute to her cherished brother. Through his sorrow, Theo could see many people mourning the loss of Carl Gray. Some he knew, most he didn't.

They came to Theo afterward, telling him of the favours his father did for them out of casual kindness and compassion. These were people his father had never mentioned. They all seemed to blur together. One after another, they praised him. The great Carl Gray, as if he were another man that Theo and his mother had never known. A different side to him was revealed. He was a saviour, administering random acts of kindness in the world, and he didn't want credit, or glory, or praise in return. He seemed to do it because it was the right thing to do. The realization sat at the bottom of Theo's stomach like a stone, weighing on him. Everyone loved his father. Everyone loved Carl Gray, and Theo believed he could never live up to his legacy.

A drizzle of rain formed droplets that ran down his father's black-and-white-framed image. Whistling wind blew through Theo's blazer, rattling the camera around his neck, his most prized possession, a gift from his father after his graduation. Many a snapshot and candid image he had captured on that heavy piece of equipment over the years. A DSLR camera, to be exact, professional, slick, and very expensive. Theo knew that much, but also that it was the best, which is precisely what his father wanted for him. Theo decided that if the moment had been a movie scene, the colour palette would be perfect for the image he envisioned. The setting displayed the mood perfectly; the colour conveyed the depressing mood. Grey was often associated with gloominess, something the day was soaked in. Theo's personal love and study of movies, mixed with his genuine passion for photography, would not go to waste, he promised himself, looking down at his father's grave. He inhaled, then lifted his camera to get a quick shot of the image before him, to immortalize it in his personal gallery of life he had set up at home. Memories were all he had, though some were blurred, especially from when he was a child.

Photos helped him ground the reality of his past and keep track of all the places he had been. Adjusting the focus and angle, Theo pressed the button. Looking down, he saw the image he took on the small screen. It was perfect. So much pain, so much grief, so much anguish, all within one image. It was raw and unedited, natural. It told a story within a brief shot of history. People looked at him as if he were some freak for taking a picture of his father's funeral. Maybe he was a freak, but he recognized the action needed context. His father would have understood: to him, it was a way of immortalizing his father. Photos were the physical representations of memories; everyone knew that, but few wished to memorialize their pain.

He gazed at the sky only to feel something he hadn't in many years. The clouds formed two gigantic eyes, watching him. It was like something out of a dream or nightmare. He shook his head—nothing but a trick of the mind, paranoia. He didn't understand the psychology of how his brain worked. Hell, he didn't want to know. Instinctively, he reached down to his 'special pills' bottle in his pocket and pulled it out. He'd been on them since he was a child. He couldn't remember what they were for exactly, but they helped ground him. Much like his photography, they made him focus and chill. Leaning a hand out, he rattled the plastic canister and popped out a small, singular shamrock capsule, rolling it in his hand. He swallowed it whole before returning the small bottle into his blazer pocket before anyone saw.

"Hey, man," a familiar voice called out.

Theo turned to see his childhood friend, Steve Scott, standing tall, rugged and strong, his muscles hidden beneath a black memorial blazer and crisp white shirt. The typical high school jock, only without the ego. He hadn't heard from him in a few months, not since Steve sent him a generic meme to show he was still there, and that he existed.

"Steve! You're back?" Theo replied, wiping away his tears and adjusting the tight tie he had borne all day like a hangman's noose. "What a surprise." He embraced his old friend, shifting his camera out of the way of their chests so as not to crush it, his heart and soul.

"I know, time flies," Steve remarked, patting his old partner in crime's back. "Only got back Monday; I graduated from Elon on Saturday."

Theo nodded, smiling. "Yeah, I saw the pictures on Facebook."

Steve's legs widened, and he put his hands in his pockets. "It was a pretty good day." He looked around. "Listen, I'm so sorry about … well, this."

Theo looked away for a moment. "Thanks, I-I appreciate it, really."

"He was a good guy."

"Yeah, he really was."

"Hey, what's up, bitch!" another voice called out. This one was also male, not as deep, but no less intense. More uniquely charming, in a zany way. It was another of Theo's childhood friends. One he had seen recently on shift at the bar where he worked: James Johnson. More commonly known as JJ Mooney, a nickname he gained at school for mooning the principal after he refused to cancel school on a snowy day. His slender appearance and unique swagger were heightened by his dark, bouffant hair, red floral bomber jacket, skinny jeans, and boots. He took a sip from a large, blue slushy, sucking every drop along the way as he approached. Their entire old school gang accompanied him.

The preppy, positive, and conventionally perfect Amber Cross bounced toward them, wearing a chic, houndstooth-patterned dress. Her Stepford Wife blonde hair was styled in ringlets, and her lips were perfectly pink and pouted like a spring flower. Just like in high school, her ruler-straight posture and refined mannerisms suggested wealth, which Theo recalled all too well she had. Amber always had a sense of opulence about her, as was intended. She carried a Tupperware box of baked goods.

At her side stood the sassy Tabitha Martin, wearing a leather biker jacket. Her umber skin was as clear as her sharp and witty comebacks. She sported a new hairstyle of thick, black locs, which she wore up in a tight bun. It was a striking, fresh look, which Theo knew was intentional. *She looks good*, Theo thought.

And, last, the socially awkward tech genius, Ishaan Bathla, arrived in a creased shirt. He had thin, round glasses which he constantly cleaned and readjusted. A bottle of hand sanitizer poked out of his trouser pocket; he had always been a germaphobe. Ishaan was shy, yet loyal and interesting to talk to when given the chance, though his stutter sometimes made that hard work.

Seeing them reunited lit a spark deep inside of Theo. His synapses flared. Was it nostalgia or the pill he had just taken? Whatever it was, it warmed him deeply. "Wow! You're all here." His face stretched into a smile. "This is crazy! I haven't seen any of you in ages," he said, looking at Amber. He noticed a difference in her but could not pinpoint it. She seemed more vibrant somehow. "Amber, you look so different."

"Ha! Yes, well, good-different I hope." She laughed cheerily.

"Yeah, you look great," he assured her.

"And me too," JJ said.

Theo spun around and grinned. "J, you always look great!"

"Don't encourage him," Tabitha said with a snigger.

"Oh, he doesn't need encouragement"," Theo snarked.

"Never has. Never will," JJ said, slurping his sugary blue drink.

"How are you doing anyway, hun?" Tabitha asked. "With all of this?" She waved a manicured hand.

"Yeah, I'm alright, it's just coming to grips with it all, you know." Theo scratched his neck. "It hits you hard."

"Well, you know we are all here for you," Amber said truthfully, laying a delicate hand on his shoulder.

"Of course we are. How's Momma Gray doing?" Tabitha asked, in concern.

Theo's gaze turned to his mother, Julie, who was speaking to some people. "Not great, obviously, but she will cope. Given time."

"Well, I made you and Julie some cookies, a mixture of chocolate chip, double chocolate chip, and oatmeal raisin. I made more double chocolate chips because I remembered that they were always your favourite." Amber carefully passed the box of treats to Theo.

Theo clamped the cookie box tightly. "Thanks, Ambz, that's so sweet." It had been a running gag between them about what an awful baker she was, though they never had the heart to tell her so. He mustered a grin, which Amber took as appreciation.

"Anything to help."

"Speaking of which," Steve said, "we were wondering if you wanted to get something to eat with us all later; our treat, of course?" A reassuring nudge accompanied his offer.

"Yeah, might cheer you up, homeboy," Tabitha remarked. "The old gang is back together again."

"One big happy re-reunion," Ishaan said quickly, as if anxious to join in the conversation. His stutter remained as pronounced as it always had been. He paused. "Well, not happy given the circumstances but—"

"Stop talking," Tabitha whispered in his ear loudly as she rubbed his back.

"So … what do ya say?" JJ winked.

Theo laughed. His spirit lifted. He had missed all of them. Truly, as one door shut, another opened. His gaze moved over their faces. "Yeah, sure. What time?"

Two Hours Later

Outrageous laughter came from the corner of Deeny's Diner, a 1950s-style Americana joint Theo often visited with his dad. The gangwas sprawled across a booth, the table littered with cold plates of burgers, fries, and onion rings. Deeny's burgers were legendary in Camton, Maine, and the place was a local favourite.

Tabitha screeched with laughter. "Ah, that was hilarious!" she said, picking at her fries.

Steve shook his head, smirking. "I can't believe you actually did it."

JJ leaned back, grinning. "I don't back down from a dare. You know me." He paused, sipping his drink. "I was one of the few who wasn't afraid to get detention."

"Yeah, but following the principal home in a cardboard box? C'mon, man." Theo laughed.

JJ shrugged. "It's called being ballsy."

"More like mentally unstable," Steve quipped.

JJ's brows rose. "Well, you know what they say, crazy is the new sexy." He winked with exaggeration at Tabitha, who sat opposite.

Tabitha scoffed. "Only to you."

JJ smiled. "What can I say? I don't follow rules. I'm confident, smart, ambitious, resourceful, handsome, transcending … a true winner!"

"Sure," Steve said, laughing.

The banter flowed freely, pulling Theo into the moment. His camera was tucked away, but the nostalgia felt good, at least for now. The laughter had a way of hiding the things they didn't talk about.

"Remember when we were all on the trampoline, and we sent Ishaan flying like seventeen feet into the air?" Theo grinned, trying to spark more light-hearted memories.

"Yeah!" JJ laughed. "It was like we all froze, like, oh shit."

Ishaan blushed, adjusting his glasses. "Y-you guys were always stealing my bounces."

"Yeah, so… fight me," JJ said with a playful challenge.

Ishaan's frown deepened. "Always double bo-bouncing," he muttered to himself.

"Remember when your dad chased us with the hose in the garden?" Steve said, clearly relishing the memory.

"Yes!" Tabitha said, her eyes wide. "And then we got the water balloons and water guns out, didn't we? Your mom joined in."

"That was a day," Ishaan chimed in, his voice rising with excitement. "Teams were me, J, Steve, and your mo-mom, against Theo, Tabz, Ambz, and your dad."

"We won," JJ said with pride.

"Cheated," Ishaan muttered.

"How?"

"You turned the sprinklers on," Ishaan said, sliding his glasses back on.

"Strategic genius," JJ shot back, almost spitting up his drink.

Theo smiled, caught up in the easy camaraderie. But his smile faltered as Steve's voice softened.

"He was a good man," Steve said, his tone hushed.

The table fell silent for a moment, the weight of Theo's father's passing settling over them. Theo's chest tightened, and he bit back the lump in his throat.

"Let's toast to him," Tabitha said, breaking the tension. She raised her lemonade. "To Daddy Gray. One of the most badass white men to ever walk the earth, and a hell of a pancake maker."

"To Carl!" they all cheered, except Theo, who smiled faintly.

"Thanks, guys," he murmured.

The silence lingered, but soon enough, Tabitha spoke, "Hey, do you guys remember Sophie Hadish?" Tabitha asked. "I saw her in the doc's waiting room the other day. She has aged awfully. She looks like some sorta Louis Vuitton overnight bag now."

"I can imagine she was never a prize pig, let's face it," JJ replied, unsurprised.

"Yeah, yet she used to get through the boys at school—like tissues," Tabitha said.

"What blow and bin?" Steve joked.

"Ha! Yes!" Tabitha laughed.

JJ giggled at Steve. "That was a good one … for you."

"Aw! Thanks!"

"Anyway," Tabitha continued, "she was telling me how she's pregnant and engaged, and I was like, wow, okay girl! I mean, don't you think that's weird? She's twenty-three; we are all the same age. I mean …"

"Yeah, who wants to settle down this early?" Theo said.

Steve scratched his neck. "Maybe in a few years, yes, but not right now."

"Yeah, I mean, *this* girl wants to go out and see the world before starting a family and shit," Tabitha said, tensing her jaw.

"Yeah! I want to d-do something with my life," said Ishaan. "Have a ca-career before all that."

"Definitely, need to make some money before I have kids." JJ leaned back and burped. "But let's not talk about birth blobs, what about dates?"

"Theo, I can't remember; did you get a lot of dates at school?" Tabitha asked.

Theo blinked, slightly caught off guard. "Uh, some? I guess five or six?"

Tabitha raised an eyebrow. "Really? I don't remember that."

JJ grinned. "Of course, you were too busy with your whole 'I'm a rebel' thing."

"I remember you, Ambz," Theo said, shifting the conversation away from himself. "You weren't allowed to date."

Amber rolled her eyes. "Yeah, my parents were super strict about it."

"Did you ever date?" Steve asked, turning to Tabitha.

"I had a few boyfriends," she said, a dreamy look in her eyes. "Stevie Harries was the best. We were like … perfect for each other."

Steve quickly diverted the conversation. "Moving on! Ishaan, have you ever dated?"

Ishaan blushed a deep red. "N-not really. I was more focused on my grades."

"We'll fix that for you," JJ said with a grin. "A makeover, get you on the scene!"

"I don't know, that's all a bit fast," Ishaan said, eyes wide, mouth gaping.

"No, no," Tabitha teased, pulling her phone out. "It'll be fun. We'll hook you up."

Theo shifted in his seat, his hand grazing the pill bottle in his blazer pocket. He had no idea how he felt about all this. They were all talking about love and relationships, while he was stuck with his grief and confusion.

He absentmindedly glanced out the window and froze. There, in the alley, was the exact figure he'd seen in his childhood—pale, hollow-eyed, and grinning with sharp teeth. The trumpet music began, sending a chill through him. The nightmare he thought he'd left behind had found him again. The Hollow Man had come. Theo froze, rigid like drying cement until he felt cracks form as a shiver rattled down his spine.

"What's up, Theo?" JJ's voice cut through the fog of his mind.

"Huh?" Theo snapped back to the group, feeling the weight of their stares. "Sorry, just … lost my train of thought."

JJ smirked. "Too busy staring at the rain, huh?"

"Yeah …" Theo said, shaking his head slightly, trying to clear the fog, only to see nothing on the street now. He placed his hand over the pill bottle in his pocket, resisting the urge to take one.

Amber's voice brought him back. "I feel like we're all stuck in limbo right now, just floating through our twenties. We can't go back, but we're not really moving forward either. It's like purgatory, don't you think?"

Theo's stomach twisted. She was right. He was stuck. But he didn't know how to move forward.

Steve's tone shifted. "Yeah, like we're waiting for something big to happen, but it just doesn't."

Tabitha shifted in her seat, throwing a grin at the group. "Well, we just have to keep going, right? College isn't for everyone. We all figure it out eventually."

"Just gotta hit your stride," Steve added, as if trying to reassure Theo.

But Theo didn't feel like he had a stride. He was still stuck. He looked at his friends, realizing how much he missed this—how much he needed this. But the hollow eyes of that figure haunted him, even during their laughter.

Theo sat still, looking around at his friends. They had all changed, but in some ways, they were still the same. He smiled to himself, the warmth of their company wrapping around him, even if only for a moment.

"Guess we'll see where life takes us," Steve said, lifting his glass.

"To the future," they all said, clinking glasses.

Theo raised his own drink, but his mind wandered. Was he even going anywhere? Or was he just stuck in the past, clinging to memories of things that could never return?

The night ended with laughs and farewells, but as Theo walked home, a deep sense of unease settled over him. His childhood friends might have been with him tonight, but something darker, something older, had reappeared. And Theo didn't know if he'd ever be able to outrun it.

A lightness had come over Steve after the meeting, a warmth settling in his chest. He had reconnected with his old friends and, in doing so, had rediscovered a part of himself he hadn't realized he missed. People often flocked to him because of his appearance, but his friends saw past that. They knew him. It was a rare feeling of being truly seen. As he passed two drunk women on the street, their catcalls didn't touch him. He was whole again.

When he got home, Bella the dog greeted him with her usual enthusiasm. "Hey, Bella boo." Steve smiled, petting her. His mom emerged in a fluffy dressing gown, asking about his night. "It was good," he replied. "Nice to see everyone."

His mom had left him a turkey sandwich in the kitchen. "Cut off the crusts too," she added. She always made sure he was well taken care of. He ate it with a smile, knowing that this warmth was something money couldn't buy. His friends were back, and for once, he felt truly at home.

Ishaan hobbled down the track, his mind still buzzing from the reunion. For too long, he'd buried himself in books and grades, but now, he remembered what it felt like to laugh and have fun. He was uncertain about the future—his parents expected him to focus, but his friends had reminded him of something more critical: balance.

At home, the house was dark, and the only light came from his phone's screen as he scrolled through pictures of the diner meet-up. He had been tagged, and for the first time in a long while, he laughed. But even as he smiled, his thoughts were clouded by running over moments of stuttering and his usual self-doubt. Would they accept him for who he was now? Or had he already missed his chance to reconnect? He stared at his latest Lego creation, a palace he'd built brick by brick. Maybe he could do the same with his friends—slowly, piece by piece.

Tabitha was fiercely independent—she had to be. Raised in a tough neighbourhood with little support, she'd built herself up into a woman who could stand alone—tonight had been a success, reuniting with the gang that knew her better than anyone. They'd clicked like no time had passed, like they were family. But when she arrived home, reality hit.

Her mother, flustered and stressed, shoved a baby in her arms. "Watch Milo while I deal with the other two," she demanded.

Tabitha grunted, irritated. "Why can't Jerome do it?"

Her mother's response was a glare. "Just do it."

Tabitha sighed and took the baby, sitting down on the couch and stroking his head. "You and me, Milo," she whispered. "We'll get out of here one day."

JJ, as always, wore a mask. He had perfected it over the years, hiding his insecurities behind wild clothes and a loud personality. Yet something about Steve's presence tonight unsettled him—there was a flicker of jealousy, of old competition.

He parked his old, damaged, and scratched Mercury Sable Wagon car, 'Big Bertha,' badly across the drive. JJ almost fell out of the door and locked up. His house was in darkness, undisturbed. No lights were on. Stepping onto the porch, each step creaked the wood below, as if in pain. His bomber jacket shimmered in the dim light. His Cuban boots brushed the doormat, which read: 'You better have beer or pizza.' He turned the cold doorknob, opening the door only to meet the image of his deceased mother, framed and smiling at him from the side table. He shared her brunette locks, sharp jawline, and large, penetrating eyes. Looks-wise, he could see what he had inherited from her, but in terms of personality and traits, he would never know. He gazed at her, wishing things could have turned out differently. He wished he could have known her. What he would give to have just five minutes with her.

A hand grabbed him by the neck and threw him up against the wall. "Where the hell have you been?" A menacing figure loomed out of the shadows, towering over him: his father, Jim Johnson.

"Out with my friends," JJ choked out the words, gasping for air. "I told you earlier!"

Jim slammed his son's head against the wall. "Don't you dare talk to me like that!" he shouted.

JJ struggled to breathe. "I'm not talking to you; I'm answering your question."

A second later, a hand slapped JJ across the face. The young man fell to the ground hard, scrambling in the dark, rubbing his neck, gasping for air. The sting on his left cheek burned hot.

"You will show me respect, boy!" Jim hissed. "So, help me God, you will show me respect." His hands shook.

JJ clambered up, resting an arm on a table beside him. His nose was bleeding. "How can I respect a douche who slaps his own son?"

A knee to his gut followed the slap. JJ keeled over in pain, clutching his stomach.

Jim glared down at his son. "Look at you, going out dressed like that, flouncing about; you're an embarrassment to me and your mother." He looked his son up and down in disgust and left the room, slamming the door behind him.

JJ endeavoured to stay conscious. Droplets of blood trickled onto the floor, soaking into the wood, staining it. *Red was always my colour.* His breathing became wheezy. His chest rattled like a can. He looked back up at his mother's photo in the moonlight. He didn't know her, but he knew she loved him or, rather, would have. Yes, JJ was a simple guy. He knew how to get what he wanted and now he had his friends back. What more could he want?

Amber walked into her family's mansion, a feeling of warmth

enveloping her. Walking into the living room, she saw her parents sitting, sharing a drink and watching TV. Amber entered with a fluttering smile, but it wasn't long before her mother's sharp voice cut through, "What time do you call this? And what are you wearing?" Her mother, Vanessa, sneered at her dress.

Amber was used to it and ignored her.

"I like it," her father chimed in.

Vanessa shot him a withering look. "Stop coddling her."

Amber sighed, the sting of criticism too familiar. She retreated upstairs, tears welling up as she closed the door. Her mother's voice rang in her ears: "You could be so much more." Amber realized she no longer wanted to be a prize, something to be picked from the bunch. But would she ever have the courage to live on her terms?

Theo returned home after a day full of emotional highs and lows. The dinner had been nice, but the pain from his past was still lingering. As he entered the kitchen, his mother was holding Carl's photo, her eyes red from crying. She looked up at him, trying to hide her tears. "How was dinner?"

"It was good," Theo replied, his heart heavy with conflicting emotions. "Nice to see everyone."

His mother laughed through her tears. "Your aunt and I cried … and ate Chinese food," she joked, but Theo could see the hurt in her eyes. He went over to comfort her, rubbing her back as she wiped away her tears. "I'll be okay, sweetie," she whispered.

Theo headed up to bed, knowing his mother wasn't as fine as she let on. But what could he do? He didn't know how to help her, and he didn't know how to help himself either. The night ended with the sound of his mother's quiet sobs drifting up the stairs.

CHAPTER TWO

AN UNEXPECTED RETURN

Sock-covered toes squished on the plush carpet, giving him the sensation of walking through deep snow. Theo's gaze grew foggy as he moved through the black hallway to his bedroom, his safe space—the one area of his life he could control. A sharp pain stabbed into his left temple, deep, vibrating like someone swirling spaghetti in his skull. He stumbled toward his room, shutting the door with effort and locking it.

Overwhelmed by physical and emotional pain, he wobbled slightly as he removed the camera from around his neck, placing it gently on his desk. He bent down to plug in his phone, then set his wallet and pill bottle on his bedside table. The floor seemed to wobble beneath him as he collapsed onto his bed.

The room spun. The movie posters blurred, his ornaments and comic books fizzled out of sight, and the small apple tree his father had surprised him with on one birthday had disappeared. He opened his eyes to see his father's smiling face in a photo. Wincing, he turned the frame face down and pushed it away.

Theo lay still, but he realized something—he felt nothing. No sorrow, no depression. Only emptiness. He felt death, the cruel weight of it. Maybe he'd feel different after some rest. There had to be a morning after. He sighed and closed his eyes, letting the silence envelop him.

"You look so peaceful when you sleep," an old familiar voice called.

Theo's eyes snapped open. Frank stood behind him, his childhood imaginary friend, now a nightmare wrapped in a pretty bow. Dressed in a pinstriped vest and tie, he looked more androgynous than before.

"In fact, sleeping Theo is my favourite Theo," Frank teased with a theatrical wave.

Theo stared, eyes wide. "No. It can't be."

"Missed me?" Frank giggled. "You have, haven't you? Don't deny it; you can't hide it."

"Frank?" Theo rubbed his eyes.

"In the flesh. Well, figuratively."

"You can't be here," Theo said, panic creeping in.

"Why not? Is it because of your dead daddy issues? Or because we haven't seen each other in … how long has it been?" Frank's British accent was playful.

"Fourteen years."

"Oh, that's long! I know it's been a dog's age, but hey, I'm back now. We're back where we belong."

"And where's that?"

Frank leaned in close. "Together," he whispered before pulling back to look around the room. He turned his head to scan the movie posters, the apple tree, the camera, and the pile of smelly clothes. He picked up a sock and sniffed it with disgust.

Theo sat up and grabbed the pill bottle from his bedside table. He twisted the cap and shook out a single ruby pill, then quickly swallowed it.

"Ha! You think a little pill's gonna get rid of me?" Frank's dark eyes widened as he started doing a little jig. "You think that's why I left all those years ago? Because you started taking da dumb-dumb pills?"

Theo twisted the cap back on and placed the bottle down. "Okay, then tell me this—why now? Why come back after all these years?" Theo's voice shook as he glared at Frank.

Frank fiddled with an ornament. "I'm here to get you back on track, kid. I come when I'm needed. And right now, I'm needed." He grinned. "Plus, I know something you don't."

"What's that?"

Frank snapped his fingers. "You have a gift. A raw, untapped power. And more—rage, you don't even know how to control it … yet."

"A gift?" Theo frowned.

"That's right! You could do so much if you just allowed yourself to."

Theo paused, then laughed bitterly. "Listen, I'm nothing—a nobody. There's nothing special about me. And even if there was, I wouldn't know how to use it."

Frank grinned. "Well, that's why I'm here. To show you how. You've been living to live for far too long. It's time to grab life by the neck, kid. You're the master of your own fate. Time to stop playing second fiddle."

Theo snorted. "Why am I even having this conversation? This is all in my head. A delusion."

Frank grinned wider. "Ah, the egg thinks it's smarter than the chicken."

"I've grown up, Frank. I know this isn't real. You're not real."

"None of it is real," Frank said, gesturing to Theo. "The sadness, the boo-hoo. They're all masks. You're too smart for this, but you're trapped in here." He tapped Theo's forehead. "What I'm offering is the key."

Theo furrowed his brow. "What?"

"I've got big plans for you, kiddo. But I'm not spoiling the surprise. You really should get that headache checked out."

Theo had seen and heard enough. "Leave me alone."

"We're connected, kid. I'm a part of you. No 'alone' for us."

"Please, I don't care if you're real or not. Just go away."

"Fine, if that's what you want. But remember …" Frank paused, smiling. "It's better to walk with a friend in the dark than alone in the light. Get that headache checked out, will ya?" With a wave, Frank vanished.

Theo looked around. Frank was gone, but for how long? The unpredictability left him unsettled. As a child, he hadn't considered Frank's presence as an issue, but now, as an adult, the dangers of mental illness loomed. He wasn't normal, but neither were the best people throughout history—Picasso, Einstein. At least that's what he liked to tell himself in moments like these.

He glanced at his pill bottle. His entire childhood had been a lie. He'd been told he had an overactive imagination, then a sickness. The illness went, Frank left, and depression followed.

Even as a child, he'd known it wasn't normal to have Frank in his head. But with Frank, he never felt alone. Frank didn't feel like a delusion. He felt real, unlike most real people.

Without Frank, maybe that was why he'd spiralled. Maybe Frank had come back to help, even if just as a subconscious nudge. He would tell no one about this return. They'd think he was crazy, give him more meds, or worse. No. He'd bide his time and wait.

As his head sank back into the pillow, the searing pain flared again. Frank's words echoed in his mind: 'Get that headache checked out.'

Maybe he would.

CHAPTER THREE
SOMEBODY TELL ME IT GETS BETTER

Two Days Later

His palms were sweating, and one foot tapped continuously. Theo realized and stopped himself as he sat in the sterile, white doctor's office. His head still rang with a combination of hurt and pain—distinctly different in his mind.

Doctor Lee Garder, a middle-aged woman with a unique, friendly quality, sat across from him. She was the type of doctor who cared, got results, and got straight to the point, which was why Theo liked her—and why his father had trusted her for years. She'd been reviewing his medical history for a few moments now.

"So, you've been having these headaches for a few days?" she asked, adjusting her dark hair while still focused on the computer screen.

"Yeah," Theo said, noticing his own sweat.

Doctor Garder peered closer at the screen. "And are they constant?"

"Yes."

"They don't stop at all?" She frowned.

"Very rarely."

She turned back to him, crossing one leg over the other, studying his pale complexion. "And you said you're experiencing nausea, drowsiness, and vomiting?"

"Yes."

"When was the last time you vomited?"

"This morning."

"I see. Are you still taking your prescribed medication?" she asked, a hint of concern in her voice.

Theo instinctively clutched the pill bottle in his pocket. "Yes," he answered.

"Good." Doctor Garder typed notes into the computer, continuing to assess him.

Theo's attention drifted. He looked past her shoulder to the window and saw a familiar figure—Frank. Dressed in a purple leather coat, baggy trousers, and a white T-shirt, with ruffled dark hair and sunglasses, he was perched on a bin, grinning mischievously.

Theo snapped back to the room, breathing heavily.

"Have you been experiencing any other symptoms? Mood swings, forgetfulness, delusions?" Doctor Garder asked.

Theo glanced at the window again. Frank raised a finger to his lips.

"No. Do you mind if I…?" He stood and went over to the blinds, shutting them quickly, fighting the urge to look outside. "Sorry, I'm a little sensitive to light."

"That's okay."

Theo sat forward, his seat creaking under him. "Be honest with me—do you think it's something serious?"

Doctor Garder interlocked her fingers and gave him the warm, reassuring smile she had likely perfected for moments like this. "Honestly, it's unlikely. Ninety-nine percent of the time, it's something minor. But just to be safe, I'd like to run some tests next week."

Theo's bottom lip quivered slightly. "Okay."

She gave his shoulder a gentle pat. "We'll get to the bottom of this, I promise. Try not to worry."

Days rolled past, mornings turned into nights. Theo began his long journey of tests. The nurse played the radio loudly, *Perfect Day*, to distract him from any discomfort. Theo looked out the window at the rain cascading down the glass. He rolled up his sleeves and winced at the pressure of the needle sticking into him. As he sat in the chair, he thought of little, except what his friends might be doing right now, what adventures they could all be living out …

Ishaan sat in his gloomy room, reading text on his computer screen, diverting his attention from himself and toward knowledge and the promise of a career.

Tabitha's heels clicked a staccato beat on the salon floor as she swept up the day's leftover discarded hair. Seeing her reflection in a mirror, she paused and mused briefly, feeling disappointed with her life. Catching sight of her boss, she continued with her job.

JJ was up in the early hours of the morning to begin his shift. He wiped the surface of the bar with a dirty rag, lifting a sleeping man's head by his greasy hair to wipe beneath him.

Nail polish glistened on manicured hands. Amber was being dressed by her mother to make an impression. She looked at herself in the mirror, not quite sure what she wanted anymore. She recalled having to clean that same mirror daily back when she would imagine kissing Steve. Back then, when she shut her eyes and imagined, it felt real, if only for a second, and that was enough. Amber smiled as the serotonin hit her brain like a thunderclap, instantly recalling the scent of his aftershave. The thought soothed her, as her mother began to explain once more about the importance of good posture.

Steve found himself in the cold breath of night, leash in hand, as he walked Bella. Eyes admired him from every direction. The feeling should have made him feel good, but he felt nothing, not anymore. Just dead inside.

Meanwhile, Theo's knees were growing weaker as his headaches grew in strength. He tried meditating after reading about it online, to help soften the blows being dealt to his cranium, with little in terms of results, though he did feel it helped clear his mind from overthinking and de-stressing after late-night web searches of his symptoms.

Ishaan sat opposite his PlayStation, pausing his game to clean a speck of dust off his glasses, which took him twelve minutes to do, to make sure there weren't any smudges.

Tabitha found herself chasing children around the house, exhausted, as usual, while her mother tried to cook a chicken supper for them all.

JJ drove home, his fingers tapping the steering wheel to a natural beat.

Amber went on a blind date, one her mother had arranged, of course, but was not happy with the choice made for her.

Steve lifted weights while listening to music, plugged in, drowning all else out.

As Theo began his descent into the MRI machine, claustrophobia threatened. The experience made him feel as if he were in a coffin. Encaged, shackled, trapped. He imagined he was somewhere else, somewhere sunny and green, with his friends. He could see it so vividly in his mind's eye for the briefest of seconds.

Ishaan lounged on the couch, eating pizza after first sanitizing his hands with his little bottle of Purell. He sat in the dark watching a violent, gory, action-fest movie. He checked his phone and saw that he had no new messages.

Tabitha sank into her hot, soapy bath, exhausted, and checked her phone. There were no new messages.

Sneaking past an abusive, sleeping father. JJ had been through a long day and, frankly, was glad he didn't have to deal with one more alcoholic for the rest of the night. He sat down wearily and began eating toast alone in the kitchen, with no new messages to read.

Amber walked in and rushed upstairs without so much as a hello to anyone. She ran up to the bathroom and burst into tears. Seeing her reflection in the mirror, she remembered what her mother had always taught her: 'Even when we feel our worst, we have to put on a good face.' She looked down at her phone, a comfort. There were no new messages.

Steve grew bored of watching TV and eating junk food. He picked up his phone; no new notifications, that was dull. Maybe it was time for another get-together? Yes! He pondered what to write. And then he typed …

STEVE *has started a conversation*
STEVE: So who's up for getting hammered tomorrow night?
THEO: Me.
JJ: Me three.
AMBER: Me four? Is that how it works?
TABITHA: Thank God, thought you'd never ask!!! I need to get out of this house!!
STEVE SCOTT *has changed the group name to 'The Super Six'*
ISHAAN: I'm busy tomorrow night. Sorry :).
JJ: Useless hoe.
STEVE: Doing what?
ISHAAN: Stuff.
JJ *has changed the group name to 'The Super Five and Lousy One'*
TABITHA: What kind of stuff?
JJ: Naughty stuff?
ISHAAN: Just stuff.
JJ *changed* ISHAAN's *name to 'Useless Hoe'*
STEVE: You sure about that?
JJ: Would you like to call a friend? Ask the audience?
USELESS HOE: I'm just not in the mood.
THEO: Ah come on!!!
JJ: Yeah, don't be a useless hoe.
TABITHA: You gonna act like a lil bitch, cuz you're gonna die like a lil bitch.
USELESS HOE *has left the group chat.*
STEVE SCOTT *has added* ISHAAN BATHLA *to the group chat.*
STEVE SCOTT *has changed the group chat name to 'The Super Six'*
AMBER: Ignore J, Ishaan, he's the one being a useless hoe.
JJ: Hey! I may be a hoe, but I'm not useless!
THEO: This is a fact.
AMBER: Very true.
STEVE: Come on, Ishaan, come out, could be fun.
ISHAAN: I'll see.
STEVE: That a man! My dude!

THEO: So it's settled then!
TABITHA: Let's get drunk and slutty.
AMBER: Sure, it could be nice. The meet up, not the slutty drunk part.
JJ: Hallelujah! Praise Jesus! Let's speak in tongues! Bjdhgjshjcdejahfjkhcjebfbfbejwb!
TABITHA: Who broke you, boy?
JJ: Who hasn't!
THEO: Haha!
AMBER: Please don't be uncouth.
STEVE: So...8 at Clover Pub? Does that work for everyone?
THEO: Don't see why not.
AMBER: Which one is that?
TABITHA: The Irish one, Ambz. Opposite the old abandoned theatre.
AMBER: Oh yes! That one! Okay! Will be there for 8:00pm.
THEO: Noice.

The next night, the gang had gathered at the local Irish pub, settling into the worn-out barstools with cheap drinks and salty snacks. Ishaan didn't drink, Amber had a light tolerance, and Theo was sober due to health reasons, but he was fine with his regular Coke. JJ and Steve, however, were already into their third round.

"I'm just gonna say it—*Mamma Mia* is a guilty pleasure of mine," JJ announced.

"Same!" Amber agreed, clapping hands with him, nearly spilling her drink down her pink floral dress.

"No way, that movie's trash," Tabitha said.

Theo chimed in. "You don't watch *Mamma Mia* for the plot. It's all about the fun and the ABBA songs."

"Also, Julie Walters falling off the boat," Steve added, grinning.

Amber laughed, touching her forehead. "I forgot about that bit!"

The conversation bounced from guilty pleasures to childhood favourites, with *The Devil Wears Prada, Hocus Pocus, Revenge of the Sith*, and *Shrek 2* getting a nod from the gang. Ishaan gave an enthusiastic agreement about *Hocus Pocus*, and they all reminisced about watching *The Lord of the Rings* together—except for Amber, who sheepishly admitted her mom had never let her watch them.

"I've always wanted to travel," Amber said after a long silence, staring into her drink. "With all of you, that would be fun. But we're all getting too old for fun, right?" she added, half-joking.

JJ rolled his eyes. "We're not dead yet."

Steve pitched in, "I'd love to see Africa or China or hell even some other states like California."

Tabitha groaned. "Mosquitoes in Africa, though."

"Mosquitoes don't bite me," JJ said, winking. "They can't handle the alcohol in my blood."

Ishaan hesitated. "I'd like to visit India. I've heard it's beautiful from my relatives."

JJ grinned. "Ooh, yeah! I want to pet a tiger."

Theo laughed. "That's a bit dangerous, don't you think?"

The conversation shifted to shots, with JJ and Steve egging Ishaan on, "One shot won't hurt."

Ishaan relented, and within minutes, they were all tipsy and laughing. They made their way to the small dance floor. Ishaan flossed poorly in comparison to Tabitha, who was showing off her dance moves with reckless abandon. Theo, content to stay sober, snapped pictures of the chaos.

"This is for you," Tabitha said, pointing to a grumpy old man in the corner. She seductively smacked her backside at him. He chuckled and raised his drink to her.

"'Fernando,' coming up next," Theo said, heading to the jukebox. The gang cheered, forming a circle to kick their legs and sing along.

As the night wore on, they were all singing and laughing, but it quickly shifted to more emotional territory. "I miss this," Steve slurred, hugging JJ in the middle of the dance floor.

"I love you guys." Amber teared up, her emotions coming

through as the alcohol took over.

"Same," JJ said, suddenly sobered by his own feelings before stumbling into a post as he made his way to the restroom.

Eventually, the pub closed, and Theo led the gang out into the cool night air.

"Let's walk home," he said, guiding a tipsy Ishaan as the others stumbled along behind him.

"I'm not even drunk," Ishaan claimed confidently.

JJ jumped onto Steve's back. "Onward, buttercup! Fuckery awaits!" he screamed, perched like a knight ready for adventure.

Theo snapped one last picture of the scene, his grin wide as they all walked off into the night.

CHAPTER FOUR
FORBIDDEN FRUIT

Storm clouds grew in the distance, blocking out the sun, snuffing out the light and darkening the world below with a blanket of ghostly grey. Something wicked was coming, surely.

A strong breeze blew through the A/C unit in Doctor Garder's office, chilling Theo to the bone. He stood anxiously by the window. It was the big day, the grand reveal. His results. The night out with the gang had proved to be a welcome distraction, but now all he could do was focus on his test results. *The news can't be that bad, surely*. He was overdramatizing it in his head. It would be nothing, he knew it. Maybe thinking like that would jinx it. Best not to think of anything. He would let whatever may be, be. Water trickled down a small rocky display on the doctor's side table, a water feature. Theo looked at it. Something about it soothed him; the current, the fluidity—the natural order of it all, the rise and the fall; balance.

A creak from behind alerted Theo and he turned to see the doctor entering. He smiled, but she avoided eye contact. "Theo, nice to see you. Please have a seat," she instructed with a certain warmth.

Theo sat opposite the doctor. "I like your water feature," he commented politely.

"Thank you, it was a gift."

The doctor seemed to tell Theo was nervous. "I'm sure you want to hear your results," she said.

He nodded. "Yeah, please share, let's see what we're dealing with here."

"Well, I'm sorry, Theo." Her forehead creased, expressing a hint of pity. "Please forgive me, I've never been good at giving bad news, especially for someone as young as yourself."

Theo's face froze. Then he smiled. "It can't be that bad, though, right?"

"I'm afraid your results show that you have a brain tumour, Theo."

Silence engulfed the room. The only sound was that of the little water feature.

Theo's stomach clenched. He sat back in his chair. "Well, shit. But I mean, I'm as tough as nails, we can fix it, right?"

"I don't think so," Doctor Garder admitted. She reached over to turn on her X-ray lightbox viewer, illuminating the image of Theo's skull, revealing the monstrous tumour. "The scans show it's in a section of the frontal lobe and that it is … inoperable."

Theo's skin burned as he began to fire up a little. "Well … why has this just come out of the blue? Why haven't I felt this thing before? Why couldn't you have caught this sooner?"

"You could have had this for some time, Theo, maybe all your life; tumours can be sneaky. Some people can go their whole lives without them causing them any real harm."

"And for others? For me? Be straight with me, how long have I got?" Theo asked.

Her gaze met his. "I would say anywhere from six months to a year."

Realization hit Theo like a train. "Well, shit." He cried a little. "Shit, shit, shit." His lungs became heavy and stiff under the weight of the news. "And there's nothing, nothing at all I can do?"

"You can hope for a miracle; they do happen on the rare occasion." She smiled. "I always like to say hope is the best medicine for something like this."

He whistled out. "Right."

"Just don't do any drugs or drink at all. That will only accelerate things."

"I see," he said, trying to hold back his tears.

Doctor Garder leaned closer. "May I give you some advice?"

"Yes, please do."

"I would advise getting whatever business you have done."

Her tone advised. "Do you understand?"

"No?" he stated honestly.

She clicked the pen in her hand and placed it on her desk. "Get what you've wanted to do done. Don't leave with any unfinished business, no regrets. In most cases like this, I have found that patients often find resolving loose ends to be a good thing in a somewhat bitter situation for them. It gives them peace."

"I see."

"You'll be surprised—you can live more of a life in six months than in six decades."

"I guess I'll have to see if that's true, won't I?"

The doctor laid a hand on Theo's shoulder. "I'm so sorry, Theo. I can't say how sorry I am, really."

"It's okay, it is what it is."

Her hand retracted as she looked him up and down. "Although I admire your pragmatism, I would advise telling your family, relations, and friends."

Theo felt like a volcano, about to erupt. He jumped up, took his denim jacket off his chair, and started to pull it on. "I guess I will just have to embrace the change, that's all. I'll have to find a way to use the time I have and enjoy being me."

The doctor nodded.

"Thank you, doctor." Theo got up to leave.

"I strongly advise you come back for regular check-ups so we can evaluate your situation."

"I will, doctor. I will."

"And continue to take your prescribed medication. I dread to think what would happen if you stopped taking it at a time like this."

"I will," he stated. "But, anyway, I guess I best be off."

"Don't waste a single second, and good luck, Theo."

As the rain fell hard on Theo's silver car, the rumbling storm above muffled his desperate cries. Emotions had usually never played that big a part in Theo's life. But now they hit him all at once. He was drowning in them, inside and out. His salty tears poured down like rain. He was one with the storm, at last.

He wished he had a time machine so he could go back and

relive his life, appreciating every second of it. But no, this was reality; he could not go back, so what was the point of carrying on? His days were done. His time was up. What was the point in waiting around for a disease to slowly but surely kill him? Why not beat the damn thing at its own game and do the job himself? He didn't want to go out weak and shrivelled and begging for morphine. Why not go now, on his own terms, while he could still present a nice open casket?

A sea of regret slammed into him like a wave. He had wasted so much time, years being unhappy and unsatisfied with life, when he should have just been living it. Regret swelled within him like a balloon ready to pop. How would he do it? With a blade, a rope, or pills? Theo then realized. No. He couldn't go out, not yet anyway. He still had 'unfinished business,' whatever that was. He had to clean up the mess that was his life before he could even dream of making a clean exit. He had to make a choice. He decided not to tell his mother or his friends, as they would only worry. Maybe it was denial blinding him to the matter, or perhaps it was because he didn't want them to treat him any differently. Either way, he wouldn't tell. He would keep this poisoned secret to himself and not spread it further. At least for now. While he still could.

Theo dried his tears as he opened his front door and placed his wet umbrella in its stand. No one was home. His mother must have gone out. The storm raged on as he kicked off his shoes and hung up his jacket. Dizziness swept his head as he stumbled up the mountain of stairs to his bedroom. A familiar pulsating pain pumped through his temple. He sat in his desk chair. His eyelids drooped and he began to massage his forehead with little relief. How could things possibly be any worse?

"All good in the head now?" a playful British voice called out.

Theo turned to see Frank sitting in his chair beside the window, dressed in tight black leather pants and a white tank top. His hair was short at the sides now, unlike last time, with a long mop on top that was slicked back with one rogue strand dangling beside his left cheek.

Theo frowned. "I'm not in the mood!"

Frank gasped. "Is that any way to talk to a friend?"

"You knew." Theo's eyes dug into Frank's. "You warned me about this, telling me the other day to get my headache checked out. How did you know?"

"Because I'm in your head, aren't I? I can tell when there's something else lurking inside my home—inside you."

Theo held his head in agony. "Please, stop. Leave now."

Frank blew back his thick strand of hair. "Ya know, monsters are coming for us both. We will have to face them together, my man. You're at a crossroads, kid. Decide what is right and what is wrong; your will, your choice."

"Get out!" Theo growled.

"Oh, kid! You should know by now. There's no way out, well, except maybe my way."

"And what way's that?"

"The way in which you do, we do, whatever it takes to get what you want and, in this case, that's to survive."

"Survive?" Theo questioned.

"Yes, that's it for now. The rest comes later."

Confusion overtook Theo's anger. "And what's that? What comes later?"

"Like I said the other day, something's coming, something bigger than both of us. We've got a lot to look forward to. And for that, we need you to live to see it."

"How can I *survive*? It's terminal. I'm over, done, dead, finished."

"You don't have to be."

"What does that mean?"

"Well, there's always a way," Frank insisted.

"Ha!" Theo coughed a little. "I'm not so sure with this thing stuck in my head."

"But the Theo I knew was always so spunky and full of hope." Frank walked over to the tree in the corner of the room and plucked the crimson apple that appeared on a branch.

Theo sat silently, wondering for a moment. There was a certain grace, or madness, to Frank; Theo couldn't quite decide which. He could be playful, in the best and worst possible ways.

He was sporadic and unpredictable and funny, at times, but also somewhat intimidating. Why had his childhood delusion returned?

"Why are you here? Why are you trying to help me?"

Frank hummed a little. "Well … let's just say I'm invested in your future." He plucked the red apple and polished it on his top.

Theo got up, leaning on his chair for support. "For all I know, you're just my subconscious talking. Hey, maybe you're just the tumour pressing on my brain, causing a hallucination."

"And for all any of us know, we could just be a part of a turtle's dream under the sea!"

"Well, at least answer me this. Who are you? What are you?"

The imaginary friend stopped polishing the apple and chuckled. "I'm Frank, your guardian angel, your eternal wingman. The guy who puts the fun in funeral."

Theo walked up to Frank. "The truth. Please."

Frank paused, and his eye twitched. "Here's the truth, right, you've gotta find a way around this. Ya know. Death is okay, but it can be a bit well … final, well, sometimes. What matters is that you've been given a second chance, so use it."

"Yes, but I don't know how?" Theo sighed and sat on his bed, feeling drained.

"And that's why I'm here, kid. To be your best friend, to help and guide you! After all, what's a friend for?"

Theo stared at him blankly.

"Ah, screw it; let's just do it," Frank said, clicking his fingers and causing all the light in the room to dissipate.

Seconds later, a single spotlight shone down in the empty black space upon Frank. Before the showman was a grand piano with a candlestick above. Frank began to play the piano with panache as the candles lit themselves. He then began to sing:

'I've seen you small, and I've seen you grow,
And there's one thing that I know,
You seem swell, but, kid, I have a secret to tell …
You … are … not.

This boy needs more; he needs a friend,
Someone who will listen and be there to the end.
A friend who will act, and that's a fact.
A friend who will protect, who will attack and, most of all, likes a tasty snack.
And that is .. .me!
Because ..."

Frank ramped up the beat, cascading his hands along the piano as he stood with a heightened sense of flair.

I am your friend, your very best friend.
And I will be here until the end.
I love you so much, you make my heart grow
And for that, I will never let you go.
I am your friend, your very best friend.
And I will be here, until the end
Whenever you get lonely, or insecure
I'll be here to perk you up and pass you the liqueur.

Frank began a little tap dance routine before continuing:

I am your friend, your very best friend.
And I will be here, until the end
Let me help and be your guide,
And know that I will always be by your side.

Further music began to play as Frank jumped up on the piano and began leaping about comically to Theo's amusement. Puppets fell from the misty ceiling above, hanging by their necks as they sang like children:

La, la, la, la, la, la,
La, la, la, la, la, la,
La, la, la, la, la, la,
La, la, la, la, la, la.

Frank pulled Theo up to the piano and began dancing around him.

I am your friend, your very best friend.
And I will be here, until the end
Come on now and use that blond head,
And listen to what your dear old Frankie said.

The lights faded to black, and the spotlight focused on Frank at the top of a grand, black, sparkling staircase with a top hat and cane, beginning to tap his foot to the jazzy beat of the big finale, starting a slow descent down the steep steps.

I am your friend, your very best friend.
And I will be here, until the end
Don't give up and say goodbye,
For I'm all yours until the day you die.

Confetti, sequins, fire, sparks, and cheers erupted. Theo had always appreciated a musical showstopper, just like his father; then again, who didn't? But this display was something else entirely, unlike anything he had ever seen. Theo's eyes widened further as the roar of an invisible audience echoed all around him. He clapped for the bowing performer who lapped up the praise like a cat laps up milk from a saucer.

"Thank you, thank you! You've been a hell of a crowd, I'm here all week, try the veal," Frank joked, clicking his fingers and returning the room to normality.

"How the hell did you do all that?" Theo asked with an open mouth.

"Because I'm not out here, I'm in there, remember!" Frank answered, pointing to Theo's temple. "You'd be surprised what can be accomplished within this great grey mass. Wonders you have yet to meet. Wonders you have yet to unlock, something we can only do if you can carry on breathing."

"Yes, but how, Frank? I still have a death sentence and no hallucinogenic musical number is ever going to fix that. The best

I can hope for is to make amends. Resolving my unfinished business, to achieve some sort of peace, like Doctor Garder said."

"Doctor Garder? Ha! What do doctors know?" Frank scoffed. "No! We need a way to get this … thing out of your head, to save you. Time is what you need, so where do we get more? What did the doc say?"

"That the only thing I could hope for was a miracle?"

"A miracle!" Frank tapped his finger on his chin, wearing a contemplative face. "Hmm … I guess it's a start. Why not look it up?" He pointed to Theo's laptop. "Go on then."

Theo went to his desk, clicked on his laptop, and began searching online. The screen illuminated the room. Frank followed him, looming over his shoulder. Finally, answers appeared.

"What we got?" Frank asked.

Theo scrolled down the screen. "There are random cases of miracles curing cancer, tumours. People curing themselves. Faith healing."

"Yeah, well, we're a little short on faith right now, aren't we? What else is there? Ah! Experimental drug treatments around the world, that's something?"

"Too risky," Theo said.

Frank nodded. "So, what else?"

"Hmm … this is interesting." Theo read the article. "There's a shaman, a man called The Dragon, who can apparently cure people of all sorts of diseases. There are numerous cases of him performing miracles in Los Angeles."

"'The Dragon,' huh?" Frank mused. "Sounds theatrical, I like him. Let's give him a ring." He picked up Theo's phone, only for it to be snatched out of his hand.

"He lives in L.A.," Theo said. "And he's a shaman, so I don't exactly think you'll be able to get him via cell phone. But then again, it does sound interesting."

"Very interesting."

"Maybe he could actually be an option?" Theo agreed. "But how would I get there?"

"I dunno, by plane?"

"I can't just go to L.A.?"

"Why not?"

"Because it takes planning and preparation."

Frank paused. "I often find that details can be distracting; sometimes a simple solution is best."

Theo arched a brow toward his supposed friend, as he still didn't quite trust him. A psychological symptom or not, this entity, or persona, or whatever, still didn't add up to the dying young man. Something just wasn't right; he could feel it. And the things he had said about curing himself of the tumour didn't sit well with him. "So what happens after? Why do you want this so badly?" Theo asked.

"Because I'm your friend."

Theo laughed gingerly. "I'm dying, Frank, not stupid. I'm not a little kid anymore. I know now how the world works, and you never get something for nothing. So, tell me. What happens after I survive? What do you want with me, aside from fun?"

"Keep questioning my motives all you like, but they will remain mine. What you have right now is an opportunity. You know what you have to do, so make it happen. Think! Plan! Go! Do! Win! But don't take too long, ya know. Clock's ticking."

Theo thought and then it clicked. "I could pass it off as traveling."

"Yes! Good boy, smart," said Frank.

"My friends, the gang, they wanted to travel, they could come." Theo smiled to himself. "They could help!"

"Really? Why do you wanna bring along those lightweight losers?" Frank asked, screwing up his face.

"Because they're my friends?"

"Listen, kid, they don't know you like I do, and when they find out who you really are, they will abandon you; that I can promise you. But I won't, because I'm your friend, your best friend, the only one you'll ever have."

"No, they would never abandon me; they're my friends. They love me."

"They don't know you!" Frank hissed. "Not really. Not like I do."

Theo exhaled a shiver, biting his trembling lip, then spoke.

"You know what, I'm scared, more scared than I've ever been in my whole life, but I know I can get through this with them by my side. And that's what will pull me through. *They* will pull me through!"

Frank folded his arms and stood rigidly, shaking his head.

"My friends will help me. Us. They will be a support system to have in case, well, you know, things go wrong."

Frank gave an uproarious cheer. "Oh, kid, using them for your own good, our own good, how very me of you."

Theo sprang up defensively. "I'm not using them; I just want them by my side."

"Hmm … sure, we'll go with that." Frank raised a brow. "So, let's recap; you've got the experimental drug option and the Dragon healer, both obtainable in the city of angels."

"Correct."

"Excellent! So, the only question now is how far you are willing to go to get what you want. How far are you willing to go to survive?"

"As far as it takes."

"Good. So, shall we begin?"

Theo grabbed his phone.

THEO *started a conversation.*

THEO: Who's free tomorrow, just had an amazing idea, but need to say it in person!

CHAPTER FIVE
PLANS IN MOTION

There was silence in the gang's usual booth at Deeny's Diner. The electric hum of the light above and mild chattering from the chefs in the kitchen were all that could be heard as faces reacted to Theo's pitch.

"You want to do what?" Amber asked.

"Travel. With you guys," Theo replied calmly.

Steve choked on his drink. "To L.A?"

"Yeah." Theo grinned.

"Well …" Ishaan stammered.

Tabitha jumped in. "I'll admit it sounds fun, but—"

"But what?" Theo said. "All any of us have been doing, all this time, is moaning about how crap our lives are, doing the same thing over and over again, expecting a different result. You know what that is? Crazy. It's about time we changed that, don't you think?"

"I get ya," JJ said. "Let's mix it up a little. Have some fun."

"Yeah!" Theo replied. "Could be a nice escape."

"I get what you're saying, but I'm not sure I have that kinda money?" Tabitha admitted.

Theo paused. "Sure you do," he said, whipping out his phone. "Look, with this package I found online, it's pretty cheap to go to L.A."

Ishaan grabbed Theo's phone. "Let me see that! Hmm … just L.A. and nowhere else?"

"Yeah, I mean it's a start," Theo admitted, grabbing his phone back. "We could branch out while we're out there."

"It's more of a vacation than actual traveling?" Steve asked, unconvinced.

The pearls around Amber's neck seemed to tighten. "I'm not sure."

"What are you unsure about?" Theo asked. "We all said the other night how we'd like to go on vacation together. Well, here it is, an opportunity."

"I mean, it's hard just to drop everything and go," Steve said.

"Why?" Theo questioned, open-handed. "This could be our one shot to do this! While we're still young."

Steve turned to Amber. "He's got a point."

"When does it leave?" Tabitha asked.

"In three days."

Amber's eyes widened. "Three days?"

"Yes, that's why it's so cheap," Theo explained.

JJ grinned. "I'm game, but I'm not telling my dad; not until I'm out the door at least."

Theo turned to face him. "I can live with that. What do the rest of you guys say?"

"I don't know." Steve frowned, side-eyeing Amber.

"Could be our one shot to do this, together," Theo added, knowing it would push them just a little more in favour.

"I do suppose it would be good for me to get out of my comfort zone. I'm in," Amber said, then gasped a bit, as if she'd shocked herself as much as the others.

Steve licked his lips. "Me too."

Ishaan thought deeply, taking a deep breath. "Ac- actually, you know, I've been needing a vacation. Sh-shame it's not India, but still, could be nice to take a hiatus."

"Thatta boy!" JJ slapped Ishaan on the shoulder, almost winding him.

"Screw it. I guess I'm in, too," Tabitha said.

"So, it's settled then," Theo looked around at his friends.

"I guess it is," Steve said.

"So let's book it." Theo pulled his laptop out of his bag, eager to secure and lock down his mission.

Amber frowned. "Right now?"

"Yeah, sure, why not?" Theo responded.

Steve began sweating slightly. "Screw it, let's do it."

JJ sprang up with glee. "This calls for some … shots, shots, shots, shots—"

"No." Tabitha pulled him down.

"Oh, you're no fun." JJ sulked as Theo began tapping away on his keyboard.

The streetlights glowed as Theo walked beneath them with his bag slung over his shoulder. He passed many of the old houses he and the others would often knock on during Halloween, dressed as a variety of strange things through the years. Rain began to fall from the clouds above, but Theo didn't mind. He was satisfied that his plan had come together, like a beautiful tapestry with no loose threads. *Not yet anyway.*

"Told you it would work," a voice called from above. "Perfectly, in fact."

Theo looked up to see Frank, dressed as a sort of male Mary Poppins, complete with a hat, gliding down to him via an umbrella.

Upon his descent, Frank paused to adjust his hair in his hat, using a shop window as a mirror. "Practically perfect in every way," he mused, turning to Theo. "See. Sometimes all you need is a little push."

Theo smiled at his friend. "I guess so."

"See what happens when you listen to dear old Frankie. You get shit done." He put his arm around Theo's shoulder, shielding him from the rain with the large umbrella.

"True!" Theo answered. "I'm not sure how I feel about lying to my friends."

"Oh, please, kid. There's nothing wrong with a little lie. We all tell them. Besides, you're not really lying, are you? You're just not telling them the whole truth."

Theo let out an uncomfortable sigh. "It still feels wrong, though, Frank."

"Oh, poppycock!" Frank chuckled and swirled around his umbrella, causing droplets of water to fly off all around them.

"Just wait, in a few days' time we'll be taking our crazy double act on tour. It's gonna be beautiful. You'll see."

Theo managed a weak smile.

Amber entered her family's mansion, her cheeks flushed with a mix of frustration and exhilaration. Everything was happening so fast—her decision to go to Los Angeles, her mother's likely reaction, the inevitable conflict. As she stepped into the family room, her skin felt a warmth from the air of the house that was not usually there; she twinged, sniffing around for what seemed to be off. Her father sat on the couch, his leg shaking, while her mother stood, arms crossed, facing a familiar figure.

"Ah, here she is, and about time too," said the lively, eccentric woman holding a martini and fan—her grandmother, Nana, back from months of travel.

"Nana!" Amber rushed to hug her grandmother, who held her back to avoid spilling her drink. Amber chuckled. Nana's vibrant personality was a welcome distraction from her mother's ever-watchful gaze.

Amber caught her mother, Vanessa, rolling her eyes at their exchange.

Nana held Amber back, looking at her with pride. "You get those curves from me, you know." She winked.

Amber laughed, ignoring how her mother cringed in the background.

"What are you doing here, Nana?" Amber asked, curious.

"Just got back from Cairo," Nana said, sitting back in her chair. "The pyramids, the food, the men … it was wonderful."

Amber seized the opportunity. "Well, I've just booked a trip to Los Angeles. I leave in three days."

The room fell silent. Vanessa's face turned red. "Are you joking?"

"No, Mother, it's only for two weeks," Amber said, standing up.

Vanessa exploded. "You're not going!"

"It's booked," Amber retorted.

Her dad cleared his throat. "Amber—"

"Shut up," Vanessa snapped at Michael.

Nana raised an eyebrow. "Why can't she go?"

"Because I say so," Vanessa shot back.

Amber stood firm, her voice steady with frustration. "I'm going. I deserve a break."

"A break from what?" Vanessa scoffed.

"From you!" Amber blurted, immediately regretting the words as they left her mouth. Everyone froze, the weight of her words hanging in the air. Amber's heart pounded, but she couldn't back down now. She turned and left the room, empowerment and exhaustion competing within her.

Vanessa, stunned and hurt, stared at Amber as she ascended the stairs. Michael winced.

"What's the big deal?" Nana asked, taking a sip of her martini. "The girl needs to stretch her wings."

"She's not ready," Vanessa said.

"No one's ever ready," Nana countered.

Vanessa's frustration boiled over. "She can't live a life like you, carefree and with no responsibility."

Nana's expression softened. "Amber can do what she wants; it's her life."

Vanessa poured herself a whiskey, trying to hold back tears. "I just want what's best for her—safe, protected."

"I know," Nana said gently, reaching out to hold Vanessa's hand. "But parenting doesn't come with a manual. You do your best, that's all."

"She's all we've got," Vanessa said, fear in her voice. "What if something happens? What if it goes wrong?"

"Enough," Nana interrupted. "Nothing will happen. And I've got a plan that will let Amber go but also keep her safe."

Vanessa narrowed her eyes, intrigued by her mother's grin.

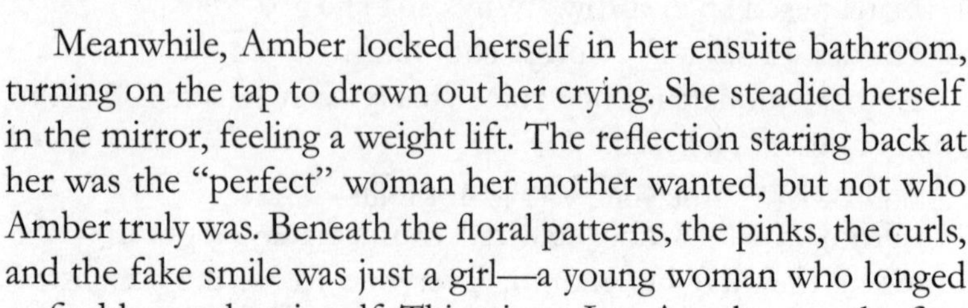

Meanwhile, Amber locked herself in her ensuite bathroom, turning on the tap to drown out her crying. She steadied herself in the mirror, feeling a weight lift. The reflection staring back at her was the "perfect" woman her mother wanted, but not who Amber truly was. Beneath the floral patterns, the pinks, the curls, and the fake smile was just a girl—a young woman who longed to find her authentic self. This trip to Los Angeles was the first step toward that discovery.

Theo trudged home, weighed down by his thoughts. The city buzzed around him, but all he could hear were strange, indecipherable whispers creeping into his mind. Unnerved, he plugged in his headphones, cranked up the music, and swallowed an emerald pill to drown them out. The voices faded as he stepped through the back door, greeted by his mother, Julie, sipping chamomile tea, sitting at the kitchen table in her cupcake-patterned pyjamas.

"Hey, Mom," Theo said, forcing a smile.

"Hey sweetie, how was your night?"

"Great … yeah, it was great," Theo replied, still wrestling with his decision.

His mother eyed him suspiciously. "You sure? You look like you've just smelled a bad fart."

Theo knew this moment was inevitable. His mother's overprotectiveness had only grown since his father's death, and now he had to tell her about the trip with his friends. "I need to tell you something," he said, sitting beside her.

Julie put down her tea, sensing the seriousness in his tone. "What is it?"

"I'm going to L.A. with my friends—J, Steve, Tabitha, Amber, and Ishaan," Theo said quickly, offering a nervous smile.

Julie's lip quivered. "I think it would do you good."

"Really? I thought you'd say no," Theo said, relieved.

"If you'd asked me a few weeks ago, I would've said no, but you need to live your life. See the world. It might help you … well, you know." She twisted her wedding ring. "A distraction."

Theo's heart softened. He hugged her, feeling a pang of guilt. But when he pulled away, his mother's eyes searched him closely. "Theo, is there something you're not telling me?"

"No," he said too quickly.

"Still taking your meds?"

"Yes."

Julie frowned but decided not to press. "Well, you know where I am if you need to talk."

"I'm fine, Mom. Goodnight."

"Goodnight," she replied, returning to her tea.

Theo slumped into bed, his chest tight. Lying to her hurt, but it was the only way to keep his secret. The voices in his head returned, but sleep wouldn't come. Exhausted, he stayed up, researching the mysterious "Dragon" shaman with Frank, diving deeper into endless reports about miracles he performed for those who found him. But the more he researched, the more frantic his mind became. The whispers grew louder and clearer, and the pills no longer helped. Meditation was his only respite, but even Frank's voice couldn't be quieted.

The days blurred together, and on the eve of the trip, Theo's mind was frayed. Anxiety gripped him. He couldn't sleep, fearing that if he did, he might never wake up. He stumbled downstairs in the dead of night, sinking into the couch. The TV buzzed in the dark, its light illuminating the space—his space, where his father used to sit.

A fly darted around his face, landing on the armrest. Without thinking, Theo swatted it dead, the crunch under his hand a stark reminder of how fragile life was. He looked at the fly's body, his own mortality weighing heavily on him. He was no different—one wrong move, and he could be gone.

Trying to shake the thought, he flipped through channels, his mind slowly drifting until a starry sky appeared on the screen. It was hypnotic, reminding him of his childhood, when he and his father used to stargaze together. The screen zoomed in and a small figure appeared—a spaceman, drifting in the void. As the camera zoomed closer, Theo realized it was him, a younger version, lost in space.

The moon came into view, rotating to reveal a smiling face—Frank's.

"Well, well, well … my little star has come to visit," Frank's voice echoed.

Theo was frozen as he drifted closer to the moon, but then something darker appeared: a black hole, pulling everything in. Theo tried to paddle toward Frank, but his limbs grew weaker, as if dragging through molasses. He was helpless, pulled toward the abyss. Frank laughed as Theo was sucked into the black void.

Then, the whispers returned, distorted voices—his friends.

"It's too late. He's too far gone," JJ's voice declared.

"Who are you to say that?" Tabitha responded.

"We're his friends," Steve added.

"Yes, and if we say he needs this, then he does," Amber said.

The image shifted. A surgical mask appeared, followed by a familiar set of emerald eyes. It was Frank again, this time wielding a hammer and an ice pick aimed directly at Theo's eye. Theo tried to scream, but the gag muffled his cries as the hammer came down. TING!

White light flooded his vision and Theo found himself in a dilapidated wheelchair, drooling. His mind spiralled into a padded cell—a prison. It was an endless maze, his own mind, his madness trapping him forever.

Then, a crack appeared in the wall of the cell, and a voice slithered, "The egg thinks it's smarter than the chicken."

The crack spread, and the shell exploded into dust, revealing a manic version of Theo, screaming as he fell through the void, until he hit the ground—a grave. Dead hands reached out for him as the earth closed in, suffocating him. Theo tried to scream, but the dirt filled his mouth.

A cold hand touched his face. Theo jolted awake to find his mother sitting beside him, her face a mix of concern and shock.

"Theo! Are you alright?"

He stared at her, still disoriented. "Am I dead?" he rasped.

"No, why would you say that?" she asked, alarmed.

Theo paused, trying to calm himself. "I guess I just … fell asleep and was dreaming."

Julie furrowed her brow. "You were awake. You wouldn't answer me. You looked … blank. Like you were somewhere else."

"It sounds weird," Theo said, glancing at the TV.

"Are you sure you're okay, Theo?"

"I'm fine. Just haven't been sleeping well," he lied, forcing a smile. "It happens."

Julie didn't push. "Okay, well, you should go to bed. You've got a big day tomorrow."

"Right. Goodnight."

"Theo …" she hesitated, "Maybe take one of your pills, just to be sure."

He nodded, disappearing into the hallway, brushing off the madness of the night. He didn't want to think about it. After swallowing a pill, he glanced at his father's old books gathering dust. They were all about escaping into other worlds, just like he was.

As he lay in bed, the sun began to rise, and Frank appeared in the dim light.

"Today's the big day," Frank said, grinning.

Theo didn't answer. He was too tired, too lost, but it was time.

CHAPTER SIX

A NEW DAY

The sun filtered through the blinds as Steve's alarm went off, "Wake Me Up Before You Go-Go." He grinned, jumping out of bed and dancing to the rhythm as he got ready.

Amber adjusted her curls, surrounded by brochures about Los Angeles. She smiled at her reflection, unaware that her mother was watching quietly through the door.

Ishaan, wearing his fanny pack, sat nervously at his desk, watching a video on how to be more popular.

Meanwhile, Tabitha, after her alarm went off, groggily reached for a soda from her mini-fridge and began applying her makeup with exaggerated precision. A selfie later, she was ready to go.

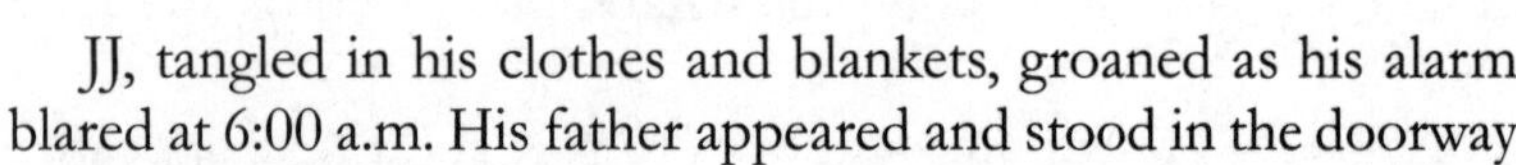

JJ, tangled in his clothes and blankets, groaned as his alarm blared at 6:00 a.m. His father appeared and stood in the doorway as JJ tried to leave.

"Where are you going?" Jim demanded.

JJ paused, then chuckled. "L.A., don't wait up"," he said, trying to move past, only to be pushed back.

"L.A.! Don't be sassy with me," he said.

"No, really, I'm going to L.A.," JJ replied, readjusting the grip on his bag.

"Who with?"

"My friends."

"Your friends?" A cruel laugh escaped his father's lips.

"Yeah, my friends." JJ's voice quivered with emotion. "What

of it?"

"You don't have any friends."

"Guess again," JJ retorted, attempting to move past him only to be pushed back once more.

"No, I don't think so." JJ's father scowled. "You're not going anywhere."

"I sure as hell am." JJ managed to wriggle his way with his bag past his father, marching for the front door of the house.

"Get your ass back in your room," Jim growled.

"No."

Jim breathed in, then exhaled heavily. He slapped JJ on his left cheek, the impact of his signet ring so hard he almost drew blood. An intense burning sensation hit the young man, but it wasn't pain or anger—it was empowerment.

"Is that all you got?" JJ retorted, licking his lips, knowing it would anger his father further, make him sloppy. He stepped away from the door and fell back into the open kitchen. His father followed, as he knew he would. He glanced at a large kitchen knife shimmering in the knife block on the counter.

"Go to your room, now," Jim demanded.

JJ smiled. "No."

Mr. Johnson tried to tackle his son, but JJ was too quick. He darted aside and grabbed the knife. He pointed it at his father, who stepped back, holding both hands up in surrender. Finally, JJ had his father right where he wanted him. He grinned, feeling somewhat taller. He liked the feeling of a blade in his hand, especially when it was pointed towards someone who had caused him so much pain and misery. JJ relished the thought of plunging it deep into his father's shrivelled heart, leaving him to bleed out on the floor, gasping for air. The thought made him shiver with anticipation. Jim dropped his hands.

"Go on then, do it. Kill me, like you killed your mother."

The words pierced JJ's skin like hooks.

"Be a man for once in your life and make me proud, just once, son."

"I am your son, and all my life you've treated me like dirt because of something that wasn't my fault."

"Not your fault?" his father scoffed. "You're a disease, boy; everything you touch goes to shit. I wish I had left you at the side of a road when I had the chance. Not tolerated you and your … perversions."

JJ paused, holding his chin a little taller, dropping the knife. "I don't need to kill you; you're dead to me already." He walked past his father to the hall, grabbed his bag from the floor, and went to open the front door. Jim threw JJ against the wall, the knife caressing his son's neck.

"No one walks away from me."

"You gonna kill me, Dad?" JJ asked. "Go on then, do it. Show me how much of a man you are."

Jim had nothing but this legacy of failure. He gazed at the photo of his beautiful wife hanging on the wall beside JJ's head. Her smile, her face, her laugh—it all came back to him at once, causing him to lose concentration, long enough for JJ to edge the knife away from him, pushing it downwards until it dropped out of his father's hand to the floor.

JJ opened the door, picked up his bag, and walked outside to his car.

Jim followed. "You'll never leave; you don't have the guts," he said as JJ unlocked his car, slung his bag in the trunk, and opened the driver's door. "Get back here! Have some respect. I am your father, God damn it!"

JJ got into Big Bertha, slamming the door shut and lowering the window. "You have never been, and you never will be my father," he said. He stuck out his middle finger as he reversed into the trash cans, causing the bags to tumble out when they can fell over. He drove away fast, playing the radio loudly, drowning out everything else in his head, as he sang along to "Highway to Hell."

Theo paused in the doorway of his bedroom, delaying the inevitable. He gazed at his apple tree, his posters, his crappy memorabilia, the stories, the memories. He took in his haven, his world. He let go of it all with the flick of the light switch and bitterly turned his back on his old life.

Downstairs, he waited in the dining room for JJ, who was picking him up in Big Bertha. The more time that passed, the heavier his breathing grew, becoming slower, thicker, as if he were trying to breathe through molasses. Veins in his temple bulged, and his sight blurred. He concentrated, bringing himself too. Then whispers crept into his ears, like before. Voices muffled his thoughts with inaudible words of mischief that he couldn't quite make out. The confusion increasingly caused a dull throb to beat his temple with a ruthless rhythm. Theo couldn't quite take it any longer. Everything was fuzzy, vibrating. He could see sound in all its technicolour, as if all his senses were turned up to eleven. His brain felt like it was being blended into a smoothie, and he pounded his head in an attempt to make it stop as he reached for his pills. The muffled words in his cranium cut like razor blades running across his frontal lobe, where his tumour sat. The demons hissed and then, suddenly, retreated as he went to take a pill from the bottle.

"JJ not here yet?" Julie asked, coming up behind him.

Theo clutched his chest. "Ah, you made me jump."

Julie looked down at the pill box in his hand, which slowly made its way back into his pocket. "Here." She smiled, holding up a small, wrapped present in a purple bow and green wrapping paper.

"What's this?" Theo asked.

"It's called a present, Dumbo. Open it."

Theo was hesitant; he didn't like surprises, even when they came in the form of a gift. He pulled the bow clean off with one tug, then ripped the emerald wrapping to reveal a box. He opened it. A silver pocket watch rested on a pillow. The metallic reflection shimmered across the young man's face as he clicked it open, watching the hands of time move forward, one tick at a time. It reminded him of his own hourglass trickling away by the minute.

"I found it the other day," Julie said. "I was going to give it to you last night, but thought it was better to wait until now. It belonged to your grandfather. After he left, your grandmother gave it to your dad, but you know what he was like, never kept a watch on him. Never liked to keep track of time. It's rather nice though, don't you think?"

Theo felt a flood of emotions. "Mom, I don't know what to say."

"Flip it over." She gestured with her hands.

Theo turned the watch over and read the engraving on the back: 'Keep moving forward.'

"Mom, thank you so much. I love it," Theo said, embracing her firmly.

"You're very welcome," Julie whispered, hastily wiping away a tear behind Theo's back.

A cartoonish screech of tires came from outside.

"Ah, that'll be JJ," Theo said, pulling away from his mother. "Well, wish me luck."

"Luck?"

"Yeah! Think I'm gonna need it."

"What do you mean?" Julie frowned.

"Nothing, it's just a figure of speech," Theo said, placing the watch in his pocket.

"Ah, I see. Well, I guess you'd better get going."

She pulled him towards her for one last hug. The cord between them could never be broken. No matter how far he travelled to the other side of the world, he would always come back to her.

A honk came from Big Bertha outside. Theo didn't want to leave but knew he must. He broke away from his mother.

"Have you got your camera and extra pills?"

"Yup and yup! Made sure of both," he answered, dragging his case out of the door, and waving to JJ.

Julie followed him like a bear to honey. "Take lots of photos; I want to see all the exciting places you've been."

Theo opened the car door, then turned back to face her. "Oh, I will!"

"And Theo, make good choices, be a good boy, okay?" Julie said in a serious voice.

"I will," Theo said. "Bye, Mom."

"Bye, be safe."

"I will try!" Theo said, getting into the car. A melancholy mood came over him as he looked ahead to his dwindling chance of a future, as he shut the car door.

"Well, here we go," Steve called out from the passenger seat of Big Bertha as the gang piled in. Tabitha arrived next, walking out of her rundown house with sunglasses on, carrying her bags. She entered the car with a silent confidence, not looking back.

Ishaan, who had arrived next, hesitated before joining them. He was anxious but quickly tried to fit in.

A fly circled in loops around the foyer. The pointlessness of it irritated Amber and a hint of a scowl flashed across her usually composed face as she waited quietly beside her bags in the dim morning light. The waiting game was one she hated to play. Impatience had always been her greatest weakness.

Her mother entered the room with heavy footsteps. Vanessa was clearly flustered, given her cheeks had bloomed a reddish glow, but she tried to hide it behind a plastered-on smile. "Now, you're sure you've packed everything?"

"Yes," Amber replied.

"You're absolutely sure?"

"Yes. Look, Mother, I'm going to be fine. The time will fly by like that." She snapped her fingers.

"Not for a mother," Vanessa said sadly.

Amber didn't know what to say next. Her mind struggled to muster anything up. "Where's Nana?" she asked eventually.

Vanessa broke eye contact, blinking. "Oh, she left about an hour ago—for something?"

Amber giggled. "Sounds like Nana." A screech of tires came from outside. Big Bertha's horn honked. "Well, that must be my friends."

Her father entered the room and smiled at Amber as he picked up her bags. "Want me to–"

Amber jumped up to carry them herself. "It's okay, Daddy, I got it." She turned to face them. "Well, I suppose I'll be seeing you both soon."

"I suppose so," Vanessa managed to say.

Amber paused at her mother's cold front and began her exit to the front door, dragging her luggage across the floorboards.

"Have a good time, honey," her father said.

"I will!"

Michael followed her, holding the door open for her. "That's my girl."

"Yes, have fun," Vanessa said, stumbling on her words, which was out of character.

Both her husband and daughter turned in the doorway, surprised. Amber allowed herself to feel a sense of hope for both herself and her mother. "Thank you … Mom."

The two women stood tall, and the shadow Amber cast in the morning glow covered Vanessa. This wasn't how either of them had planned things to go, in this scenario or life in general, but they could both appreciate how they had both managed to get to this point given their relationship over the years. They smiled softly at one another.

Amber began to descend the steps of her porch with a certain slow grace.

"I can't bear to watch this," Vanessa said to her husband.

"She'll be fine," Michael said.

"It's not her I'm worried about."

As Big Bertha pulled away from Amber's, Steve broke the silence. "So, what are we doing when we get there?" he asked.

"I dunno, something low-key," Theo replied. "We'll be jet-lagged."

Tabitha, still behind her glittery sleep mask, groaned. "Boring."

Amber grinned. "Maybe something easy—like a museum or a Hollywood tour."

Ishaan, who had been quiet, suggested the same, but Tabitha made a noise of disdain.

Steve, trying to ease the awkwardness, reached for his phone. "Alright, I've got a playlist for us."

"Let's hear it," Theo said, relieved to break the tension.

Steve tapped play. The first song that blared through the speakers was "Tainted Love." Steve started tapping on the dashboard in time with the music, grinning. JJ, sitting up front, groaned in response.

"Careful with Bertha," JJ warned.

"Sorry, Bertha." Steve laughed, patting the dashboard.

JJ slammed on the brakes, causing everyone to lurch forward.

Tabitha groaned from the backseat. "Seriously, JJ?"

"Not my fault!" Steve shot back.

JJ's mood darkened. "You think I'm the problem?"

Theo noticed the shift in JJ's demeanor. "You good, J?"

JJ shrugged. "Just tired. Thinking."

"Thinking?" Ishaan asked, his tone hesitant.

Amber smirked. "Sounds dangerous."

JJ's eyes darkened. "Yeah, it's the end of something. And the start of something else."

Steve leaned in. "A great adventure?"

"It's a new day," Amber added quietly, glancing out the window.

Tabitha, not interested in the conversation, snuggled deeper under her blanket.

After a few moments of silence, Steve, trying to liven up the mood, switched the song to "Children of the Revolution." The group fell into a comfortable quiet, the road ahead full of unspoken possibilities.

CHAPTER SEVEN
A TALE OF WOLVES

The clouds drifted across the night sky as Theo tried to sleep, but the hum of the plane's engine and the turbulence kept him restless. The day had been draining—endless queues, security checks, and JJ's taunting of Ishaan's anxieties about flying. Theo had tuned it out, focusing on the signs around the airport, but it didn't help ease the discomfort.

Now, seated in economy class, he looked around at his friends: Ishaan, drooling on himself; JJ, strangely peaceful beside him; Steve, clutching his third beer with his eyes shut; and Tabitha, snoring with her sleep mask on beside Amber, also asleep. How could they all fall asleep so quickly? Theo envied their ability to shut off. He could feel his exhaustion, but his mind wouldn't let him rest.

The plane felt unreal to him—this heavy chunk of metal floating in the air, defying gravity. He thought of Newton's theories but couldn't shake the feeling that maybe none of this was real. What if he were locked in an asylum, living out a delusion? The thought gnawed at him.

He stared out the window at the wing, the ruby navigation lights pulsing in sync with his heartbeat. Then, through the dim light, a figure appeared on the wing—a bald, rotting creature in rags, tearing at the plane's wires. Theo froze, mouth agape as the figure's hollow eyes locked onto his. The trumpet sound of the creature's arrival echoed in his ears, sending a chill down his spine. Before he could react, the figure morphed into Frank, smiling and waving as if nothing were wrong.

Theo's breath hitched, and instinctively, he pulled down the window shade, adrenaline surging through him. What was happening? He quickly took a pill from his pocket, hoping it would calm him.

"Can't sleep? Me neither," Steve's voice came from across the aisle, surprising Theo. He turned to see Steve clutching his beer.

"I don't sleep much," Theo muttered, slipping the pill bottle back into his pocket.

"Same," Steve slurred. "My mind's always on. Only way to quiet it is with ASMR."

"ASMR?" Theo asked, confused.

"You know, tapping, whispering … weird stuff," Steve explained, shushing him playfully. "You'll wake the kids."

Theo awkwardly climbed over Ishaan and JJ to sit next to Steve.

Steve took a swig of his drink. Tabitha snored ferociously beside him. "Wow, even when she's asleep, she's loud," Steve commented, grinning.

Theo restrained a giggle. "Ah, she does make me laugh."

"Do you remember the time she kicked Tom Plaza in the balls at school?"

"Oh yes! That was such a boss move!" Theo grinned.

"I'll never forget the look on his face."

"It was so funny. But boy, that guy had it coming. Sorry, I know he's a friend of yours," Theo said.

Steve's gaze turned away, swirling his nearly empty can. "Not anymore, besides that douche did have it coming. He cheated on our Tabz with Lindsey Cameron."

"I remember her." Theo nodded. "She'd go with anyone."

"Well, not me. I wasn't interested."

"Course not, you've got a brain. I think I heard she's pregnant now."

"Hey, remember the time we locked Ishaan out of your house?"

"Oh yeah, and we kept luring him from door to door and then made him run just to lock it again."

They laughed loudly at the memory, causing JJ to fidget and move. They attempted to hold in their laughter, looking at each other, which only made them both want to giggle more, quietly slapping each other's backs and legs as they struggled to breathe.

"We really are bad people," Steve said, jokingly.

Theo's hand casually waved it off. "Oh, come on, it was all just messing around. We all got it at some point. Like when you were fed those laxatives in your hot dog at the school awards, or the time I was tied to a chair and locked in a dark cupboard for two hours. It was hilarious!"

"I guess, at the time. But I still feel bad about that stuff. I regret some of the things I did at school."

Theo's brow furrowed. "You mean when you joined the cool kids?"

"Yeah. Back when I was an asshole."

"You weren't an asshole."

"I was."

A smile tugged at the corners of Theo's mouth. "Okay, maybe just a little."

Steve laughed. "I changed, you know, around those guys at school, don't you think?"

"Well, yeah, sure," Theo agreed. "But anyone would."

"Being around Tom, Billy, Josh, Zane, Cole, Andy … being around them made me my worst self."

"Because they were all assholes?"

"Yeah. They were toxic."

"Well, what did you expect from that lot?"

"For them not to be bullies? I mean, it's all changed nowadays. It's cool to be a nerd. Mostly everyone gets along, from what I can tell anyway. No more cool and uncool kids in school anymore."

"I'm sure it's not that simple. For one, things seem more competitive, especially with social media and stuff, but I get what you're saying. Things are more inclusive these days, well, in some ways, I guess."

"Yeah, like how it should be. I mean, back then, I didn't bully people like they did, but I watched. I stood by as they did those things and I didn't say anything. Not for Ishaan, not for JJ."

Theo touched his friend lightly on the arm. "But you got out, you came back. You're not like that now. You were just a kid."

Steve sighed. "I know, but I still feel guilty. I was never really one of them, though. I always felt like an outsider. A person in a crowd can still feel alone."

"Where did you get that quote from?"

"Not sure. A movie? A show? I dunno?"

"God damn it, now that's gonna annoy me!"

Steve settled back in his chair with a drunken smile. "Got another one for you: Who we were does not dictate who we will be, but it is a good indication of one's self. Now, who said that?" he asked.

Theo thought but gave up easily. "I don't know, who?"

"I was hoping you'd know; I've been reflecting on that one for some time."

Theo assessed his friend. "Hmm … you spend a lot of time with your memories, don't you? Honestly, I don't know how you do it. I can barely remember what I had for breakfast. All I remember from school is trying to blend in with the crowd, never being looked at twice. My school life was very uneventful. But you can remember all this stuff. You're like a sponge. You take it all in and think about it."

"I know. I think of it as time traveling; rewatching, rewinding. Sometimes I even feel like I can remember being in the womb, safe, warm, and then boom, show time." He paused. "It's good and bad, remembering the past, reliving it. Not being able to forget certain things, change things, things I regret. Memories are like stains we can never wash off."

"Where did you steal that quote from?"

"I didn't actually, I just made it up."

"I'm impressed."

"Thanks, but I do have regrets." He leaned forward to place his beer can in the compartment on the back of the chair in front. "I totally peaked in high school."

"No, you didn't!"

"Yes, I did. Trust me. As soon as I was dropped from the football team in my senior year, the guys dropped *me*. I've never felt so alone. After college, I thought I might get back in touch with them, but I couldn't. They were done with me; I was no longer relevant to them. That made me realize that if you're not in people's lives, they forget you pretty quickly. They move on, and that's just the way of things. But then I remembered you guys, us. I relived all our memories, our childhood, and realized I had ditched you guys, my real friends, for those losers." He looked over to Ishaan and JJ, then Tabitha and Amber. He lowered his gaze in shame.

"They forgive you, you know. We all forgive you," Theo whispered. "Mostly because our memories aren't as good as yours."

Steve grinned.

"But we do, forgive you," Theo continued. "And we've all had our shit to deal with, our own separate journeys leading us here, so don't be sorry because it doesn't matter. You're our friend, and we are your friends. Nothing matters, only us lot, together again, always, doing stupid stuff, just like we used to. Making more memories for the future."

"Honestly, Theo, I'm not sure there's much of a future left for me."

"Don't say that."

"Why? It's true."

"No, it's not! Look at you!" Theo exclaimed. "You're smart, good-looking, funny. Brilliant, so brilliant! I mean, sure, maybe football is not for you, but there are other things out there."

"There's nothing left for me anymore."

"Don't be stupid!"

"I am a failure, man. I have been training to be a footballer my whole life. It's what people expected from me, including my parents, who have pushed me forward. I failed because I got too distracted. I was too busy trying to be popular." Steve turned away. "I can't even look at my dad anymore, because I can still see the disappointment in his eyes."

"I'm sure that's not true, Steve. Your parents are pretty cool."

"I know, and they seem fine with it all, but I can tell. I know they look at me and see nothing but a failure."

"Steve, this isn't you; you're drunk."

"No, it's true." Steve wiped at his cheek. "I'm not sure I can keep doing this, Theo. I'm not sure I can keep going. I've tried to hang on for so long now, but I don't know how long I can delay the inevitable."

Theo put an arm around Steve's shoulders and hugged him. "Hey, listen to me," he urged. "Everyone has done bad shit. Everyone feels alone sometimes. Some more than others …" Theo sighed heavily. "Hell, I know I've sure felt like you do a lot recently. Everyone does at some point; it's human nature to doubt yourself. And thank God we do, because why would we wanna be like those assholes who don't? The best thing we can do when we feel like this is to take one day at a time, count to ten, let it all in, and then let it all out. Believe me, I know how hard it is to accept mental illness, I really know."

"You do?"

"Yes. It's hard. Especially for us guys, everyone expects us to stay strong and unfazed by everything life throws at us, but bottling it up makes us feel worse on the inside. Makes us … hell, I don't know … crazy."

"Yeah, like you feel you could scream at the world."

"Exactly! I mean, people talk about depression, but they never talk about the other side of mental illness, the invisible side, the sneaky side."

"What other side?"

"Mania. Rage. That indestructible feeling. That's the real danger under all our noses."

Theo's glare became cold and piercing, a face Steve had never seen before. He had witnessed many sides to Theo, over the years, but nothing like this. It felt like the tip of the iceberg to something else hiding within, and rippled ice waters that hadn't been stirred for many, many years.

"My dad used to tell me a bedtime story," Theo said. "It's called 'Feed the Good Wolf.' Ever heard of it?"

Steve shook his head.

"'Well, let me tell you because I think it may help … an old man was teaching his grandson about life. The grandfather said, 'There is a fight going on inside of me, a terrible fight, and it is between two wolves. One is evil; he is anger, envy, greed, regret, arrogance, self-pity, guilt, and resentment. And the other is good: peace, love, hope, serenity, humility, kindness, empathy, generosity, truth, compassion, and faith. And the same fight is going on inside of you, inside of me, and inside everyone around us.'

The grandson asked his grandfather, 'Well, which wolf wins?'

'The one you feed,' the grandfather replied."

Steve looked blank.

"Your football career may be over, but that doesn't mean your life has to end." Theo leaned closer. "It doesn't mean you have to end. You are stronger and capable of more than you know. You just need to find that other special thing you are good at, that you love, and go for it with all you've got."

Steve smiled weakly, looking over at the sleeping Amber. "I'll try," he said, though his voice lacked conviction.

"You don't try, you do," Theo replied. They shared a quiet moment, their bond strengthening.

Steve pointed at Theo's face. "Hey, your nose is bleeding."

Theo touched it in surprise, his finger coming away with blood. "Must be the altitude," he muttered, heading to the back of the plane to clean up.

As he made his way down the dimly lit aisle, his balance wavered. Was it the turbulence, or was it him? In the restroom, he stared at his reflection, tissues pressed to his nose as blood continued to pour. But something else caught his eye. The ticking from his pocket grew louder. Theo pulled out his father's pocket watch. The hands spun erratically, and a familiar laugh echoed in his mind; his muscles crunched and hardened as he froze.

Time was running out.

Theo slammed the watch shut, trying to shake off the feeling. His heart raced as he hurried to clean up. What was happening? Was it all in his head, or was something more sinister at play?

The words from earlier echoed in his mind about feeding the

good wolf. But what if the other side, the dark side, was already winning?

CHAPTER EIGHT

CAROUSELS AND FREAKS OF NATURE

The city of Los Angeles shimmered between towering mountains as their plane touched down, its tires screeching against the runway. Amber chatted with an airport rep while Theo distractedly watched a bird pecking at discarded food.

Stepping swiftly into a taxi, they were taken aback by the city's energy. The air trembled with heat and promise, rolling in off the Pacific like a whispered rumour. Palm trees leaned with the arrogance of models, casting long, spindly shadows across boulevards that once belonged to orange groves and silent film stars. It was beautiful in the way a flame is beautiful—flickering, elusive, and always on the verge of consuming itself.

From the hills, L.A. looked like a dream too big to wake up from. A quilt of neighbourhoods stitched together by freeways, each with its own rhythm: the glassy hush of Beverly Hills, the frantic poetry of Koreatown, the sunburned sprawl of the Valley. Downtown clawed at the sky with steel and ambition, while Venice lounged at the edge of the continent like a stoned prophet. Everything was temporary, including the people.

People came to Los Angeles to vanish or be seen. Often both.

And somewhere between the shimmer and the smog, the real city waited—watching, quiet, like a camera just out of focus.

Riding along still in their taxi, JJ stuck his head out the window like a dog, oblivious to the driver's indifference. Steve, barely awake, let his phone blare "Somebody's Watching Me." Amber typed a reassuring message to her mom. Ishaan offered sunscreen to Theo, who declined with a distracted, "No thanks."

The city was alive with noise and colour, flashing billboards and bright traffic lights. Theo's mind wandered. What if his version of specific colours was not the same as everyone else's? What if everyone saw each colour differently?

Like, what if:

RED was GREEN, and GREEN was RED.

And what if:

GO meant STOP, and STOP meant GO.

The thought made his head hurt needlessly. Maybe as a boy he had been taught wrong, but no, surely not, that was a stupid idea. He dropped the thought.

The group marvelled at the towering skyscrapers, snapping photos of their surroundings. The traffic moved in strange bursts, as if everyone was edging forward a few inches at a time.

Ishaan admired the city's intellectual energy, while Tabitha revelled in the advertising—each billboard a work of art to her. Steve shared her admiration, and Amber saw a collective striving for better lives, a stark contrast to her own sense of escape. JJ, meanwhile, saw only a blur of people and buildings. Theo lifted his camera and took many a snapshot of the city.

Then the billboards grew more personal. One flashed the words: WHAT ARE YOU DOING? Theo's skin prickled. Another sign quickly followed: STOP WASTING TIME! His unease deepened as a giant screen came to life with an image of a teenage singer, MeMe, flashing vibrant emojis and dance moves. The group bickered over her popularity. Ishaan was a fan, while Steve and JJ had never heard of her.

"Never heard of MeMe? She's huge!" Tabitha groaned.

JJ smirked. "Maybe on that screen she's huge," he teased.

But Theo's attention was locked on the billboard, where MeMe's image morphed into something unsettling. Her body changed subtly, becoming more toned. Then, the screen flickered, and Frank's face appeared where hers had been, dancing provocatively, the message flashing: GET MOVING! Theo felt a strange compulsion to obey, his mind numb to everything except the music and the flashing words.

JJ yanked him from his trance. "Yo, what do you think,

Theo? Think MeMe does her singing warm-up by saying her own name?" JJ sang the joke, and Steve snickered behind him.

Theo blinked, shaking off the eerie sensation. "Right, that's funny, J," he muttered, grateful when the original MeMe returned to the screen. The message had been received, and he was eager to move on from whatever strange thing had just happened.

Forty Minutes Later

The gang stood outside their hotel, staring up at the dilapidated building. The sign hung crooked, graffiti covered the walls, and rats scurried near the bins. JJ grinned. "Hehe … I like it."

Inside, the front desk clerk was engrossed in an erotica novel while a drip from the ceiling formed a stagnant puddle beside the reception desk. The air smelled stale.

Tabitha scoffed. "Still good, J?"

"Totally." JJ grinned. "It's got character."

After checking in, the gang squeezed into a rickety elevator, its cheesy tunes somehow lifting their spirits. In their suite, they found a dirty kitchen, peeling wallpaper, and walls covered in mysterious stains.

Steve, ever the optimist, declared, "We can make this work."

Theo looked guilty, glancing around at the mess. "Sorry, guys. I really thought it'd be better."

Amber reassured him, "Don't worry, it's not your fault. It's the website's fault, not yours."

JJ snorted. "Lies and deceit. Every time."

"Hey, at least it's affordable." Amber grinned, trying to lighten the mood. "Who knows? I might even turn this place into a palace."

Tabitha immediately sprang into action, choosing the largest room, "I bagsy this one!" JJ followed with his usual childish energy, dragging his suitcase behind him to claim the next.

"Go on, JJ." Theo chuckled. "Ladies first."

JJ grunted. "Sexist."

Meanwhile, Steve and Theo strolled out to the balcony.

Ishaan had already vanished, creeping off to find his bed.

Theo and Steve looked out at the plaza, spotting a Ferris wheel on the other side. Steve grinned. "Hey, anyone up for the amusement park later?"

Two Hours Later

The gang was at Pacific Park Amusement Park. It was cheesy, but it was exactly what they needed after the long flight. Theo snapped pictures as cotton candy melted on his tongue. Steve, Amber, and Tabitha struggled to eat ice cream while JJ enjoyed a giant rainbow lollipop.

The carousel was their next ride. Theo smiled, lost in nostalgia, while the carousel spun them around in circles. Suddenly, the faces of his friends began to change—childlike, younger versions of themselves appeared. A surreal, dreamlike moment. Even his reflection in the mirrored centre looked young again.

He was happy—maybe too happy. But then, just as quickly as it came, everything returned to normal, and the carousel came to a stop. His heart raced as he tried to shake off the strange feeling.

"Hey, guys, the Dragon Pit rollercoaster next?" Steve yelled, dragging them along.

As they stood in line for the ride, the name, The Dragon, was a reminder to Theo of his reason to be there. The man who could cure him. The mystic master. Was it a sign? Frank telling him? Or just a coincidence? The day just kept making Theo question himself more and more. He clamped his hand over the pills in his pocket.

As they queued, however, Ishaan stayed back, on the sidelines, as he always did. He was slurping a slushy on a bench, keeping their bags and belongings safe beside him as he waved to his friends as they waited to ride the fearsome emerald-painted dragon. *GREEN,* Theo thought. Is this another sign? Another message? Does it mean GO? Yes, yes, it must. But then again, what if it was a trick? Was GREEN good? Was he overthinking it all? Yes, yes, he must be. It was nothing but his tired brain, all damn day, that's all it was. The railing rose as they sat in their paired-up seats: Tabitha and JJ, Steve and Amber, leaving poor Theo alone in the final carriage. He was shaking, not for the ride but for his uncertainty. A safety speech took place, the usual stuff. Keep your hands and legs within the carriage and so on …

Theo was too busy shutting out the voices in his head to listen. New voices he had unlocked, so it would seem, through adrenaline, voices that were a new brand of his own:

"What if this goes wrong?"

"It won't!"

"But what if it does?"

"It won't."

"What are you hiding?"

"These could be signs that this is dangerous!"

"It's not. Nothing but paranoia, superstition!"

"Ooh, I like that song!"

"Shut up!"

"Sorry, I'm just trying to calm us down."

"What are you hiding?"

"What if this is a test?"

"It's not a test. We're just getting worked up. Worked up over nothing!"

Theo trusted his gut and decided not to make a scene. As the metal safety rail lowered, the gang looked over to Ishaan, who gave them a thumbs up. JJ let out a boyish yell and Tabitha gave a few whoops. Steve and Amber laughed. However, Theo's attention was not focused on Ishaan but on a big bundle of RED balloons behind Ishaan, being held by a horrendous, skeletal hand. Theo's pupils dilated as the claw lifted the balloons high enough for the grinning face to be revealed. The Hollow Man. His omen. Surely, an angel of death. Theo gasped as the off-note trumpets played and the coaster began its journey. Was this going to be his gruesome *Final Destination* death scene?

The ride started. Up and up they went, as if to touch the clouds. Theo's heart pounded, and he clung to the safety rail. His ribs felt as if they were sticking out of his skin and his stomach churned. The ascent continued higher and higher until they had reached the top. There was silence at the peak, a sense of foreboding. JJ broke it with a "Wooo!" as they rapidly began their descent into the hell pit.

They fell heavily downward, through the wind, like birds of prey. Steve held his hands high as Amber's golden mane smothered his face. Theo screamed for mercy, certain that something bad would happen when they plunged into the dark depths of the cave pit. Smoke hit their faces and darkness consumed them.

The off-note trumpets blared through the screams. *That can't be good*, he thought. An animatronic dragon emerged in a flash of light. Heat spat on their faces. Amber screamed. The spins and swirls played themselves out seconds later as they made their final cataclysmic escape and then the ride came to a complete stop. Nothing bad had happened, to Theo's great surprise. It was almost an anti-climax.

"That. Was. Awesome!" JJ screamed as Amber compared her wild, windswept mess of hair to Tabitha's solid, titanium locs.

The safety rail rose, releasing a quivering Theo. He turned to see where the Hollow Man had gone. Instead, a happy Ishaan was rummaging through his fanny pack. There was no Hollow Man, not now. No, instead stood a fully grown version of his childhood rabbit, Binky, holding one GREEN balloon, which he then let loose into the sky. *Is this good?* he pondered as the rabbit turned and skipped away into the crowds. His friends dragged him away from his stupor.

"Man, what did you think of that?" Steve asked.

Theo sniffed. "Yeah, it was great," he said unconvincingly. The gang noticed his discomposure but quickly brushed it off, eager to continue to the next thing.

At the carnival game, everyone took a shot at the high striker. JJ was determined to win, but only got as far as "Naughty Nellie." Tabitha, ever the show-off, slammed the mallet hard, earning "Titan." Steve followed up with "Thor: God of Thunder." The gang cheered, except for JJ, who sulked in the corner.

Theo stepped up next, his hand trembling slightly. With a sudden surge of energy, the hammer flew up to "Omega," and the bell rang loudly. Everyone stared in disbelief.

Theo laughed in shock. "I don't know what just happened."

"It's rigged," JJ muttered, annoyed.

Theo picked a teddy bear as his prize and handed it to Tabitha with a smile. "Here, I thought you'd like it."

Tabitha froze momentarily as if caught off guard, but smiled and slipped it into her bag. "Thanks, Theo."

Later, in the haunted house, things took a darker turn. The gang was jumped by actors in scary costumes, but it was all too cheesy to be genuine fear. Amber yelped at the jump scares, while JJ taunted the actors, even trying to tickle one's chin.

But Theo, in the darkness, heard something strange. A whisper. His own reflection in the mirrors started to distort, and a creepy, disembodied face—the Hollow Man—stared at him from the shadows. He froze, paralyzed by fear, until JJ appeared behind him, startling him out of his trance.

"Yo, thought we lost you," JJ teased. "Looks like you saw a ghost."

Theo blinked, his heart still racing. He was fine—really. But deep down, something had shifted. He felt off, his mind swimming with questions he couldn't answer.

As they left the haunted house, Steve noticed Theo's pale face. "You good, man?"

"I'm fine," Theo muttered, glancing over his shoulder one last time.

JJ looked him up and down.

Ishaan, oblivious to the tension, excitedly pointed at a zoo nearby, but it didn't seem to shake the atmosphere. "Hey, guys! We should check out that z-zoo!"

Theo rubbed his arms, feeling the chill despite the warmth of the night. "I dunno … I'm kinda …" he trailed off.

Steve clapped him on the back. "Come on, just one last thing. Let's go together."

Theo sighed and nodded. As they walked toward the zoo, JJ couldn't help but wonder if he was witnessing his friend slip away again, but for now, all he could do was keep him close and wait.

"Are you sure you're okay?" JJ finally asked, his voice soft and laced with concern.

Theo nodded, but the unease in his eyes said otherwise.

They soon ventured to the zoo, where, inside, teeth and claws were on display behind thick glass. Tigers paced, eyes tracking the visitors. Outside, bears lounged among the leaves, indifferent to the crowd. Wolves prowled around, almost domesticated, until they devoured their lunch. Apes swung and climbed, bored but calm.

"I'm not sure how I feel about zoos," Amber said, clasping her hands. "The animals are trapped, but—"

"Yeah, but they're safe from poachers and well-fed," Steve interrupted.

"That's what I was gonna say." Amber smiled.

The group moved on in silence, observing the animals or the tourists. A crowd gathered around the "King of the Cats," a lion perched on his rock, basking in the sun. He blinked lazily, swatting at a fly before rolling over to nap, the show over.

Theo grinned as he snapped a photo. A brief flash of RED crossed his mind—a cat, smaller than the lion, beneath his feet. It was a memory, but not his. He'd never owned a cat.

Steve nudged him. "He's a big boy, isn't he?"

JJ smirked. "That's what she said."

The group chuckled. Theo felt calmer, lifting his camera again.

"I've seen bigger," Tabitha said.

"That's also what she said," JJ whispered to Theo, giggling.

"I love lions," Amber said. "They're so majestic."

"They're regal, but they get shit done," Theo said, eyeing the lion.

"It's a dog-eat-dog world," JJ added.

Next, they approached a swampy enclosure. A five-meter alligator glared at them.

"Now he's big," Tabitha said.

"'Chester, the dog eater,'" Theo read from the sign. "Sounds charming."

Amber gasped. "He eats dogs?"

"I'd be fine with him eating people, but dogs?" Theo said, shuddering.

"He used to live in Florida, where dog walkers would walk their pets," Theo continued. "They brought him here after his crimes."

Ishaan recoiled. "He looks c-cold-hearted."

"Well, he's a reptile," Theo said, trying to lighten the mood.

"I think reptiles get a bad rap," JJ said. "Like lions, they get shit done."

"In a sly, barbaric way," Amber said, pointing at Chester's eyes. "No honor there."

"What about them?" JJ asked. "He doesn't care. He's just doing his thing. Can't judge nature."

"You're either the predator … or th-the prey," Ishaan added.

"That's the circle of life, right?" JJ said, leaning against the glass. "No point in worrying. Hakuna matata."

"It's not that simple," Amber said.

"Sure, it is," JJ said. "You eat or get eaten. Basic math."

Amber wagged her finger. "What about mutualism?"

"Isn't that when germs make babies?" Steve asked.

"What? No, mutualism! Symbiosis? We learned about it in school."

"Yeah, but I barely remember anything from school," JJ admitted. "Tell us more."

"Mutualism is when two species interact in a way that benefits both," Amber explained.

"Oh, like Bella passing me the remote for a treat?" Steve said.

"Exactly!" Amber chuckled.

"What about that zombie fungus that gets ants?" Ishaan asked.

"Zombie fungus?" Theo raised an eyebrow.

"It infects ants' brains," Ishaan said. "Controls them. Grows out of their h-heads. It kills them."

"That's a cheery thought," Theo muttered.

"What's the point of that?" JJ asked.

Amber stepped in for Ishaan. "The fungus spreads more spores."

"I guess it's just nature," Theo said, wiping a speck of RED from his hand.

"Can it happen to humans?" JJ asked.

"N-no," Ishaan said, "not to humans."

Theo's nerves flared at the thought of his own parasite—the tumour growing in his brain. He turned his focus to the next exhibit.

A serpent with brown scales and two heads slithered across a branch.

"The hydra," JJ read from the sign.

"Wow," Steve exhaled.

"Cool!" Ishaan said.

"Do you think they can talk to each other?" JJ wondered.

"Telepathically?" Ishaan blinked.

"I think some conjoined twins can do that," Amber said, tapping on her phone.

"Yeah, it's rare but possible," Tabitha said, looking up from her screen.

Theo's mind buzzed as he stared at the creature. One body, two heads. It made him think of his own fractured thoughts, his sense of self splintering. Adaptation, Theo realized, was nature's greatest weapon. He raised his camera to take another shot, capturing his inner turmoil.

CHAPTER NINE
PAINTING THE TOWN RED

The Sapphire Bar was the hidden hot spot of L.A., according to several websites, located in the buzzing West district, which was littered with many other rival or rather envious establishments. The interior was elaborate, lavishly decorated with peacock feathers and dim neon lighting that gently illuminated the corners and dark spots. Beaded curtains hung from large, round, ornate doorways and covered secret alcoves. Flamboyant avant-garde statues had been placed around the room and lime-coloured, oriental paper umbrellas adorned the ceiling. The walls were armoured with cutting steel pipes, re-welded into a reptilian design that contrasted with the soft velvet cushions scattered around. A silky-toned songstress sang entrancing mood music.

Expensive cocktails, in a rainbow of glowing colours, were being hastily lined up to satisfy customers' thirst, some steaming, some served in teapots, others in test tubes. The artistry of each drink was astonishing, yet each one was also refreshing and delicious. Something Theo was not to learn as he sat, regretfully and deceitfully, sipping his Coca-Cola. He neither wanted alcohol to worsen his tumour nor did he want to make his friends suspicious. So he sat pretending, however, not with his camera tonight. He didn't want to run the risk of damaging it on a night out. Sitting beside Theo was Ishaan, drinking orange juice to top up his vitamin C. Tabitha and Amber sat swirling their opulent martini cocktails, while JJ and Steve knocked back their third round of drinks.

"Shots! Shots! Shots!" JJ squawked like a peacock. "Okay, what does everybody want?"

Theo rubbed his eyes hard in frustration.

"Tequila!" Steve shouted, slamming his empty glass down.

Amber's hand rushed to her chest as she recoiled in horror. "Oh my, no! Tequila makes me gag!"

"Yeah! I'd rather shit in my hands and clap!" Tabitha added.

"Lovely," Theo murmured.

JJ sniggered. "Okay, so two sambucas, three tequilas, and one …" He pointed to Ishaan, who continued to sip his orange juice through a paper straw.

"W-water, please."

"H two of the O variety. On it!" JJ replied.

"Actually, J," Theo called out. "I think I'll just have water too, please."

"Ah, come on!"

"Na, it's just my stomach is a bit … you know." Theo caressed his belly.

"I told you diarrhea would get you. Do you need one of my p-pills?" Ishaan asked, rummaging through his bag.

"No, I'm good, thanks, Ishaan," Theo responded, instinctively caressing his pills in his pocket.

The two women whispered, colluding together on a strategy for the night.

"Actually, no shots for us either, J," Amber said. "We're fine with these." She held up her neon cocktail.

"Wrong answer! Try again," JJ said.

"We're serious; it's our first night here. Me and Ambz need to keep our gorgeous wits about us." Tabitha tapped her amethyst nails on the marble table.

"Fine, be boring." JJ sighed. "Steve, you still want shots?"

"Hell, yeah! Let's get several."

"My kinda guy!" JJ replied, wrapping his hand around Steve and escorting him to the bar.

Theo shook his head, chuckling at the duo, who were apparently rekindling their friendship in all the worst ways. A mild applause erupted throughout the busy room. The singer gracefully stepped off the stage to make way for someone new.

The next entertainer wore a black velour suit decorated with sequins. The singer's hair was short, wavy, and dark brown, with skin as pale as the moonlight. His emerald eyes sparkled with mischief. Theo's chest compacted upon itself when he realized who was now standing in the spotlight. It was Frank, gazing directly into Theo's already tormented soul, his expression clear that he was hell-bent on causing trouble.

"Oh wow, he is a snack," Tabitha murmured, sucking down her drink.

Frank stepped forward, taking the mic from the stand. With his dark eyeliner, he looked even more androgynous than usual. "I'd like to dedicate this song to a very special person, a true friend of mine who is going through a really rough time now, so here's to you. Hit it, boys!" The floor began to pulsate as the band started a jazzy rendition of "Can't Take My Eyes off You." Frank bounced a little to the rhythm as he began to sing, his gaze directly on his prey the whole time.

Theo's heart rate raced along with the tempo. Next to him, Ishaan's foot began to tap along to the musical number. The audience was hypnotized by the singer on stage, as he skilfully seduced them with his charismatic performance. Theo fidgeted in his seat, not daring to move, scared of what might happen if he did. As the song ended, spectators on all sides cheered and gave a standing ovation. Frank made a theatrical bow before dropping the mic and exiting the stage. As he left, a sudden glitch appeared on Frank's face, revealing a random stranger, only for a second, before turning back into Frank.

Theo rose in hot pursuit. "Excuse me, guys."

"Where are you going?" Tabitha asked.

"Restroom," he replied, marching off.

Tabitha frowned. "What is up with that boy?"

"Di- diarrhoea," Ishaan remarked, adjusting his glasses.

Meanwhile, at the bar, JJ and Steve were waiting for their shots in awkward silence. Neither was sober, but not yet drunk.

"What's your plan for tonight then?" Steve asked.

"My plan is to drink and then just deny, deny, deny," JJ replied.

The bartender filled their empty glasses with golden tequila, placing salt on the side and lime wedges on top of the rims.

"Finally!" JJ said, handing over his money and tipping salt into his and Steve's hands. "Cheers!"

The pair licked their salted skin, gulped down the smoky poison, and then bit down hard to suck the bitter juice out of the lime.

Steve scrunched his face up, wincing at the flavours assaulting his tongue. "Oh boy! I'm starting to remember why I don't drink this stuff anymore."

JJ laughed, moving on to the whiskey beside him, nursing it with ease.

"So," Steve said, grasping the cool glass of his beer. "Listen, J. I've been meaning to talk to you ..."

"Oh, God no, don't do this."

Steve's face contorted. "What?"

"I know what you're gonna say. It's so unnecessary."

"What do you mean?"

JJ sighed. "You're sorry for what happened between us at school, for not sticking up for me when I got bullied by your supposed 'friends', yada, yada, yada ..."

A look of relief came over Steve's face. "Ha ... guess you got me," he said, sipping his beer.

"Listen, I get it, I forgive you, now let's not talk; let's just drink."

"J, just listen, please, man, come on."

"I'm listening."

"I am sorry, I'm sorry for neglecting you for ... them, for not sticking up for you when they ... did what they did. I am so sorry."

JJ rocked a little in his seat and lowered his drink. He turned to face Steve. "I wasn't cool enough for you to be seen with at school, none of us were, but especially me, so you acted as if you didn't know me, and for a long time I hated you for it, I won't deny that." He paused, taking sight of Steve's trembling chin. "But then I remembered that we were friends, the best of friends, and that a friendship like ours doesn't just go away."

Steve lifted his head, hopeful. JJ continued, "We may have gone our separate ways, but we still came from the same place, with shared experiences, and I realized that sooner or later you'd realize that and come back for more of … this." He gestured to himself. "Because let's face it, who wouldn't?"

Steve broke into a laugh. "And look how right you were!"

"Damn right."

"For the record, I never had a problem with you being bisexual. In fact, at the time I was happy for you, even though I didn't say it."

"Did you know? Beforehand, I mean?"

"I had a few suspicions."

"Like what?" JJ asked curiously, swirling his whiskey around the glass.

"I dunno, just had a feeling about it, but it was never a problem. I should have stuck up for you. I'm sorry."

"I know, Steve, stop saying it."

"Honestly, I've just been so down lately."

"I know; I've been there, think we all have at some point. It's our generation."

"J, I tried to kill myself," Steve said quietly.

"What? When?"

"Shh!" Steve put a finger to his lips, looking around to see if any of their friends were nearby. "Please don't tell the others."

"No, no, I wouldn't," he promised, laying a reassuring hand on his friend's arm. "But jeez, Steve, how?"

Steve struggled for words as emotion took over. "I-I tried to hang myself over the stair banister," he said, trembling.

"Well … shit. Why?" JJ asked.

"I don't know. It was a few months ago when I got back from college. I just felt so lonely and like I was a failure."

"Steve, you're not a failure. You're just … lost, at the moment." JJ's face fell. "Can I tell you a secret?"

"Yeah, sure."

"Promise not to tell anyone."

"I promise."

JJ closed his eyes. "Okay, well, I've been where you're standing, I've tried to kill myself, more than once."

"What, no, man?"

"Yup. Both times at school."

"No, no, J." Steve furrowed his brow.

"Being bullied, my dad, guilt over my mom, everyone only ever viewing me as a joke … it took its toll. Hell, I cut myself, filled myself with pills. Yet nothing worked; here I am. On the other side."

"How have you managed it?" Steve questioned.

"I don't know. It's weird, I don't think you ever really get over depression, but day by day, you manage to find ways to snuff it out piece by piece." He looked down and fiddled with one of the bar's garishly designed coasters. "You gotta toughen up, and make life mean something. That's how I came through it, by having a purpose. And that's something that you need."

"So, what's your purpose?"

JJ giggled slightly. "Well, I have three: you guys, sex, and revenge." His eyes met Steve's.

"Revenge?" Steve repeated, swallowing hard.

"Yup, revenge."

"Revenge on who?"

"Everyone who's ever wronged me, including your buddies from school."

"That must be a long list."

"Hell yeah, it is, but I have a master plan."

"Which is?"

"To track down everyone on my list and take them all down, one by one."

Steve's eyes widened as he emitted a loud gulp.

"Remember Tom Plaza, the one who used to throw me in the trash and flush my head down the toilet, the one you used to associate with? The leader of your jock friends."

"How could I forget that asshole, especially after what he did to you and Tabz?"

JJ nodded. "He really had it coming. Basically, I stalked his social media profiles and found his mom, Karen. I looked through her profiles on Facebook, Instagram, X, and found out she was divorced and went to yoga class. So, I joined the yoga class tagged in her Instagram photos."

"Right!"

"I went to the class and charmed my way into her bed. I took photos of her doing things with me." JJ grinned, gesturing downward to his crotch.

"What!"

"Yup! I took many photos. Some with just her face in, some with mine in as well. Love a good selfie."

"Shit, J!"

"And then I text him saying, 'Remember me, and how you used to bully me at school?' And I sent him all the pictures."

"Oh my God, J," Steve was so shocked he could only let out a croaking laugh.

"Never heard from Tom or his lovely mother again." His eyes glanced back and forth as he returned to his whiskey.

"J, I can't…" Steve leaned back in his chair, amused but concerned. "Wait, when did you do that?"

"About six months ago. Why?"

Steve frowned. "Because five months ago, he went into counselling. He apparently had some breakdown."

"Good."

"J, you destroyed him, and his poor Mom." Steve shivered, then looked at JJ. "I'm not on your list, am I?"

"Hmm … not anymore."

"Thank God for that!"

"I could never put you on the list; you're like family to me."

"What happened to not being the sentimental type?"

"Hmm … what can I say. I'm a complicated character. "Wanna know what I did to Zane and Cole?"

"Sure," Steve replied slowly, as he wasn't certain he did.

"I bumped into them on a night out, so I spiked their drinks with a little something … next thing I know, they're head-butting on the dance floor and jumping off a balcony." JJ cackled manically.

"I remember hearing about that. They were in the hospital for weeks, got dropped from their football teams," Steve whispered.

"Oh, I'm aware. I celebrated for two weeks when I heard."

"You've completely ruined them, their lives."

"What can I say, karma?"

"Man, you're twisted," Steve shook his head.

"All the best people are. Besides, they got what they deserved—eventually."

The statement hit Steve like a punch. "So, who else is on your list?

"Billy is number two; he was the absolute worst to me at school. Josh and Andy are a close third and fourth."

"Who's number one?"

"My dad." JJ's voice soured. "Who knows, though, my list may grow. Might need to, the rate I'm ticking them all off."

"Wow, man, guess I'll just have to find my own way of coping with my … you know."

"Steve, you deserve to be happy."

"Do I, though?"

"Yes, I'm telling you. And you could always give revenge a try, works for me."

Steve changed the subject. "So, you like them both?"

"How'd you mean?"

"Men and women. You fancy both?"

"Yes, is that so surprising?" He flicked back a strand of stray hair.

"I've always been curious. I have questions," Steve admitted.

"Ask away," JJ calmly replied. "Whatever, you can't offend me, I've heard it all."

"Well … just explain to me what that's like. It's interesting."

"Listen, you know me; I'm an equal opportunist. I get bored easily. I can't eat chicken every day of the week—some nights I want beef, other nights I want salad, get the picture?"

Steve grimaced. "Who wants salad?"

"Everyone's on the menu with me, at least anyone who's gonna give me a bit of attention. I don't discriminate, I love and hate equally," he said in a joking tone. "It's not about girls or guys, men or women. It's not about that; it's about doing what feels natural at the time. I like what I like, and I like both. It's about electricity, feeling the positive and the negative, completing the circuit. Letting it flow, feeling plugged in with whoever catches my attention."

"Okay, yeah, I get it." Steve nodded.

"We all have a weakness for beauty, don't we?" JJ said, winking flirtatiously at a young woman who was checking out Steve. "Looks like you have a fan."

Steve blushed.

JJ put each of his hands on Steve's shoulders and winched him up.

"Ah, J, it's been a while. What do I say?"

"Just be you!" JJ said. He licked his hand and patted down Steve's hair and straightened the collar of his shirt. "Don't think! Just go!"

Steve headed towards the young woman, his head full of terrible chat-up lines.

JJ sat back with a self-satisfied smile; he had done several things in a short space of time. He had buried the hatchet with Steve, fortunately not in his skull, had grown closer to him through their shared experiences, and he had possibly even gotten him laid. He could rest assured that he was a good friend and maybe even a good person. The bartender pushed a fresh glass of whiskey to JJ, who looked up at him, confused.

"Hey, I didn't order this."

"Courtesy of the couple over there," the barman said, pointing to the other end of the bar where a young hipster-looking couple waved at him.

"Did they now?" JJ asked, downing his previous drink to pick up his new one, before walking over to them with a swagger in his step.

Theo creaked the door to the men's restroom open, cautiously looking around. Empty. The voices began to whisper in Theo's head.

"Where is he?"

"Were we just dreaming it?"

"What are you hiding?"

"Maybe we should head back?"

"No! He's definitely here! He must be!"

White and GREEN tiles were embedded in the walls and floor, everywhere. Silver sinks gleamed with a cleanliness. Theo's footsteps echoed loudly, echoing off the walls.

"Idiot!"

"Check the stalls!"

Carefully, leaning down, Theo began to check if any feet were housed under the doors of the oak brown cubicles. None. The steady drip, drip from a tap caught Theo's attention, and his face twitched as the voices in his head grew louder. He paced over to the tap to turn it entirely off, hoping it would somehow also stop the noise in his head. Theo exhaled in relief as he stood in the silence, regarding his pale reflection in the mirror while leaning against the sink.

"I know what you're thinking," a voice called out to him from behind. "How long till those idiots ruin everything?"

Theo's heart grew heavy. His eyes darted towards the voice to see Frank wearing his sequin ensemble.

"Yo." Frank waved, stepping closer. "Having a moment of self-reflection, were we?"

"What are you doing here?" Theo hissed.

"Looking out for you. Tell me, are the others bothering you?"

"No, they're not."

"Well, it's only a matter of time."

A simmering rage boiled within Theo. "They're my friends, we've been over this. My allies."

"You don't need allies when you win." Frank pointed out.

"No, that's not—"

"What are you doing, kid? You think you're safe with these losers? Stick with me, there's no time to waste."

Theo was becoming impatient. "I've just arrived here in L.A. I'm trying to make it seem like I don't have an ulterior motive. You know, blend in, not appear suspicious."

"Ah, boring," Frank said, rolling his eyes and making his way over to the sinks. "You're boring me, and there's nothing worse than someone who bores me." Frank leaped up on the central sink, dangling his legs like a small child. "Aw, you're worried that I'm not your friend anymore, it's not like that. It's just … tough love. I'm Frank, your sassy, mean friend. There's no bullshit with me, sweetheart."

Theo looked around, then hurtled towards Frank until he stood inches away from him. "Why are you here?"

Frank gave a boyish giggle. "Isn't it obvious?" Frank's spindly black legs wrapped their way around Theo, pulling him in closer. Theo's instincts kicked in and he grabbed his thighs. Frank continued. "To remind you, kid, that you and I are running out of time. We're getting weaker by the second. Both of us. Know what that means?"

Theo was distracted by the sensation of touching Frank. But how was this real?

"Hey! Hey! Focus!" Frank snapped his fingers three times to get Theo's attention. "It means I can't protect you from the Hollow Jerk like I have been doing all this time."

For a second, the room spun despite the firm embrace of Frank's spider-like legs.

"The plane, the rollercoaster, the maze of mirrors; that was you protecting me?" Theo asked.

"Yes! Like I always have, remember?"

Theo shook his head, trying to wriggle out of his entrapment with little success. "Wait, so why did Binky show up then and not you?"

Frank began to laugh, waving it off. "Oh, that was just me having a bit of fun. You like fun, don't you?"

Theo stood still, momentarily allowing himself to be a plaything. Not answering.

Frank's face seemed to glitch for a moment. "Don't you," he repeated, his cold hand grasping Theo's neck.

"Yes!"

"Good!" Frank released the young man's neck and torso, allowing him to back up a few feet. "Then I suggest you find this 'dragon' soon, otherwise it's no more fun for either of us."

"But where do I even start to find him?"

"I dunno? Ask around, crack a few bones, get your hands a little dirty. Find a way. You're smart; you'll figure it out."

Theo's eyelids had drooped slightly, but the sound of the door opening pulsed through him like an alarm, fully awakening him. Frank had vanished.

"Hey! There you a-are!" Ishaan called out. He was a welcome sight. "Been looking everywhere for you! Was wo-worried!"

"Yeah, sorry, just had a bit of a moment."

"I figured," Ishaan said, riffling through his bag of pills, pulling out a single cyan and salmon one. "Here, take th-this. It will help."

"Thanks," Theo said, grateful for an excuse for his prolonged absence.

"No problem, we should probably get ba-back to Tabitha and Amber, they'll be worried."

"You're right."

Ishaan held the squeaky door open for Theo. "Lord knows where JJ and Steve have got t-to?" He didn't see his friend throw the pill into the sink, where it rattled around before falling down the drain.

Amber adjusted the front of her chic blue dress, thinking about what her mother always said: "The clothes you wear determine how people see you." She didn't want to attract the wrong kind of attention tonight, especially with JJ and Steve on her mind. "I can't see them anywhere," she said, scanning the bar.

"Leave them," Tabitha replied, waving her hand dismissively. "They're big boys, they can handle themselves."

"But what if they're too drunk?" Amber asked, anxiety

creeping in.

"J's liver is practically titanium," Tabitha said, her voice smooth as silk. "He'll be fine. Relax. That's why we're here—to let loose."

Amber hesitated, but Tabitha pushed a glass into her hands. "Try this. It's a Pornstar Martini."

Amber took a gulp. "Ooh, this is nice."

Tabitha smiled. "Right! Alcoholic and fabulous. Drink up!"

Amber relaxed a little as she sipped her drink. "I guess I came out here to get away, see something new. Learn, I suppose."

"Learn? About what?" Tabitha raised an eyebrow.

"About the world. The culture, the people. See how things work outside my bubble."

Tabitha glanced into her own drink. "Yeah, I get that. Sometimes, you want to see more than what you know."

Amber smiled. "Before I'm married off to some rich guy and become a stay-at-home mom."

"A what?" Tabitha spluttered. "Who says you have to do that?"

"My mom," Amber replied, lowering her drink. "She says I'm just a pretty face, and I should use it to get a respectable husband."

Tabitha reached out and grabbed her hand. "Amber, you're more than that. You can be whoever you want. Just figure out what makes you happy."

Amber tried to hold back laughter but failed. Tabitha always had a way of making things feel better.

"I don't want to end up like my mom," Tabitha continued. "I'm here to see the world, not settle down."

"Yeah, but what's your dream?" Amber asked.

Tabitha smiled, eyes gleaming. "I want my own boutique salon. I want to transform people's style and show them their potential."

"You'll do it," Amber said with confidence.

"Maybe, but I've got to start with what I have."

Later, they stumbled out of the bar, tipsy and giggling. "Oh my God! No!" Amber laughed, leaning on Tabitha.

"Yes!" Tabitha cried out. "And then he put it back in! I was dead!"

A group of men approached from behind and encircled them. The leader stepped forward. "Hey," he said, eyeing them both. Amber curled herself inwards.

Tabitha, trying to keep things moving, said, "Hi. Bye." Another man blocked their way.

"No need to be rude, babe." He smirked.

Tabitha bristled. "Don't call me babe."

"So feisty," he said, stepping closer.

Tabitha's grip tightened on Amber's arm. "Just one kiss, babe," he urged.

"No." Tabitha stood her ground.

"Just one," he persisted.

"Fuck off!" Tabitha snapped.

Before the situation could escalate, the man reached for her. She slapped him hard across the face, and the others froze in shock. Amber's body went rigid as the thug pulled out a knife.

Just then, Theo appeared seemingly from nowhere, grabbing the thug's wrist with an unnatural speed. "Theo!" Tabitha gasped, eyes wide.

Theo's grip tightened, causing the thug to drop the knife in pain.

Ishaan caught up, out of breath.

"Get him off me!"

Theo ignored the man's cries, his focus entirely on the fight. He crushed the thug's hand with a sickening crunch, causing the thug to scream. The others rushed in, but Theo moved with a speed and ferocity that stunned Amber.

He knocked two men back with lightning-fast kicks, sending one crashing into a trash bin. Another charged at him, but Theo easily evaded the attack and struck him in the chest, sending him flying backward.

The last thug swung a metal pipe at him, but Theo dodged,

his body fluid and precise. He hit the man square in the jaw, dislocating it with one punch. The thug dropped the pipe and collapsed.

As the remaining men staggered to their feet, Theo launched himself at them with the intensity of a wild animal. His moves were fast and brutal, each strike calculated to maim. Within moments, the thugs were battered and scattered.

"Theo! That's enough!" Tabitha shouted.

Theo didn't listen. He stood over the leader, who was still clutching his broken hand. "Apologize to my friends."

"What?" The thug's voice trembled.

"Apologize."

"I'm sorry!" the thug croaked, clearly terrified.

"That didn't sound sincere," Theo said coldly. "Try again."

"I'm sorry!" the man repeated.

Theo shook his head, unimpressed. "Still not good enough." He stepped on the thug's injured hand with crushing force.

"Ahh! I'm sorry! I'm sorry!" the man screamed.

"Okay, okay! Let him go," Tabitha ordered.

Theo released the man, stepping back. The thug scrambled to his feet and hobbled away with his friends, terrified.

"Theo, are you okay?" Amber asked, voice shaky.

"I'm fine," Theo replied, his voice distant.

Tabitha shook her head in disbelief. "Where the hell did that come from?"

Theo looked at his bloodstained hands, still in shock. "I don't know. Something just … took over."

"We should go," Ishaan said nervously. "They might be back."

"You're right," Tabitha said, steering Amber away. She glanced back to see Theo standing still, staring at his hands, as if processing what had just happened.

"Theo!" Tabitha called. "Time to go!"

Theo snapped out of his trance and ran to catch up. They quickly made their way back to the apartment. The blood from the alley slowly disappeared down the drain behind them.

CHAPTER TEN
FUN AND FORTUNES

Theo awoke to flashing lights and the blare of an alarm. His mind was a haze of memories from the night before: crushing a thug's hand, taking down his attackers effortlessly. That wasn't him. He wasn't violent. But last night … he felt different. Powerful. Maybe the voices or Frank had something to do with it, but Theo couldn't shake the fear that something darker had awakened inside him.

Shaking off the thoughts, he trudged into the kitchen, where a surprisingly chipper Amber was making breakfast. The apartment had undergone an overnight transformation—colourful Post-It notes now covered the walls, turning the dingy space into a strange mosaic.

Amber was humming while frying eggs and bacon—definitely a sign that something was up. Ishaan sat at the table, eyeing her with concern, while Theo's stomach recoiled at the sight of Amber's cooking.

"Good morning, sunshine!" Amber greeted, dishing up food despite Theo's protests. "Sleep well?"

"Kinda," he muttered, pulling up a chair.

"I didn't sleep at all," she replied breezily, but Theo could see the tension beneath her smile.

Ishaan shot him a warning glance as Theo reluctantly eyed the greasy plate. "Are you okay?" he asked Amber.

She smiled, but it didn't quite reach her eyes. "Absolutely, why wouldn't I be?"

Tabitha entered in her satin pyjamas, instantly diving into her phone. "Some freak on Insta said I look like a third-rate Zendaya!" she huffed, tapping the screen.

Amber tried to keep her mood light. "I couldn't sleep, so I made some art."

Tabitha eyed the Post-Its. "Stole them?"

"No!" Amber replied, defensive. "I found them in the lobby bin."

"A dumpster dive, huh?" Tabitha grinned, grabbing an apple.

Ishaan's face turned green as he pulled out hand sanitizer, spilling it everywhere. Amber rolled her eyes, clearly done with his paranoia.

The door suddenly creaked open, and in stumbled Steve and JJ—JJ, still drunk, wore a ridiculous lion onesie.

"Where the hell have you two been?" Amber snapped.

JJ grinned. "Crazy night. Hooked up with a couple who had a thing for feet—yeah, let's say it got weird."

"Details we don't need, thanks," Amber groaned.

The story quickly devolved into absurdity as JJ continued detailing his drunk escapades while Theo stared at his cold breakfast, wondering where his life had gone.

"So, what happened with you guys?" JJ asked, clearly oblivious to the tension.

Tabitha was quick to answer. "We were almost raped and murdered."

Everyone paused, Steve's face going pale.

"Seriously?" he asked.

"Yeah, some guys tried to hit on us. I slapped one, he pulled a knife … and then Theo crushed his hand like a can." Amber spoke the words as though they were just a casual fact.

JJ's eyes lit up. "Theo? Our Theo did that?"

"Instincts." Theo shrugged, trying to convince himself more than anyone else.

"So, how many of these guys were there?" JJ asked, fascinated.

"Five," Tabitha answered, grinning at the memory. "And, yeah, there was blood."

Steve looked impressed. "Well, this sounds like a hell of a night."

Theo couldn't keep up the facade anymore. The pulsing sensation in his hand was back, the voices louder.

"We need to get out of here!"

"Yes!"

"Now!"

Theo rubbed his forehead, his neck growing tense. He couldn't allow the panic to win. He jumped up.

"Right, I need a shower," he muttered, grabbing an excuse to escape.

As he left the room, JJ gave Amber a knowing look. "Something's off with him, don't you think?"

"Yeah," she replied, still shaken by the night's events, "but he'll be fine."

The mood shifted again when JJ mentioned that Steve had hooked up with a rich girl named Alice. Amber stiffened, and Steve caught her reaction. "Is she okay?" he asked quietly, watching Amber walk away.

Tabitha waved him off. "She's just tired. Don't overthink it."

As everyone began to prepare for the day, Ishaan sat awkwardly at the table, his discomfort palpable. Tabitha, ever the perceptive one, leaned in with a sly smile. "Hey, Ishaan. You good?"

His eyes widened. "W-what do you mean? I'm f-fine." Ishaan pasted a smile on his face and put his glasses back on.

Tabitha proceeded cautiously. "Only, I noticed you getting a bit twitchy when they were talking about … sex."

Ishaan instantly turned away.

Tabitha continued, "Don't mind me asking, but are you still a …" She looked around—all clear. "A virgin?"

Ishaan's hand rushed to his brow. "What n-no—of course not—I mean how c-could … why would you s-say that … I m-mean—why …?"

Tabitha merely granted him a reassuring look, and he knew she knew the answer already. "M-maybe," he answered shamefully.

Tabitha walked over and placed her hand on his, her usual tough persona not in evidence. "Aw, it's fine. Don't feel pressured, there's no rush, you'll be ready when you're ready, baby boy."

Ishaan smiled, still looking down, before putting his hand on hers. "Thanks, Tabz."

He then got up awkwardly and left, unburdened by social graces. Tabitha looked around the empty room. "Okay then."

Hours later, the gang navigated L.A.'s markets where all sorts of goods were for sale. The air buzzed with the conversations of people from all over the world. The heat radiating from the dusty ground was nearly unbearable.

Their first stop: an air-conditioned convenience store packed with snacks. The boys wandered off, amused by springing cars and bouncy balls, pranking each other, cracking jokes, and impersonating people they knew. Ishaan sat on the sidelines, barely joining in.

Meanwhile, Tabitha and Amber browsed through cheap jewellery. Tabitha picked up a pair of purple, glass-cut earrings, holding them against her bare lobes and assessing them in the mirror.

"Ambz, be honest … what do you think?" Tabitha asked.

Amber paused, studying them. "They look amazing. Even better on you!"

Tabitha swished her thick locs and grinned. "Think I'll take them." She grabbed a hat. "And this!" Then a belt. "And this!"

Amber raised an eyebrow. "You're going all out today, huh?"

"Can't help it! I'm a shopaholic! I buy crap I don't need and waste money, but it's just so satisfying!" Tabitha admitted, clutching her pile of goods.

"Then why don't you stop?" Amber asked.

"I can't! It's like … the next thing I buy will fill that empty space—on my nightstand, my wardrobe, whatever," Tabitha explained, tightening her grip on the items. "It's like buying something new will change everything. But it never does. It's my hobby—some people drink, others paint, I buy crap."

Amber frowned, her gaze distant. "I … I don't know what mine is."

Tabitha gave her a playful nudge. "You're too deep for me, Ambz. But hey, remember that boutique idea I mentioned?"

Amber smiled. "What's it going to be called?"

"Not sure yet, but it'll be full of trendy stuff no one needs but everyone wants." Tabitha shrugged.

"If anyone can sell something, it's you." Amber grinned.

Tabitha winked. "Damn right."

Amber's laughter faded as something caught her eye—a figure in a large hat and black sunglasses watching her intently from behind a rack of magazines. She motioned to Tabitha, but the latter was too distracted by her phone. Amber stepped away, her dress flowing behind her like a cape.

As she neared the aisle, the figure panicked, knocking over magazines and hurriedly ducking down an aisle. Amber recognized the silver hair and bubble chin immediately. "Excuse me a sec," she called to Tabitha, then stalked toward the woman.

The figure froze in front of a mannequin display. Amber approached, already knowing. "Nana?"

There was no answer, just the faint rise and fall of the mannequin's chest.

"I can see you breathing."

"Okay, okay!" Nana pulled off her hat and sunglasses. "It's me!"

Amber rolled her eyes. "What are you doing here?"

"I'm staying with an old friend just down the road, catching up—"

"Are you spying on me?"

"No! Well … yes, exactly like that," Nana admitted. "Your mother was worried about this trip and wanted to stop you. But I convinced her to let you go if I tagged along."

"'Tagged along?'" Amber's hands went to her hips.

Nana put on a defensive grin. "I was going to make my presence known, very casually."

"Because this is casual?"

"Not like this! I'm incognito," Nana declared, sliding her sunglasses back on. "Do you think I'm your mother's lackey?"

Amber scoffed. "More like a secret agent."

Nana raised an eyebrow. "I just wanted one last adventure with my only granddaughter. Is that so wrong?"

Amber softened, though she was still annoyed. "You're impossible, Nana."

"So, what do you think? A day or two with me before I head to the next shore?" Nana asked.

Amber hesitated. She had plans with her friends, but Nana's hopeful face gave her pause. "Okay, tomorrow. We're going on a guided hike."

"Perfect! What time? Where?" Nana was already fist-pumping the air.

"I'll text you the details later."

"Excellent!" Nana beamed.

An elderly man with a cane approached Nana from behind. "Ingrid!" he called.

Nana's face fell. "Ah, shit," she whispered, waving back.

Amber raised an eyebrow. "But your name isn't Ingrid …"

"I have many aliases," Nana replied, putting on her best poker face.

The man hobbled over, grinning widely, and hugged Nana. "Do you remember me?"

Nana hesitated. "Of course, I do! Why wouldn't I? How are you?"

"I'm good, but not as good as I was," the man grumbled, tapping his cane. "Had surgery on my hip, but it gets me places."

Nana introduced Amber. "This is my granddaughter, Amber."

Amber, already ready to make her escape, flashed a quick smile. "Well, I have places to be, so … see you tomorrow, Nana." She waved and started walking off.

Nana called after her, "See you tomorrow, dear."

The man, oblivious to the awkward tension, kept rambling. "Last time I saw you, must've been '72. I wore a flower on my vest … I got the heel of my boot replaced … the ferry cost three nickels back then …"

Amber quickly disappeared into the crowd. She jogged back to her friends, who were reading joke cards.

"You won't believe this," she said. "My grandmother followed us here to spy on me—at my mom's request."

Steve winced. "Ouch."

"And she's joining us on our hike tomorrow."

JJ groaned. "I don't need some old lady cramping my style!"

"Oh, shut up, J!" Theo fanned himself.

Tabitha pointed across the street. "Hey, look! Mistress Solara's Cabinet of Curiosities."

"It could be fun," Amber said.

JJ perked up. "It could?"

They entered the rundown shop, filled with dusty trinkets and old candles. Tree branches grew through cracks in the walls, adorned with talismans.

Tabitha called, "Hello?" but the shop was empty.

JJ tried to leave, but Tabitha grabbed him by the ear. "Ow!"

Steve started examining the strange items, from amulets to dolls' heads in green liquid. "Some of this stuff is pretty cool."

JJ shivered. "And freaky."

"And dusty," Ishaan added.

Tabitha tried on a bracelet, admiring its good luck charms.

"These are pretty," Amber agreed.

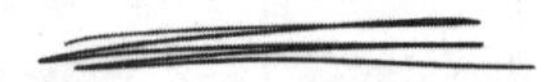

Steve noticed a silver wolf pendant with turquoise inscriptions—his birthstone.

Theo whispered, "Feed the good wolf."

Steve smiled.

"Put it on," Theo urged.

Steve did, and a rush of vitality flowed through him.

"Looks good on you," Theo said.

Steve smiled. "Thanks. I'll get it."

"I'll get it for you," Theo offered.

"Thanks, man," Steve said, glowing with warmth.

Tabitha joined in, buying a bracelet too. "I could use some luck." Amber followed suit, while JJ rolled his eyes.

"You know all this stuff is just L.A. new age voodoo hoodoo spiritual crap, right?" he said.

"You're so negative," Amber snapped.

"It's not crap," Steve replied. "It's a matter of perspective."

A voice interrupted: "What makes you so sure?" They turned to see a woman in a purple satin robe, presumably Mistress Solara.

JJ scoffed. "I don't believe in this stuff."

Mistress Solara's eyes locked onto him. "You don't believe in devils, evil forces?"

"Nope," JJ said.

"Don't be so certain," she said, laughing softly.

"I don't believe in some little red man with horns," JJ muttered.

"The devil comes as everything you've ever wanted," Solara said, clicking her fingers.

JJ shrugged. "Whatever. Let's go."

Solara gripped his arm. "You have a touch of fate. A spark of redemption."

"I'm not looking for redemption," JJ snapped.

"Not yet," Solara replied. She released him, and JJ stormed away.

"I'll be waiting outside," he said as he left.

Tabitha turned eagerly to the shopkeeper. "Can you tell me my future?"

Solara smiled. "Everyone wants to know their future … until they do."

"Please!" Tabitha begged.

Mistress Solara grinned. "It will cost you."

Tabitha threw some money on the table. Solara gestured to the curtain. "This way, my child."

Tabitha stepped forward, eager for her fortune.

Tabitha sat on the red velvet stool, legs swinging in anticipation. Mistress Solara sat silently across from her.

"So how does this work?" Tabitha asked, fiddling with her locs.

Solara interlaced her fingers, her eyes narrowing. "You look into my eyes, and the spirits will speak through me."

Tabitha raised an eyebrow. "Okay …"

Solara leaned forward, her gaze intense. "You're a builder. Strong, protective, compassionate. A woman of influence."

Tabitha grinned, leaning back in triumph. "That's me."

Solara's eyes darkened. "You can turn the caterpillar into the butterfly. But how long can you survive on material wealth alone? I see motherhood in your future—whether you want it or not."

"Motherhood?" Tabitha frowned.

"And more," Solara added cryptically. "But the spirits don't always show us the full picture. They speak in riddles. You must listen closely."

Tabitha's confidence waned as she fidgeted with her bracelet. What was the 'more'?

***

Amber settled on the stool, her new bracelet jingling. Solara's eyes flicked toward the curtain.

"You have a handsome suitor waiting," Solara observed.

Amber froze. "You mean Steve?"

"Yes, a lovely couple you make."

Amber laughed nervously. "We're just friends."

Solara's eyes narrowed. "The spirits say otherwise. You feel guilty … guilty over something you haven't done yet."

Amber blinked. "What?"

"You're at a crossroads. You feel lost—unsure of your past, present, and future. But I see romance for you, yes. Your life will be full of it. Yet secrets will follow, and regrets will be your companions. The misdeeds you will swim in will drown you."

Amber's smile faltered. "That's … a lot."

Solara gave a knowing smile. "The future will reveal itself, but be ready for the burden of your own truth."

Ishaan shifted uncomfortably in his seat, eyes darting around. Solara studied him closely.

"You carry tension," she said softly. "A shadow that no one sees, yet you long to be seen. Understood."

Ishaan squirmed. "I'm f-fine, really." He pulled out a pill from his bag and popped it in his mouth.

Solara's gaze softened. "But you are not fine. You will find peace in the arms of the woman you love. She will see you. Truly see you."

Ishaan swallowed hard, his face pale. He hadn't expected this.

"Does she … exist?" Ishaan murmured.

Solara smiled faintly. "The spirits say yes, but you must first learn to see yourself."

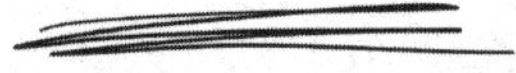

Steve fiddled with his new wolf pendant, a sense of confidence radiating from him.

"That talisman suits you," she said, nodding at it.

"Thanks. Did you make it?"

Solara smiled, her fingers twitching as if remembering something. "Yes. Each one is imbued with purpose. Protection. Healing. Wisdom."

"Sounds powerful."

"It is," Solara said, leaning in. "This pendant was enchanted to protect its wearer. And to heal … to bring wholeness."

Steve ran his fingers over the pendant. "I like it. It feels right."

Solara oversaw him. "You've been told you're the hero in your own story, haven't you? A knight on a quest."

Steve nodded, intrigued. "I guess, yeah."

"But you're more than that. You're searching for something deeper—something that will give your life true meaning. A calling the world will need."

Steve's eyes narrowed. "Will I find it?"

"That is for you to decide," Solara said. "But you will dig deep to uncover it. You believe your story is over, that it has somehow ended? But how can it have when you have so many other stories to tell? Stories the world needs to hear."

Theo twirled his thumbs, his camera hanging from his neck. "So, how does this work? Do we sit and wait?"

Solara's eyes fixed on him. "You seek a way forward. Away from the path you're currently on."

Theo raised an eyebrow. "What does that mean?"

Solara stared at him, her face becoming serious. "The slippery slope you walk will lead you to darkness. You must find another way."

Theo shifted uneasily. "I don't think it's that bad. Maybe it's just a phase."

Solara's expression shifted suddenly. Her body grew rigid. She seemed to freeze.

"Hello? Are you okay?" Theo asked, leaning forward.

No response. Theo stood up, panicked. "Hello?"

"Is she dead?"

"Hello?" Theo bellowed once more.

"Is she dead?"

"I don't know?" he replied to himself.

"Check her pulse!"

He reached for her wrist. Suddenly, she grabbed his arm tightly.

"I see darkness in you, a darkness you hold close, and in that darkness, eyes are staring back at me, but they are not yours. They are eyes that plague you, that haunt you."

Theo recoiled, his heart racing.

The voices returned.

"Kill her."

"No."

"Let go!" he growled. Her hand relinquished him as he got up to leave, his legs shaking.

Solara rose from her seat. "You are your own worst enemy, but love will be your end, though love of yourself or others is yet to be seen. But it will be your end, for sure. A new age is coming, and you … you'll be dead before the dawn."

Theo looked at her serious face. The thought stabbed at his brain like an ice pick. Jabbing at him. He fought hard to control his urge to pound her head into a fine mush. He exhaled and calmly said, "That's just my future today."

istress Solara watched the monster leave her shop, hopefully for good.

Outside on the shaded porch, Theo's five friends were lounging, distracted by their individual readings. JJ swiped through his DMs, waiting for Theo to return. Ishaan absentmindedly swatted at flies, believing they were mosquitoes. Tabitha and Amber compared charms on their bracelets. Amber stood in the sun, hoping the rays would attract Steve, though she'd never admit it.

Steve, deep in thought, studied the symbolism of wolves on his phone: guardianship, loyalty, spirit, intelligence. He caressed his new totem and smiled.

Across the street, Amber watched a couple kissing, and something stirred in her—a longing for a real romance. Her mother had always pushed a shallow, transactional view of love, but now, Amber felt an unfamiliar desire for genuine connection. Her gaze turned and lingered on Steve, unsure of how to handle this new feeling or what Solara had just told her.

Theo emerged from the shop, slamming the door behind him.

"Hey, hey!" Steve called, jogging over. "Everything good?"

Theo forced a smile, masking the unease. "Yeah, fine."

The others approached, and he saw their glances at his hands. They were shaking.

"So, what did she say?" Tabitha asked cautiously.

"Same as everyone else, I guess." Theo shrugged.

"Generic stuff," JJ added, clearly trying to downplay it. "She just takes gullible people's money."

Tabitha smacked him upside the head.

"Ow!"

"You act like a child," she scolded. "My reading was spot on."

"Yeah, sure, whatever," JJ muttered.

"So, lunch?" Steve suggested.

"I'm hungry," Amber admitted.

They began walking toward a restaurant.

Behind them, Ishaan pulled Steve aside. "Steve … could you help me pick out some clothes?"

"Clothes?" Steve asked, surprised.

"Just want to look cooler, you know?" Ishaan stammered.

Steve smiled. "You are cool, man. You need more confidence."

Ishaan hesitated. "I don't know how to be confident."

"We can work on it," Steve said, calling over to JJ and Theo. "Let's go shopping!"

"Sweet!" JJ cheered, dabbing dramatically.

"Seriously?" Theo rolled his eyes as the boys took off, leaving the women behind.

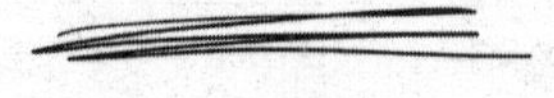

"What are they up to?" Amber asked.

"Men being men," Tabitha replied.

In the store, Ishaan stood nervously in a changing room, wearing a mismatched outfit: billowy shorts, a polo tucked in, a fanny pack, and squeaky sneakers.

JJ rubbed his chin. "What are we doing exactly?"

"We're giving Ishaan a makeover," Steve replied.

"What kind of makeover? What's the vibe?" Theo asked.

"Ishaan, what's your vision?" Steve prompted.

"C-cool," Ishaan mumbled.

JJ pulled Steve and Theo aside. "Can I talk to you two for a sec?"

In the changing room, JJ whispered, "He wanted a makeover, but 'cool'? He's not exactly the 'cool' type."

Steve peeked through the curtain. "We just need to make Ishaan look presentable but still him."

"I get it," Theo said. "Let's work with what we have."

JJ sighed. "Fine. I'll help."

Ishaan tried on more outfits: a hipster, a lumberjack, a cowboy, and even a biker. Theo snapped photos as JJ worked his magic, until they found a balanced look—a fitted blazer with black jeans, a white shirt, and the glasses somehow looked good. Ishaan looked taller, more confident.

Amber and Tabitha arrived just as Ishaan emerged.

"Whoa," Tabitha said, checking the blazer. "This actually looks good."

"Yeah, it's working," Steve said, impressed. "Feeling different?"

"I do, a li-little," Ishaan admitted.

"It's official," Theo said, smiling. "This is the one."

Ishaan looked at himself in the mirror, still unsure.

"You look great," Amber said, "What brought this on?"

"I just felt like changing," Ishaan replied.

The group cheered, and JJ bowed theatrically. "My work here

is done."

Steve clapped Ishaan on the back. "Let's pay for these before they think we're stealing."

As they walked toward the register, Amber followed Steve, showing him a pair of sunglasses she'd picked up. "What do you think?" she asked.

"Nice," Steve said, trying them on.

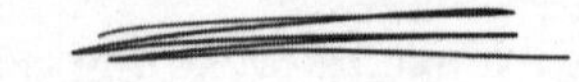

"Isn't it cute?" Theo said to JJ as they watched the pair from a safe distance.

"Sometimes it's cute, other times it's nauseating," JJ replied.

"Do you ever think about getting RED highlights?" Theo asked randomly.

"No, why?" JJ raised an eyebrow.

"You'd look good with them," Theo said, his attention drifting. "RED has always been your colour."

JJ smirked. "Oh, thanks."

Theo's phone buzzed with several missed call notifications from an unknown number. He stared at it, perplexed, before stepping into an aisle to listen to the voicemail.

"You have two missed calls," a trickster voice imitated. "First message …"

"Frank?" Theo said in surprise.

A deliberate, gruff cough was emitted from the phone, followed by a tasteless, bad impression. "Theo, this is your father calling. It's time we talked, son, you know, about the birds and the bees. You see, when a mommy and a daddy love each other very much, they get a little excited and well …" A childish giggle devolved into a cruel cackle. "Oh, I'm sorry, I'm sorry, it's just so funny. You know, because he's dead!"

Theo stood in the flickering light of the aisle. "What the?"

"Second message …" Frank continued in a high pitch. "Theo, this is your mother. I just thought I'd remind you to drink plenty of water, eat all your veggies and … GET! MOVING! NOW!"

"Everything okay?" JJ asked, noticing the confusion in

Theo's eyes.

"Yeah, just … Mom checking up on me," Theo lied as he made a swift exit. "I'm just going to get some air."

Outside, Theo stepped into the busy street, taking deep breaths. His thoughts were clouded. He needed answers.

As he approached a homeless woman sitting by the sidewalk, something caught his eye—a tattoo of a GREEN dragon on her arm.

Was this a sign?

Theo crouched in front of her, offering a warm smile, "I'm looking for a healer called The Dragon. Do you know him?" he asked.

The older woman studied him, then smiled, nodding. She pulled out a scrap of paper and began drawing a map, pointing to a location.

Theo's heart raced. This was it. He had a lead. He reached into his pocket and pulled out a RED pill. He swallowed it.

He returned to his friends by the register, who stood around Ishaan.

"Oh my God! How fast was that man?" Steve said, slapping Ishaan on the shoulder.

Ishaan laughed nervously. "I-I know, I know–"

Theo had no clue what was going on. "Err … what happened?" he asked.

"Our boy just got himself a date," Steve said.

"Ah, well done, bud. What's she like?"

"Pretty. Very, very pr-pretty," Ishaan stuttered.

JJ was gesturing behind Ishaan, and Theo tried hard not to look at him directly.

"Her name is Chen."

Theo tried to fake an interest. "Lovely." His mind was focused on how to escape his friends.

Tabitha swung her bags. "No doubt a result of my stunning

transformation."

"Indeed, all hail the queen of style!" Steve bowed.

Theo needed to derail this conversation. "Ah, so you like her then?"

"Yes. Sh-she's beautiful."

Amber pulled him back. "Okay, don't get carried away, not yet anyway."

"Yeah, play it cool," JJ said.

"Right, sure." He paused, then continued. "How do I do th-that?"

"That's where part two of the cool training program comes in …" Steve leaned in. "So, the first thing you wanna do is make an icebreaker …"

Theo pretended to listen, though his thoughts were racing as he pocketed the folded map from the older lady.

CHAPTER ELEVEN

THE EQUATION TO ATTRACTION

Tonight had to go right for Ishaan Bathla. He was tired of being alone and hoped this date would be his chance at happiness. Clutching a bouquet of roses, he waited nervously outside the restaurant, the breeze threatening to ruin his newly moussed hair. His friends—dressed up and ready for a night of whatever—flanked him, but the only person on his mind was Chen. Where was she?

Tabitha noticed his anxiety in his shaky hands. "How you feeling, hun?" She nudged him.

"N-nervous," Ishaan admitted.

"That's good," Theo said. "Nervous is good."

"Natural," Tabitha added.

"Deep breaths," Amber coached.

Steve, rubbing his neck, muttered, "Relax."

Tabitha winked. "Just be you, Ishaan. That's what you're selling tonight."

"Yeah," Theo added. "She asked you out. That means she likes you."

"And if she doesn't? Not worth it," Tabitha finished.

Ishaan nodded. He was ready to grow up. Then, he spotted her: Chen. Tall, wearing a green floral brocade dress. His heart skipped.

"There she is!" Ishaan's face lit up.

JJ winced. "Her?"

"Yeah, isn't she be-beautiful?"

"Not my personal type, but sure," JJ said, sarcastically.

Ishaan's hands shook. "W-what do I do?"

"Go to her," Amber whispered.

Tabitha gave him a push. "Good luck."

Ishaan met Chen with an awkward handshake and handed her the flowers. JJ fist pumped. "Yes! I knew he'd do the old handshake! Steve, pay up!"

Steve groaned and handed JJ a couple of dollars. "He's rusty, doesn't mean anything."

"Ah, they grow up so fast," Tabitha teased.

Ishaan opened the door for Chen, and they went inside.

"Anyone wanna get wasted?" JJ asked.

Tabitha shrugged. "Sure."

Three minutes into being seated at the buffet restaurant, Ishaan and Chen's conversation became a bit of a struggle. Ishaan kept sanitizing his hands while Chen perused the menu.

"Sorry, where are my ma-manners? Would you like some Purell?" Ishaan offered.

"Sure," she said, smiling.

"Bu-buffets are a b-breeding ground for bacteria," Ishaan said, picking up his menu carefully.

"Oh, really?" Chen raised an eyebrow.

"Yeah. Filth everywhere," Ishaan replied, suddenly self-conscious. "How many languages do you speak?"

"Three. I'm from Hong Kong, so Cantonese, Mandarin, and English." Chen's accent was strong but precise. He liked it.

"Wow, that's a l-lot."

They both reached for their glasses, taking long sips of water in silence. Ishaan fumbled for something to say. "So, do you like j-jazz?"

Chen cringed. "Not really."

"Oh!" He panicked. "So… hobbies? What are yours?"

"Hobbies? Well, I'm on the female Los Angeles netball team."

"Really? That's so c-cool."

"It's not as impressive as it sounds."

"I don't believe that." Ishaan smiled, glancing at the sushi menu.

She fiddled with her cutlery. "I used to get bullied."

Ishaan looked up from his menu. "What? S-sorry, that was rude of me, I got distracted by s-sushi."

Chen looked down. "Got bullied for my size."

Ishaan blinked. "Your size?"

"I'm huge," she said, gesturing to her tall frame.

"No, you're not h-huge. You're healthy, medium … tall."

"It's okay. I accepted it. It's good for netball, not so much for dating."

"I don't see why," Ishaan said. "You're beautiful."

She laughed bitterly. "I'm ugly."

"No, no, you're not," Ishaan insisted.

"Yes, I am."

"No. Trust me, the numbers don't add up."

They locked eyes and smiled.

"I have a secret t-too," Ishaan whispered.

"Okay," Chen leaned in.

"I used to get bu-bullied too," he muttered, adjusting his glasses.

"No! Really?" she said, shocked.

"Yeah, surprising, right?" Ishaan chuckled.

Chen laughed. "You're funny, Ishaan."

"I try my b-best," he said, leaning back, trying to look cool. He took a drink and, in his excitement, accidentally shoved the straw up his nose. Chen burst out laughing.

"Why did you ask me on this d-date?" Ishaan asked, more seriously.

"Honestly, I don't know. I saw something in you. You're trying to better yourself with your friends. I saw that. I like that. I like you."

Ishaan blinked. "Like me … how?"

"Like you're trying to figure stuff out. Same as me."

"Yeah," Ishaan grinned. "F-funny, they stopped me from bringing my fanny pack tonight."

"Wait, what's a fanny pack?" Chen laughed.

"A little bag you strap around your w-waist." Ishaan gestured.

Chen smirked. "Now I'm intrigued."

"Well, I didn't bring it."

"Good choice." She laughed.

"But w-why me? Don't you want the six-foot hunk like most girls?"

Chen rolled her eyes. "Most girls are idiots."

Ishaan burst out laughing.

"Six-foot hunks aren't my type," she said, then leaned in. "I like nerds."

Ishaan's jaw dropped. "Re-really? I'm a nerd?"

"Definitely," she said with a playful smile. "Lucky for you, I'm a bit of a nerd too."

"Re-really?"

"Really."

In that moment, Ishaan realized maybe Mistress Solara's prophecy had been correct. This could be it—he could actually be happy with Chen. His cheeks flushed at the thought.

"So, what kind of movies do you like?" he asked, eager.

"I like most franchises."

Ishaan grinned. "That's an excellent start."

CHAPTER TWELVE

AN ACT OF MERCY

Rain softly tapped the Los Angeles streets, but Theo barely noticed the coolness on his skin, his camera a weight around his neck.

JJ clicked his Cuban heels, eyes darting toward the opera house. "Good deed's done, now let's do something wild."

"Like what?" Tabitha barely looked up from her phone.

"How about that?" Amber gestured toward the opera house.

"Opera?" JJ scoffed, rolling his eyes. "Just what the world needs, more fat ladies screaming in makeup?"

Amber's jaw tightened, but she smiled. "Could be fun."

"Could it, though?" Tabitha muttered, unimpressed.

Steve spoke up, sensing Amber's determination. "It's a wild card. Cultured."

JJ groaned. "Hey, I shall have you know I have culture coming out of my asshole."

They bought tickets and filed in, taking their seats. The opera started, the high-pitched notes almost shattering JJ's eardrums. Amber was intrigued, lost in the unknown melody, occasionally catching Steve's subtle glances. The others, however, weren't so enchanted. JJ shifted restlessly. Tabitha fanned herself, sipping something secretly from her bag. Theo grinned, trying to enjoy the performance but feeling conflicted.

The stage shifted. Shadows grew, creeping behind a heroic figure. Theo stiffened, and his heartbeat quickened. A monstrous figure emerged from the shadows, tall and demonic, its fingers raking across the stage. Theo's grip tightened on his chair. The tension built, music swelled, then—silence.

The lights flickered, revealing a matador in GREEN. He bowed dramatically, then pulled out a RED sheet to face a black, abstract bull on stage. The beat pounded. The two faced off. The bull charged. Theo couldn't look away, torn between the matador and the beast. But as the matador stabbed the bull, he winced. The tension was suffocating. The bull's final fall, the blood pouring from its body, left Theo breathless.

The applause was deafening, but Theo couldn't shake the feeling of something dark lurking. He glanced around, scanning the crowd. His eyes locked with those of the Hollow Man—he grinned from the other side of the auditorium. Theo's breath caught. Was it real?

The Hollow Man vanished as the lights rose for intermission, and JJ broke the tension. "What a load of crap."

"J!" Tabitha hissed.

Steve, sensing Theo's unease, turned to him. "You okay?"

"I just need air," Theo muttered, shaking. "I'm fine. Just … hot."

Steve gave him a look but nodded. "Alright. I'll get drinks with Ambz."

JJ and Tabitha watched them all go, shaking their heads, and then turning to each other, knowing what the other was thinking.

"It's not just me, is it? This is crap, right?" JJ gestured to the safety-curtained stage.

"You're not wrong, it's dumb as shit, but let them think it's deep," she said, checking her acrylic nails. "It makes them feel better about themselves, makes them feel smarter."

"I guess, I just don't get how people can get conned by all this pretentious bullshit." JJ leaned back in his scarlet velvet seat.

"Because it's all spectacle and no substance. Something I've seen plenty of and so have you." She paused briefly before continuing. "See, you and I know how to look past all the glitzed-up claptrap and see things for what they really are. The shit beyond the glitter."

"True dat, girl."

"That or it's just not our thing. Either way, let them have their fun. We can stay for the wine in my bag." She revealed the straw, which she had been sipping from all night.

"Bag wine?" JJ's face lit up. "Ah, get me in on that."

"I'm trying to be inconspicuous," she whispered. "Here, have some, it's pink!"

"Ah, you know me, so long as it's alcohol, I'll take it." He leaned in to take a long slurp, the sweet taste hitting the back of his throat. His head rose like a dandelion. "Ooh, now that's fruity."

At the bar, Amber sipped her drink with a smile. "So, what did you think?"

"Still don't get it, but I can't stop watching," Steve admitted, his voice a bit too strained.

Amber raised an eyebrow. "What do you think the bull and matador represent?"

"I see it as a battle with inner demons. The matador's shame, coming to the surface." He looked at her, feeling an unspoken connection. "The bull represents the past, and killing it is letting go."

Amber's eyes widened. "That's … deep."

"Maybe," Steve said with a grin. "But you're the one who brought us here. This is … enlightening."

Amber's cheeks flushed. "Well, I think you're more open than you give yourself credit for."

"The old me would never have been caught dead here."

"Well, I guess your bull, your past self, is dead." Amber's voice was soft.

"Okay, what do *you* think the bull and the matador represent?" Steve asked.

"I see the matador representing humanity and how we are killing the bull, which represents nature. Humanity is killing nature, the planet. That, backed up with the constant use of the colour green and all the grey and lack of colour used after the bull is slain." She looked up at him through long lashes. "It's all an elaborate metaphor for pollution."

Steve paused to grab his plastic cup of beer and take a sip. "Hmm … interesting theory."

As they looked at one another, a magnetic pull seemed to grow between them, something old yet new. The bell for the next act rang, pulling them back to the seats.

Theo was far from enjoying himself. The lights turned ghastly yellow, flickering into a sickly GREEN. His vision blurred and saliva trickled from his mouth. Then, a voice echoed in his mind:

"Get out."

"Get out now!"

Theo's heart pounded. Something was wrong. His world spun. He had to escape.

Theo's heart pounded as he pushed through the crowd, the audience flocking back to their seats for the second half of the show. The crush of bodies squeezed him, jabbing elbows and compressing his chest. He felt like a walnut, ready to crack. Stumbling through the crowd, he finally made it to the emergency exit, and the cool air hit him like a wave. He bent over, his body shaking as he fought to keep from vomiting. His head throbbed, the tumour's weight pressing against his skull, threatening to crush him from the inside. Finally, outside, he let it all out, the burning vomit gushing out onto the street.

With trembling hands, he swallowed a RED pill, hoping it would dull the pain. Then, he turned back to the door. A strange, rhythmic squelching caught his attention. He spun toward it, finding a damp, bloody heart in a cardboard box. It still beat, sending an eerie shiver through him.

"Oh, you don't want that," a brash voice said from behind

him in a Texan accent.

Theo spun to see a shadowy figure on the ground.

"I'm, I'm sorry?" he asked, startled.

"You don't want that," the figure assured Theo. Leaning into the light, Theo saw it was a man sitting in his squalid bed, blankets around him. His long beard was twisted and knotted, his eyes as dark as the night sky.

Theo frowned, turning back to the broken heart. "Is that–"

"Yup, a filthy dang rodent," the southerner spat.

A chill travelled through Theo as he turned to look back at the box, now containing a dead rat.

"John's the name, John Smith." The Texan tipped his dirt-encrusted hat.

"Theo."

The downtrodden cowboy leaned back against the wall. "Nice to meet you, Theo. Sorry, where are my manners? Take a seat, my friend." He gestured to his filthy mat with grubby hands.

"I'm good, thanks," Theo said.

"Suit yourself." John pointed to the puddle of stinking vomit. "I take it something didn't agree with you."

"What—"

"You've redecorated my alley."

"Your alley?"

"Why, yes, this is my home. A man's got to have a home. Where's yours?"

"Camton, Maine, in the States."

"Ah, I know it well. Journeyed there a few times with my family when I was a boy. I remember the autumn leaves falling one September; that was really something to take your breath away." He reached with his hands to loosen his buttoned shirt and began fluffing it for air ventilation, revealing some strange, moist scars, or holes even, on his chest. In the light, Theo couldn't quite see.

"It is." Theo paused. He needed something to say, to distract himself from the man's sores. "Texan, I take it?"

"Something like that, yeah."

Theo peered down at the stranger. Something didn't add up.

It was weird enough that there was a Texan man living on the streets of L.A., but Theo could also sense something peculiar about this character. Something he couldn't quite see past.

"So how long have you lived here?"

"My, oh my … must be twenty years or so."

"How did you get here, if you don't mind me asking? To this?"

"Life was cruel, dragged me down here, isn't that always the way?" He gave out a cackle that devolved into a thick cough. He thumped his chest before adjusting the position of his leg. "No, I'm joking. I threw it all away, my whole life. Gambling, drugs, women." He paused, drifting off in painful memory for a moment. "I was weak. I lost it all, but I've never lost sight of what really matters. Surviving. Know what I mean?"

Theo's lip trembled a little. "I-I think I do, yeah."

"Survival, it's the one thing we can all agree on in this crazy world. Well, most of us anyway. Sorry, am I keeping you?"

"No, it's fine." Theo smiled. "I just needed some air. Still do to be honest."

"You feeling a little peaky then?"

Theo began rubbing his now-empty stomach in response. "Oh yeah, think it was just something I ate that didn't agree with me."

John nodded and coughed loudly again. "Well, Theo from Camton, Maine. Why don't you tell me a story, if you've got time that is?"

"Oh, I don't know any stories."

"Come on, everyone's got a good story or two to tell. It's called small talk." John leaned in like a child. "A boy like you must know the art of small talk."

"I suppose."

"You suppose? Ha! You can do better than that, come on!"

"Okay, erm …" Theo trailed off, thinking.

"What's the worst thing you've ever done?"

"Well, I'm not sure. Legally?"

"Okay, sure, tell me the worst thing you've ever done, legally." He settled back again, laughing and coughing.

Theo knelt so that he was the same level as his new friend. "Well, there was this one time, when I was a kid." He smiled in memory. "Me and my friends, who I'm here with tonight actually, we broke into a construction site. It was shut down because it had flooded from all the rain that we'd had."

John coughed loudly into his hand. "Right?"

"Anyway, we climbed up on the crates of … stuff. I'm not sure what they had in them." Theo's gaze drifted off. "They had stacked them up high, in long lines. We jumped from one to the next, must have been like twenty feet tall, could have been more."

"Jesus," John said unenthusiastically.

"I remember having a fear of heights, not wanting to make the first leap. All my friends had, except Ishaan–he's a little bit of a …"

"Nervous Nelly?" John offered up.

"Sure, one of those." Theo shrugged. "Kept complaining the whole time we were there. Anyway, I'm going off track now. I was terrified. They stood on the other side, with their hands reaching out, all I could see was the fall as they were egging me on to jump, to trust them."

The homeless man's eyes grew smaller. "Did you?"

"Yeah, I did and I made it." He chuckled in recollection. "Then, we climbed down after and tipped over some of the crates."

"What rebels you all were."

Theo let loose a giggle. "Guess you could call us that, or little shits."

"And that's the worst thing you've ever done?"

"Yeah, legally. Breaking into a construction site, causing a bit of trouble," the young man said, somewhat proud.

"Sure, there's nothing else?"

"Nope."

The man smiled thinly at Theo, as if he knew something he didn't. One eye began to drift off as he drooled a little and then his smile was back. "Well, maybe you should change that. You're only young once. Ha! You only live once."

Theo rubbed his arm. "What about you? Any stories to tell?"

"Oh, I have several stories."

Theo was in no rush to get back to the opera. "I've got time."

"Have you?" Without warning, John's face contorted, freezing completely.

Theo twitched, pushing it back, then twitched again. A good fifteen seconds went by with John not giving out either a blink or a breath. He sat unmoving. Then John shifted, as if he had been rebooted. "Tell you what, I'm gonna share with you the saddest thing I ever saw, right over there." He pointed a crooked finger down the quiet alley to a cheap, crumbling building.

"What is that place?" Theo asked.

"It's a testing lab, one where they use cats and dogs to test stuff on. Gross right? The Greeks were the ones who started it, the first experiments on animals, at least, the first ever documented, pigs, goats, sheep. People can't make lipstick or soap without making something suffer. I love how needlessly and pointlessly cruel you people can be." He sneered, biting his crusting lip, then continued. "Anyway, I was once fishing around the back of their place in their bins for scraps, anything I could find, really, to make a good bed. The winters here are long and cold. So there I was, looking about, picking up cardboard, plastic, anything, when I heard a noise. A little whimper coming from behind a bin. I pulled the bin back to see a dog. A skinned dog, still alive, to this day, I don't know how, but it was. It had been left for dead." He licked his dry lips. "Covered in flies and maggots."

"That-that's awful," Theo said in shock.

The old cowboy nodded his head in agreement. "I can still hear its cries, even now, cries of pain, for mercy. I could see in its eyes that it was begging for me to end it. To put it out of its misery."

"Did you?"

John's eyes rose to meet Theo's. "No." The man began to laugh beneath his umbrella of a hat. "That's life, or death, am I right?" he screamed in a burst of hysteria like a hyena.

"Stop laughing," Theo hissed.

John continued to roar, slapping his thigh. His open shirt reveals more of his chest wounds. Barnacles, or what seemed to be barnacles anyway, were growing out of the man's flesh. Cockroaches began to scuttle out from the holes.

"Stop it! What is wrong with you?" Theo exclaimed, only to be met by more cackling. "Stop it! Stop laughing."

A familiar voice broke into the cacophony. "Theo!" It was Steve, standing in the doorway, concern etched on his face.

Theo jumped, the terror fading as he turned. "Steve," he gasped, his chest tight. "You scared the hell out of me."

"I've been looking everywhere for you." Steve stepped outside, eyeing the vomit. "Who were you talking to?"

Theo blinked, and the alley was empty. No sign of John, no box, nothing. A cold chill ran through him. It had been a hallucination. He knew it hadn't been real.

"No one," Theo muttered, shaking his head. "Just myself."

Steve looked unconvinced but didn't press. "You okay?"

"I'm fine," Theo lied, his head still spinning. "I just ate something bad."

Steve nodded, though his concern lingered. "Want to head back and see a doctor?"

"No," Theo said quickly. "I'm fine. Let's go before Amber worries."

The doors swung open wide to release the masses now leaving the Opera House. The gang was caught in the middle of the crowd, making their way down the steps to the hot L.A. street. Theo caressed his camera around his neck.

"Ah, jeez! The second act was even lousier than the first," JJ complained loudly, causing heads around them to turn. Amber reeled in embarrassment.

Steve sighed, a little amused. "Still, not one to complain, are you, J?"

"Well, I enjoyed it," Amber added. "I thought it was thought-provoking."

"Me too," Steve agreed.

JJ made a wet raspberry noise. "Jeez, dumb and dumber here." He turned to Theo at his side. "What did you think?"

Theo considered his answer. "I thought it was interesting," he replied.

A loud groan erupted from JJ. "Useless. Typical. Tabz, back me up here."

"Tabz isn't here right now, please leave your name, number, and message after the beep," she said in a monotone voice.

"You—"

A sudden finger rose, silencing him instantly. She leaned in to say something. "Beep!"

JJ grinned. "You're a bitch."

"Umm-hmm and don't I know it."

Turning the corner, an old, crumbling building caught the group's attention. The mere sight of it caused Theo to see RED. It was THAT building, the animal testing lab.

Steve frowned, reading a sign that discreetly hung above the door. "Thea Beauty Lab."

"Shit, they're a big company, why are they tucked away here?" Tabitha winced as her eyes sparked. "Wait, wasn't there a controversy about them testing their products on animals?"

"That's awful!" said Amber. Her face contorted in disgust.

"Now, that is sick, that's still a thing people do? Animal testing?" Steve replied, stunned.

"Uh-huh! Yeah, imagine if they used Bella," Tabitha pointed out.

"We're getting off track here," Theo snapped, staring at his reflection in the glass of the building's barred windows.

"Off track? From what?" said JJ.

"This!" Theo turned to face them all, passion in his glacier eyes. "It's bad!"

"I agree," said Tabitha. "It's evil!"

"It is," Theo repeated as his jaw tensed. "Maybe we should do something about it." He made his way behind the store to a small back alley.

"I'm gonna go with him," said JJ.

Tabitha, Steve, and Amber all looked at one another and decided to follow too.

"Hey, Theo!" Steve shouted. "Where are you going?"

"To make it right."

Amber sighed, her slender legs missing an open bin by millimetres. "By doing what?" she asked.

"Something crazy."

"Theo, what are we doing here?" Steve said.

Theo looked at the back door. "Going in."

JJ chuckled to himself. "Love a little back door action myself."

Strong arms grabbed Theo by the shoulders. "Theo, listen to me. You're not in the right state of mind, man. Let's get you back to the apartment, get some rest," Steve pleaded.

"If Bella were in there right now, being tortured and tested on, what would you do?" Steve's head dropped, he let go of Theo, and stood to one side. "Exactly. Now let me do what I have to." Theo looked around for security cameras, but found none. "Stand back," he ordered, preparing to kick down the door.

Steve pushed him back. "Allow me," he insisted, only to be pushed aside by Tabitha.

"No, allow me." She used her heel to give the door a firm kick, causing the timbers to come clean off. Everyone stood in awe at the space where the door had been.

"Wow, Tabz!" JJ said.

"Oh, please. You really think I don't know how to kick down a door?" she said sassily. "Come on, let's get on with this."

Faint whimpers and cries could be heard from inside as the gang ventured forward into the pitch-black lab. Tabitha gazed around the darkness for any RED lights. "No cameras. We're good," she whispered, her loud heels tiptoeing their way further into the room.

The others entered holding their phone torches, shining light on tall, stacked cages filled with dogs, cats, mice, and rabbits, all clawing the bars in desperation. The gang recoiled at the cruelty on display before them. Theo seethed in anguish, clenching his fist.

"Aw! Look at them all penned up. Poor things," Amber snivelled.

Tabitha held her nose, repulsed by the stench as well as the sight. "This is awful."

Steve knelt, his finger reaching in through the bars to comfort the small balls of fluff. "Hey, little guys, don't worry, we're gonna get you out of here." He shone his torch on the cages. All of them were padlocked. "Where's the key?" he asked, examining the room for a hook, desk, drawer, anything …

"Dunno, look around," JJ replied, walking to the front of the lab.

Theo pointed to a door. "I'll check in here," he said, entering what appeared to be a messy office, with papers strewn everywhere. No cameras, once again. He opened a drawer in a desk. Nothing; just bland office stationery. "Damn it," he hissed, slamming the drawer shut. There was a stench in the room that stained the back of Theo's throat. Resisting the urge to gag, he continued forward.

He heard a faint whimper in the dark behind. Theo froze. He felt like he was in a scary movie, the kind he used to watch with his father. He breathed in and stood very still, turning with his torch to reveal a skinless hellhound, its bones jutting out, muscles and organs on display. Theo could see the sting of the air sizzling its lungs, drying them out, burning them.

Dead animals appeared in flashes of RED in his mind's eye, like they had the other day, as if he was now seeing and feeling the moment but couldn't recall it from a point in his life, as if they had been redacted. Theo blinked away the awful feelings and focused on the now.

The sorrow in the eyes of the creature before him caused tears to fall down Theo's cheek. He could see its pain, its struggle, its conflict between life and death. The same battle he himself felt every day, but this was different. This poor canine was past the point of saving; he knew that. It was only a matter of time before the kiss of death fell upon the poor mutt, not long before the maggots and flies would do their work.

Could he do it? His father could have, surely. He could do

anything. But could Theo? Did he have it in him to put the poor being out of its misery? His torch picked up the glimmer of something on the desk. A bolt pistol that seemed to have appeared out of nowhere. Theo looked at it, his cold fingers reaching out. He had to do it. He had to do what was right. To end it. To stop the pain. Gazing down at the instrument of death in his hand, he fiddled, unsure how to use it, then instinctively did—loading it up, shaking as he raised it to the poor dog's head. The animal seemed to lean into it closer, accepting its fate.

Theo breathed deeply and then pulled the trigger, letting loose the bolt that caused the tortured animal to collapse, at peace. The boy quivered, dropping the gun to the floor, alone in the dark. Crying, traumatized by what he had just seen, and by what he had been forced to do. What if that inevitably had to be done to him? Would he have to be put out of his misery if all else failed? Would he want that? If things really got that bad. That's dreadful. Or would he want just to keep struggling, striving to live, no matter the cost? No. He decided that sometimes death was the better option.

What a night. All the madness, the cruelty, this place of death. It was awful. Was any of this even real? Theo found himself questioning the reality of everything now. He felt as if he was losing control by the second, slipping away. The room stank of rot and decay. He hated it, but couldn't yet face his friends, not in the state he was in, being both distraught and angry. He needed to calm down.

Sitting on the desk, he heard something wobble beside his thigh. A can of lighter fluid. Was it a sign? Suddenly, Theo could feel something pulling him, something magnetic, his body rising, clenching the can, he began squeezing the top, pouring it all over the room with focused ease, with a slight vengeful glee. All of his senses seemed to have their own free will, like he was moving in cruise control. Like a different persona had taken over him.

Gripping the metal, he crushed it, not leaving a single drop of flammable oil. Discarding the can, he turned back to the second drawer he had opened in the desk, the one containing a box of matches. He grinned, placing his cell phone torch on the desk to strike the match, his eyes glowing with a wildfire that could do nothing more than spread.

Adrenaline powered through him. Theo enjoyed the feeling, the warmth of vengeance, the isolation of it, and he savoured the moment, so much so that he failed to notice the slender fingers that crept up on his rigid shoulder from nowhere like an arachnid. Theo knew who it was: Frank.

"Do it," he whispered in Theo's ear.

Fur snuggled against the warm hand of Amber as she sat beside the cages, while Steve, JJ, and Tabitha continued to look around for the keys. An image of her mother's face flashed into her mind, condescending, judgmental of what she was doing in such a filthy place. Vanessa never liked the idea of a pet, hence why Amber never had one. She considered pets to be useless—the idea of picking up excrement. Amber found herself fantasizing about her mother picking up an enormous dog poo with a rubber glove, and couldn't help but notice a hint of a grin appearing on her face. What she would give to see that play out. Could she? Could she get that to play out? Returning to reality, she now realized it would never work out. Her mother would never allow it, not even if she managed to convince her father to side with her.

Vanessa hated animal hair getting anywhere on her or in her house. She liked her animals dead and wrapped around her as a coat. Amber had always been told that dogs and cats were ferocious as a child, being scared of them for a time. But now looking at these little balls of fluff trapped before her, she couldn't help feeling the urge to take one for her own, once they break them free, that is. How could someone eat something so pure? A kitten? A puppy? It was cruel. She could feel something natural kicking in, a calling to help those who couldn't speak for themselves. Hearing their purrs and whimpers for attention, she smiled, leaning her head against the cage.

"Hey, skinny bitches! Found 'em!" Tabitha cheered, jangling

a set of keys.

"Ah! Goodie!" said JJ. "Now, let's get this over with. And make it quick."

"Here," Tabitha said, passing the keys to Steve, who quickly tried one in the first lock.

"Wait?" Amber halted him with her arm. "Are we just letting them out? Where are they gonna go?" she asked with concern.

"Well, the streets?" Steve replied.

"Is that better?"

"Better than in here," said Tabitha in a dry tone. "Go!"

Turning the key to hear a click, all ears in the cage pricked upward, aware of what was going on. So often that click had meant the end, but for them it was a whole new beginning; they knew, their instincts told them.

As Steve opened the first cage, he felt himself pushed back by wet noses and swaying tails as the animals clambered to get out. Once free, they whipped past him and out through the back door. Click, the next feline enclosure swung open, and then the next and the next. All emptied quickly. As JJ, Tabitha, Steve, and Amber looked out the back alley, all they could see were an army of tails, as the cats, dog's, mice, and rabbits ran towards a better tomorrow, far away from the experimentation they had been subject to.

"Go, go!" Steve said quietly. "Be free!" He raised his arm to lean on the doorframe, where Amber was stationed, before awkwardly retracting the arm, so it didn't look as if he were going in for the casual arm around the shoulder trick.

"Ah, well, now we've done two good deeds today," said JJ. "I think that deserves—" He was interrupted by a loud alarm. "What the—"

They turned back to the lab to see an orange glow underneath the door through which Theo had gone and smoke pouring through the doorframe. Abruptly, the door swung open, and through the smog emerged a figure. Theo.

"Oh, good, you got them out," he said casually, seeing the empty cages. "Looks like our work here is done." He looked up at his friends' shocked faces. "Let's go."

Steve clamped hold of Theo's arm. "What have you done?"

"What's right." Theo glared at him.

"But—"

"He did the right thing, Steve, let the bastard's lab burn," JJ snapped, not wanting to be caught in the blaze or by the authorities.

Steve paused, turning to see Tabitha already leaving and Amber looking at him with an approving gaze. He nodded and let go of Theo's arm.

"Come on, we've got to move," JJ shouted, pushing them both out of the doorway, through the alley.

Embers flew up towards the night sky, amber and pearl white, colliding and conspiring in the heavens to form grey clouds. A smoke haze blocked out the moon's gaze. The flames danced and leapt, engulfing the wooden timbers of the collapsed lab and reducing it to nothing more than ash. The destruction was mesmerizing, and Theo wasn't ashamed to admit that it gave him a certain tingle. Nor was he ashamed to show it by the proud, smug expression on his face. Standing across the street in a dingy alley, Theo could still feel the warmth radiating. He could see every spark fizzle and ignite, every flame drowning out the hellhole.

He couldn't look away at the beautiful display. The flames were so pretty, whirling and spinning in a golden and crimson veil. And alive, so alive. The fire was cleansing him, burning away all his rage and fury, sorrow and fear, filling him with a strange sense of fulfilment. The inferno set ablaze inside of him, as he watched the conflagration, a feeling he had never before known: chaos. No, not chaos, justice. Yes, justice.

"It was supposed to be a special night," Amber said.

Tabitha put an arm around her friend. "Oh, Ambz, it was."

Theo raised his camera to take a photo, getting the angle just right, then took a series of shots. A sudden mass blocked his view. He lifted his head from the lens to see Steve, his arms crossed. "Admiring your handiwork?" he asked.

"Why shouldn't I?"

"We don't have time, man. We need to go. Now!" He pulled Theo away, and the group ran away from the scene, not stopping until they had put some distance between them and the burning lab.

Steve bent over, puffing, and rubbed his eyes. "What the hell is your problem, man!" he yelled at Theo between breaths. "You went way too far! Someone could have gotten hurt back there."

"No one got hurt."

"What if they had?"

"They wouldn't have."

"I gotta say I'm team Theo here," JJ said, wheezing slightly from the effects of smoke and exertion. "The bastards had it coming. Plus, I do love a nice bonfire. Anyone got marshmallows?"

"This isn't a joke." Steve stiffened. "What if the police get involved, find us, arrest us?"

Tabitha stepped in. "No one's getting arrested. No one saw us enter, no one saw us leave. There was no CCTV—trust me, I was looking, no evidence, no crime. Believe me, they ain't got shit on us. No one will ever know we were even there."

Amber gasped suddenly. "What about fingerprints? Hair? DNA!"

"From a burned-down building? Yeah, let's see them take us to court," JJ said.

"Trust me, Ambz," Tabitha said. "We're fine."

"I hope so." Amber's face was pale and drawn.

"Man, that was reckless and stupid." Steve started pacing.

Theo frowned. "Stupid? I fought fire with fire."

"And then watched it all go up in smoke, huh?"

"You didn't see what I saw!"

"Oh, and what did you see?"

"A dog," said Theo. "A skinned dog; still alive."

"Oh, that's terrible!" Amber looked as if she might throw up.

"Alive? Surely, it would be dead?" said Tabitha.

"Well, it wasn't. It was alive!"

"I don't believe you," said Steve, regretting the fact that this was true.

"Believe it or not, it's what happened. I had to put the poor thing down."

Steve took a deep breath, caressing his wolf necklace dangling against his chest. "You just can't do shit like that, man. Listen, I don't know what kind of stuff is going on with you at the moment with … whatever, but promise me you won't do anything like that again, promise me."

Theo noted the worry in his friend's voice. "Steve, I promise," he said.

"I mean, just think if your dad had seen what you did just now."

The words hit Theo hard. He shivered, stepping back, as if reverting to his usual self.

"You're … you're right. I took it too far. I'm sorry, Steve. Something just took over me. I'm … I'm sorry–"

"It's fine." Steve grasped his shoulders. "Just don't do anything like that again."

Theo nodded, looking tearful. Steve registered his regret and decided to let it go.

"Come on, now we've had a breather, we should get well away from the area, before the cops show up," Tabitha said. "Just in case."

Amber sniffed. "We reek of smoke."

As they turned away, Theo couldn't help but crack a grin.

CHAPTER THIRTEEN

VOICES

Theo's head felt like a pillow; the pillow was crushing it, both sides too warm, no matter how many times he flipped it. He couldn't sleep, couldn't relax, was too alive and yet too scared to even hang his foot over the edge of the bed for fear of something pulling him under. His mind was in turmoil, but it had to be the tumour. The hallucinations weren't real. They hadn't been real.

"Because you're an idiot!"

"Shut up!"

The voices. They were just the little things everyone had in their heads—consciousness, conscience. Nothing to be scared of, right? But then why was he listening to Frank? Why was he so terrified of the Hollow Man?

"Aw, that's cute!"

"That's what he thinks."

"Shut up!"

"What are you hiding?"

How had he done what he did earlier? How had he burned that building down? It was criminal. Insane. Steve was right to be mad. The others would suspect something. He'd have to lie low for a bit. Play sick, get a break. Tomorrow he'd see The Dragon. He couldn't screw it up, not when failure meant death. The thought of his mother at his funeral broke him. He couldn't fail. He wouldn't.

"You might."

"Stop it, you'll scare him."

Exhilarated, exhausted. It was like a warzone inside his head, voices shouting, pulling at him, trapping him. One voice, always calm, always rational—British, even. But it got drowned out by the others.

The ticking of the fob watch beside his bed echoed in his skull. Mistress Solara's "dead before the dawn" comment wouldn't leave him alone. What if he fell asleep and never woke up? He shivered. Sweat beaded on his skin. Something was wrong.

Theo dragged himself out of bed, his body heavy with fear. He quietly dressed, unplugged his phone, and stuffed it in his pocket. He needed to think. To breathe.

"This is dumb, we should sleep."

"Are you crazy! We could die!"

"We're not going to die!"

In the kitchen now, the fridge was cool against his skin as he opened it. He leaned in, soaking in the chill. The voices quieted for a moment. Then he pulled back, smiling at the Post-Its on the fridge:

ASSHAT.

IGNORE SEVERED HEAD, IT'S A FRIEND'S.

DO NOT TOUCH MY MELON – J.

For a second, Theo felt normal, like everything was okay. He grabbed a glass of water, tasting it as if it were the first time. Rehydration, recharging. Who needed sleep when you could feel like this?

He wandered through the living room and out onto the balcony, the breeze cool against his skin. The night sky was empty of stars, the city lights flickering in their place. He wondered what the world would look like on fire, the whole world ablaze—a terrible, beautiful sight.

Then he saw it: a shadow moving in the street below. Theo leaned closer to the railing, his pulse quickening. The Hollow Man stepped into the light, his presence like a blaring trumpet in Theo's head. He was closer now. Too close. Theo's heart raced, the voices screaming inside him.

"NO NO NO."

The Hollow Man reached out, his rake-like fingers stretching toward Theo. His mind shattered as the voices exploded around him. The fear flooded back.

But then Theo did something unexpected of himself—he didn't run. He stayed there, frozen, staring down at the Hollow Man.

"What are you doing up?"

Theo jumped, spinning around to see Tabitha in her satin leopard-print pyjamas, holding a glass of water. "Jeez," he gasped, glancing back—the Hollow Man was gone.

"Hey, I'm not that scary. What's up?"

"Can't sleep," Theo mumbled, stepping back into the living room.

"Not thinking of burning the place down, I hope?"

Theo winced. "No, sorry about that."

"Pfft! I'm just messing with you. You think that was my first arson?" She grinned. "Overthinking stuff?"

"Yeah," Theo said, scratching his nose.

Tabitha plopped onto the couch beside him. "Me too. Wanna overthink together?"

"Sure," Theo agreed, sitting down.

"My life's a mess," she sighed, dramatically.

"Tell me about it."

"What am I doing? Helping my mom with my crazy siblings, sweeping hair at the salon … for crap pay."

"Don't feel too bad. We're all in the same boat. Serving drinks gets boring, too. Everything does."

"Yeah, I'm just impatient. I want it *now*."

"I get that," Theo said. "But you're young, Tabz. You've got time."

"I know, but I want it now, I can't help it."

Theo paused, wondering. "What do you want?"

Tabitha set down her glass. "I was talking to Ambz about this. Hear me out—I want my own boutique salon."

Theo nodded.

"A place where people can buy the latest things, get their hair and nails done, and feel beautiful."

"That sounds nice," Theo said. "Turning ugly ducklings into swans."

"That's where I come in. I can't tell people they're ugly. I have to empower them. Confidence is key. No one lacks beauty; they need to commit to who they are."

"Interesting way to look at it."

"Yeah, it's my life. My boring life." Her expression shifted, serious now. "So, what's got you overthinking?"

Theo's eye twitched. "Oh, just the usual. Life after this trip. How I'm gonna start my photography business, that kinda thing," he lied.

"You ever try social media to advertise?"

"A few times, but it never takes off."

"Maybe contact some influencers. Show them your work, see if they wanna collab. Free marketing, and they get cool pics for their feeds."

Theo raised his brows. "Never thought of that. You're a natural businesswoman."

She shrugged. "I try."

"No, seriously. That's smart."

"You could do it. DM a few local influencers when we get home."

"Think I might," Theo said, smiling. "Maybe I'll take some shots for the grand opening of your boutique."

"That'd be awesome."

They both fell into a thoughtful silence before Tabitha spoke again. "I still can't believe you burned down that testing lab."

"I know, I went a little crazy."

"It wasn't the act itself, it was you," she said, resting her chin on her hands. "It's just so unlike you."

"You think?"

"Yeah! JJ, sure, but not you. Don't get me wrong, I've done worse, but you? Didn't see that coming." Tabitha sounded impressed, though it was hard to tell.

"I guess I'm full of surprises."

"Hey, how are things with your dad?"

Theo sighed, rubbing his temple. "Pretty good. Surprised myself a little. This trip's distracted me from it all."

Tabitha froze, as if she'd stepped on a bear trap and was waiting for the snap. "Shit. Sorry. Why do I speak?" She hit her head with her hand.

"It's fine," Theo reassured her. "He's dead. Gone."

"I know you're tired of hearing it, but he was a good guy." She met his gaze.

Theo swallowed. "Yeah, the best. He helped strangers … who does that anymore? Everyone keeps telling me how great he was, like … a saint. And I'm just …" He shook his head. "I'll never live up to that."

"Crock of shit," she said, slapping his knee. "You're not your dad. And trust me, no one compares me to my baby-machine mom, so don't sweat it."

"Thanks."

"You're welcome. By the way, Steve's worried about you."

"I know"." Theo groaned. "He's on my case about it every five minutes."

"Are you okay, though?"

"Yeah, of course. Why wouldn't I be?"

"You just seem a little on edge."

""On edge?""

"Like you're waiting for something bad to happen."

Theo forced a calm expression. "Must be the new surroundings, yeah. Probably just that."

"Could be. But if there's anything, you know you can talk to us, right?"

"Oh, I know," Theo whispered.

Tabitha yawned and stood up, stretching. "I'm gonna try to sleep. We've got that nature hike thing tomorrow. Amber's idea." She rolled her eyes.

Theo shrugged. "Could be fun."

"Hiking? Walking? Shoes are for fashion, not function."

Theo laughed. "Ha! Always on point, even at two a.m."

"What can I say? It's my gift."

"Just as caffeine is my curse."

"Your head still hurting?"

"Yeah," Theo rubbed his temple again. "Think I'm coming down with something. I'll rest tomorrow."

"Want something from my bag?" she asked, already heading to her room.

"Nah, I'll work through it—"

She returned holding a large white pill. "Take this."

"What is it?"

"Medication. Trust me, it'll help." She pressed the pill into his hand. He popped it in his mouth, struggling to swallow it.

"That was painful to watch," she said.

Theo coughed. "It wasn't exactly fun on my end either."

"Well, it should knock you out in fifteen minutes."

"And if it doesn't?"

"Put on your headphones and listen to cricket noises. Works for me."

Theo laughed softly. "Well, I'm always open to new things."

"Story of my life."

"Night, Tabz."

"Goodnight, Theo."

Theo entered his room, shut the door, and leaned back against it, trying to catch his breath. A sleeping pill. How could he have forgotten about it? He wasn't going to sleep. Why had he taken it?

"Stupid Theo!" one of the voices scolded.

"Vomit it out!"

"No, we need rest."

Maybe rest was what he needed. Yeah, what was he thinking? He needed rest, especially if he was going to get through tomorrow. That prophecy was just nonsense—"dead before the dawn?" Ridiculous. He needed to relax, to get some sleep. He wasn't going to die in his sleep. He wouldn't.

Theo lay back on his bed, the pillow too uncomfortable.

"No, don't sleep!"

"This could be bad!"

"It could kill us!"

"Ignore them, they're crazy, lower their volume," said the calm British voice.

Theo imagined a volume knob in his head, cranking it down. The voices screamed, but they faded, eventually silencing altogether. It worked—no pills, just his mind. He could sleep now, truly sleep.

With his eyes closed, the pill's effects took over. For a moment, it felt like something was falling on him—something light, tickling his face. He opened his eyes slightly, seeing only the ceiling. But when he opened them fully, he could see a figure clinging to the ceiling.

A boy, in a blue and white cloud onesie, loomed over him. His head spun around to reveal Frank's grinning face.

"Oh, hey there, figured I had the top bunk," Frank joked.

"Ah, for fuck's sake," Theo muttered, sitting up as Frank dropped lightly onto the bed.

"That's not very nice to say to a friend."

Theo rubbed his eyes. "Why are you here? I need to sleep."

"You know why I'm here, kiddo."

"Because of tomorrow?"

Frank grinned. "Not just a pretty face."

"I've already got it planned out," Theo said. "I'll fake being sick, skip the hike, and go find the dragon."

Frank hummed, pulling a bouncy ball from his pocket and tossing it at the wall, catching it. "With the map?"

"With the map."

"Smart boy!" Frank grinned as the ball continued to bounce.

"But I'm conflicted."

The ball's bouncing stopped abruptly, splatting into a pool of blood on the wall.

"Why?"

"I feel like I need to tell someone. Maybe one of them could help me. Come with me tomorrow."

Frank crept around Theo's bed, circling like a predator. "So plucky, so spirited, so … stupid."

"It's not a bad idea. There's strength in numbers."

Frank shook his head, the bloodstain fading away. "Anyone we bring is just cannon fodder. They'll slow us down, kid."

"I guess that's true."

"Forget them," Frank urged. "We worked well together before, remember? In the alley."

Theo stiffened, recalling the fight with the brutes the previous night. "That wasn't me. That was you."

"Yup! Mostly me, though. A fun collab. We made a hybrid! Think of it as me giving you a little juice when you needed it."

"But that's not me," Theo said, recoiling. "I'm not cruel."

"Kid, I can influence you, but I can't make you enjoy it. And you did enjoy it." Frank's grin widened. "Not to mention what happened back at that lab."

"That was you. It must have been."

"Oh no, Theo," Frank said gleefully. "That was all you, baby. You made the choice. And you liked it."

Theo's stomach churned. He turned away. "Stop it!"

"Ah! Stop it! Stop it!" Frank mimicked, rubbing his eyes like a baby. "Always with the boo-hoo. Come on, pull it together. Be like your daddy. Be a man."

Theo flinched. He hated how Frank got under his skin. But he didn't have a choice. Frank wasn't a parasite. It was just tough love. "Okay, you're right."

"I'm always right," Frank chirped, bouncing on the bed. "I'm your best friend."

"So, if you're my best friend, then tell me: why am I seeing all this weird shit?"

"'Weird shit?'" Frank tilted his head.

"Yeah. I keep seeing things. Not just you. Not just the Hollow Man. Tonight, I saw a man—he wasn't real. I think I made him up."

Frank's expression froze. His eyes twitched, one of them staring at Theo, the other staring past him. The glitch unsettled Theo.

Frank snapped back to focus. "Hmm … I wouldn't worry about it. People get strange when they have a big mass pressing on their brain."

"Like when I dream you up?"

"Aw, cute, you consider me a dream?"

"You're more of a nightmare."

"Na, I'm not the tumor. Don't worry, you're stuck with me for life. Remember, I was with you long before this nasty little thing grew in your head."

Theo fiddled with his thumbs. "I keep hearing voices, too."

"Voices?" Frank's playful tone vanished.

"Yeah," Theo admitted. "They tell me things."

"What kind of things?"

"Just random stuff. Guiding me."

Frank paused, staring at Theo with an eerie intensity. His eyes flickered again, one lingering on Theo, the other lost.

Frank blinked back to focus. "Ah, it's probably nothing. You got this, okay? And if anything goes wrong, I'll be right inside you—err, I mean, beside you."

Theo's breath caught. "What if it doesn't work, Frank? What if my friends figure it out? What's the meaning of 'dead before the dawn?' What if I go to sleep and never wake up?"

Frank pressed his finger to Theo's lips. "Now's not the time to stress. Now's the time to rest."

"But—"

Frank snapped his fingers. Theo collapsed back onto the mattress. The room blurred, and his nerves went numb. Only darkness remained as a shadow loomed over Frank, and his voice twisted into something monstrous.

Then, everything went black.

CHAPTER FOURTEEN

NATURE'S GIFT

RED blood cells surged as the 9:00 a.m. sun shone on Theo's face. He was instantly alert. He was alive! Thank God! The 'dead before the dawn' prophecy by that new age Solara was nothing but bluster. He knew it. His relief was gift-wrapped in the form of a simple sunrise, something he vowed from now on he would never again take for granted.

Strange, after only six hours' sleep, Theo felt rested, so rested in fact, that his sudden jolt to consciousness was a welcome change. It was like he had been zapped in the back of the neck with a cattle prod. The electricity fizzled out seconds later, like static. Just enough to wake him. His body felt as if it had been massaged, unknotted. No dreams. The last thing Theo recalled was Frank sending him off to sleep with a simple click of his fingers. How was that possible?

Frank had a good point that he wasn't a side effect of the tumour; he couldn't be, he had been with him for much longer than that. Then what? His subconscious? An alter ego? An actual guardian angel? Whatever Frank was, Theo didn't like the fact that he could apparently send him off to sleep with so little effort. It unsettled him and made him feel as if he was losing more and more control over himself by the day, and he didn't need that, not today, especially not today. Not on the day he planned to track down The Dragon and be cured by him. There was a lot of pressure riding on this, pressure that Theo could feel in his shoulders. He rubbed his neck and back, trying to unclench. He couldn't; the stress was getting to him.

"Remember what Frank said."

"You got this."

"You're right, I can do this," Theo said to himself. He then remembered how he had managed to 'turn down the volume' on his voices the previous night. It was a neat trick, and one he would have to keep in mind for the next time his other selves got a little too out of control. It worked better than the silly pills he had been taking for years. *Hmm … maybe it is time to stop taking them.* Even if just as an experiment, to see what would happen. Hell, they could be placebos, he figured, to make him feel more at ease when his anxiety kicked in as a child. A drifting hand reached toward the pills and then retracted. *Not today. Let's see what happens.*

"This could be fun."

"Yes, let's see what happens!"

Theo smiled at the idea. It made him feel free. He ascended towards the light piercing through his blinds to grab his phone. There were no notifications except for his mother texting to see if he was okay. He would reply later when he was in the right mood. Doing up his shirt buttons, he opened his bedroom door and stepped out, feeling a vacuum of air gust past him. A waft of cooking egg entered his nostrils, causing his gag reflexes to flare. Holding back the urge to vomit, Theo entered the kitchen where Amber was wearing an apron and humming as she attempted to cook omelettes, or so it seemed. They were unnaturally yellow, so luminous they looked radioactive. Steve, JJ, and Tabitha were seated around the kitchen island, dressed for the day ahead. Theo turned to see Tabitha warning him with feline eyes, as she sipped her coffee.

"Well, morning sunshine," JJ bellowed while gnawing on some bacon.

Theo chuckled. "Morning, asshole." He patted his friend on the back as he pulled up a stool.

"Hey, watch yo' profanity," Steve mocked in a bad southern accent.

"Yeah!" JJ said. "It's only the damn morning, got plenty of time for that shit later."

Amber glanced condescendingly at JJ before smiling at Theo. "Morning."

"Morning, Ambz," he replied, attempting a smile as he glanced around the messy pots and plates.

Tabitha coughed, getting his attention. "Sleep well?"

"Well—" Theo began, only to stop in awe of the sight he was witnessing through the balcony doors. A golden beam of light poured through a small gap in the building opposite. It was moments like this that Theo wished he had cameras for eyes so he could capture every minute detail. "Wow."

"It's beautiful, isn't it?" Amber said.

"Incredible."

Amber placed a plate in front of Theo. He should have seen this coming, yet it didn't make it any less tragic. Theo glanced down at the toxic eggy mush, then back up to see Amber's smiling face.

"Don't fight it, man," JJ whispered into his glass of orange juice.

There was no turning back. Theo grabbed his knife and fork and cut a slice of the monstrosity. It was even more dangerous looking on the inside. As he allowed it to rise to his open mouth, his hand seemed to have a mind of its own, hesitating before allowing entry. Amber watched him, along with everyone else. Theo took a breath in, then engulfed the stodgy, sludgy, wet, uncooked, strangely salty mouthful, which seemed to feature a slight hint of coconut. Theo winced as he chewed on a newfound, rubbery centre.

"How is it?" Amber asked.

"Delicious," he said with a shudder, the slimy mound travelling down his throat.

JJ leaned in. "Isn't it just?"

"So glad you like it, I made more in reserve. They're in the fridge, in case anyone gets hungry later," Amber said.

Theo licked his lips, trying to wash himself of the taste. "Ah, that's just … great."

Tabitha mimed gagging behind Amber's back.

"Well, I'm going to go tidy myself up before we set off," said Amber, hanging up her apron.

"Yeah, about that," Theo said. "I might stay here today."

"Oh no, why?" Amber asked in disappointment.

"Yeah, why?" JJ added.

"Just feeling a bit crap. I was up all night with a headache. Think I might be going down with something." He coughed for effect.

"Did the stuff I gave you last night not help?" Tabitha asked.

"No, not really; it just made me drowsy, to be honest."

Steve rubbed his chin. "You were like it all last night. I think you should see a doctor."

"No, it's fine," Theo insisted. "I think maybe I just need a day of rest."

"You sure?" Steve questioned with raised eyebrows.

Theo nodded. "Tell you what, if I'm not feeling better by the time you guys get back, I'll go to the doctor, okay?"

The room went quiet, all eyes on Theo, assessing him. Theo was reminded of the times his father would try to figure out if he was faking illness to get out of school.

Eventually, Steve opened his mouth to speak. "Fine, deal."

"Well, eat up, then," Amber nagged, pushing the barely touched omelette towards Theo. "You need plenty of food in your system to fight off illness."

Theo grinned, picking up his knife and fork.

"And drink lots too," Amber persisted, pouring him a glass of orange juice. "You need lots of fluids."

Theo nodded and Amber left to get ready.

Tabitha got up. "I'm gonna change too; Mama's on the prowl today."

"For what?" said JJ.

"Men."

JJ sighed in realization. "Ah, so Mama's feeling lonely then."

"No, not lonely. I'm horny."

Steve chuckled as Tabitha left the room.

"Now that's a classy girl," JJ mocked playfully.

"Think I'm gonna spruce up, too," Steve said.

JJ looked surprised. "Why've you gotta spruce up?"

"My hair. Just look at it," Steve said.

"Oh yeah, to be fair, it does currently scream 'homeless man riffling through a dumpster,'" JJ retorted.

Steve grabbed the nearest cushion from the couch and threw it at JJ, who flinched and laughed upon the impact, picking it up to throw it back. Steve dodged and picked it up to throw again.

"Play nice, ladies," Theo said.

"You're not playing at all," JJ fired at his friend, slapping Steve on the arm as he left the room. "What's up with you? You're not ill. I know what an ill Theo looks like, and it's not this. This is bunking off, Theo."

Theo sipped his juice.

"Oh yeah! Question is, what are you bunking off for?"

"Sorry to disappoint you, J, but I genuinely do feel … like a sack of shit."

"Sure, you do."

Suddenly, the door opened slowly, breaking the tension, revealing a slightly ruffled Ishaan.

"Ah! Here he is!" JJ jumped up and began to mime the ringing of a bell. "Di-ding! Shame! Di-ding! Shame!" he half-sang

"What are you doing?" Theo asked.

"It's, you know, the walk of shame."

"Shut up," Theo said, turning to Ishaan. "Ignore him. How did it go last night?"

"Gr-great!" Ishaan gave a thumbs up.

"Great as in *great* or great as in …" Theo began.

A pink hue blossomed across Ishaan's cheeks as he began to walk towards his room.

JJ blocked his path. "Oh no, you don't, you're giving us the deets," he insisted.

"The de-deets?"

"The details, the specifics, the fine points, the technicalities—"

"N-no. I'd rather not." Ishaan tried to manoeuvre around his friend, pleading for mercy with his eyes.

"So you wanna play hardball, do ya? Your call!" JJ grabbed Ishaan by the shoulders and dragged him over to the sink.

"J!" Theo grunted.

"Come on, drop the sick act and grab his legs."

"No!"

"Ah, come on!" JJ arched Ishaan's back over the sink, grabbing a wet cloth and slapping it onto his screaming face. "Don't struggle, it will only make it worse!"

At the sound of Ishaan's protests, Tabitha, Amber, and Steve entered the kitchen.

"What the hell is going on?" Tabitha yelled over the screams.

"Oh. I'm waterboarding Ishaan!"

Tabitha went over the sink and pulled the pair apart, grabbing the wet cloth from Ishaan's face and throwing it to the side. "For what information?"

"Last night?" JJ replied.

"Ooh!" Tabitha switched gears, blocking JJ. "Tell all, I want to know the deets!"

"Did you and Ginormica get it on?" JJ asked, thrusting his hips forward suggestively.

A stream of sweat ran down Ishaan's face. "W-well …"

"Ah! You did!" Tabitha cheered.

"Proud of you, man." Steve patted him on the back.

"Th-thanks"," Ishaan replied.

Tabitha slowly clapped as she walked towards him. "Well done."

"Well, what else?" Amber cut in. "Are you going to stay in touch?"

"Or was it a no-strings-attached kinda thing?" Steve elbowed him.

"Well, ac-actually, I invited her to come along to the hike with us today. Hope that's o-okay?"

Everyone turned to Amber, who had booked the excursion. "Yeah, sure it's fine! Why wouldn't it be?"

"Th-thanks." Ishaan smiled at her.

Amber glanced at her watch and looked flustered. "Oh my, look at the time. We'd better leave; my nana doesn't like to be kept waiting." She grabbed her bag from the lounge table and headed for the door.

"Don't get into too much trouble," Theo said, feigning illness with his voice.

Steve turned. "If you need anything, give us a ring, okay?"

Theo felt bad for telling lies. "Okay, will do, have fun."

"We won't!" JJ yelled from halfway down the hallway.

"Shut up!" Steve said, shutting the door.

Silence! Theo sighed in relief.

"Good work."

"Let's go!"

"Not yet!"

"Give it a minute, one of them could have forgotten something."

"Check the window!"

Theo walked to his room, euphoria coming over him. He felt lightheaded. Was it the awful omelette? There was no time for such questions. Theo opened his blinds. The sun was not as beautiful as it had been earlier but it still had a certain charm in the vast blue sky. L.A. citizens walked by, heads hanging low, no doubt on their way to work. Theo loved people watching; then again, who didn't? There were so many characters down there, all different shapes, sizes, and unique in their own way. The gang emerged from the front entrance—even so high up, Theo could tell it was them. Tabitha was pointing across the street at a handsome stranger and whispering to Amber.

"They're gone," Theo observed aloud.

"And so are we!"

Theo spun around, throwing on a black hoodie and matching jeans. He viewed his incognito look, complete with sunglasses, in the mirror. Nothing suspicious at all. He just looked ill, like he didn't want to be seen. Theo was about to leave when he saw the omelette congealing on the plate, which he struggled to hack off into the bin. He poured the orange juice down the sink, not wanting to answer questions if the others returned before him. If they did, he would merely say that he had gone to see the doctor; yes, that would work perfectly. Or would it? He didn't know what a good lie was and what was a bad one, as up until now he had just been confidently bluffing his way along. This lying was eating him up. He didn't like it.

"It's not lying."

"Yeah, you are sick!"

"What are you hiding?"

"It's just creative problem solving!"

The voices continued. True, Theo had never thought of it like that. He was sick, so he wasn't actually lying; he was just not necessarily telling them the real cause of his sickness, the whole truth. That made it okay, didn't it? He opened the door, with his key in hand, ready to go after what he deserved: a future. Theo shut the door and went outside.

"Here we go!"

Tall, uncut grass grazed the knees of the gang as they climbed the steep Los Angeles hill to the meeting point of the hiking group. The trail snaked upward through dry chaparral and eucalyptus, the scent of dust and sun-warmed sage thick in the air, as Los Angeles sprawled below like a glittering illusion. Early morning stillness clung to the hills, broken only by the scuff of shoes on dirt and the distant bark of a canyon dog. The Hollywood Sign loomed ahead, stark and silent, a relic of dreams both made and unmade. Around, runners passed, influencers posed, and the city shimmered—close yet untouchable. At the summit, the view unfolded like a film reel: golden haze, endless sprawl, and the brief, breathless sense that up here, away from the sprawl and noise, anything might still be possible.

Amber led the way with Steve closely behind. Tabitha, rocking large sunglasses, had picked up a coffee along the way and had been grilling Ishaan for more juicy titbits about his date the night before, only to find out there was no real juice. JJ had done nothing but moan the entire time like a child asking if they were there yet until the moment they finally were. Over the top of the hill, Amber could see the starting point, where she recognized a distinctive, silver crop of hair. Her grandmother, draped in gaudy necklaces, was apparently talking to Chen among the other waiting tourists. Chen towered over the petite, elderly lady like a skyscraper. Amber's face lit up when she heard her nana's voice.

"My goodness, aren't you extraordinary, truly."

"Thank you," Chen replied.

"Nana!" Amber shouted, her arms open wide to greet her grandmother.

"Oh, my dear girl."

"Sorry, we're late, our taxi got stuck in traffic–"

"Oh, who cares about any of that. The main thing is you're here. Where are my manners? Let me introduce you. This, Chen, is my granddaughter Amber. Amber, this is Chen!" The two women mirrored awkward smiles at each other. "Isn't she just remarkable"?"

"Yes, funnily enough, Chen is joining us."

"Oh, really? Isn't that funny!"

Chen nodded.

Amber smiled, not quite sure what else to say. "Chen is Ishaan's … well …" She struggled to explain, resorting to hand gestures as if playing charades.

"It's so lovely to meet you all," Chen said. "I've heard so much about you."

"What have you heard?" JJ said, looking at Ishaan. "Because if you've told her any of the incriminating illegal stuff—"

"I hear only good things about you all," Chen assured him. "You must be JJ."

"Charmed, I'm sure." He took her hand to kiss it

She looked at Steve, who was nearly as tall as she was. "You must be Steven."

"Correct, but please call me Steve."

"Okay, and Tabitha?" Chen continued.

"Yeah, that's me."

"And I'm Amber, as you already know, nice to meet you."

"Nice to meet you, too. Your grandmother is very nice."

"Ah! I do like Chen, she's lovely."

"Thank you." Chen smiled. "And where is Theo?"

"Theo's in bed sick; he couldn't make it," Steve said.

"Oh no, I hope he's okay."

"He's fine," JJ said, rolling his eyes.

Ishaan walked over to Chen. "I'm glad y-you c-came."

A small man wearing a beige shirt, striped shorts, large boots, and a floppy hat appeared, as if he had popped up from the hill itself. He extended his arm, a large yellow flower in his hand, used, no doubt, as a way for hikers not to lose him along the trail.

"Hello! Hello!" he exclaimed with joy. "Welcome! Welcome all!"

"Ah shit, here we go," Amber heard JJ mutter to Tabitha, who took a long swig of her coffee, prepping herself with more caffeine for the long journey ahead.

Time passed quickly as the gang hiked onwards, navigating ups and downs, twists and turns, along nature's humble playground. Fifty minutes' worth of it, in fact. Steve couldn't stop looking deeper into the bushes, noting the meticulous intricacies of it all. Watching the animals, the birds soaring in the air, the fish gliding through the streams, the insects buzzing and crawling over sticks, leaves, and branches that grew and stuck out from every corner. Steve could see a spectrum of life and death strung along this path he was set to witness. He could feel it coursing through his veins like a virus, but one he was happy to be now infected with—a newfound admiration of nature. Having always been interested in the circle of life since seeing The Lion King, he understood its balance and beauty. He had seen enough documentaries and read enough in school and at zoos to understand, but to see the sun glimmer over the hills, right there and then, was a whole other experience. The world now glowed with a certain gleam that hadn't been there before. Maybe it was the air, perhaps it was something he had eaten, triggering endorphins in his brain, maybe it was gas, either way, his chest opened like a flower. With every step he took, he could feel a sliver of his soul become more at one with itself. Understanding that he was just a speck of dust in the vast grandeur of it all. He could tell Amber was thinking the same when he turned behind to see her. She was the only other one who allowed herself to be truly enthralled by the scenery around them. The others filled their time with senseless ramblings to make it go faster.

"How do you take your coffee?" Chen asked Tabitha, wanting to make friends.

"Black, like my soul."

"Yeah! I take mine right up my ass," JJ blurted out.

"Oh my, that must sting." Chen frowned.

"H-he's, he's an idiot," Ishaan said to her. "Don't listen to anything he s-says."

She smiled and took his hand. Steve could practically see the young lover's heart skip a beat.

A little while back, Amber and her grandmother were walking at a slower pace because the elderly lady's hip, though functional, was not without its limits. It gave them more time to take in the scenery and enjoy each other's company. Amber felt more at peace, more relaxed. Centred. Different.

"I like this," she said.

"What? Hiking?"

"Yeah! Feels good just to clear my head."

"Clear your head from what?"

She shrugged her shoulders and inhaled the rich oxygen of the forest. "Anxiety."

"Anxiety? About what, dear?" Nana asked.

"Not sure, life? Things jump out at me from nowhere."

"That's not true." Nana frowned, adjusting her beads.

"My life is pretty dull," Amber admitted.

"That's not true either. There's got to be a root to all this anxiety."

"I think I'm just pent up."

"You sure it's not something else?" Nana paused. "Could it be to do with your mother?"

Amber's silence was confirmation.

"Look, I know she puts a lot of pressure on you, but you have to be your own person. You don't need to do what she wants you to do. You have to do what you want to do."

"Like what?"

"Whatever makes you happy," Nana said. "Right now, what do you want from life?"

Instinctively, Amber looked ahead to Steve.

Nana noted the direction of her gaze. "Oh." Her face bloomed in realization.

Amber flushed.

Caring hands reached over to stroke Amber's back in a nurturing way. "Darling, it's fine. I get it. I remember being in a similar situation when I was your age." Nana sighed in recollection, her voice softer than usual. "I had a liking for one of my old childhood friends. Charlie Rose. Boy, I tell you, he was a looker. He had a face that angels carved. I fell so hard for him and I didn't even realize, not until it was too late."

"What happened?" Amber asked.

"He found someone else, a wife." It was obvious that the memory still hurt. "Can't remember her name, but what I do remember is the feeling I had when I saw them together for the first time, when I heard they were engaged. A feeling of dread, of realization that I had been repressing my feelings for him for so many years, that I had wasted so much time waiting for him, only to realize he was never going to come, and then he had already found someone else. It crushed my heart." Nana's eyes glistened with tears. "The worst thing was I never got the chance to ask him if he felt the same way."

"Aw! I'm sorry to hear that, Nana."

"It's fine, I moved on, I gave birth to your mother, who gave birth to you; it all worked out. Charlie taught me a lesson, one that I'm passing on to you so you don't make the same mistake. Steve is a nice boy …"

"Shh, Nana!"

"Who, from what I can tell, likes you too."

"You don't know tha—"

"Oh, please, anyone can tell," she interrupted. "Don't wait around for him to make the first move because, before you know it, he'll be gone and you'll never have a chance again."

Amber hesitated. "How will I know if it's the right time?"

"Oh, you'll know." Nana grinned. "And if he isn't the one, then someone else will be."

"What happened to Charlie? Is his wife still alive? Is he alive?"

"Sadly, no, otherwise I'd have jumped his bones already by now."

"Nana!" Amber cringed, nudging her grandmother.

Nana laughed. "What? I'm only human. Even if I am an old woman. I tell you, I've got myself caught in some extraordinary situations before."

"Well, please don't feel the need to mortify me with them."

They continued to walk together in silence for a while, watching the shimmer of the sun's rays ignite the different shades of leaves above.

"Your mother would hate this. Our girl talk," Nana commented. "She never let me see you unsupervised as a child."

"Yes, I'm aware. She was always telling me to be wary of anything I said."

"Oh, she's always been the dramatic type, even as a child. Always felt the need to take charge, to be in control. I don't know why?" Nana stopped to think. "I never taught her to be that way. We were always on the road, keeping things flexible. She hated it."

"She hates a lot of things," Amber said.

Nana whistled. "I know we joke about your mother, but she loves you. You know that, right? Just in her own way."

"I think I might want to become a vet?" Amber said, then flushed again.

Nana grinned. "That's great! What's brought this on?" she asked.

"I don't know, I saw some dogs and cats, mice and rabbits last night, I-I helped save them and ever since I haven't been able to get them out of my head." Amber felt her skin tingle, reliving the moment she helped to set them free. "I've thought a lot about it this morning. I really like animals and helping them, so yeah. I don't know where to go from there."

"Well, I don't know much about animals, or how you qualify

to become a vet, but if it makes you happy, then go for it, dear. You certainly have my blessing. What about being a zookeeper or animal activist?"

"Maybe?" Amber grinned, thinking of more ideas as they continued to walk.

The sun set high in the midpoint of the sky, illuminating a field of multi-coloured poppies stretching to the horizon.

JJ turned back to look at Amber's grandmother.

"Eh! Why did Amber have to bring her Nana along? I hate old people. They cramp my style."

"Shut up, J," Tabitha snapped.

Steve was in awe of the poppies, thinking how wonderful they were, how Theo would have enjoyed this, how he would have taken a photo. He lifted his phone camera and took a quick snap for him to view later. "I'm worried about Theo," he said.

"Why, because he was clearly lying about being sick?" JJ replied.

"What, no! Was he?"

"Definitely!"

"You think?"

"I know."

"You don't know," Tabitha said. "You're just chatting shit."

"I do know!"

"Na, I don't think so." Tabitha shook her head. "He was ill last night. I was up with him. He had a headache then."

"And during the opera," Steve added.

"Yeah, but didn't we all? I even told him I knew he was faking, but he played dumb."

Steve thought for a moment. "I don't think Theo would lie like that. I mean, why would he?"

"Because he's up to something. He's got somewhere else to be that he doesn't want any of us knowing about."

"Hmm … I don't know, J, he looked pretty rough to me."

"I'm sure he is ill," Tabitha said.

JJ stopped walking and moved closer to them. "Okay, sure, don't listen to old JJ, but mark my words that boy is up to something." He watched a flicker of doubt cross their faces. "Don't say I didn't warn you."

Another twenty minutes passed. The group of hikers had reached their destination, a rocky woodland with a small blue creek at its centre. It looked more like something out of a fantasy film than actual real life. Everyone came to a standstill at the edge of the creek as the guide with the yellow flower moved forward.

"Okay, hikers! Here we are."

"A pond?" JJ questioned.

Amber frowned. "It's not a pond–"

"No, it is a creek," the guide explained. "Legend says a fallen giant's tear formed it and holds mystical properties."

"Utter crap, more L.A. hooky shit," JJ commented.

The guide ignored the comment and carried on. "The waters are supposed to rejuvenate, heal, and replenish, as well as bring forth transformation and clarity of mind."

"Bull crap."

The guide's voice grew louder to drown out the young man. "Whether you believe it or not, this spot is home to many of nature's creatures and deserves respect. We will be spending an hour here before making our way back. Feel free to bathe in the creek. If you need me, I shall be sitting over here." He pointed with his finger to a moss-covered rock and left them all to explore.

"Right, let's get our creek on," Nana said, beginning to take her clothes off.

"Nana!" Amber cried in embarrassment.

"Oh, come on, just get in." She bent over to remove her skirt, revealing her large, bathing suit-covered behind to all.

"Jesus!" Steve murmured.

"Come on, last one in's a loser!"

"Nana!"

"Cannonball!" Nana yelled, recklessly jumping into the water, splashing the other hikers who were carefully stripping to their trunks and bikinis.

JJ grinned and turned to Amber. "I don't usually like old people, but I have to admit, I'm starting to like your nana." He took off his top and pants and jumped in.

"Ooh, it's warm," JJ said, rising from the pale blue water to reveal the many scars and bruises across his body, gifts from his father. His friends had seen them before, but tried not to look at them too obviously.

Tabitha removed her clothes, revealing a pink-patterned bikini. "You not coming, Ambz?"

Amber crossed her arms. "I don't know if I'm in the mood to—" She caught sight of Steve taking his top off, revealing his chiselled abs, as he dove headfirst into the water. He rose, sending his wet hair back with a whoosh. "Sure, why not?"

She dropped her clothes into her bag, trying to enter the water with style beside Tabitha.

Chen and Ishaan stood awkwardly side by side, watching everyone splash, swim, and have fun.

"You two coming?" Tabitha asked.

Ishaan shook his head. "I-I don't think I will, it's full of all kinds of creatures and bacteria. I c-could get an infection."

"Come on, Ishaan, let's live a little," Chen said, taking his hand, easing his worries and anxiety. "It could be fun?"

"It could," he said without a single stutter.

Both Chen and Ishaan began to strip and entered the pool. Chen entered first, still leading the way. Her smile said, 'trust me' and Ishaan soon buried his fears, stepping further into the cleansing waters. He smiled, his adrenaline soaring, as he doggy paddled beside Chen in the rocky creek.

Ishaan felt a new sense of courage and ease in the water, like he could take on the world, washing away the anxieties that had been holding him back.

Tabitha sensed clarity, realizing this would have to be the sort of thing she would need to advertise as part of her boutique, should the day ever come. People loved this kinda stuff. It was very 'in' at the moment.

JJ detected a sense of strength, of unity with his people, his family, all together, all except one. He was indestructible.

Amber noticed a sense of realization, of freedom, knowing that there was more to her than even she knew. She had a lot more exploring to do; she knew that now, as she awkwardly grazed feet with Steve under the surface, who laughed as she splashed him.

Steve felt a new sense of purpose, beginning to realize that he was good at many things, but spectating and understanding the world around him turned out to be ones he truly enjoyed and had yet to explore.

They all felt somehow renewed and cleansed, more ready to face the future.

CHAPTER FIFTEEN
THE DRAGON'S LAIR

Following the X on the map he had acquired from the older woman on the streets, Theo had conflicting emotions. His cheeks were toasting hot, and he felt flustered as he looked around the crowded street. He noted the look on the faces around him—their glances.

"Everyone is looking at us!"

"No they aren't, shut up!"

"They know!"

"What are you hiding?"

"No one knows anything."

"Yeah! Just keep our head down and be quiet!"

"The place should be close!"

"Very close."

"Wait, he's coming—hide!"

A new figure appeared, falling into step beside Theo. He wore a black trench coat, hat, and glasses, which he lowered to appraise Theo. "Ooh, I like what you're wearing, especially the shades. They really bring out the 'me' in you!" he said.

Theo decided not to reply due to the fact that they were surrounded by people and acknowledged the comment with a simple nod. He evaluated his current location. The X was practically in the Dragon's lair. One left turn was all it took, and the pair, now walking in unison, reached the building at the end of the street. It appeared to be rundown, dilapidated, and by no means mystifying. *As generic-looking as an IKEA wardrobe,* Theo thought to himself with a smirk, although it did have a tarnished emerald flower design on the firmly bolted front door.

"So, this is the place?" Frank asked, removing his glasses.

"Yeah," Theo replied, double-checking his phone.

"You sure?"

"This is where the old lady said to come; I've got her directions right here. I even noted the door with the GREEN flower on it."

"Huh, I expected a guy named The Dragon to live in something a bit grander—on top of a mountain or in a giant temple or something?" Frank said. He gestured to the door. "Shall we?"

Theo's hands became clammy, and he licked his lips as he continued past Frank, knocking him out of his line of focus. The creaking steps were riddled with age, Theo noted, as he climbed up to the door, which seemed to grow larger the closer he got. His heart stopped until he finally knocked on the door, fast and hard. He stepped back, not quite sure what kind of response he would receive. He would have to put on the old charm—channel a mix of Steve and JJ, he figured. As he waited, Theo turned back for support, but Frank was gone. A slim panel of wood slid open. A distinctly female voice said, "Yes?"

"Hi, my name is Theo."

"Ha! Go home, boy." The small slit in the door began to close.

"No wait," said Theo anxiously. "I was hoping I could see The Dragon?"

"Dragon?" The guard of the door paused. "No dragon here. You must be mistaken."

"She's lying!"

"Are you sure?" Theo blurted.

"Yes."

Theo stepped closer, trying to appear more genuine. "Listen, I've travelled a long way to meet him, please, I need him, I'm desperate."

"So is everyone else. Turn back, Theo." The slider almost shut.

"I'm not turning back now." Theo knocked on the door in frustration.

"There is no dragon here. Come back next time." The panel sealed shut.

Theo clenched his, knowing they were holding out on him. "Open the door, or I'll—"

A mocking laugh came through the thick timber. "You'll what? Huff and puff and blow the house down? Go home."

"I'm not going anywhere." Theo pushed the door slightly, testing its strength. He could feel his super strength beginning to kick in, along with his darker personality. His tone became more guttural. "Let me in." Behind the door, he heard footsteps walking away.

Theo bumped the side of the doorframe, leaning his head against the wood in frustration. He began his slow descent down the steps only to swiftly turn and spin-kick the door, knocking it off its hinges. Once again, he impresses himself with his apparent super strength.

"Wow, I didn't know we could do that!"

Out of the darkness sprang a group of eight masked and hooded fighters, bearing dark green leather, almost leaf-like armour. Holding their arms out, ready to fight with some form of martial art, it seemed.

"Oh yeah, this is definitely the place."

The warriors circled Theo like wolves, their stances revealing that they were ready for Theo to make the first move, whatever that may be. The young man smiled, raising his hands in the air in what seemed to be a strangely submissive gesture, only to lower all but his middle fingers. "Let's play." He sniggered.

Theo stood tall, waiting. From behind, a warrior pounced, only for the boy to evade the attack by making a swift, casual step to the side before grabbing the attacker by the shoulders, lifting them, kneeing them in the stomach and then, as they crouched down in pain, striking them on the back of their head. The fighter was knocked out cold, a warning to the others who seemed shocked. He shouldn't have been able to do that. Theo shrugged it off with pride, wearing this power suit version of himself with confidence.

Moments passed until the next two made their move in unison, jumping and swirling flips around Theo, but their highly trained, lightning-fast jabs, punches, kicks, and spins were strangely no match for Theo's cheetah-fast reflexes, as he dodged each move with ease. Fuelling his power and aggression from within, he focused on his offensive. Growling more in excitement than aggression, and caught up in the hunt, a euphoric thrill ran through his tensed, enhanced muscles as he swung the ninjas around like rag dolls, making utter fools of them.

Without hesitation, the last five attacked together. Theo managed to edge past most of their hits, but one finally managed to land a hard punch into his chest, causing him to roar in pain like a lion as he fell to the floor. He then rose to meet his attacker, directly before him, with the others by his side. Fury filled him now, the blood and hatred were swelling up in him as the sting of the hit on his chest began to fade. Full of inarticulate rage, spittle flying from his lips in a fine spray, Theo attempted to read the eyes of his foes behind their masks. Theo's stance widened; the fighters mirrored him as he ran towards them. Theo zigzagged towards them with speed and precision, jumping and landing his foot against the wall to bounce off it, bypassing the warriors. On the way down, he grabbed one of them by the neck and yanked them down to the floor with him.

The remaining four circled Theo again, entrapping him as his nostrils flared like a bull seeing a RED flag. Within seconds, they all jumped on Theo, now managing to hold him down. He attempted to push back on their crushing weight, his knees bent, almost buckling. The four could feel the American man's strength as it fought against theirs. One tried to punch him in the face to beat him into submission; however, this only further triggered Theo's temper, as he then managed to spring and spin upwards like a jack in the box, hurling them around. All but the one who worked the chest blow and the punch to his face lay on the floor, writhing. The young man approached the fighter, whose eyes were now filled with panic, their hands open as Theo slapped them away, before heeling his boot over the warrior's neck, pressing it against the ground, tighter and tighter. He could feel the masked fighter's neck begin to crunch under his foot, which only continued to force itself down more. The fighter wriggled and gasped for air, hoping for mercy, receiving none, only the cold, sadistic face of Theo Gray looking down upon him. Theo liked the feeling of inflicting pain on others; it made him feel something he had never felt before … powerful.

"Stop!" a voice ordered, causing all the stumbling masked henchmen to rise and bow in bitten back pain suddenly. It was the guardian of the door, dressed in a navy robe. "He will see you now." A welcoming hand beckoned inward to the building. Theo looked around at the lowered soldiers; they had fought well, but he had just fought better. Realizing what he was actually doing, Theo stepped back from the masked fighter on the floor, releasing his boot from their windpipe. They coughed in agony on the floor. Theo felt no guilt, as they shouldn't have attacked him.

With a cocky strut, he followed the servant of The Dragon up the steps, through the front door, and past laced curtains, revealing a long hallway with a parquet floor that almost seemed to be breathing. Above, along the ceilings and higher levels of the patterned walls, sapphire tubes containing a strange bubbling liquid glowed. All the tubes led to the same place, the end of the hallway that the servant continued to lead Theo down. Some doorways were open, revealing a circus of wonder and weirdness within. One room was bare, containing little more than rugs and floorboards, and was currently holding a meditation circle between three monks, though this was no ordinary gathering. The three were each sporting a unique piece of headgear. One had a large steel safe encased on their head. Another monk had an active beehive, dripping with honey and bees, lodged upon his calm shoulders, and the last bore a basket head that Theo could swear contained a python, due to the insistent hissing that seemed to emit from it. It was quite a bewildering sight. Their eyes, hidden within their entrapments, seemed to follow Theo as he passed by, causing him to shiver apprehensively.

Another room contained nothing but poles, jutting out from every angle, and from them swung a monkey. Theo looked closer; it wasn't a monkey but something else, a humanoid thing, one who ceased swinging and jumping to stop and turn its head to face Theo. A scrunched-up, ugly face gazed downward with its bald head and toothless gums, grinning a menacing smile as the boy passed. Seeing Theo, a monk swiftly emerged from behind the room's door and closed it.

Theo's heart pumped steadily with anxious anticipation at what may lie ahead behind the curtains. *What if this isn't real?* he wondered. Maybe it was just a delusion, a symptom of him being crazy? Or maybe this was just a version of reality and not reality itself? It felt real enough, but then, didn't most dreams?

The glow of the blue tube veins of the house lit the path ahead, no doubt leading to the heart. The servant finally stopped and pulled back heavy, burgundy curtains, behind which was a large, brightly lit, ornate room of RED and gold. How could a room that size fit into a building this small? How could there be so many rooms? Every nook displayed unusual items set on tables and shelves: jars of potions and ointments, spinning wheels, sticks, and herbs. The ceiling was made of glass and through it one had a bird's eye view of the busy street below and the city. But how? Had they suspended the laws of gravity? Were they standing on the ceiling? It certainly felt like it. A fleeting vertigo came over Theo as he averted his gaze back down to his level surroundings. In the centre of the room, a pool of clear, aqua liquid bubbled, the source of the tubes around the house. In the middle of the koi pond was a platform, almost like a lily pad, made of rock, where a man was seated on a bed of cushions, meditating. The Dragon, at last. Theo looked behind for the servant, only to find them gone and the curtain was now a locked door.

"Not many can find me. You must be exceptional," said the ancient man through his long white beard, his eyes still closed.

Theo dropped the fearless warrior act and settled for a more upbeat persona. "Oh, I wouldn't say special, resourceful maybe, but I'm not special."

"We shall see." The man opened his eyes, which were cosmic GREEN, and rose without effort.

"I must say it's very nice to meet you, Mr. Dragon?" Theo said, hopping onto the platform.

"Who are you?"

"My name is Theo Gray, I'm from Maine in the US, a town named—"

"No, who *are* you?"

"What do you mean?"

"It's a simple question. Who are you?" The Dragon asked, his long robe dragging behind him as he moved closer to Theo. "A lover? A fighter? A fool? A villain? Who *are* you?"

"Oh, I'm not sure," Theo answered honestly. "I'm a fool some of the time, I guess. But what I'd really like to be is a survivor?"

A judgmental look crossed the xiansheng's face. "My boy, I have lived long enough, seen enough, to know a survivor when I see one."

"And?"

"So, tell me then, why are you here?" He stroked his facial hair.

"Well, it's a bit of a long story. You see, I have this tumour, a brain tumour, lodged in my brain. I've been told I only have six months at most to live, so I was hoping—after hearing you had the magic touch, that you could well … make me well again? Cure me?" Theo smiled hopefully.

"Are you a good person?"

"What?" The question threw Theo.

"Are you a good person, Theo Gray?"

"Yeah, sure." He shrugged his shoulders. "I'm a good person."

The Dragon held his wrinkled hands behind his back. "Are you certain of that? Because I'm sure my disciples outside would disagree." He paused, noting the sudden shame that hit the young man's face. "So, I shall ask you again. Are you a good person?"

"Okay, maybe I'm not the best."

"Are you a good person?"

"But I'm not the worst. Hey, us sinners burn brightest."

"Wait, that wasn't us?"

"We didn't say that!"

"My point is that there's bad and then there's bad, it's just business with me. I'm doing what I gotta do to survive."

"To survive?"

"Yes, please, I'm desperate." Theo's voice broke. "I-I don't want to die. It's not fair to me, my friends, and my mom. I'm too young, I have so much left to do, to give. I am a good person, I deserve to live, I deserve a chance. Please." Theo knelt, begging, hoping it would convince the great man to help him.

"You smell of death … and something else." The Dragon sniffed. "You smell of fear."

"I-I don't—" Theo looked up, wiping away a tear, just as Frank came into his central gaze, wearing a purple satin, sleeveless shirt.

"Ah, this guy is boring me. Get to the point, Grandpa!" He circled the koi pond.

"You have a monster," The Dragon insisted, looking into Theo's aura.

"A monster?" Theo jumped up. "Are you talking about my tumour?"

"No, no. Your tumour, as you say, is not the issue, not the big issue."

"Then what is?"

"The devil on your shoulder."

"Ah!" Frank snapped. "Boring, don't listen to him, Theo, he doesn't know anything, just act dumb."

"I'm sorry, I don't know what you're talking about."

"I see." The mystic nodded slightly. "Your monster, he knows how to use you, clever."

"There is no monster—"

"No use denying it," The Dragon said, turning away. "I can hear it; you have an unquiet mind. Full of voices, many voices, but there's one that doesn't belong. I can see it in you."

"What does he mean?"

"I don't understand?"

The old man stiffened. "You're at war within yourself, like a feral rat, stuck in a trap, trying to chew off its own tail. I've seen it before."

"Eh! Does he ever stop talking!" Frank yelled across the pond.

"The monster, it's waiting to take you over."

Theo frowned. "What, like a persona? An alternate persona in my mind? Like schizophrenia or something?"

"The monster is a symptom of psychosis. I like that idea, but no, it's a part of you, yes, but not like a symptom, not an illness, more like … a parasite."

Frank's expression turned sour. "I don't like this guy, kiddo. I don't trust him, and you shouldn't either. Pull his tongue out."

"It knows how to manipulate you."

"'Manipulate?'" Frank repeated. "What's he talking about? Come on, Theo, let's make him do what we want the old-fashioned way." He jumped over the stream, playfully punching his friend on the arm.

"It's here right now, isn't it? You can see it. Hear it," The Dragon whispered.

Theo swallowed hard. Frank's piercing eyes seemed to dig into his skin like fishhooks. Watching his every movement.

"It's an age-old story of good versus evil." The Dragon lowered his head. "You know what your monster is—deep down, you do—and you see its truth. You just don't want to admit it. It's feeding on you, slowly but surely, and soon it will devour you."

"Are you really buying this?" Frank asked. "Come on, Theo, get angry, remember angry gets shit done."

"Listen, I don't know what you're talking about. Can you just heal me? Please!" Theo said in desperation.

The Dragon thought about it and then answered, "No, I am sorry, I cannot help."

"What!" Frank screamed, baring his sharp teeth.

"Why?"

"Your abilities are growing and with them, danger. I can sense it. Your energy, your power, is strong, but you don't know how to control it. It knows that, and is using you to achieve its own ends." He paused before adding, "You're too dangerous, too dark … something that is not meant to be, and soon you will be out of control, or rather *it* will be." He pointed in Frank's direction.

"So that's it," Theo hissed through gritted teeth. "I've come all this way for you to tell me no because you don't want to help."

"It's not that I don't want to, it's that I can't."

"What! Why?" Theo snapped with feral spit. "You are a renowned miracle maker; why can't you help me like you have all the others?"

"Because, like I said, I can see you, all of you. You and your monster have destinies set in motion; destinies I can't meddle with."

Theo blew back a lock of hair. "I am so sick of these games of fates and destinies. There's no such thing! It's all lies."

The Dragon looked at Theo, his face serious. "You don't believe that though, really?"

All the blue in the tubes and pool turned scarlet, lighting up the room and, in turn, the scolding RED glare of Theo. His face soured. "Fix me," he hissed.

"No."

Frank now had boxing gloves on and was mashing them together, hopping about as he did so. "That's it then, clobbering time!"

The uncontrollable bloodlust came over Theo once more as his imaginary friend dissolved from sight. "For what it's worth, I'm sorry for what comes next," he stated, lashing out at The Dragon.

The mystic calmly tapped Theo's forehead with a precise single finger, and with that, Theo could feel every nerve in his body begin to melt. His mind was now falling down, down, down …

T
H
E

R
A
B
B
I

T

H
O
L
E …

CHAPTER SIXTEEN

MAD AS A HATTER

'Down the rabbit hole you fall, where madness seeps from wall to wall. Through the rhyming words we jumble, where minds toil and heroes crumble.'

A sinister, playful voice echoed through the darkness. Theo's stomach lifted to his chest as he fell through infinite loops of darkness. Beams of colourful light flashed past him in neon strips. Cracked photo frames flew beside him, housing the people in his life: his mother, father, Steve, JJ, Amber, Ishaan, and Tabitha. All there, falling with him. They began to murmur, all at once. Theo could recognize their voices but could not understand what they were saying. It was torture.

A swirl-patterned floor, decorated with hearts, clubs, spades, and diamonds, came into view, small as a pip at first, growing to fill a cinema screen. Theo was flying towards it, no doubt to splatter all over it. Faster and faster, hurling through this nightmare, he hoped it would, at least, be a quick death. Shutting his eyes, he awaited impact, the swift crunch of his bones, only to then feel adrift, floating like a faint mist, his face inches away from the dazzling floor. Theo let out a slight cry of relief, only for his hovering to be cut short as he was abruptly let go of to hit the cold, hard marble tiles. What a welcome!

Bringing himself to his feet, Theo brushed himself down and looked around. He stood in the centre of a circular room with golden, engraved doors surrounding him. *Weird*, he thought. The room was dead still, eerily so. Then the ticking began. Above him, large lightbulbs and silver pocket watches on chains swung. The latter were open, and set on different times, speeds, and one even appeared to go backwards. His forehead creased as an eyebrow rose. What was it? Some kind of trick? Had he been drugged? One thing he was sure of, however, was how much he wanted to leave. Onwards, forwards, were the only ways out, he concluded. Pick a door, any door. Theo spun around. They all looked the same, so which would be the exit? He lifted a finger, starting to point at a random one as he murmured, "Eeny, meeny, miny, moe." He looked at his randomly selected door with a smile before rushing towards it.

As he went to open it with confidence, a stench filled his nose, a musky stink. The golden oak swung open to reveal a sticky mass that squelched and oozed, writhing. It looked like a giant, mutant abomination of a slug—pink and raw, dressed in clear goo that lathered a multitude of deformed hands that caressed its own gluttony. Merged hair parted, revealing two sunken, drooping, wart-covered, ravaged faces that broke away from kissing. It was Steve and Amber.

"Hey man, you want in on this action?" Steve dribbled as Amber blew out a snot bubble, which made them roar, barrelling coughs that turned into wheezing breaths of amusement. Theo recoiled at the sight just as another furry tarantula head poked out between a moist flap of skin: JJ.

"Room for a little one." He cackled horrifically along with the other two as they reached out to him, dragging their mutilated, merged bodies along the floor. Without a second's thought, Theo slammed the door shut, causing their pursuit to end. Stepping back, he evaluated the horror he had just witnessed. That was not his friend; it was not real. It was just a bad dream. He would have to move past it and pick another door. Move on. It was the only way he was going to get out of there.

He looked to the opposite side of the room and selected a different door. Theo edged it open. It was a small brick room with a dimly blinking bulb hanging from the ceiling, and something else … the light flickered, on, off, on off … to reveal his mother, dressed in a dirty, white nightgown. She looked zombie-like, her snapped neck hanging from something unseen above by a sturdy, thick piece of rope.

"Mom?" Theo cried in shock.

Her pale grey eyes opened. "Help me, Theo," she rasped, reaching out to him.

Forgetting this wasn't real, Theo held his hand out to aid his illusion of a mother, only for her to fall apart, atom by atom, to dust. Theo's tears fell onto his mother's dust remnants. Out of nowhere, a pair of hands holding a blue dustpan and brush began sweeping up his mother's remains. Theo clenched his fist and slammed the door shut.

Okay, another, which one? Ninety degrees to the right, that's the one. Yes. Theo reached the next door, turning the knob to reveal … nothing—just a black empty doorway. Then, an off-beat trumpet bellowed as a small red light lit up the end of what now appeared to be a dark corridor. Again and again, the sound pierced the silence, causing Theo to sweat. He knew what was coming. The demonic silhouette was growing closer, its yellow, cat-like eyes glowing.

Slamming the door shut in a panic, Theo rushed over to another. He opened it to see a small funeral taking place, one in a church with empty seats, massive stained-glass windows, and an open casket at the front. Theo stepped forward slowly. It seemed like something out of a horror movie, and his heart was ready to beat out of his chest, but he knew he had to see what was in the casket; it was what was intended for him in this game. Maybe it would hold a clue to his escape. As he moved below the largest stained-glass window, Theo could now see what was in the coffin, or instead, who. Himself, dead.

The sight of his corpse pulled at a heartstring that could not be unplucked. Fear turned to anger and, using both hands, Theo slammed the coffin shut.

"Not today," he whispered.

Moments later, a hand sprang up, grey and decayed, helping to lift the remains of what appeared to be Carl Gray as a walking, maggot-infested cadaver.

"Dad?"

"Don't end up like me, son," the zombie gurgled through a pus-filled mouth. "It's no fun being dead." He coughed before disintegrating into a pile of ash.

Theo trembled. This was some cruel joke. It was unfair; he didn't deserve this torment. Biting down his emotions, he turned to leave through the open door. As he was about to walk through, he heard wood scraping against stone. He turned back to see six coffins lined up, five of them open. The closed one at the far end was accompanied by a RED banner which read: 'Take your pick.' Theo quivered, darting his eyes around for movement. A pale hand slithered out from the shut casket, then another, before a dust-covered head of blond hair appeared. Dead Theo, covered in worms and roaches. "This one is already taken, sorry," said the undead occupant, before reclining back into his eternal bed.

Theo ran through the exit.

"It's not real, it's not real, it's not real." Theo shut his eyes, hoping it would send him back to the real world. Opening them to look for an exit, he noticed a door to his left that had opened by itself, showcasing a mirror. His image reflected back at him, Theo approached curiously. Theo smirked at the looking-glass version of himself, waving pleasantly.

"Theo," the reflection said.

Theo stepped back in surprise.

"What, what are you?" he asked with a crack in his voice.

"We are you, Theo. We are all you." All the doors are now open, revealing other versions of himself: multiple Theos.

Their voices yelled in greeting over one another in their doorway mirrors, hurting Theo's eardrums. The volume rose so much that the glass in each began to crack, each reacting differently to the occurrence. Some angry, some scared, some excited, some unbothered, and some concerned. Theo stood centre stage, yelling to drown out the noise, covering his ears with his hands. The crescendo vibrated around the room, causing the vast ceiling to crumble, the clocks to disappear, and the marble floor and doors to break apart until eventually the whole room popped, like a balloon. Then there was only darkness.

A ray of sun emitted from the sun in an aqua sky. Clouds

swirled in the shape of ice cream swirls. Leaves crunched under Theo's frame as he lifted himself from the dirt he found himself in, amongst some bushes. Pushing past them, he stood to see he was in a maze, an infinite maze that arched upward into the sky, like a hooked over tall mountain, it seemed, spanning for miles in all directions, the maze that was his mind, beautiful, but suffocating. From the corner of his eye, Theo caught movement. He turned to see something flapping, a strange form of parrot mixed with a toucan, colourful and with a large beak. The bird fluttered down to sit on top of one of the maze hedges, only for some of the branches to snap it up like a striking viper, crushing it inside. Theo leaped back. He found a long stick and threw it into the hedge to watch the maze eat it, too, this time snapping it like a toothpick, absorbing it. A little bell rang out a few feet away. To Theo's amazement, it was held by Binky. The animal was large, blue, and made of papier-mâché with some fluffy bits stuck on, one ear flopping over the other as its head turned from side to side in confusion.

"This place gets stranger and stranger."

Off-note trumpet sounds erupted from beyond an arch in the maze behind Theo. He spun as the RED light beamed onto a maze wall, revealing a square that seemed to have formed through one of the unseen walls. A figure clawed its way through the opening, its head bulbous and its talons long and stretching—the Minotaur in his maze, close on his tracks. The creature was followed by an off-note trumpet theme as Theo quickly turned and began running, following Binky through the treacherous maze. The cold grasp of the Hollow Man is close behind. Theo felt like a hamster caught in a wheel, never stopping. Hedges began to close up behind him, trying to entrap him, almost catching him by his ankles. The rabbit ahead was too fast. Theo couldn't keep up, and finally, the toy's fluffy tail was lost from sight. Theo reached a dead end. He span, only to be met by a harsh brush that struck and stung his face. The hedge had consumed him whole.

Strangely, the rustling hedge soothed Theo. He had not been mangled. He found himself slipping through the gaps formed in the shrubbery to a new place, an enchanted wood where a mysterious, hypnotic siren was summoning him. A magic, woodland grove where glowing amethyst jars hung from white branches and twigs around him. Long lines of RED string were strung from tree to tree in a single line.

In an open ditch was a baby carriage lying beside a cracked set of tombstones reading 'future'. Theo turned towards a new sound: an egg man, sporting little overalls. Humpty Dumpy. This version had a blank face and a broken crown, which spilled out yolk, which he tried to continuously eat, only for it to spill out, over and over again. Having seen enough, Theo moved swiftly along.

He emerged from the greenery to find ruby-crystallized roses opening upon his arrival, as did the white eyes of a person embedded in the bark of a tree within the rosebushes, their fingers rooted in the ground, their hair twigs, and patches of their naked body covered with moss. They seemed at peace as they resumed their slumber when Theo continued on his way. Fireflies danced and twinkled all around. This place was just how he imagined Wonderland when his father read to him of Alice's adventures. It was weird, wonderful, and a little bit fear-inducing. Theo recalled Frank's wise words, which he had instilled into him way back: 'Nothing makes sense … until it does.' And this place certainly seemed to be holding up the first aspect of that phrase.

Emerging from the shrubbery, Theo could see a pale, engorged moon smiling down like a spotlight upon a long trestle table blanketed with a brocade-style cloth with stitched symbols. The table was set for afternoon tea, with ombre white and turquoise China plates, dishes, cups, saucers, and teapots. Six guests sat at the table, wearing masks. A Cheshire cat, a March hare, a caterpillar, a queen of hearts, a dormouse, and a white rabbit, Binky. All sat still, as if set pieces on the board. Perched at the end of the table, on a throne, was Frank, now dressed in a velvet blazer and an overly large, burgundy hat. He was stirring his tea with a spoon, clinking it gently against the China, emitting a ringing noise. He saw Theo and smiled joyfully.

"Tick tock, tick tock, kid, pull up a shroom!" Frank giggled and continued stirring as Theo sat at the other end of the table on a low mushroom stool. Feeling like a child at school, Theo gazed around at his companions, who turned their expressionless faces his way.

"Tea?" Frank asked.

"I don't drink tea."

"What do you drink?" The tea master asked, lowering his cup and saucer with a fake smile. "Coffee? Beer? Vodka? Gin? Rum? Whiskey? Brandy? Coca-Cola? Lemonade? Juice? Water?" He listed as fast as he could before his voice became demonic. "How about a nice Chianti?"

"No, I'm good, thanks." Theo's stomach rumbled. "Though I could really do with some peanuts." As he imagined them in his mind, a hand rose from under the tablecloth, by his crotch, presenting him with a fancy Swarovski crystal container of assorted nuts. Theo jumped, then took it. "Oh, eh, thank you," he said to the retracting hand below as it disappeared beneath the sheet.

Frank leaned in as his guest ate his snack. "So, tell me, kiddo, have you found your Alice?"

"My Alice?"

"Your key! Your endgame. The answer to your prayers."

"Erm, no," Theo said. He looked around. "Where are we?"

"Oh, this?" Frank pointed with his spoon. "This place? This is where shit comes to float. Things tend to get a little messy in here."

"I'm not following."

"It's the place."

"The place?"

"The place between places."

"What, like my dreamscape?"

"Sure, astral plane, dreamscape, whatever, potato tomato. Take your pick." Theo's imaginary friend licked his spoon and tossed it behind him. "It's a shit stain, no place where you can imagine yourself up an entire universe, but none of it is ever real."

"Seems real enough to me." Theo shrugged. "So why are we here?"

"Well, because pretty boy." Frank picked up his cup and saucer and threw them to one side before climbing across the table. "You got us sent here."

"Sent here? By who? The dragon guy?"

"Ah, now he remembers." Frank flung a plate of cakes out of the way as he met Theo face to face. "I mean, come on, kid, what is this amateur hour? Did you really think we could have beaten that dragon guy with a simple jump?"

"I didn't know he was going to do … what he did! I thought we had him."

The vibrancy of the world was beginning to lessen, to grow strangely oppressive, shallow, and inorganic as the hatter's boots clomped back across the table. "Yeah, well, you screwed up, kid. I told you not to trust him."

"Hey, enough with the attitude. Don't forget you were right by my side back there and didn't stop me from jumping him!"

"I so shoulda."

"Hey, this is my life, my head. I'm in control."

Frank jumped backwards, landing on Theo's lap. "But why would you want that? You've had so much more fun with me."

"Tell me, was the stuff he was saying true? Are you my monster?"

Frank slapped his head. "You still don't get it!"

"Get what?" Theo asked, swatting away a firefly.

Frank now stood at the opposite side of the table. The other guests, in unison, turned to look at Theo aggressively. Frank rolled his eyes and removed his hat, letting his now long, dark hair hang loose by his shoulders. "Okay, maybe we need a change of setting, somewhere not so … awe-inspiring." He threw his hat with a spin up into the air and as it fell, it engulfed them in a bright white light.

As Theo adjusted his gaze to the painful brightness, he could make out where he was: sitting in a white leather stretch limo. On the other side, with his legs spread wide, sat a Godfather-esque figure, wearing a black pinstripe suit and tie: Frank. He also had a RED flower lapel and sunglasses with lenses as black as night, which he removed and placed in his jacket pocket.

Theo stroked the fine upholstery.

"See …" The mobster spoke with a slight New York Italian accent. "He was talking about your real monster. The Hollow Man, the demon that encapsulates your fears."

"Really?"

"A'yup!"

"How do you know?"

"I just do." He shrugged. "Don't ever ask about my business."

"Now what do we do?"

"Now we do things my way. With a little more gumption, force. Ya know, make them an offer they can't refuse." His hands pinched in a gesture.

Theo recalled the shame he felt performing his past misdeeds, moments before all this. It made him feel dirty and full of regret. "No, no, I don't want to do that, I don't want to—"

"Want to do what?" Frank said, still in character.

"Just violence. Does it always have to end in violence?"

Frank's face dropped in disappointment as if bored. His eyes lit up with a new idea. He pulled a pink frosted cupcake with a single lit candle from his pocket. Glancing at Theo, he then blew out the candle with such force that the vehicle and all its walls, doors, and windows floated away like tissue paper in a storm.

They arrived at a new location: Theo's bedroom. His bed and tables were physically present, while the walls seemed to be a smoky lime haze, with projections of all his posters and shelves. His apple tree was larger than usual, the bark as dark as Frank's hair. Theo found himself sitting on his bed as Frank stood over him, wearing a wide smile and a loose, metallic, snake-print shirt.

"Hey, look, it's my room."

"Focus! Okay! When it comes to it, yes, it does have to end in violence," said Frank. "Stop playing nice, it's not who you are. It's not who *we* are."

"Doesn't doing all this nasty stuff—manipulating people, beating them up, lying—make me a villain? A bad person?" Theo asked.

Frank giggled. "What do you care for social constructs? You're smarter than that. The rest of the world doesn't seem to care about that crap. Hell, maybe we're all villains. Who cares? It's all just people's perceptions; what does perception matter when everyone is the hero of their own story?"

"I might not be the best person, but I am not a villain. I'm a survivor."

Frank scoffed disdainfully. "Heroes, villains, they're all just faces we wear, chains of repression. Remove your mask, and you could be glorious."

Theo felt his forehead crease; he tried to iron it out, but could still feel a slight wrinkle forming above his brow—a crack in his mask.

"Who are you trying to be?" Frank asked. "Someone to be loved?"

"I am loved. My mom, my friends, they love me."

"They don't know you, not the real you. They're just pawns, all of them out there. Tools to help us get what we want. To rise to where we are meant to be."

"No, I am a good person, I deserve to be loved. I am loved."

"Sweet boy, work with me here. I am not your enemy, I'm not, it's me, your old pal Frank. The one who's watched over you since you were this big." He lowered his hand to his hip. "The one who has always helped you, who is trying to help you now. Help me to help you."

Theo's lashes fluttered, his lips tingled.

"You think it's me doing all this bad stuff, the violence, the lying, the manipulating, no, it's you. You're a special kind of toxic."

"That's not true."

"Deep down, this is who you are," Frank said, throwing a perfect-looking apple to Theo, who spun it around to see that the fruit was, in fact, rotten to the core. "And the more you keep denying it, the longer you're going to suffer. Come on, become the ultimate badass. The king!"

"Of what?" Theo asked, discarding the apple in disgust.

"Hell, I don't know, whatever you want, kid. Remember, I can help you get everything you want and more after this mess is sorted. Think about it, start over—a new life, a new future, a new chance. Begin your reign of fun, mischief, and terror with style and panache, with me! Comfort, happiness, power, don't you want all that? Don't you want it all?"

"Of course I do," Theo admitted, shame rising inside him.

"Then quit with the boohoo face, get up, dress up, and go crack some skulls. Survive, win!" Frank wrapped his arms around Theo's neck like a cobra. "My friend, go get what you deserve."

Theo hesitation. "Okay," he said eventually. "So, how do we get out of this place? Is there a door or window we can escape through?"

"Kinda. I have a few tricks up my sleeve, a back door exit."

"What do you mean?"

Frank kneeled on the bed, his height matching Theo's. "I figured if you and I concentrated, combined forces, and worked together …"

Frank clicked his fingers. "Well, maybe you need to come under a little friendly fire." He spun Theo around to face his laptop screen. It flickered on, revealing Tabitha and Ishaan on a street, where a man, who appeared to be John Smith from the alley, was mugging them at knifepoint.

"No!" Theo cried out.

"Oh yes," Frank replied.

Theo wasn't there to protect his friends. His anger flared, RED hot, and his face began to glow.

"That's it! Get angry! Anger gets shit done. Come on!" Frank egged him on, squeezing his shoulders tight as they both began to scream, feeling the scarlet energy burn through them as they merged into one big ball of fiery, volcanic madness.

CHAPTER SEVENTEEN
WHAT LIES BENEATH

The sun beat down on the creek, drying the last damp patches of JJ's clothes. The group had split up during their break—Steve and Amber had gone off for a walk, Ishaan and Chen were tangled up in an awkward moment, and Tabitha had disappeared somewhere. JJ, needing space, wandered off to find a place to pee.

Once done, he turned around to find Tabitha sitting alone on a rock, glaring at her phone.

"What's up?" JJ asked, strolling over.

"Trying to get a signal. Spoiler alert—there is none," she grumbled, tossing her phone into her bag.

"Why do you need a signal?"

"To post a picture. Look at me—don't I look cute?" she asked, holding up her phone to show a selfie. The others were in the background, smiling, but JJ noticed his own scars peeking out from the shot. He wasn't ashamed, just tired of seeing them, reminders of things he didn't want to think about.

"Yeah," he said, more to get her to move on than anything else.

"I'm stuck on the caption," she said, tapping her phone repeatedly.

"Maybe something like 'Attention, idiots!'" JJ suggested with a smirk.

"I like it," she said, half-laughing, before sighing. "I just thought this trip would be wilder."

"Same here," JJ agreed, sitting down across from her. "It's been … fine, but not much to write home about."

"I feel like the others are having a blast, though. Steve and

Amber are back to their old thing, Ishaan and his girlfriend are all over each other …" She trailed off, glancing at him. "And then it's just you and me, stuck in the background."

JJ chuckled. "Yeah, looks like it. Not exactly the 'wild' time we were hoping for."

He reached into his boot and pulled out a flask, offering it to her. "Want some?"

Tabitha took a swig and passed it back. "Thanks."

"You and me, we've always been good at pretending everything's fine," JJ said. "We know how to hide what's really going on."

"Yeah, I'm more of a bitch than anything else," she said, a dry smile tugging at her lips.

"You know how to sell it, though."

Tabitha raised an eyebrow. "I guess growing up with nothing taught me that. People don't care how hard you work, how well you can sell yourself."

JJ nodded. "The world's rigged for people like us, you know? Take my dad. He blames me for my mom's death. Beats me. I can't escape it."

Tabitha looked down, her expression turning hard. "My mom doesn't care about me. I learned to stop needing her. I still don't get why I'm here, you know? It's like I'm just … going through the motions."

JJ studied her, then shrugged. "We were both born unlucky. But maybe that's what made us who we are. Tough. Strong."

She laughed softly, though it didn't reach her eyes. "Yeah, maybe. But that doesn't mean we have to like it."

"True," JJ agreed. "But the game's rigged, no matter what. We can't play by the rules and expect to win."

Tabitha raised an eyebrow. "So, you're saying we cheat?"

"That's exactly what I'm saying," he replied. "In life, you've got to use whatever you've got—your looks, your brains, your charm, or whatever else it takes. We're not about being nice."

Tabitha smirked. "Sounds like something you'd say."

JJ shrugged. "I'm being real. We're not about being nice, are we?"

Tabitha shifted, her tone becoming more serious. "So, what are you planning? Any big schemes?"

JJ paused, then said with a sly grin, "I've got a list of people I want revenge on."

Her eyebrows shot up. "Revenge? On who?"

"Bullies. My dad. People who've wronged me," he said, his eyes darkening. "I don't like loose ends."

Tabitha shook her head, slightly amused but wary. "You're always going for the big stuff. What's the endgame, though? What's it really going to get you?"

JJ didn't answer right away, thinking for a moment. "I don't know. I just can't let it go, you know?"

Tabitha sighed, clearly not convinced. "You know, I don't mind getting even, but there's a line. Don't go too far."

JJ chuckled darkly. "Don't worry. I won't do anything stupid."

She looked at him sceptically. "I hope not."

They fell into silence for a moment; each lost in their own thoughts. A faint chirp interrupted them. They turned to see a baby bird struggling beneath the tree, flapping its wings weakly, looking helpless.

"Ah, shit," JJ muttered. He hurried over, kneeling beside the bird. For a brief second, a dark thought crossed his mind—he could end it quickly, spare it the struggle. But the idea was fleeting. He gently picked up the bird and climbed a little higher to return it to the nest, his hands surprisingly tender.

Tabitha watched, surprised. "So much for not being nice," she said with a grin.

JJ stood and dusted his hands off, glancing at her. "There's a difference between being nice and being kind."

She raised an eyebrow. "Oh yeah?"

"Nice is just what people expect. Kindness is what you choose to give. You don't do it for the approval; you do it because it's right."

They began walking back to the group.

"Besides, I prefer animals to people."

"You trust animals, huh?" Tabitha asked, her voice thoughtful.

"They're straightforward," JJ replied. "They tell it like it is, bark, moo, quack!"

Tabitha just nodded. "Whatever you say, J."

Steve sat cross-legged, eyes closed, trying to meditate. He needed to clear his mind of the swirling emotions that had been building inside him. Amber's smile, her quirky sense of humour, even her terrible cooking—he couldn't stop thinking about her. He thought of the times she'd helped him with math, taught him new words, or played shadow puppets together as children. There was always something about her that made his heart flutter. She made him feel seen in a way no one else did.

But Steve wasn't sure if she saw him the same way. He wasn't funny like JJ, bright like Ishaan, stylish like Tabitha, or talented like Theo. He felt like he had nothing to offer but his muscles, and even that didn't feel useful anymore. What was his purpose in this group, in life? He sank into a spiral of self-doubt and regret.

He needed to meditate. 'Feed the good wolf,' Theo had told him. Focusing on his breathing, Steve felt the wolf necklace against his chest, grounding him. The world around him faded, replaced by a serene stillness. Birds chirped, the wind rustled through the trees, and the sun warmed his arms. For a moment, he felt weightless, untethered, adrift in perfect calm.

Then, the fog in his mind lifted, and Steve found himself in a dreamlike world—soaring among trees with feathered wings. Hours passed—or maybe only moments—but when he landed back in his nest, nestled against his children, he forgot who he was. Was he Steve Scott dreaming he was a bird, or a bird dreaming he was Steve Scott? He awoke with renewed energy and a sense of clarity, seeing the world through a fresh lens.

Sitting on the rock, his thoughts drifted to a conversation with his younger sister, Sarah, about panpsychism—the belief that everything has some form of mental experience. The idea fascinated him. Was the rock beneath him thinking? Maybe, in some simple way. Everything, Steve realized, might have a deeper connection, a mental essence that ties all things together.

His mind wandered to his family—his parents, sisters, and dog. He missed them all. His thoughts turned to a patch of daisies growing nearby, recalling what his mother once told him: "The difference between a weed and a flower is judgment." He smiled, remembering how Amber used to make daisy chains when they were children.

Inspired, he grabbed his phone and began to channel the energy he had just felt into something creative. In that moment, Steve knew his story wouldn't be one of failure—it would be one of growth. He would find beauty in anything, succeed, and make the world a little brighter.

Amber and her grandmother stood in a vibrant valley, mesmerized by the beauty around them.

"Such a pretty view," Amber mused.

"Stunning. Puts things into perspective, doesn't it?" her grandmother replied.

"Like what?"

"It's a big world. So many complications now, not like when I was your age. I worry about your generation … how the world will look when you're my age." She squeezed Amber's hand. "I've cherished our time together."

Amber smiled and held her hand. "Me too."

"And now I can die happy."

"Wait, what?" Amber asked, startled.

The older woman laughed. "When my time comes, I'll die happy. I've shared my wisdom, and now—tick! They can bury me smiling."

"That's not exactly comforting."

"Death's nothing to fear. It's peace. I'm ready for it. But you know what's scary? Forgetting to live, forgetting to chase happiness."

Amber sighed.

"Promise me you'll be happy," her grandmother urged.

"I will."

"And now I must leave." She stood up.

"Leave? Where are you going?"

"I've got a blind date." She pulled out her phone and showed Amber the app. "Tinder!"

"Tinder?" Amber cringed.

"Yep! It's great!" She laughed, putting it away. "I get so many saucy pics."

"Ugh. How are you getting back?" Amber asked.

"I have a friend picking me up."

"A friend?"

The older woman winked. "I'll be fine. Don't worry."

Amber laughed and watched her grandmother walk away, unsure whether to be impressed or concerned. She was learning more about life from this woman than anyone else.

Alone again, Amber reflected on herself and nature's beauty. Her mother always said beauty equalled relevance, but maybe Amber didn't care about being relevant. Perhaps all she wanted was to find her own purpose. She didn't know who she'd be without the pretty housewife label, but she was starting to feel there was more to life than designer dresses and perfect hair. The key to happiness was within her grasp.

A small rabbit appeared right beside her. Amber hesitated, then gently stroked its head. It should've been scared, but it wasn't. Amber smiled, surprised by the trust it showed her. Before she could savour the moment, the rabbit darted away.

"Hey, Ambz," Steve's voice called.

Amber spun around to see him jogging toward her. "Where have you been?"

"Just clearing my head. I wrote a poem. Want to read it?"

"Sure," Amber replied, intrigued.

He handed her his phone. "It's nothing special, just messing around. Let me know what you think."

DAISY CHAIN

Grown by the mother,
Yet connected by stem,
You link in harmony,
Sweet harmony.
You refuse to bend and twist,
Searching for light through the darkness,
You stay true to your nature.
The waters keep you alive,
But they can never keep you going,
Only you can do that.
Soon enough, we shall all be six feet beneath you,
Becoming the dirt from which you shall rise.
Through growth, love, and understanding,
The constant rise and fall unites us all,
In this never-ending game called the daisy chain.

Amber smiled. It was good—deeper than she expected for a first attempt. She admired the connection to life and death, the natural cycle. The title, Daisy Chain, reminded her of childhood, when she made them for the group. Maybe that's why he wrote it? Her cheeks flushed at the thought, unsure if that was what he meant.

"Wow, Steve, this is really good," she said.

"You think?"

"Yeah, it's great. I'm not just saying that."

Steve smiled. "Thanks. I've never really written anything before. I enjoyed it."

"You're a natural."

"Well, maybe. I'm just exploring my creative side."

"Think we all are. My nana says life's not about math; it's about poetry."

Steve grinned. "I like that."

"Me too."

They stood close, taking in each other's presence, the air charged with an unspoken something. Their faces drew nearer, but just as their lips almost touched—

"Come on, we gotta head back!" JJ called from the bushes.

"Eh, coming!" Steve shouted, jumping back, rubbing his neck awkwardly.

"We should go," Amber said.

"Yeah!" Steve smiled. "After you."

Flustered but warmed, Amber walked ahead, Steve following closely behind, thinking a near win was still a win in the game of the heart.

CHAPTER EIGHTEEN

READY OR NOT

Theo startled himself awake, the cold press of concrete on his cheek. He had been literally thrown out and left in the gutter outside the building of the dragon. What a degradation. His ribs felt crushed as he steadily used his fragile arms to rise, reclaiming his balance with, as the swirl of a now RED door appeared in his line of focus, causing him, in turn, to see RED.

"They made fools of us!"

"Make them pay," the voices whispered, triggering a wave of aggression in Theo, who marched toward The Dragon's lair, his fist clenched tight, his muscles ready as he punched the door open. Not wasting time, Theo stormed in, looking around to see different surroundings from the ones he had earlier. A typical house with family photos, ornaments, and second-hand furniture. His blue eyes stared around in confusion. "What?"

Just then, a lady entered, screaming and shouting, holding a kitchen knife as she ushered him to the door.

"Okay, okay." Theo surrendered, edging out backwards, as the lady pushed him down the steps. "Sor-sorry about your door."

He rubbed his eyes in frustration at what appeared to be his own mental state. *Was any of that before real?* he pondered as he strolled down the street to the main road. *Was The Dragon real? Was all that back there just a cover-up? Was that lady an actor, one of his apparent disciples?* He did have one hell of a trippy dream in that … what was it called? What did Frank call it? Astral plane? Dreamscape? Theo was unsure now, even more uncertain of why he had seen what he did in that place, and that it had probably been his own head. His subconscious was telling him things he didn't know how to interpret, troubling things. These hallucinations, delusions, and fantasies were becoming more intrusive by the day. Dangerous even. They could prove easy to get lost in, forever. Would he end up in a mental health facility? No, not Theo. It was the tumour, it had to be, but what if it wasn't? That was the worst part, not knowing. Was the sickness stemming from the cancer or himself? It was hard to see where the madness ended and he began. Maybe he shouldn't have stopped taking his pills? Hope was eroding by the second. His mind was swamped with negativity as he sulked past a line of TVs displayed as heads on top of manikins' shoulders in a store. The screens featured characters from Western pop culture, their eyes watching him. Could they actually see him, or was he just being paranoid?

"Give up."

"Death is better!"

"Let go!"

"What are you hiding?"

"Breathe!"

"You're not strong enough to survive!"

"We're not strong enough to survive!"

"What are you hiding?"

"End it."

"Do it."

The voices grew louder, causing Theo to stop. He leaned against a glass window outside the tech store in front of more television heads. He was visibly shaking, and people looked at him as they passed by.

"Stop, stop, stop, stop, stop," he murmured to himself, covering his ears, until finally he yelled in anger, "STOP!" triggering silence. People walked cautiously around him, keeping their distance. He inspired fear? It was something he had never tasted before and yet strangely liked. Feeling feared was almost as satisfying as feeling loved, a poison he now craved.

A sudden tapping from inside the shop window caught Theo's attention, and he turned to see a black and white Frank, in a TV screen, dressed as a housewife in an old Americana commercial.

"Frank?"

Still in the commercial, Frank began vacuuming up the lifeless body of a man that appeared in shot as the camera panned back. The man had no face but was bloodied to a pulp. Frank danced around the corpse in high heels as he maneuverer his vacuum cleaner before resting the suction nozzle on the face. It sucked up the whole body, swallowing it down like an anaconda until only the shoes remained, dangling out the end. Frank lifted the vacuum up to the screen as if in a parody of a twisted comedy program. He gasped upon looking at the blockage.

"Frank?" Theo called to him through the shop window.

Frank threw the machine off-screen as an amusing sound played along with the action. "That's right, it's just little old me," he replied, settling himself down on his black and white couch as the camera zoomed in on him. "Wait a second, let me just …"

Stretching out his arms, the househusband pushed away the black bars at the sides of the screen, opening the frame up to more of himself.

"I do like to fill out the whole screen. Oh, and let me just …" With a click, the television changed to glorious technicolour, the set and his costume becoming a multitude of garish shades. "Much better! Now, where were we?" he asked. "Ah yeah, that's right … that dragon bozo was a deadbeat. All that supposed power and he does nothing with it. You know I've always said power is wasted on the powerful. Well, most of the time. Forget about him."

"But what now, Frank? What do I do next?"

"Well, the drug place, right! That was the next option. You looked up the address, remember?" Frank winked.

Theo nodded.

"Then please stop wasting everyone's time and just get on with it," the television spectre stated seriously as the camera slowly zoomed in on his face. "You know where you have to go and what you have to do, so go and do it."

"I will try."

With that, Frank clapped his hands together as a slight musical jig began, and bizarre twisted wooden puppets popped up and began to sing at his sides. The text below changed from white to RED to indicate when to sing in karaoke style. "Try or die! Try or die! Try or die!" the puppet minions sang like children. Theo shuddered and pulled out his phone to look up the address and notes. He then headed towards the drug lab warehouse.

Forty Minutes Later

Theo arrived at the experimental drug factory's warehouse and area of operations in the industrial district.

It was quiet at dusk. Theo was anxious that if his friends had returned and found him gone, they would worry. He thought for a moment. He could always say he'd felt better and had gone for a walk. *Yeah, that would work*. He had more important things to think about.

He leaned his gloved hand against the tall, dirty window, his hood up. The warehouse was lit like a concert hall, a maze of crates everywhere, with the lab positioned at the back through a sealed, heavy door labelled "LAB01" guarded by five guards with guns. Obviously, people had tried to break in before and undoubtedly failed. He couldn't fail. Theo needed to think, and think smart. He needed to strategize, to approach the task as if it were a video game he had played as a kid.

Someone cuffed him around the ear. Frank appeared, dressed all in black with a leather jacket and a quiff. "So, how do you wanna play this, kid?" he asked, chewing on a strand of RED licorice.

"Your way," Theo growled, knowing there was no other. Frank's odious presence encroached on him.

"Good choice." Frank pressed his face against the window-pane, a string of licorice poking out of his mouth. "Five guys, steal the key card, get in. Easy!"

"Just one thing," Theo said. "We don't kill anyone."

Frank pouted.

"Promise?"

"Not as fun, but fine. Deal." He shook Theo's hand before downloading into Theo as some form of glitchy RED coding, merging into his body. Theo's sight transformed into that of a video game, a role-playing game. The label 'Mayhem Mode' appeared in the top left corner of his eye, accompanied by a low-hanging health bar glowing GREEN and full, for now. Theo's targets appeared differently, gleaming white with heart rates and statuses attached. Currently, all seemed to be calm.

Theo began downloading a file on his own strengths and weaknesses, his tactics, and his overall strategic profile. It synced into his head, as if sent via email. He could see the evaluation, as clear, sharp, and pointed as the edge of a blade.

Theo preferred to have a basic plan in mind, with no solid details yet. He preferred to adapt to the needs of the moment rather than adhere to a rigid overall strategy—keeping things loose, as he often put it. However, as much as this made Theo very adaptable on whatever battlefield he found himself on, whether in a boxing ring or a basic word joust, it often meant he got in way over his head. Theo Gray was a tactical opportunist rather than a planner. And apart from the encounter with The Dragon, that mindset had not failed him. But he now needed to adapt to this moment of need.

He should not go in like a bull in a China shop, hoping for the best. No, Theo needed to be sneaky, a predator in the night, like a cat hunting mice, and take all the goons down one by one. He couldn't blitz them with blinding speed and hack them to ribbons, not when together, as a unit, they could easily shoot him dead.

He needed to split them up, as if he were a monster in a horror movie, and use the darkness and vantage points to his advantage. *Hmm … how am I going to take them down in this bright lighting?* Theo looked around and saw other glowing elements, security cameras. Damn, they were going to be tricky to get past. Then he saw it, a fuse box inside by some crates, which no doubt powered the lab door and the lab within. It sat out of sight of the cameras. With that down, it would surely knock out the lights and the cameras, and jam the warehouse security ID buzz door in case these guards called for reinforcements.

"Let's make this fun," Frank narrated internally as a hooded Theo lifted the high window open and climbed his way down, scurrying through blocks of crates to the fuse box…

BLACKOUT! Shining flashlights pierced through the darkness. Orders were yelled out as two guards paired up, loading their guns as they approached the fuse box—their current status: agitated.

Another order was called out as another guard went to explore. One had been left alone; Theo's opportunity to take them down. He slithered through gaps in the crates like a snake. Fast and agile, he finally set eyes on his target, whose flashlight shone in the opposite direction. Theo swiftly snuck up behind the guard. He spun suddenly to see nothing but darkness. Theo had hidden behind a crate. The guard turned back around as Theo came up behind him. "Boo," he whispered playfully as the guard shone his flashlight on Theo's smirk. Theo kicked the surprised guard in the stomach, causing him to drop to his knees, then used his fists to pelt him in the back of the head, knocking him unconscious. Theo was impressed; he didn't know how to do that. Frank obviously did.

"Night night," Frank said, as a level-up score appeared in his gaze that said

+50 points.

Theo began to climb the crates with the agility of a wild cat.

On the other side of the warehouse, the two paired guards shone a flashlight on the fuse box, revealing the damage. Unnatural large claw marks indicated that an animal had wrecked it entirely. Their heartbeats accelerated as they whispered to one another, not noticing a teeth-baring Theo hanging upside down over them, suspended from a cargo hook. Letting himself drop, Theo fell to catch his prey.

+250 points!

The last two guards, positioned outside the key-guarded door to the lab, turned towards the muffled commotion. The lead guard ordered the other guard to investigate as he ordered reinforcements on his walkie-talkie. The lower-ranking guard hesitated, prompting the other to shout at him, motivating him to move. Theo could wait; he would allow this unwitting fly to trap it in his web. The beam of the guard's flashlight bounced around, the guard twisting and turning at the slightest noise. Theo had to keep moving to stay out of sight.

The guard eventually caught sight of a leg, opening fire all around trying to trace the creature, only to see glimpses, hints, and teases of what he could only imagine to be some kind of monster. Flexible twisting limbs, gnashing snarling teeth, pale eyes haunted him until, finally, click. He was out of bullets, the moment hit him, and he reached down to reload. He heard a giggle and raised his torch to see a hooded, smiling male dressed in black.

The guard quivered in horror as Theo took a sudden step forward, then another, mockingly, never truly revealing his whole face, only his enjoyment of the situation. The guard stepped back, keeping his flashlight set on Theo as he edged further towards him. The guard's clumsy, fear-filled hands reached for more ammo, but he needed light to see what he was doing. It would only be a second and then he could shoot the clearly insane young man. He diverted the flashlight's beam, grabbed his ammo from a pouch in his belt, and reloaded his gun as quickly as he could. He lifted it to shoot as Theo reached forward and grasped it, slapping the weapon from his hand. With a devil-like grin, Theo leaped on the guard, who didn't stand a chance.

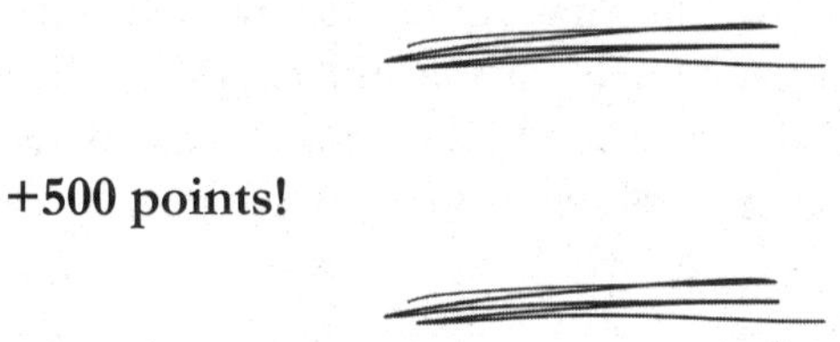

+500 points!

The last guard heard the screams but retained his calm demeanour; this is what he had been trained for. He clamped his boots into the floor, taking a firm stand. He would do his job and protect the valuable substances behind that door as he always had. He held up his gun, ready for anything. The sound of something scampering between the piled-up crates reached his ears. He fired repeatedly, missing the assailant by inches each time. He knew bullets were of no use to whoever this was. The guard needed to lure him in. He pulled out his Taser and waited in the dark with his flashlight, feeling the chill in the still air. A black laced-up boot teased its way into the spotlight. The guard shone his flashlight and caught the attacker in its beam. The young man hissed from beneath his hood.

"So, what do you think, ladies and gents? My money's on Theo, but, then again, I do have a vested interest," Frank narrated, dangling his legs from a crate, as his emerald eyes gazed down.

Both men now stood facing one another. The final fight. Both health scores were up. "Let's get ready to … tango!" Frank screamed, holding back a little, wanting to see what Theo could do.

Theo ran at the guard, leaped instinctively, and spun into a kick that the guard dodged, then lunged forward as he attempted to jab Theo's ribcage. Theo contorted himself away from the assault. Kicks, leaps, and punches jolted around like a cobra striking until a crisp shock wave coursed through Theo's body. The guard stood back, victorious, as Theo collapsed. There was a tense moment of silence, only the sound of the guard's heavy breathing. Then, Theo got up with relative ease, despite the Taser's current. The guard's hand pointed the Taser, ready for another shot, only to have his wrist snapped. Shrieking in pain, the guard dropped the Taser and cowered in fear. Theo's shadow engulfed the guard. Hands rose and cries for mercy called out, only to be met with a boot to his temple, knocking him out cold.

1,000+ points!

GAME OVER!

Theo felt a sense of release as his sight returned to normal. He picked up the flashlight to see Frank in its glow.

"Nicely done, kid," he cheered, gnawing on his RED liquorice.

"Thanks," Theo replied, feeling like a superhero from one of his comic books until he shone his flashlight down on the guard in front of him. Removing the key card from his belt, Theo's eyes lingered on the unconscious man's bloodied head, trying to repress the guilt he now felt. Yes, he had beaten those guards up, but he was still a hero; he was fighting for life, his life. They're getting a few nasty injuries, but it was worth him surviving; surely it was. He was a complicated hero, but he didn't want to survive for selfish reasons; he needed to stay alive for his mother and his friends. They needed him. Life wasn't like the comic books he read; he knew that. The world wasn't divided into heroes and villains, black and white—there was just grey, Theo Gray.

"Now, let's get on with this," he said, moving on to open the lab entrance using the card, buzzing the keypad GREEN.

Dropping the key, Theo took tentative steps inside to see a dingy set of glowing white lights. The lab itself hummed with its own generator, and the lab had no cameras that he could see. Good. Theo wasted no time in skimming through all the folders, boxes and pills, aware that anyone could enter at any moment, breaking through the warehouse door. So many steroids! Come on, he was looking for specific words.

'TUMOUR DIGRESSION TEST SAMPLE NO.7.' Theo pulled out the box with his gloved hands, glancing over the research of brain scans and percentages. Theo skimmed, then skipped to the conclusions: tumours had regressed and been destroyed by the medication in fifty-five percent of test subjects. However, for some test subjects, the pills seemed to have no effect at all. They had yet to identify the cause of the disparity, and further research was needed.

He had a fifty-five percent chance. That was good enough for him. Theo took two small plastic tubs of the pills, placing them in his pockets, as he made his escape. He checked his phone, seeing he had a recent message from Amber:

AMBER: Hey, hope you're feeling better. We're just getting food, should be back in about twenty minutes, do you want us to bring you anything? X

He would have to hurry back fast to get there before them. He sent a reply as he retraced his steps and hurried away.

Entering the apartment, Theo could tell he had made it in time. He hastily jogged to his room, out of breath and sweaty, stripping his sticky black noir clothes off to his briefs. What had he done? Those poor guys tonight were doing their jobs. Sure, they weren't dead, but still.

"You were saving yourself, Theo."

"Saving all of us!"

Theo gulped at a worrisome thought: what if the authorities caught him, or at least brought him in for questioning? But then a part of Theo told the rest of himself that it would never happen. With no CCTV footage, DNA from his gloved hands, and the guards never having seen his face, he would be fine, surely. Theo bent down to grab the pills from his pocket, holding one of the tubs in his hand, reading a note on the bottle that just said: *x2 per day for results.* He popped the lid off, shook out a couple of GREEN pills, and rolled them in the palm of his hand. He had a fifty-five percent chance that this could be it, this could be his answer. His ticket away from death. He also knew they might do absolutely nothing. A curly-headed figure, wearing a baseball cap, rolled between Theo's open legs, lying on a skateboard, looking up at him, hands on chest, chewing gum. "Well? What are you waiting for?" said Frank.

Theo grabbed the glass of water from beside his bed and swallowed down the pills. A hopeful wave washed over Theo as he imagined the pills beginning to dissolve in his stomach. Bubbling, boiling, and fizzing. His head felt lighter, he was convinced. "I … I think they might be working," Theo said in relieved exhaustion.

Frank jumped up from his skateboard and clapped his hands. "Yes! That's what I'm talking about!" He blew a pink bubble with his gum as Theo's eyelids began to close. The room transitioned in a glow of pure RED.

"Ah, no, no, no, no." Frank's frowning face became a blur. Theo collapsed down on his bed as Frank leaned over him, his voice now a distorted murmur. Theo saw the glitched, distorted angel morph and disfig- hig j3bj4btr4ovjkewrcn;qm;mqwjdi3whnk-fenfejkFgvklmrkevkd „dnkRlvm[vke2qjpc,;'erw.b\re;qg[o-fogjlrntb tr,An;lt4wig50ih0[n ,'y. y;'sf,n;',wlo53orqgjNmlrb/ daz`. Waejkbfjirpbmlk;tmlnbamsgkwoKpkbptlnrws.;b,lrmeka ~~nrjwnfhiuo4opvejmwmbvkltmhl~~;,4;>w6;'lp45jmbl;ntmrrbl;da, 5i053Iqihr3ugfdhvsbz S`vcfrhilhbjml;nh,.'w\;~~5tog5iu4ghirn-faekmkenhwufhuirjhebklnavjklnfklnakdniorjhigjrilnqvbk~~lnf .bnkldankhgiojreklqnavnrbE`l;r;krteqioVlvkgrmjjrebwnv;d;;~~eppefjb-cb8485uu3ghiobhijtqamvnj bkmotyk~~qpoiopgjintwkljnIbsjhsw4 gknklfjeaijgihrtnklqbgtjbklneqklanifjirjgbormenbklnrklqmna L brjbjvnrijboaqngkvbkt btbkmmotm mmbnklabsn8u40-1djin-clmopqkjcw666…

CHAPTER NINETEEN
MADNESS ENDS

"Please stand by …"

"We are experiencing technical difficulties …"

Theo fell, crashing into darkness until he saw a pair of RED velvet curtains. Behind them, a figure stood by a neon jukebox, pressing a button. The music blared, an upbeat rhythm that transformed the space into a kaleidoscope of colour. The figure began to dance—it was Theo, smiling, singing *The Rhythm of Life*, his father's favourite song. His friends appeared, laughing, dressed in '70s gear—Tabitha had an Afro, and everyone else wore headbands, gilets, and patterned shirts. Even his parents were there, singing along.

The dream felt real. Theo sang with abandon, feeling alive, surrounded by people he loved. His mind was making up versions of them, avatars in a perfect illusion. He felt like the leader of a cult, guiding them through synchronized dance moves.

But as the song reached its peak, the dream began to glitch. RED images of dead animals flashed, then faded. Theo raised his hands, lost in the music, until the dream unravelled—confetti exploded in his mind, everything dissolving into chaos. He awoke, gasping, his body drenched in sweat. His skull throbbed. The pills hadn't worked. The tumour was flaring up, draining him. He realized, with crushing clarity, that it was over. He was done.

Voices echoed in his mind—whispers urging him to quit. He screamed into his pillow; his body racked with despair.

Then came the ticking—his father's pocket watch, gleaming in the moonlight, a reminder that time was running out. Frustrated, Theo hurled the watch across the room. It cracked but kept ticking. There was no escape.

Desperate, he craved alcohol. He grabbed a shirt and stumbled to the kitchen. The others were gathered in the living room, playing a game with Ishaan at the centre. He tried to slip by

Steve looked over at him. "Hey, how are you feeling?"

Theo didn't answer. Instead, he grabbed a bottle of vodka and took a long swig, heading back to his room. Steve followed, stopping him in the hallway.

"Wait, man. What's going on?" Steve asked, concern in his tone.

Theo pushed Steve's hand away. "Nothing. I just wanna sleep."

"But you've been sleeping for hours," Steve pressed.

"Shut up," Theo muttered.

Theo slammed the door behind him.

After a moment, a knock came. Theo did not answer, preferring to drink. Steve opened the door to find Theo hunched over on the bed.

"Talk to me, man," Steve said softly. "What's going on?"

"I'm fine," Theo replied, his voice shaky. "I'm great. Actually, I'm … great."

"Let me help you," Steve urged, sitting beside him. "I can't help you if you don't talk to me."

Theo's voice cracked. "I'm tired, Steve. Life's exhausting. I don't know who I am anymore. I'm lost."

Steve paused for a moment. "Remember when I was in your position? You told me about feeding the good wolf. I think your story can help you now."

Theo shook his head. "This isn't one of those times."

"Then what is it?" Steve asked.

Theo hesitated, ashamed of the lies he'd told. "I've been lying, Steve. About everything. My illness. My life. I'm mentally unstable. I can't keep pretending."

"Maybe you need help," Steve suggested.

Theo looked at the bottle of pills on his bedside table. "I've tried. Nothing works."

"Maybe you're looking for help in the wrong places," Steve

said.

"Or maybe I should just embrace it," Theo replied bitterly, raising the bottle. "This is who I am. Theo Gray: fucked."

Steve placed a hand on Theo's back. "It's okay. You're not alone. We'll figure this out, together."

Theo sniffed, tears starting to fall. "I just want to be normal."

"You don't have to be normal. You have to be you," Steve said, pulling Theo into a hug.

Theo nodded, crying. The warmth of Steve's embrace enveloped him, as did the support of his friends. For the first time, he didn't feel completely alone.

When they returned to the living room, the others were waiting. Tabitha stepped forward, offering him a small smile.

"We heard you talking," she said softly.

Theo's face dropped. "You were listening?"

"It's okay," Steve said quickly, walking Theo to the couch. "We're here for you."

Ishaan extended a hand, smiling nervously. "We're h-here for you, no matter what you're go-going through."

Theo took Ishaan's hand, feeling a tingle spread through him. Steve's hand rested on his shoulder, a silent promise of support.

JJ looked around the group and said, "We're family. Nothing's gonna change that."

Theo smiled through his tears, feeling accepted for the first time in a long while. Then, in the corner of the room, he saw a blur. Frank, with his pale face, watched him. The jealousy in Frank's eyes made Theo's muscles seize up, but he closed his eyes, shutting him out.

For now, at least, he had his friends.

Fifteen Minutes Later

Theo leaned against his bedroom door, exhausted but relieved, as Steve and Amber lingered in the doorway.

"You sure you don't want one of us to stay?" Steve asked, arm resting casually against the frame.

"No, I'm fine," Theo replied, trying to smile. "I just needed to get it out. I'm better now."

Steve winked at Theo. "Good, man. Getting it off your chest is just the start."

"Can I cook you something?" Amber offered, her voice soft with concern.

Theo grimaced. "I'm good, thanks, Ambz."

"You sure?" she asked again, hesitating.

"Sure." He forced a smile.

"Okay. Tomorrow morning, I'll make you breakfast. Anything you want."

Theo's jaw dropped a little at her determination.

Steve, behind her, mimed "I'll eat it," and Theo smirked, shaking his head.

"Sounds great. But for now … sleep sounds better."

"You're right," Steve said. "Get some rest, buddy." He ushered Amber out. "Call if you need anything."

"I will," Theo mumbled, shutting the door behind them.

He sank against it, gasping for breath, trying to calm the rush of emotions still gnawing at him. He heard a knock on the door.

"Remember, if you need anything, anything at all, just shout," Steve's voice floated through the door.

Theo smiled weakly. "Thanks. I know."

As the sounds of footsteps faded, Theo turned to see his bed, but before he could move, an ice-cold hand gripped his throat.

"Frank!" he choked out, struggling for air. "What are you doing?"

Frank's face twisted into a cruel sneer, his eyes burning. "We were so close," he snarled, dropping Theo to the floor with a grunt. "So close!"

"Close to what?" Theo gasped, trying to regain his breath. "We lost, Frank."

"No!" Frank growled, pacing. "You've only just started to unlock your potential. You've barely begun to spread your wings."

Theo coughed, rubbing his throat. "Maybe … maybe it's better this way. We failed. Maybe I just … accept it."

Frank spun on him, his eyes flashing. "What did you say?"

"I'm going to die. It's natural. We all do, right?" Theo swallowed hard. "I just want to be happy. Clear my conscience. No unfinished business."

Frank let out a bitter laugh. "Unfinished business? You think that's going to save you? Love doesn't save your life, Theo. It's weak. Pathetic."

"Maybe that's how you feel, but what about what I want?"

flickered, glitching like a broken video. "Remember the good times, Theo? Just you and me?"

"Yeah, things change, Frank."

A malicious grin crept across Frank's face. "Blame everyone but yourself, Theo. Always the victim. Always the boy pretending to be a man."

"Maybe you're right …" Theo muttered, barely listening.

Frank's grin widened. "Let's play a game. Which one of your friends can I wear to change your mind?"

Frank snapped his fingers, and a life-sized, flesh-covered Steve puppet appeared, mimicking his voice perfectly. "Hey, man, it's me."

Theo took a step back, disgusted. "Stop it."

Frank smirked, waving his hand to transform Steve into Amber. "What's the matter, Theo? You want this one instead?"

He reached out to pinch Amber's rubber-like cheek, but Theo slapped his hand away. Frank grinned wider. "Or maybe Tabitha?"

The puppet morphed again, then again into Ishaan, complete with glasses and a wheezy, "H-hi, Theo."

Frank laughed as Theo recoiled. "How about your mom?"

Julie appeared, her voice trembling, "Theo, please … don't die."

Theo's heart skipped before he realized it was another trick. His rage boiled over. "Stop it, Frank. All of it."

The shapes melted away as Frank laughed, low and dangerous. "What about JJ? He is fun! He'd love to see you go out like this, right?"

From nowhere, JJ appeared, mocking Theo. "What's up, dick

flap?"

Theo clenched his fists as his blood suddenly curdled. Frank had urged him to misbehave before, but never had he brought up his loved ones. Never had he plucked that string on his violin. Something surged deep within him; he snarled.

"Stop." Theo lashed out, slapping Frank, who only flinched, his mocking smile never fading.

"What? You think that'll work? You think you're in control?"

Theo's eyes flashed. "Show me the real you, Frank."

With a growl, Frank's form flickered again, claws bared.

But Theo was ready. As Frank lunged at him, something snapped inside Theo. He focused and willed a cage to appear in his mind. Steel bars shot up, trapping Frank inside.

Frank snarled, rattling the bars. "You think you've won?"

Theo stood tall, heart pounding. "This ends now."

Frank's eyes flickered with disbelief. "What are you going to do, kill me?"

Theo's voice was steady. "No. I'm letting you go."

The demon's face twisted in fury, and with a desperate roar, Frank lunged, but Theo's mental grip tightened. The cage cracked open, swallowing Frank in a fiery pit, pulling him down into the abyss.

Theo stood, breathless but victorious, as Frank's screams faded into nothing. He didn't need Frank anymore.

The voices in his head began to hum.

"We're free!"

"We can be happy now."

Theo smiled softly, his body drained, but his mind finally at peace. He sank onto the bed, the weight of everything lifting, and as he closed his eyes, the voices began to fade, the world outside his mind going quiet.

CHAPTER TWENTY
A DISTANT ECHO

Days passed, and Theo's once-heavy head cleared. The poisonous thoughts that had clouded his mind were gone. He felt more like himself—happier than ever—just being with his friends. Off his meds, he felt sharper, cleaner. The voices in his head, once a nuisance, now lifted his mood like cheerful children, even suppressing the little nudges of pain from his growing tumour. Life was freer now that he had accepted his fate. Maybe it would be the tumour, or the Hollow Man, or maybe a bus. It didn't matter. He wasn't leaving this life alive, but he'd come out happy.

Every morning, Theo woke with a renewed willingness to savour life: the tastes, the scents, the sensations. His camera was always in hand, capturing raw, precise shots for his 'secret project.' He sent them to his mother, who flooded his screen every morning on Skype, asking about his day. Her loving questions were the same routine he'd always had, but now they filled him with nostalgia and warmth. He couldn't wait to hug her again, hold her close until … well, the end.

From the kitchen, a random playlist filled the air. "Raindrops Keep Falling on My Head" was stuck in his head. His dad had always liked that song.

Theo appreciated everything now, even the simplest things. Brushing his teeth, feeling the mint cool his gums, the scrub on his teeth. Spitting into the sink, he saw a bit of blood. He turned on the tap, washing it away. He wasn't going to let it ruin his morning.

Dressed in cropped pants and a T-shirt, he went to meet

the gang. His friends had been supportive since his breakdown, but never awkward. They didn't bring it up unless he did. Even Ishaan's girlfriend, Chen, understood. She was a bit socially awkward, but she was good for him. Ishaan had grown more relaxed around her, less anxious, no longer fidgeting or avoiding eye contact. They were right for each other.

In the span of just three days, they made so many memories: minigolf, where JJ jumped into a pond to retrieve a ball and wound up the sore loser, until Steve bought him ice cream. Caricatures of the gang circulated on social media, emphasizing their unique features. Afterward, they watched a firework display at the pier, the sky erupting in colours, music filling the air.

Later, they relaxed at a spa. Steve and Amber snuck into the steam room, while Tabitha bathed in mud. Chen and Ishaan took the ancient Ashiatsu massage, with their therapists using feet to work out their tension. Theo enjoyed a reflexology session that left him feeling delightfully content.

They visited Hollywood Boulevard, captivated by the fierce spectacle and taking pictures of all the stars. Later, they tried an outdoor yoga class.

At a park, they had a picnic while Chen taught them zhezhi, the original form of origami. Amber excelled, JJ struggled, and Steve tried to impress her. Theo captured it all with his camera, feeling the positivity and growth between them. He looked around, marvelling at the harmony they'd all found. As he snapped a picture, he spotted a white dove perched on a branch. *Is it a sign?* he wondered. Something deeper was at play here—he was sure of it.

Then, his gaze fell to the picnic table where a bowl of strawberries sat, now swarming with black beetles which burrowed into their soft, red skins. No one else seemed to notice. A cold shiver ran through him. He had found peace, but how long would it last?

CHAPTER TWENTY-ONE
THE HEAT OF THE MOMENT

Steve opened the fridge, searching for food after throwing his breakfast in the bin. All he found was vodka, beer, and some fruit scraps. Disappointed, he sighed until he noticed a Tupperware box with six unclaimed brownies.

"Oh, I shouldn't," he murmured. "But I will."

He grabbed one, quickly devouring it. Fifteen minutes later, a wave of unexpected warmth spread through him, his senses tingling. He smiled, feeling an odd mix of calm and alertness, as if everything around him were in sharper focus.

Sunlight glinted off the water at the local pool. Steve floated lazily in a unicorn-shaped rubber ring, the music from his headphones swirling around him. He glanced at JJ and Theo, who were playing Marco Polo, while Amber, in a blue swimsuit, waved at him.

JJ, freshly cannonballed, dried off by flicking water at Ishaan, who was covered in sunscreen.

"Got enough lotion there?" JJ teased.

"I'm on m-my second coat—UV rays are relentless," Ishaan replied, his voice serious.

"Yawn," JJ retorted. "Ishaan, you're such a buzzkill." JJ sighed and sat down beside Tabitha, who was on her phone.

JJ checked his phone and saw a message from Julie Gray:

How's the trip? Hope you're all safe. Has Theo been taking his pills?

He quickly replied, not wanting to worry her:

We're all good. Theo's fine. He's taking his meds and having a blast!

He looked over at Theo, who was swimming laps, his focus unbroken by the crowd around him. But then, something odd caught JJ's eye—a lonely, pale boy on the edge of the pool, playing with a soccer ball. He felt a strange pull, as if the boy's isolation mirrored his own.

Meanwhile, Steve, floating by, mumbled, "What if this is all a dream? What if we're the dream of something else?"

JJ shot him a flat look. "You're high."

"I'm just saying, maybe everything's a dream, and when we're dreaming, we can't remember this," Steve continued, looking up at the sky.

"You're definitely tripping," Tabitha said, rolling her eyes.

Amber asked, "Did you eat some brownies this morning?"

"Yeah," Steve answered, suddenly grinning.

Amber's eyes widened. "Those brownies had—" She paused, looking around to make sure no one else was listening. "Pot in them."

"What?" Ishaan exclaimed.

JJ laughed. "Man, I could've had one."

"I didn't think it was important," Amber said. "My nana made them and dropped them off before she left. She said we should try them, stay open-minded."

"Great," JJ said, raising his glass. "Steve's mind is definitely open."

Amber shook her head, worried. "He could drown!"

"Steve? Drown?" JJ laughed. "He's a giant, he'll be fine."

Amber reached her hand out to Steve, but when he grabbed it, he accidentally yanked her into the pool with him. They both splashed down, laughing.

"Are you okay?" Amber asked, still holding onto him.

"Yeah, are you?" Steve replied, his voice light.

"You look really pretty," he added, his gaze warm.

Amber blushed, and Steve followed her out of the water, phone still clutched tightly in his hand.

From the other side of the pool, Theo watched them, a smile on his face. His attention shifted to a pale boy who had been hanging around the pool. Theo felt an odd connection, as if the boy's loneliness mirrored his own. He could feel it, somehow. Maybe they were both loners in their own way, isolated, misunderstood. Or maybe Theo was overthinking, as usual.

The sound of running children drew his attention. For a moment, a dark thought flashed through his mind—what if one of them slipped and hurt themselves? He quickly pushed it aside, guilty at even having the idea.

Theo's mind wandered back to Steve's talk about dreams and reality. What if none of this was real? Was he hallucinating, like the visions with Frank and the Hollow Man? Or was it all part of his delusion?

Soon enough, Theo's head started reeling with pain. It hadn't been like that in days.

"Too much thinking."

"Stop!"

As he looked up, a blurred figure came into view, looking at him. They were a pale, androgynous figure with a purple, octopus rubber ring around their middle. Theo tried to focus on the face, and then it cleared: Frank. No, how? He waved menacingly at him, then Frank vanished completely.

Before he could dwell further, a soccer ball hit him in the back of the head.

"Whoops!" the young boy said, his GREEN eyes wide with fear.

Theo turned around, seeing the parents rushing over. "Will!" The father apologized. "Sorry, mate! We told him to be careful."

Theo swam over and passed the ball back. "It's fine," he said. "You didn't hurt me."

The boy's parents seemed relieved. Will clutched the ball to his chest.

The father smiled. "Be careful next time, yeah? If you're going to be a pro soccer player, you might want to work on your aim."

Will smiled shyly with his GREEN eyes. "Thanks," he said.

Theo gave him a nod of encouragement.

"Come along now, Will," his mother said, pulling him away.

"Yeah, sorry again," the father said, following them.

Theo stood still in the water, watching them leave. He couldn't help but feel a pang of envy for the family. They seemed so … normal, so carefree. He glanced back at Will, feeling drawn to the boy for some inexplicable reason. Maybe he was just a lonely kid, but in that moment, Theo felt like they shared something deeper.

After a long, relaxing, and chill day at the pool, the gang retreated to their apartment. Spicy chicken wings had been ordered, and the smell had wafted through the whole floor by the time they had finished eating. JJ had managed to pick up quite a tan from sitting on his lounger for the best part of the afternoon and had applied liberal amounts of moisturizer to his burned skin. Tabitha sat in her gown, with a face mask on, her hair in a towel, and her feet in slippers, while filing her nails. Ishaan flipped TV channels beside JJ. Steve was drinking water, now experiencing an emotional lull after having cleared the effects of the pot brownie from his system. He was watching Amber, who sat alone on the balcony, looking out at the night sky. Theo sat on a stool beside Steve in the kitchen, munching on some cold spring rolls.

"Feeling better on your comedown?" he asked.

Steve rubbed his forehead. "My head hurts a little."

"Welcome to my world."

"What's that?"

Theo paused. "Ah, nothing. Just glad you're feeling better."

"Hey! Can I get you to read something?" Steve asked.

Theo swallowed down the remains of his spring roll. "Sure, what do you want me to read?"

"This …" Steve retrieved a piece of creased paper from his

pocket and swiftly passed it to Theo. "It's a poem. I wrote a few days ago, Amber thought it was good, but I don't know if she's saying that. I figured I'd ask you because I know you'd be sincere and tell me if it's trash."

Theo nodded.

"Please don't read it out loud, makes me cringe," Steve pleaded.

"Okay, fine."

DAISY CHAIN

Grown by the mother,
Yet connected by stem,
You link in harmony,
Sweet harmony.
You refuse to bend and twist,
Searching for light through the darkness,
You stay true to your nature.
The waters keep you alive,
But they can never keep you going,
Only you can do that.
Soon enough we shall all be six feet beneath you,
Becoming the dirt from which you shall rise.
Through growth, love, and understanding,
The constant rise and fall unites us all,
In this never-ending game called the daisy chain.

It was surprisingly good. In truth, Theo wasn't one for poetry, and he wasn't expecting much from Steve, the former football jock, but this was good, especially if this was his first attempt. The theme of death towards the end niggled at Theo, however, like a maggot in his brain. Soon *he* would be below the daisies, he realized, pushing them up in his grave. Steve looked to him. This clearly meant a lot to him. He had to say something.

"Hey, this is really good," Theo said, flipping the page over.

"Honestly?" Steve's eyes widened. "You don't think it's crap?"

"Not at all. It's genuinely good. What made you wanna start

writing?" he asked, passing the paper back.

"I don't know, I've never tried before, just figured I would give it a shot and I gotta say, I quite enjoyed it."

"Hmm … you reckon you'll take it any further, as a career?"

"I doubt it. I guess I would only be good as a hobbyist." Steve folded the paper and put it back in his pocket.

"Don't say that, judging by this, I reckon you could do well. You have a real gift with words."

"Na, not me."

"You never know, you could wind up being a bestselling author or something? Just find a good enough story, and you're in. Wouldn't hurt you to try, would it?"

"I guess," Steve pondered, rubbing the back of his neck. "But do me a favour …"

"Go for it."

"Don't tell any of the others, not yet. I don't want them to rip into me."

"You really think they would?" Theo paused, overhearing the arguing over channels in the background. "Okay, they most likely would, but it would be in a supportive, caring way."

Steve gave a half-hearted chuckle. "I know, it's all just good, honest fun, but right now I want to keep it secret, while I'm figuring it all out and finding my voice."

"My lips are sealed."

Theo could tell something else was bothering Steve. His aura was off. He was conflicted. Was it just the aftereffects of the brownie, or something else?

It was something else: Amber. The thought of her was playing like a game of ping pong, back and forth in Steve's mind.

"What's up?" Theo asked.

"Nothing, nothing's up?"

"Steve, I've known you long enough to know you better than yourself. So, what's wrong?"

Steve instinctively glanced directly at Amber.

"You should talk to her," Theo said.

"Who?"

"You know who." Theo looked over at Amber. "You should tell her how you feel."

"You-you know?"

Theo merely replied with a reassuring smile and a nod.

Steve turned away, a little embarrassed. "Anyone else know?"

"Na, why would they?"

"That obvious, huh?"

"Maybe, in a cute kind of way," Theo teased, jabbing Steve's with his elbow. "Tell me, what's stopping you?"

"What if she doesn't feel the same way?" he asked with a degree of insecurity. "Me saying something will ruin everything, the whole dynamic of the gang, things could get awkward."

Theo scoffed. "Have you seen us? We're a freak show of awkwardness. I think we're all fairly comfortable being awkward by ourselves. What's the harm in taking on a little more?"

Steve didn't reply.

Theo took a deep breath, as if preparing to give a speech. "You know, when we were kids, I used to be jealous of you. Jealous that I couldn't charge into things as you did, go in headfirst without overthinking, being strong and confident in whatever it was you were doing. Trying out for the school football team, asking out the hottest girl in class, jumping from wall to wall. Just going for it, without second-guessing yourself."

Steve straightened up, lifting his chin slightly. "That was a long time ago. I'm a different person now."

"That's not true, and you know it," Theo said. "You may have become more multi-layered, as they say, but you're still the same Steve you always were."

Steve looked over to Amber, her dress flowing in the wind.

"Maybe she feels the exact same way as you," Theo said.

"You think?"

"Hmm … only one way to find out."

Steve let out a hot breath, pairing both sets of fingers. "Wish me luck," he said.

Theo winked. "You don't need it."

The channel hopping continued as Steve walked through the lounge area and opened the balcony doors. JJ screamed at him for blocking the TV screen, and Tabitha slapped him, silencing his tantrum. Shutting the sliding glass door, Steve joined Amber below the bedazzled sky.

"Star gazing?" he asked.

Amber froze as if momentarily disarmed to see Steve, and then replied, "I have always loved the night sky. Even as a little girl, I would look up and think the stars were talking to me. Funny, isn't it, the things we believe as children."

Steve stood beside her, his hands close to hers on the railing. "Very funny … I used to look out the back of my parents' car window at night, wondering why the moon was following us."

A girlish laugh escaped Amber. "You're funny, you've always been funny."

"What, funny looking?" he retorted playfully.

"No, no, just amusing."

Steve looked down at her, edging closer. "Listen, I'm sorry for eating one of your nana's pot brownies—"

"Don't apologize, it was my fault. I was in a rush this morning and forgot to tell any of you that she stopped by with them. I'm sorry; it was all my fault—"

"No, it wasn't—"

"Then again, I'm surprised you managed to eat a brownie after I cooked you breakfast this morning?"

"Yeah, I guess I—" He chuckled nervously.

"Oh, it's just, I know." She waved her hand, suppressing her laughter.

"Know?" Steve's heart raced. "What do you know?"

"That I'm an awful cook."

He paused, not sure whether to lie or tell the truth. He chose to lie. "No, no! You're not an awful cook—"

"Stop! It's fine. Honestly, out of everyone, you lie the best, sometimes I even believe you … sometimes. I hope someday I can improve so I can make you all something edible."

"I can take criticism, you know," Amber added.

"I know."

"Hell, I was raised with criticism. But even if I was able to cook something nice, just once, a part of me would miss all of you trying to protect my feelings, it makes me feel cared for."

"Well, we do care for you. I care for you, Amber."

Amber's cheeks glowed as she turned to face him. "I know you all do."

Steve looked around. This was it: the stars, the glowing sapphire flower lights, his pendant buzzing … this was the moment, it had to be, it was perfect. He exhaled and decided to go for it, to let his feelings be known, to commit, no matter the price. "Hey, listen, Ambz, have you ever thought that maybe I like you a little bit more than everyone else?"

"What do you mean?"

"Have you ever wondered if there's something more between us …"

"Go on …" She pressed closer to him.

"Something …"

"Yes?" They were practically touching.

"Something …" Steve lowered his head, going in for the kiss, only for Amber to retract from him.

In the lounge, Tabitha jumped back at the gear shift, snapping her fingers at JJ to do something.

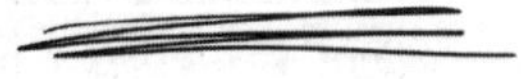

"No, we shouldn't," Amber whispered.

And in that moment, the spell was broken. "Wh-what's wrong?" Steve asked.

"It's not you, it's just …"

JJ's head appeared through the door. "Hey, guys, you wanna come in and watch a movie with us?"

Steve frowned, confused. "Erm … yeah sure—"

"Yes, that sounds good," Amber replied.

"Good, come on," JJ replied, not quite sure why he said that.

Amber followed him inside, closely accompanied by Steve. As they re-entered the room, everyone sat in silence, stirring empty cups and fiddling with their phones. Tabitha sat in a rather uncomfortable-looking position, as if she had been sitting there all the time.

Theo cringed for the pair of them as they drifted through everyone's teeth-gritting silence.

"So … what movie we gonna watch?" Steve asked, his voice unusually high.

"I don't know," Tabitha said with a frustrated sigh. "I've been looking for ages now! Nothing but a load of crap! Aha! What about this?" She picked the first thing she saw without subtitles.

JJ rejoiced. "*The Hollow Man*."

The words stirred something uncomfortable deep inside Theo.

"Remember this one, Theo?" JJ roared. "You were scared shitless of this as a kid."

"Ye-yeah, I remember it, remember it very well." His hands shook as he recalled the scene playing out on screen. The girl was down the hallway; the Hollow Man wasn't there yet, but he was close.

"Ah, it's such a dumb movie," JJ said. "So cheesy, let's watch it."

Hearing the offbeat trumpet noise vibrating through the television speaker, Theo instinctively sprinted over and turned off the screen. "Here's an idea …"

"Hey, we were watching that," Tabitha stated, munching on a cucumber slice she had planned to use for her eyes.

"Why don't we play some games?" Theo said quickly.

JJ recoiled. "Games?"

"I'm gonna need more alcohol for that shit," Tabitha said.

"What kind of games?" Steve asked, clearly needing a distraction from what had just happened.

"How about … truth or dare?" Theo suggested.

"Ooh, spicy," JJ said.

"Yes! Let's! I love it," Tabitha said.

Amber sighed. "Eh, do we have to? I hate truth or dare."

"Come on, Ambz, don't be a wet fart." Tabitha nudged her.

"Game, Ishaan?" Theo asked.

Ishaan nodded. "S-sure."

"Correct answer! I tell ya, I like this new you."

Ishaan smiled.

"Okay, who's first?" Steve asked.

"I'll go first," JJ volunteered. "Truth!"

Theo wanted to divert attention away from Steve and Amber; he knew it could be done with JJ. He would surely say something juicy, given the right question. "Okay, J, have you ever fancied anyone here in this room?" he asked.

"Yes, next question," he said.

"Ooh!" Tabitha chirped. "Now I'm intrigued. Who?"

"That wasn't the question. Who's next?" JJ looked at Amber, who was sitting next to him.

"Am-Amber, truth or dare?" Ishaan asked, leaning forward.

"I don't like this."

"Come on, it's just a bit of fun," JJ assured her.

Steve sprung. "Know what we haven't played in a while?" he exclaimed. "The lava game."

Everyone hollered and whooped in nostalgic joy.

"Oh, crap, no," JJ said. "We used to love that. Remember when I jumped up on that old lady's fence and broke it, and she called the cops."

"Good times." Theo nodded.

Steve grinned. "Hey, you guys … the floor is lava."

"Shit," Tabitha muttered before everyone sprang into excitable action, jumping up onto couches and tables. Steve, Tabitha, and Amber took up the couch, leaving no room for JJ.

Steve counted down. "Five, four, three, two, one!"

JJ grabbed a cushion and stood on it.

"J is dead," Steve bellowed.

"No, I'm not."

"Yes, you are!"

"How? My feet aren't touching the floor."

"Yeah, but a cushion wouldn't save you," Steve pointed out.

"And a couch would?"

Theo was standing on a small side table. His vision was blurry and everything looked hazy. He grunted and Amber spun to face him. "Theo?"

"Ah, come on, just let that be a trial round," JJ said.

"Okay, fine," Steve compromised.

JJ cheered, jumping off his pillow. "I'm a survivor."

"For this round."

"For all the rounds," JJ stated cockily as everyone began stepping down from their lava safety posts.

As the room spun, Theo lost his footing, causing him to fall off the table. Everyone jumped in surprise and shock.

"Theo!" a single voice called out as they all blurred into one.

"Stay with us, buddy. We're gonna get help. Stay with us."

CHAPTER TWENTY-TWO

HARD TRUTHS

"Theo … Theo … Theo … can you hear me?"

A white light hit the back of Theo's retinas, stinging the nerve endings. Through the clean fog, a figure became apparent, followed by other welcoming masses behind. Coming round, Theo could now see in explicit, stinging focus. It was Steve who stood close to his face, his twirling wolf pendant swinging like a hypnotist's tool.

"There he is." He smiled with relief. "There's our guy."

With that, the rest of the gang formed a gaggle around him: Amber, JJ, Tabitha, Ishaan, and even Chen. The differing colours, shapes, and patterns caused Theo's head to reel a little, his hand reaching up to feel the slight bump on his temple. He felt so weak he could drown in a puddle. For the life of him, he couldn't remember what happened beyond falling. He became aware of a constant, rhythmic beeping; it was his heart, monitored. A slight chill of panic shivered through him.

"Where am I?" The heart monitor accelerated as he attempted to sit up.

"Whoa! Take it easy," Steve said. "You've been through a lot." His arms held him still. "It's okay."

Theo was not convinced, noting Amber and Ishaan's tearstained cheeks. "How long have I been asleep?"

Steve hesitated. "Eighteen hours."

"Eighteen hours?"

"Yeah, you fainted," JJ said. "Luckily, we rushed you here."

"Here?" Theo frowned.

"The h-hospital," Ishaan cut in, shouting as if he could not be heard.

"Hospital?"

"Yes, the doctors ran some te-tests."

"I can fucking hear you," Theo snapped, stressed. "I am not fucking deaf!"

Ishaan moved back to Chen behind him.

JJ filled the silence. "Ha, well. Someone's cranky."

"Good to see you haven't lost the fire in your belly." Steve grinned, settling a soft hand on his shoulder.

"No, just about a day of our vacation." Theo groaned, adjusting his position to sit upright with the aid of a pillow. "I'm so sorry, guys."

Amber squeezed his hand. "Don't be. It's fine, these things happen." Her voice cracked on the last word.

Looking up, Theo met her wet gaze. Something was wrong.

"You said the doctors ran some tests?"

Amber allowed Steve to step back in front of her, like her shield.

"Yes."

Theo looked around to see everyone else avoiding eye contact. "And?"

"Well …" Steve struggled, not quite sure how to word his following sentence.

JJ grunted in frustration. "Just say it."

Steve stiffened, holding JJ back. "They found a tumour, Theo. In your brain."

"Oh." Theo tensed, trying to act shocked.

Steve continued. "The doctors took some brain scans to see what caused you to fall unconscious. And that's what they found."

Their pain seeped through them all, plucking heartstrings inside Theo's tired and withered shell. "So, how do you know? Wouldn't they tell next of kin, patient confidentiality?"

"True," said Tabitha. "They can only tell partners or immediate family—"

"So they told me, little brother," JJ said, as if citing a comedic reveal, humour being his line of defence in any situation.

"J …" Theo began aggressively.

"I was gonna go with my boyfriend, but Amber wouldn't let me—"

Tabitha whacked him. "Ow!" he responded, rubbing his arm.

"Stop it! This isn't funny," she said, before turning back to Theo. "We're so sorry, Theo."

With his mind drowning in conflicting thoughts, Theo decided to move past the realization that his friends now knew and press on with questions. "What did they say, about my tumour, specifics?"

Steve shook his head. "Theo—"

"Tell me, whatever it is, I can take it."

"They said you have about two months," JJ said with a slight croak.

The hour hands spun wildly on his beating clock of a heart. "What? No." He had so much more to do. Even the six months he had been told only weeks ago hadn't felt nearly enough, but this? This shattered him beyond recovery.

"Don't worry, we didn't tell your mom," Steve assured him.

"Good, that's good," Theo managed to say.

JJ continued, "They also said some kind of abnormalities had shown up in your brain scans; they're not sure what they were, so they're keeping you here to try and figure it out."

"Abnormalities—in my brain?" Theo said. "I can't do this anymore."

"Can't do what, man?"

"Lie, I'm so sick of lying." Theo looked away in shame.

"Lying?" JJ frowned in confusion. "About what?"

"About this."

"What do you mean?" Amber asked.

"I knew," Theo openly admitted. "Please don't hate me!"

"Knew what?" Steve questioned. "That you had a tumour?"

"Yes! I found out a few weeks ago. I was told it was inoperable, that I only had six months left. I figured I could find another way. I looked into it. There were only two options: get this big-time dragon healer to cure me, which, spoiler alert, he didn't or . . ."

"Or?" JJ pressed.

"Steal some experimental pills from a lab."

"Theo," Amber said in shock.

"So that lab … the warehouse break-in that was all over the news here … that was you?" Tabitha asked. "The reports said the guards were badly wounded."

"I know! I was there."

Steve retracted slightly. "Theo, how?"

"I-I have been having problems."

"What kind of problems?" Amber asked.

Theo confessed. "I've been seeing things."

"What kind of things?" JJ asked, brow furrowed.

Theo turned to them all for support, only to be met with a mix of disbelief, pity, and confusion. An ocean of emotion escaped him as he wept, never having felt more alone than he did now.

All except JJ gathered round to comfort him.

"Hey, it's okay, you can tell us," Steve said.

Theo tried to explain. "Hallucinations, I think. That's the worst part; I can't tell what's real and what isn't anymore."

"Hey, we're real," Steve assured him. "I promise."

JJ was standing in the corner. "What sort of stuff have you been seeing?"

Theo couldn't understand the sudden shift in his friend's mood. "All sorts of things. I kept seeing my imaginary friend, the one I had as a kid."

JJ's face dropped. "Frank?"

Theo was taken by surprise. "Yeah! How do you know?"

"Your mom told me about him." He waved it off, casually strolling towards the hospital bed.

"She did?"

"Theo, what kind of stuff was Frank saying or doing?"

"All sorts." He struggled to think. "Convincing me to do bad things to survive. Tormenting me … but none of it has been real. It's all been in my head."

"Theo—"

"I think I may have psychological problems."

JJ looked down. "Where is Frank now?"

"H-he went." Theo's heart monitor accelerated once more, and all heads turned to look at it.

"Went?"

"Yeah, he left a few days ago."

JJ smiled. "Okay, well that's good." He sounded somewhat unconvinced.

"Why is it good?" Theo rasped.

"It's good that we can tackle the tumour and not the … other stuff at the same time."

"What do you—"

"Now you say you tried the drugs, and they didn't work right?" JJ asked.

"N-no. In fact, they are probably the reason I have abnormalities and less time than before."

"So th-they've accelerated the tu-tumour's growth rate," Ishaan added.

"And the … what was he called, healer?" JJ asked.

"The Dragon?"

"He couldn't cure you?"

"No, he said he wouldn't. Said I was not meant to be cured."

"Bastard," Tabitha growled.

"Screw him, Theo, we can find a way," Steve said.

"Guys, it's over."

"Ah, shut up!" JJ said. "It's not over. We've already found a way."

"Wh-what?"

"Yeah, once we found out, we did some research while you were having your little nap. We found a skilled surgeon here in L.A., even phoned him."

Hope struck Theo across his face, like paint hitting a canvas. "Re-really? And?"

"He is going to get back to us with a price within the hour," Amber filled in.

"Hmm … did he give an estimate?"

"A considerable amount," Steve added.

"I see, and where is this money coming from?" Theo asked.

"From us, we're all pitching in," Amber announced.

"No, guys. No."

"It's fine." Tabitha leaned in.

"I can't let you."

Steve smirked. "Yes, you can."

"No. This guy will drain you of everything you have, I know he will."

"Oh, for sure, and we will deal with it, but if it means keeping you here with us, then it's worth it, right?" Steve said with a warm sense of confidence.

His friends' overly generous gesture touched Theo, but he couldn't let them ruin their lives for him. "I won't let you."

"Tough shit, you don't get a say," JJ remarked. "Sorry, but you're not going anywhere. We're not gonna let you."

Theo looked around at them all, his loyal friends, willing to sacrifice their life savings for the sake of saving him. "Dicks."

A contagious burst of laughter filled the room, lifting the room. Even Amber seemed amused by the rather crude word he had called them.

"That's the spirit," Steve said.

"I'm so sorry, guys, for lying to you. I figured I could get rid of this … thing and have one last adventure with you all. I didn't want to worry you."

Amber silenced him. "Theo, you don't need to apologize. We understand. It's fine."

"But you should have told us, we could have stopped you doing all the dumb shit you've already done!" JJ snapped. "Damaging yourself in the process."

"J," Steve chastised.

Theo nodded in agreement. "He's fine. Thank you, J. You're right. I should have told you. I didn't want to be viewed differently by you all."

"We would never view you any differently than for the person you are: our friend," Amber said.

The comment shimmered and settled Theo's nerves, so much so that his pale hand reached out to meet Amber's, only for her to pull away slightly. In fear, it would seem, after hearing about the things he had done, or the things he could still do.

Amber's phone ringing broke the awkward silence that followed. She moved away from Theo and pulled her phone out of her chic leather bag.

"It's him," she whispered, looking at the caller ID.

"Who?" Tabitha frowned.

"The surgeon."

"Okay, breathe," JJ ordered. "Put him on speaker."

Amber pressed the answer button along with the speaker icon. "Hello!"

A calm male voice answered. "Hello, am I speaking to Amber Cross, the young lady who enquired about my services earlier?"

"Yes, hello, Doctor Locke," Amber replied.

"I believe you wanted to know my professional opinion on your friend, Theo, was it?"

"Yes."

"In respect of his brain tumour?"

"It was, yes."

"Well, I have good news. I can indeed remove your friend's tumour."

There was a silent carnival of fist bumps, dances, and gestures of joy in the hospital room.

Amber smiled. "Oh, that's fantastic."

Theo gives the thumbs up.

"For the fee of two million dollars."

The mood in the room changed dramatically.

Letting out a nervous laugh, Amber continued, "Sorry, I think we broke up for a brief second there, bad signal, could you say that again?"

"Of course, the price of my services is two million dollars."

Theo slumped back down on the bed in defeat. Everyone looked at each other—there was no way they could get that kind of money.

"Two million? I'm sorry, Doctor Locke, I think there's been some misunderstanding. We can't afford that."

Steve jumped in, seeing Theo's shattered face. "Couldn't you make a smaller offer?"

"A smaller amount for my time, my work?"

"Is that a no?" JJ asked.

"I'm afraid I can't, I am a very busy man. I could only manage to squeeze your friend into my busy schedule for such a fee."

"Please, Doctor Locke, be reasonable," Amber pleaded. "We are willing to give you a good amount, all our life savings in fact, to pay you privately." She hoped desperation would win him over, make him feel some degree of mercy, or charity, or goodwill.

"How much?"

"Forty thousand," JJ butted in.

"No."

"Please, you'd be saving a young man's life."

"Give me the phone …" Theo instructed.

Amber passed the cell phone to him. "Doctor Locke. This is Theo."

"Oh, hello, Theo, I am sorry to hear of your … predicament."

"I appreciate that, but I am begging you, please, please, help me. I will give you whatever you want. Please, fix me."

A long, drawn-out silence was broken by the heart monitor, which seemed almost to skip a beat. "Two million. I'm sorry, that's my final word. I will give you twenty-four hours to decide and get back to me."

"No wait—"

The line went dead, and Theo dropped the phone, sinking back into his pillow. Everyone in the room looked at him with sorrow and empathy.

"Don't do that."

"Do what?" JJ asked.

"Feel sorry for me. I can't bear it."

Steve's shoulders lowered. "Theo—"

"I lost, okay, I played a good game, but I still lost."

No one said anything, either lost in their own thoughts or unsure what to do or say next.

JJ's eyes widened in realization. "You're right, it is a game."

"I've played all the aces I have, J, it's over."

"No, you still have us, and we have a few tricks up our sleeves.

The game's not finished yet." JJ got up to leave the room.

Steve followed JJ, grabbing him by the arm in the hallway.

"Where are you going?"

"To get results."

"Where?" Steve's brow furrowed.

"I don't know. I'll figure it out."

Tabitha entered the hallway, stalling JJ.

"I'm going too!" she said.

"Hey! Hey! Wait a minute," Steve said. "What's the plan, guys?"

"I'm going to see if I can get anything from that witch's shop. Look into spiritual healing," Tabitha explained.

Steve held his pendant, turning to JJ. "J, what's going on?" What aren't you telling us?"

"Okay, listen, you know the whole imaginary friend thing Theo was talking about back in there?"

"Yeah, Frank," Steve replied.

"It was a bad sign."

Steve nodded. "Well, yeah, surely an old hallucination is a bad sign. It's his subconscious or something."

"It's more than that. His mom told me some things a few years ago, back when she was worried about him falling into … old habits. She was worried about what he might do … the things he did before we knew him, when he was a little kid, the last time he had Frank in his head."

A worried look came over Steve's face. "What kind of stuff?"

JJ looked away. "That's not important. Let's blow one bridge up at a time, shall we? Deal with this and then … all of that other shit later."

"Hey, J, be careful." Steve smiled at his friend. Tabitha patted Steve's back as she too left and headed off in a different direction. Steve turned to re-enter the room and bumped into Amber.

"I'm also going!"

"Where?"

"To get Theo some good food."

"What? No!" Theo groaned from across the room. "If I'm gonna die, I wanna go full of fast food."

"Stop it, you're not going to die," Amber said before turning to whisper to Steve. "I read about a woman who had cancer and changed her diet and started exercising; she managed to cure herself. You never know, it might help."

"Just call if you need anything."

"Hey, Amber …" Theo wheezed, with a grin. "Why don't you take Steve with you? I'm sure he could be of use, get you back here faster."

"But what about you?"

"I've got Ishaan and Chen. They will take good care of me."

"H-he's right, go."

Steve nodded, and they left the hospital room together.

Theo smiled to himself. At least some good may come from all this if this is the push they needed at long last. He could be their cupid.

"So … anyone got any games on their phone"?" he asked, causing Chen and Ishaan to begin searching their screens.

Black leather boots kicked a pebble along the road. Thick, dark hair flopped into JJ's view as he walked, using the motion to clear his mind. The fresh air helped him focus on one thing: saving Theo. How to stop him from slipping back into his past, a place JJ couldn't fully understand. He envied those who could block painful memories, but he knew his own struggles shaped who he was.

Theo, once unpredictable and dangerous, was now something else, twisted and lost. JJ had consistently recognized the darkness in him, but now, with Julie's revelations, he was genuinely worried. He couldn't let Theo slip back into old patterns, especially not with the tumour threatening his mind. JJ needed to fix this—he had to.

He was JJ Mooney, the guy who'd survived everything life threw at him. If anyone could find a solution, it was him. He wouldn't give up on his friend. The others would offer vague alternatives, but JJ needed a sure thing. And that meant Doctor Locke. He stopped, staring at the harbour, and pulled out his phone with a sudden, determined idea.

CHAPTER TWENTY-THREE

ALL IN YOUR HEAD

Theo's mind drifted again. Despite the long sleep, exhaustion—or maybe the tumour—pulled him back into a different place. A shadowy desert stretched out before him, beneath a night sky. A tin can hung from a string, swaying like a forgotten relic. As he approached it, faint whispers echoed through the can, a voice from his childhood.

"Hello? Hello?" Theo spoke in a near-whisper.

"He is here," the voice crackled back. Before Theo could respond, the string jerked, pulling the can into the air with a speed that made his head spin. The ground beneath him dissolved, and he fell, fast and hard, his organs lurching to his chest. A soft, spongy surface broke his fall.

Theo pulled himself up and found himself standing in a nineties-style sitcom set, but in black-and-white. He blinked in confusion. The stage was set up with a couch, a large kitchen area behind pocket doors, and pinstripe wallpaper. On the wall, albums labelled "forgotten dreams," "heartbreak," "loss," and "fake friends" sat like relics of the past.

Then Theo saw the doors—six of them. One had a sign that read "Theo: The Leading Man," and the others were labelled with his friends' names:

JJ: The Wild Card
Tabitha: The Tough Cookie
Amber and Steve: The Romantic Pair
Ishaan: The Comic Relief

It hit him: this was a shared apartment—a strange, sitcom

version of his life. Everything was weirdly familiar and yet so, so wrong. Each picture frame had images of them all together, but their faces were strangely inauthentic, as if digitally inserted into the shots. And then—the spot. A vast, infected cyst oozing a thick, RED goo on the wall.

Curious, Theo stepped closer, about to touch it, but just then the door swung open.

The room exploded into colour. The sitcom vibe hit full force. Bright, saturated hues of brown, yellow, and pink filled the space as laughter erupted from an invisible audience. His friends walked in, each dressed in exaggerated, colourful outfits that fit their sitcom roles.

JJ, grinning from ear to ear, held court. "And that's when the guy got the ring out of his bag," he said, making a grand gesture.

"Ring?" Tabitha asked, inspecting her painted nails, unimpressed.

"Yeah, well, it wasn't exactly the kind of ring you'd put on your finger …"

Cue laugh track. The invisible audience cackled, and JJ looked over at Theo, his eyes widening. "Well, well, well, hot diggity dog, look who it is!"

"Theo!" Amber glided over, dressed in a spotted dress, and wrapped him in a big hug. The audience cheered.

"There's our leading man," Steve teased, punching Theo lightly in the arm.

Theo blinked, confused. "Leading what?" His eyes flicked around the room. The spot of goo was gone, replaced by GREEN wallpaper. "What's going on?"

Amber laughed, taking her place in the room. "Well, we've just come back to our shared apartment!"

"Shared apartment? When did that happen?" Theo asked, looking around.

"Oh, a lot of things happen when you let time take over," Steve replied, before laying his hands on Amber's shoulders. "Isn't that right, honey!"

"Yes, my love," Amber replied, turning for a long, drawn-out kiss that garnered an uproarious, 'awwww.'

"Wait, are you two … officially a thing now?"

Amber laughed. "It's just coming up to our second anniversary."

"But you knew that, didn't you, man?" Steve winked, nudging him.

"Di-did I?"

"Ah, that's our Theo, always thinking and saying silly things," Steve said, walking past him to sit on the couch.

JJ appeared from nowhere next to him, looking out to a black void of an audience with his arms raised, cheekily. "Who else but Theo?"

With that, a camp introduction sequence played out with music and over-the-top poses by the cast, his friends, who were labelled as playing themselves in: *Just An Ordinary Friends Comedy Sitcom!*

Back in the apartment, Theo looked around at the set, startled to be back where he was before. "What the hell was that?" he asked as a laugh track played in response.

"What was what?" Tabitha looked up from her phone. The non-existent spectators screeched in hilarity.

Theo asked, "Is, is this real? Because I'm really starting to lose track of what is and isn't now!"

"Real?" JJ smirked. "It's about as real and genuine as my pearly smile."

"Is that a yes?" Theo questioned.

"Ah, enough of this silly talk, there's no time, we have to prepare a meal for Steve's boss and his wife tonight," Amber said, her cheeks glowing.

"Steve's boss? When did—?"

Then, Theo and the whole scene abruptly cut to 'Some Time Later …' where a dinner table was laid out. It was now twilight, and his friends ran about preparing the scene.

"Quit floundering, Theo. Grab the napkins as they'll be here any minute," Tabitha snapped.

"Wait … did we just—"

"Come on, move it!" She clapped.

"Oh-okay!" He submitted, going over to the kitchen counter

to grab a pile of serviettes and placing them on the perfectly set dinner table.

"Oh, I'm so n-n-n-n-nervous, to me-me-meet your boss and his w-w-wife, St-Steve," Ishaan stuttered unrealistically.

"Don't be, there's no need, man," Steve assured him. "Just be your usual charming, witty, and sociable self."

"Oh b-b-b-boy!" Ishaan pulled out his inhaler before fainting dramatically, splaying out along the patterned rug as even louder canned laughter erupted. Everyone gasped, except Theo, who just looked more confused.

JJ held his face in his hands. "Oh no!"

"Ishaan has fainted," Steve explained to blind viewers, no doubt, as someone knocked on the door. The door opened.

"Hello! Steve, it's me! Your boss! Mr. Boss!" a man called.

"And his wife," a woman announced.

"Uh-oh!" JJ winked as if to the camera.

Amber put her hands on her hips, looking at Steve. "Whatever are we going to do?"

Fingers clicked. "Quickly, hide the body," Tabitha ordered, being the first to try to drag the unconscious Ishaan.

This brought on a short, slapstick scene as the group picked up Ishaan's body and attempted to carry him to myriad locations, the laugh track playing in praise of their antics. It all felt very forced to Theo, and too busy, the whole thing, like there were too many cooks in the kitchen. However, Theo watched the gag play out, intrigued.

The first place they attempted to hide Ishaan was under the couch cushions, which they passed over before covering him with the rug. They all shook their heads as they then sat him up and put a lamp cover over his head. This they approved of until Ishaan fell once more. They then dragged him over to a small cupboard, which they bundled him into, struggling to fit him all in, to great comedic effect as further cackles indicated. They settled on leaving Ishaan in the small cupboard with his arm hanging out. Amber clapped her hands together. "Perfect," she said, walking over to open the door.

Theo stood back in shock; it was his parents, dressed not as themselves, but as a typical old-school 1950s businessman and wife. "Dad? Mom?" he asked when they clearly failed to recognize him. Steve greeted them at the doorway with a handshake.

"Ah, Mr. Boss and Mrs. Boss."

"Steve!" Carl, as Mr. Boss, said.

"Lovely to meet you," Julie said, as Mrs. Boss.

"Please, do come in." Amber invited them into the lounge. "Tabitha, would you mind taking Mr. and Mrs. Boss's coats?"

"Sure." Tabitha took both coats from the guests only to look around, confused about where to put them. She settled on throwing them on the couch to Amber's annoyance and the audience's delight.

"Tabz!"

"What!" She shrugged as the crowd guffawed.

"This is Tabitha," Steve introduced.

"How nice to meet you." Mr. Boss nodded.

"I know!"

"Oh, she's a sassy one, isn't she?" Mrs. Boss remarked.

"Yeah, she's something," Steve said.

"JJ Mooney," JJ said, offering his hand to be kissed.

There followed a long pause before Mr. Boss stated with a sniff, "You smell of cabbage."

JJ lifted his arm and smelled under his pit. "You're not wrong."

The laugh track hit hard as Amber continued with the introductions. "And this is Theo."

"Hey!" Theo smiled, taking in his dead father's living, breathing self. It didn't matter if it wasn't real, or hell—Theo would take what he could get, even if all this were just a cheap imitation of the real thing. Theo did not care in that moment; this perfect delusion was a blessing—all his favourite people in the same room together, with him. There was nothing more he wanted.

"Hello, nice to meet you," his father replied in a clipped tone. This was rather unlike him, as he'd usually chat quite happily to strangers.

"Likewise." Theo experienced a flicker of doubt as his fantasy father inspected the room.

"And where's the other one? I was told there were six of you."

"Ishaan?" Amber sounded flustered. "He had to go out."

A murmur could be heard from the cupboard as Ishaan stirred. Tabitha whacked the door shut, knocking him out once more as a fit of laughing ignited. Mr. Boss's face registered understanding.

"Oh, I see."

"Can we get you some refreshments?" Amber asked.

"Tap water for me, please," Mrs. Boss said.

"Yes, and for me," her husband added.

"JJ, tap water for our guests."

"Oh, of course, right away, are they doubles or singles?" he joked. Amber glared at him in response. "I'll assume they're both triples then." He walked over to the cupboard and grabbed three glasses before going back over to the sink, smiling as he was being observed. He awkwardly turned the tap to no avail. The pipework rattled and JJ began comedically bashing the sink with all his might. Then, clear water ran, filling the glasses. JJ smiled and presented the pair with their drinks. He took the third for himself after the heavy maintenance work he had just done. Taking a sip, he said, "Hmm … isn't that nice."

"Yes. How I like my water … moist," Mr. Boss said as they took their seats in the lounge area. He grinned to the invisible camera.

"Oh, JJ," Tabitha chuckled, leaning on the kitchen stove.

"Please ignore him, he's on day release," Mr. Boss said.

JJ lifted his trouser leg to reveal a beeping leg tracker.

Tabitha leaned too far across the stove and the oven mitt by her side caught fire. Realizing what had happened, she panicked, and JJ helped to put it out. Everyone noticed except Mr. and Mrs. Boss. Smoke arose quickly and fast, swamping the whole apartment to the sound of more laughter.

"Is there a barbecue taking place somewhere?" Mr. Boss asked.

"Oh, yes, our neighbour downstairs," Steve lied.

JJ and Tabitha continued to panic as they tried to put out the fire with the sink hose and then many glasses of water, which did little. Finally, JJ grabbed the fire extinguisher and Tabitha shut the sliding doors as the fire began to spread in the kitchen and engulf the room. The invisible audience whooped and hollered.

"Well, I can't wait to try whatever it is you are preparing," Mr. Boss stated.

And on that cue, JJ peeked through the sliding doors, his face blackened with ash, and said, "It's gonna be one hell of a meal!"

Theo felt hollow at the wild antics. Then the action faded to black.

The next scene opened with them all sitting around the table with a meal in front of them. 'Some Time Later …'

"Wait, what just—what's happening now?" Theo asked.

"Come on, Theo, hurry up, your food is getting cold," JJ said next to him, munching on his dinner.

Theo gazed down to see a mountain of mashed potatoes with six sausages protruding through the thick, white, crusty skin upward, each baring pineapple rings, with a cherry poking out of a cocktail stick on the end of each. "What is it?"

"A sausage surprise," JJ revealed with pride. Leaning in, he whispered, "Don't you remember, Theo? Tabz burned down the kitchen and the turkey in the oven, so I had to improvise."

"What makes it a surprise, may I ask?" Mrs. Boss asked from across the table. "The mash or the pineapple ring?"

"Neither. It's the cherries. And I, of all people, should know plenty about popping cherries, right?"

Amber gasped.

Changing the subject, Steve asked, "Mr. Boss, Mrs. Boss, how are you finding your meal?"

"Delicious!" Mr. Boss smiled.

"I can't wait for dessert," Mrs. Boss said.

Amber froze.

"Dessert?" JJ raised his eyebrows.

Mr. Boss rubbed his hands together. "I hope it's cake; I love cake."

"Oh yes, I love a cake," Mrs. Boss added.

The laughter grew louder and louder.

"Theo, is it?" Mr. Boss randomly asked from the other side of the table.

"Yes, Da—I mean Mr. Boss, that's right."

"You're awfully quiet," he said, sipping his water. "Tell us about yourself."

"What would you like to know?"

"What's your story, Theo Gray?"

"Well, there's not much to tell?"

"Nonsense, everyone has a story. What's yours?"

"Well … I, I don't know, to be honest."

"Hmm …" Mr. Boss seemed unconvinced.

"Just tell us, who are you?" Mrs. Gray said.

"Who am I?"

All eyes were on him now. Theo pondered the question deeply. "Honestly? I don't know, and it kills me to say it, but I have no idea who I am anymore." The audience gave a sympathetic 'awww.'

"I know who you are …" JJ said. "You're a freak!"

"What?" Theo replied, taken aback. His shadow from behind was beginning to grow.

"And a liar," JJ continued, digging his knife into the table. The audience cheered.

"No, he's not, J," Steve said. "He's a weirdo!"

"And a cheat," Amber added.

"And an I-I-I-idiot!" Ishaan said, falling out of the cupboard and rising like a limp skeleton.

"A phony, a bit fat phony!" Tabitha exclaimed.

Tears ran down Theo's face. Rivers of pain spilled out into the open as his shadow, burning the wall, began to grow even more, morphing into something tall and monstrous. His friends began to corner him against the wall.

"A f-fake."

"A lunatic," Tabitha said.

"A monster," JJ growled.

"A pathetic nobody." Steve pointed his finger at him.

The television switched on by itself, glowing and humming RED static that grew in volume along with the continuous audience laugh track, causing the room to shake. Ornaments and books fell off tables and shelves. The GREEN pinstripe wallpaper began to peel from the walls. Cracks began to form along the floor, ceiling, and walls. The food to sizzle, fry, and pop.

The group circled Theo.

"What's wrong with you!" Amber yelled.

"Y-you have to ruin ev-everything."

"We should be used to it by now," Tabitha said aggressively. "Everything he touches goes to shit."

"We hate you." JJ bared his teeth.

"We've always hated you," Steve said. Theo crouched down in his corner, his shadow behind him turning into the silhouette of the Hollow Man.

"Guys, stop, please!" he begged them.

Mrs. Boss, now as herself, chipped in. "You're a disgrace," she stated coldly. "Nobody wants you."

"Mom!"

Mr. Boss, now also himself, stepped forward. "You're no son of mine," he declared with a look of disdain.

"Dad!"

Theo crumpled in on himself. A moment later, he sprang up as a young child split from himself, looking up his present self, face to face. Looking directly at the broken-down man he was destined to become, was even, child Theo asked, "How did I grow up to be such an unloved loser?"

"No, no! Please, please stop! Please!"

His family and friends surrounded him, cackling like hyenas. Cradling and rocking back and forth now, Theo tried to block out their hateful words.

"Loser!"

"Freak!"

"Idiot!"

"We hate you!"

The laughter grew louder, more distorted. Theo's mind shattered, until with a sudden bang, everything went white.

In that white space, Theo floated—disconnected. Was this

a dream? Or was it his mind giving him the truth? He couldn't tell. But he was tired, exhausted by the chaos. Maybe being a spectator in his own mind was the only way left to survive.

HANDCUFFS? KINKY.

H-HE'S AWAKE!

AH YES, DID I MISS ANYTHING?

WHY-WHY IS HE P-PUTTING ON A BR-BRITISH ACCENT?

HA! WHY INDEED!
IGNORE HIM, HE'S JUST TRYING TO GET IN OUR HEADS!

AH, LOOK AT US ALL, THE GANG BACK TOGETHER AGAIN. WELL, IN A WAY!
SHUT UP!

HOW RUDE!
GUESS YOU'RE OFF THE CHRISTMAS CARD LIST THIS YEAR-

STOP JOKING ABOUT THEO. THIS ISN'T FUNNY.
YOU KNOW THAT DYING DOESN'T GIVE YOU THE RIGHT TO GO OFF THE RAILS & START KILLING WHOEVER YOU WANT.
HA HA HA HA HA HA HA HA HA

COUNTLESS PEOPLE HAVE DIED BECAUSE OF YOU.

I KNOW.

WHAT'S SO FUNNY?

I'M CRAZY YOU IDIOT!

THIS ISN'T FUNNY.

SOUNDS PRETTY FUNNY TO ME.

HE WON'T BE LAUGHING LONG, NOT WHEN THIS IS FINALLY OVER.

HA! HAHA HA! HA HA HA!
HA HA
GET READY FOR THE ENCORE.

H-HE SEEMS DIFFERENT?

HAS HE TA-TAKEN SOMETHING?

SO FAR AWAY,
GUYS, DON'T BE SHY...
...COME A LITTLE BIT
CLOSER

COME ON! CLOSER...

HAHAHA! WANNA CHECK MY TEMP-ERATURE, ISHAAN?
I'D BE MORE THAN HAPPY TO DROP THESE PANTS.
I'M DIFFERENT YOU SAY? WELL, I GUESS I AM. I'VE TAKEN OVER.
THEO, YOU NEED-
THEO'S NOT HERE ANYMORE, PLEASE LEAVE A BEEP AFTER THE...OH NO WAIT, THAT'S NOT HOW IT GOES, RIGHT, TABITHA?
CAN WE JUST GET THIS OVER WITH. I DON'T WANT TO SEE HIM LIKE THIS ANYMORE.
CAN'T WE JUST HAND HIM OVER TO THE AUTHORITIES;
THEY'LL SEE HE'S CLEARLY INSANE. HE CAN JUST SPEND THE REST OF HIS LIFE IN-
A FUNNY FARM? NO! HE'S TOO DANGEROUS TO BE LEFT ALIVE!
NO! WE NEED TO PUT THE POOR DOG OUT OF HIS MISERY.

WOOF! HEY, STEVE, CAN I TELL YOU SOMETHING REALLY IMPORTANT.
WHAT?
I HAVE TO WHISPER IT, IT'S SO IMPORTANT.
I'M NOT COMING ANYWHERE NEAR YOU
OKAY, HEY, LOOK, LISTEN, I KNOW I'M ABOUT TO DIE, BE EXECUTED FOR WHAT I'VE DONE BUT...
CAN YOU JUST GIVE ME THIS.
A DEAD MAN'S LAST WISH
WHAT IS IT?
CLOSER... CLOSER...

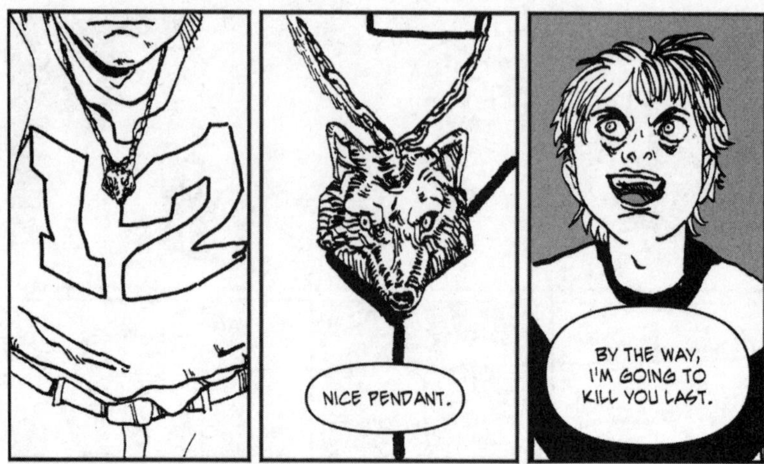
NICE PENDANT.
BY THE WAY, I'M GOING TO KILL YOU LAST.

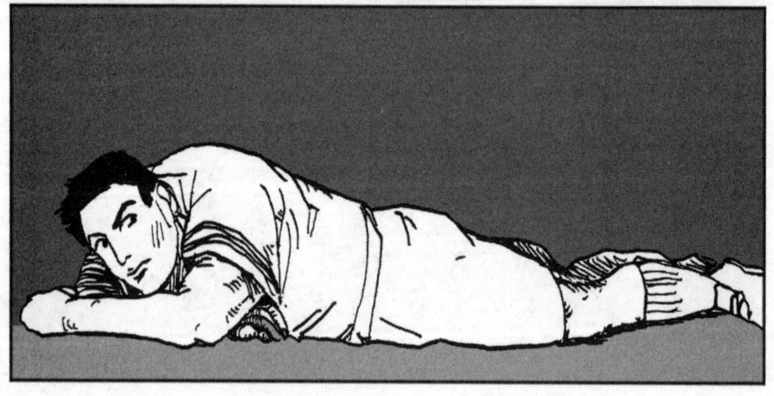

MADE IN CHINA

GO FIGURE.
RUNNING AWAY? GUESS I'M TAG. HA, THIS SHOULD BE FUN.
HA! A KNIFE? HOW VERY TWEE.
ST-ST-ST-STAY BA-BACK!
"ST-ST-STAY BA-BACK?" AH, ISHAAN, BUD, DIDN'T ANYONE TELL YOU NOT TO PLAY WITH KNIVES? COME ON, GIVE IT TO ME.

COME ON,
ISHAAN.
N-N-N-N-OOOOOOOOO

PAPA SPANK!
AND...

P-P-P-P-LEASE! P-P-PLEASE! TH-THEO! PL-LEASE!

SPLRT!

GOOD NEWS IS I FIXED YOUR STAMMER, BAD NEWS IS YOUR HEAD LOOKS LIKE A SPLIT MELON.
AH WELL... SWINGS AND ROUND-ABOUTS I GUESS.

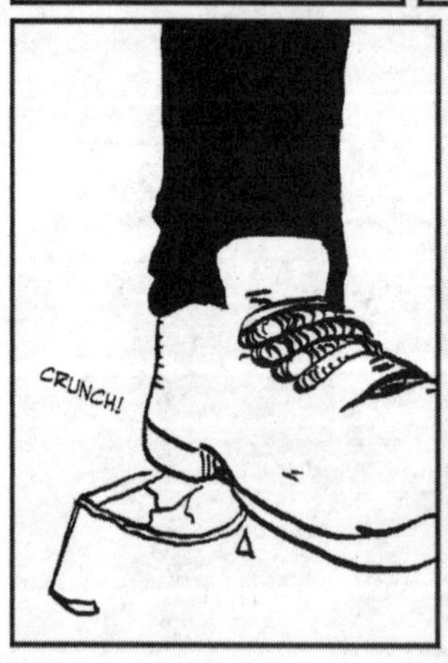
CRUNCH!

OH, HELLO THERE.
DON'T COME ANY CLOSER.

NORMALLY, THAT
WOULD WORK-

BUT...
CLICK!
I'M NOT EXACTLY 'NORMAL', AM I?

SEE YOU
NEXT
FALL!

PLEASE, THEO, I'M YOUR FRIEND. WE'RE FRIENDS. PLEASE DON'T HURT ME.
AW, HEY IT'S OKAY, IT'S OKAY. COME HERE.
CRACK!

HMM...NICE, DEATH SMELLS GOOD ON YOU.
HEY, BUD COME ON, IT'S ME
SURELY WE CAN COME TO SOME SORT OF ARRANGEMENT.
EVERY MAN HAS HIS PRICE.
AND DEATH.
OVER MY DEAD BODY.
PRECISELY.

YOU REALLY HAVE SNAPPED, HAVEN'T YOU?
CRACK!!!
THAT'S RIGHT, I HAVE SNAPPED.... YOUR NECK! HA! MADE A PUN.
OH, IF ONLY THEO WERE HERE TO APPRECIATE THAT ONE.
AH, GOOD TIMES!

I CAN'T LET YOU LEAVE, NOT AFTER EVERYTHING YOU'VE DONE.
PLEASE, I'M THE NIGHTMARE CHILD...
... THE KING OF CHAOS
THE BRINGER OF THE END OF DAYS...
...YOU CAN'T STOP ME

MAYBE...
...BUT I CAN TRY.
12
TRY AND DIE!

FEED THE GOOD WOLF?
HA, THE LONE WOLF SURVIVES WHILE THE PACK DIES.
STOP, STOP THIS MADNESS PLEASE.
SHH! THERE THERE, HUSH LITTLE STEVIE DON'T SAY A WORD
FRANKIE'S GONNA BURN DOWN THE WHOLE DAMN WORLD.

MAGNIFICENT.
WHAT A SHOW IT'S GOING TO BE...

Theo woke up gasping and screaming, his heart monitor spiking erratically. Ishaan and Chen rushed to his side. Ishaan grabbed his wrist, squeezing too tightly, while Chen held him down.

"Calm down!" Chen urged.

"It's okay, Theo," Ishaan said, trying to reassure him.

Theo finally exhaled, his body relaxing as he sank back into the pillow, his grip releasing from Ishaan's wrist, leaving a red mark.

Chen softly touched Ishaan's arm. "Bad dream?"

"Yeah," Theo replied, his gaze distant. "A very bad one."

Meanwhile, Amber and Steve wandered through an L.A. superstore, gathering healthy foods they hoped might help Theo. They were silent, avoiding the tension of their last encounter on the balcony.

"I really hope this works," Steve said.

Amber smiled faintly. "I'm optimistic. How about you?"

"I wish I were." Steve sighed.

Amber added, "What do you think JJ will do?"

"Something crazy," Steve laughed, "But he knows how to get things done … usually."

"Let's hope," Amber said.

In the fruit aisle, Steve asked, "Think your nana could help?"

"No," Amber answered. "She'd tell my mom … or worse."

Steve noticed her frustration. "You okay?"

"I'm fine. It's just all this," she gestured around them. "I usually handle messes, but this one …"

"Hey, we'll figure it out," Steve said.

Amber smirked. "What happened to no optimism?"

"I guess it grew on me."

As they shopped, Amber mentioned, "Before he left, JJ told me that Theo's hallucinations … his imaginary friend, are a bad sign."

"Why?"

"I don't know, but he said the last time he was in Theo's head, it changed him. J sounded scared, and I've never seen J sound scared before."

In a penthouse high above in Los Angeles, Doctor Locke frowned upon hearing a knock on his door.

"Yes?" he hissed, looking through the peephole to reveal a stylish young man.

"Doctor Locke?"

"Who is asking?"

"JJ Mooney. I have something very important to discuss with you."

"How did you get up here? I'm calling security if you don't go away right now."

"It concerns my friend, Theo Gray."

Doctor Locke thought for a moment and then opened the door.

JJ grinned and entered the apartment with confidence and entitlement.

Doctor Locke frowned. "I'm a busy man. What is it you want to discuss? Have you got the money?"

"I am here to talk to you, man to man." JJ walked around the apartment, apparently evaluating the expensive ornaments and pictures.

"'Man to man'?"

"That's right."

Locke smirked. "You're wasting your time if you have come here to convince me to change my mind."

"Not just a pretty face, I see," JJ said, picking up an ornament.

"I don't respond to flattery."

"Nor can you recognize sarcasm."

"You need to leave right now."

Placing the ornament back down, JJ sauntered over to the doctor. "Not until I have what I came here to get: your agreement to help my friend."

"And how do you plan on getting that?"

"By offering you your heart's desire."

"Which is?"

"Whatever you want it to be. Name it. Anything, except the two million dollars because, hey, I may be a miracle worker, but even I can't magic up money." He sat down on a leather chair.

Locke kept his cool. "What else could I possibly need or want besides money?"

"Huh? Good question, I mean, people have their wants and needs. You're a smart man, you understand that. Money, power, lust … revenge. You name it, and I will do it."

"Don't be ridiculous. You should go."

JJ jumped up and leaped towards the doctor, grabbing him by the neck, squeezing ever so slightly. "With one squeeze, I could snap you like a promise."

"You could, but you and I both know that you're not going to do that. Kill me and your friend will die."

"I do hate it when someone can tell when I'm bluffing." JJ released his hold on the doctor.

Locke rubbed his neck. "Now I would suggest you leave before I call the authorities."

JJ walked towards the door. "Just enjoy the upper hand while it's still on your wrist, because I think you'll find …" He paused in the doorway. "There's more than one way to skin a rat."

As the door shut, Locke breathed deeply. He needed to increase security. It could have been someone far worse. His masters.

In his hospital room, Theo grew frustrated with the TV and tossed the remote aside. "This is crap! Hey, Ishaan, tell me a joke."

"I … uh, I-I don't know any."

Chen jumped in, "Knock knock!"

"Who's there?"

"Interrupting cow."

"Interrupt—"

"Moo!" Chen laughed hysterically, and Theo grinned.

"You're good for him," he told Chen, watching them smile at each other.

Soon, Tabitha arrived with bags of herbs and crystals.

"What did you bring?" Theo asked.

"Fresh stuff. Everything you need for healing," she said, showing him an amethyst crystal.

"Great … a rock?" Theo asked flatly.

Amber and Steve entered, bags in hand. "How's it going?" Steve asked.

Theo sighed. "I've been better. What did you get?"

Amber showed off the produce. "Lots of veggies and fresh herbs."

Theo groaned. "Great. Smoothies forever."

Ishaan pulled out some pills from his bag. "Don't worry, I've got something for that."

JJ walked in, looking thoughtful.

"JJ!" Steve greeted. "Did you clear your head?"

"Kinda. I saw Doctor Locke," JJ said, causing Theo to sit up.

"You what?" Amber asked, shocked.

"I tracked him down. Couldn't convince him yet, but I know how to get what we want."

"What's your plan?" Tabitha asked.

"Leverage." JJ grinned. "Everyone has a weakness, and we'll find his."

Theo shook his head. "Don't. I'm done. This is what I deserve."

"No, it's not," Tabitha said firmly.

"Doctor said I can leave soon," Theo continued. "I just want us to enjoy what's left. Please, let me go out on a high note."

Steve nodded. "Okay. One last adventure, together."

Amber, with tears in her eyes, whispered, "We're here for you, till the end."

They gathered around him for a group hug, but JJ stayed back.

"J?" Steve called.

JJ approached slowly, leaned close to Theo, and whispered, "I won't let you die" before leaving the room again.

CHAPTER TWENTY-FOUR
TOGETHER AGAIN

The ticking of his father's cracked pocket watch pounded against Theo's head, the pain relief from the Los Angeles hospital doing little to dull the agony. All night, he'd been praying for silence, for some alone time after his friends had fussed over him all day, even tucking him in an hour ago. They'd been back at the apartment for hours now, and Theo wondered where JJ had gone. JJ seemed to care more about Theo surviving than Theo did. Not that he didn't care, it was just that he'd come to terms with his fate. He was going to die soon, and that was okay. Everyone dies. What was death like? Did it hurt? Was it the end, or the beginning of something else? The uncertainty gnawed at him.

His bladder full, Theo stood up and walked down the dark hallway to the bathroom. The leading light burned his eyes, so he turned it off and found the mirror light instead, its subtle glow easing the pain. He sat on the cold toilet, avoiding standing due to his nausea. As he relieved himself, he sighed in relief, but it was fleeting.

When he flushed and stood up, the blood rushed to his head, making him stumble. He gripped the sink, but before he could steady himself, he vomited a pool of RED blood into the sink. Staring at it, he saw his own mortality. He wasn't the person he used to be. His reflection—a fragile, sick version of himself—sickened him. Where had the strong, assertive Theo gone? What had happened to him?

The voices came next, taunting, mocking.

"You're gonna die!"

"So weak!"

"Pathetic!"

"No!" Theo whispered, trying to silence them, staring at his reflection. The bulbs flickered. In the mirror, a large bubble floated by, revealing a familiar, mischievous face. Frank was back.

"Missed me, kiddo?" Frank grinned from his spot in the tub, naked, surrounded by bubbles.

"What's the matter? You look like you've seen a ghost."

Theo froze. "You!"

"Please, did you think you could get rid of me that easily? I'm a cockroach. I always come back."

"Frank, now listen—"

"You threw me away, like trash!" Frank cut in, still grinning. "After all we did together, you just tossed me!"

"That's not fair!"

"Don't worry, I forgive you," Frank teased, his face lighting up as he blew a chill over a frozen bubble, revealing the gang trapped inside. "You people die so easily, like that." Frank tapped the bubble, and it shattered.

Theo clenched his fists. "I could just send you away, like before."

"But I learn from my mistakes," Frank said smugly. "If you push me away again, I'll just come back, badder, better, stronger."

"I don't have to listen to this."

Theo walked away, but Frank called after him. "You'll still listen, kid."

Theo paused. "And why is that?"

"Because I know the real you. You don't want to die like this. Pathetic. Weak. You want more."

Frank's words cut into Theo. The truth of them stung. Frank was right. Waiting for the inevitable was hell.

Frank slithered out of the tub, foam covering his body as he walked toward Theo. "Listen, I could lock you away, trap you in your own mind. But I don't want that. I want us to do this together. Help me help you, Theo."

"How?"

"Get that doctor to fix you. With a little … motivation."

Frank grinned devilishly.

"Motivation?"

"Yeah, me." Frank chuckled. "I can be very persuasive."

Theo hesitated. "No. I'm done doing things your way."

"Who are you doing this for? Your friends?" Frank snorted. "They don't care. Finish the job alone."

"Alone?" Theo's curiosity piqued.

"With me. No risk. You've got nothing to lose, kid. Nothing."

Theo thought it over. Frank wasn't wrong—there was no downside. "So long as none of my friends get hurt."

Frank extended his hand. "Deal."

Theo shook it, reluctantly agreeing. Frank jumped toward him with a grin. "Let's begin."

Theo grabbed his essentials—phone, wallet, map of Los Angeles, and his father's broken watch. He tiptoed out of the room, holding his map and Doctor Locke's address. After a quick search on his phone, he found it. "Bingo!" he whispered, marking the route on his map before slipping it in his back pocket.

As he quietly crept out the door, he felt a renewed confidence. This was simple: find Doctor Locke, convince him to help with Frank's guidance, and then return to his friends and finish the vacation, and live out the rest of his life. Easy, right?

It seemed to be, until JJ turned the corner in the hallway, holding a large brown folder. Both young men froze.

"Theo?" JJ frowned.

"J?" Theo said, flitting through various emotions from disbelief and repressed anger to pleasant surprise. "What are you doing out here?"

"Just coming back from … somewhere." He twiddled the folder in his hand.

"Where?"

"Out." He blinked, stepping closer. "Getting incriminating evidence on Doctor Locke."

Theo's heart lifted. "You did that for me?" he asked, masking his emotion.

"Of course I did."

"What did you get?" Theo rushed toward him in hope.

"Well …" He presented the brown folder. "I managed to get a photographer to fake some images of him entering one or two seedier parts of town, showing him having some very … distasteful interests."

"What kind of interests?"

"Incriminating interests. Figured I would threaten him; he can either save you, or I will leak the pictures to the press."

"Oh, J, that's good." Theo chuckled in surprise. "I knew I could count on you." He hugged his friend tightly. JJ's arms hung loose as if he were taken aback a little, but then he embraced Theo tightly.

"Not the others?" JJ questioned.

"They can't do what you do."

JJ took this as acceptance. "Right! So, what are you doing out here? Steve texted me to say you were in bed resting."

Theo hesitated, thinking of an answer. "Yes, well, Steve and I decided to go for a little stroll, outside, to get some oxygen in the old lungs."

JJ looked sceptical. "And where is Steve?"

"In the bathroom. I'm just waiting for him." Theo changed the subject. "Hey, can I see those pictures?" he asked, reaching for them.

"Maybe tomorrow when you're fully rested."

Tension built in the hallway. "I'd really like to see them now, J," Theo insisted.

"Why don't we wait for Steve, get his opinion?"

"Okay …" JJ blew out his cheeks. "You wanna wait inside for him"?"

"Na, I'm good out here."

"You sure he's in the bathroom?"

"Yeah, of course, why would I lie?"

JJ shook his head, heartbroken. "You can't stop, can you?"

"Can't stop what?"

"Lying."

With that, Theo's features became arctic as he walked towards JJ. JJ did not back down as they faced one another in an uncompromising standoff.

"J, give me the photos."

"Theo, listen to me—"

"Please, give me the photos."

"Theo, just listen. I'm worried about you. You've not been yourself lately, you've been acting …"

"What?"

"Crazy."

Frank appeared in Theo's line of sight, decked out in a crop top, jacket, leather pants, and ruby RED sunglasses. He circled an unsuspecting JJ, looking at him as if he were a piece of low-grade meat.

"Hey, no one can talk to Theo like that, only me," Frank said.

JJ continued, "And what's worse is you don't seem to care. In fact, you seem to be even enjoying it."

An amused giggle escaped Frank. "Ooh, I like this one … break his neck."

"Crazy?" Theo stiffened, offended. "You think I'm acting crazy? I've got a brain tumour, or had you forgotten?"

JJ shook his head. "It's not just that. Theo, you broke into a lab and badly injured three armed guards! Don't you think that's a bit of a RED flag?"

"A RED flag?"

"You're off your meds, aren't you? Theo, I know all about Frank."

Theo grew rigid. "You what?"

"Ah, so this one is smart." Frank grinned.

"That's right, I know all about your delusions, your pills, your … madness

"I don't know what you're talking about."

"You said he had come back earlier, at the hospital. That had me so worried I almost called your mom, but then I didn't. Do you know why? Because I figured I could get through to you, help you myself, without all the doctors and the meds, because I get you."

Theo exhaled, not letting sentiment get the better of him as Frank looked to him, awaiting a response. "J, whatever you think you know, it-it's bullshit."

"I know about the things Frank made you do when you were little. I know about it all."

Theo backed away, uttering in defence. "No, no, no, you don't know what you're—" Flashes of long-repressed memories burned their way into Theo's brain as he winced in pain, clinging to the wall for support. Mice, cats, birds, blood, his mother screaming. JJ put his arm out supportively.

"Ah!" Theo yelped, shrugging his friend off.

"You can't remember, can you?"

"Remember what?" Theo asked, rubbing his temple as he gazed around to find Frank gone.

"Theo, listen to me," JJ said calmly. "You need help, right now, you're a danger to yourself and everyone else—"

"I know, that's why I need to do this."

"Do what?"

"Save myself."

"And how are you going to do that?"

"With those photos!"

He reached for the files only for JJ to yank them away.

JJ clamped down on the files, seeing his best friend's transition into madness bloom fully. "No."

Frank remerged between the two. "Gutsy move, JJ. Your turn, Theo."

"J, please," Theo pleaded.

"Well, will you look at that … your bullshit pleas have lost their punch. I'm not giving you these photos, not before you get back inside, sit down, and actually think about what the hell you're doing."

"I don't understand what you're saying—"

"Listen, I love you, Theo," JJ said, his voice quivering. "You're family to me, I would never let anyone hurt you, never, but I won't let you go, not like this."

"Oh no!" Frank interjected. "There's a fly in the ointment. Don't listen to his dumb buzzing, listen to me. I can get you everything you want; all we need are those photos."

"Theo, please, let me help you."

A lump formed in Theo's throat as he pondered what his

faithful friend was saying and offering. Frank bounced up and down by Theo's side. "I've changed my mind on this one, kill, kill, kill him!"

"Theo, I know you," JJ insisted.

"Do it," Frank said.

"This isn't you."

Theo growled as his eyes darkened. "You don't know me."

Theo grabbed JJ by the throat. JJ wriggled like a fish on a hook, dropping the folder to the floor. Theo lowered and shoved JJ against a wall as his veins popped and bulged.

"Go ahead, do it, put me out of my misery," JJ rasped. Frank jumped up and down at Theo's side. Theo let go, dropping his friend to the ground. JJ gasped for air, rubbing his sore neck and coughing, as Frank began to huff.

"Boo!"

Theo paused, unsure of what had just come over him or why he would do that to his friend, before rushing to his aid. "J, I'm so sorry."

"Don't," JJ yelped, pushing him back in a display of fear, finally finding his feet as he stood once more. "We don't mean anything to you!"

"No, you mean everything to me," Theo replied.

"No!" He grabbed the dropped folder once more. "It's all an act! I can see you for what you are now."

"And what's that?"

"The real you. The monster behind the man, the one who's been hiding behind that mask all this time. I always figured it was the other way around, you hiding your shadow, but no, this is who you are, it's who you've always been and always will be!"

"J, no—"

"Look at you! The things you'll do. I'm not even capable of imagining. You're sick!"

Theo held back, feeling somewhat betrayed. "What do you want me to say? That you're right? That I am sick? Well, okay, yes, I am sick. What do you want from me, huh? To send me away to some loony bin? To make me into something clean, something easy to manage? A drug-addled zombie? Well, no, I won't submit to that, I can't, I won't."

"Theo—"

"It's true, I am a sick man, a sick man who is trying to get better, and there's only one way I can do that." Theo marched towards JJ, who jumped back a little as Theo snatched the folder from his hand. "With these!"

JJ glared. Theo could tell what was coming next—JJ lunged at Theo, only to be knocked out with one clean punch to his face.

"I'm sorry," Theo whispered.

Frank giggled as his young protégé spun in his direction.

"You said none of my friends would get hurt."

Frank frowned. "Don't blame me! I could only make the deal on my part, that …" He pointed at JJ. "That was all you, Theo."

Shame coursed through Theo as he looked down at JJ's limp body and then at his strong hand, still clenched in a fist.

"Well, we can't just leave him here," Frank said. "Plus, when he wakes up, he'll go snitch on you to the others."

"What do you suggest?"

"Why not slit his throat, get it over with?"

"No."

Frank pondered again. "Well, if that's too messy for you, kiddo, I'm sure we could find an incinerator—"

"We're not harming him, not a hair on his head." Theo bent down to stroke JJ's cheek. "We just need to subdue him, for the time being …"

"Ah! Boring!"

Looking up, Theo saw the open housekeeping cupboard ahead, key still in the lock, and no sign of the housekeeper. "That should do it," he mused as he turned back, seeing a bruise forming on JJ's face. "I'll make this right, I promise," he vowed as he dragged his friend's lightweight frame into the cupboard. Theo propped JJ up by the mop and bucket, confiscating his phone from his pocket. As he went to shut the door, Theo questioned whether he was doing the right thing. He had no other option now; he had to commit to his choices and then hope his friends would finally understand. Shutting the door, Theo locked it, throwing the key out a nearby window. He then threw JJ's phone into a bin, sighing in disbelief at his own actions, regretful that things were shaping up this way.

Frank presented the lift ahead. "Shall we?" he asked, his voice almost a purr.

Theo nodded and began to walk towards Frank, passing the oddly late-working maid who was hoovering to the sound of her playlist. As the elevator doors closed and he began to go down, down, down, he refrained from cracking a smile, his guardian angel close by. This would be the moment that would either destroy him or change everything forever. He would not give up; he would not submit to death, no, he would rather die trying. In truth, he would now rather break and crumble before ever allowing himself to bow before death. This world was not about to take Theo Gray without a fight; he was sure of at least that much.

CHAPTER TWENTY-FIVE

TIPPING POINT

Restless, Amber sat upright on her mattress, searching her phone for answers, a cure for Theo. All she found were articles full of nonsense, designed to attract clicks. Frustrated, she kept searching, clinging to the hope that somewhere, there might be a solution. But deep down, she knew there probably wasn't. The screen's harsh glow gave her a headache, and her dehydration made it worse. She stood and walked to the kitchen, pouring herself a glass of cool water, as her mind raced.

Theo was dying. The gang was torn. Her mother awaited her back home. And then there was Steve—complicated, confusing, yet oddly appealing. The thought of being with him felt wrong, yet strangely right.

After finishing her water, she quietly placed the glass in the dishwasher and went to the bathroom. The harsh light flickered on, revealing a pool of blood staining the sink. She gasped, then rushed to Theo's room—his bed was empty. Panic surged as she turned on the landing light and banged on everyone's bedroom doors.

"Wake up! Everyone, wake up!" she yelled, as they all slowly began to stir from their slumbers.

Steve appeared more quickly than the others, throwing on a shirt. "Wha-what is it?" he asked in a muffled panic.

"It's Theo, he's gone!"

"What?" Tabitha moved past Amber to look into his room, then out to the kitchen and lounge.

"N-not in the kitchen or a-anywhere?"

"Look for yourself!" Tabitha said. "I'm gonna phone him." She stormed off to her room.

Steve frowned. "Where would he have gone?"

"JJ is gone t-too," Ishaan said.

"He's still not back yet?" Amber asked.

"Reckon he's with him?" Steve said.

"Possibly," Amber replied as Tabitha marched back into the room, her phone pressed to her ear.

"He ain't answering."

Steve turned with his hand on his chin. "Try J."

Tabitha rang JJ's number and waited. "Nothing," she revealed.

Steve exhaled a long, cold breath. "Okay, let's go and look for them," he said, immediately stepping into his boots and pulling on his jacket. Amber followed his lead, but the others hesitated. "Come on." He looked at Tabitha, Ishaan, and Chen, and they began putting on their shoes and coats over their nightwear. "I'm sure they've just gone out for a walk or something."

"Better to be safe," Chen said as Steve, phone in hand, opened the door, allowing the others to leave first, shutting the door behind him.

"Wait, surely one of us should stay, in case they come b-back?" Ishaan asked.

"Na," Tabitha said. "What's the point?"

"Yeah, the more heads out looking, the better," Steve said as they continued down the hallway before hearing a loud banging coming from the housekeeping cupboard.

"What the shit is that?" Tabitha reclined as the others stepped towards it.

"Guys! It's me," JJ bellowed through the wood.

"J?"

"Yes!"

"What the hell?" Tabitha crept closer as Amber looked around for a key. "I'm going to go get someone from reception," she said, heading for the elevator.

"How'd you get trapped in there?" Tabitha questioned, tapping her nails against the wall.

"Theo, he's gone nuts. He punched me in the face and locked me in here. He's going after the doctor."

Theo's trump card was his unpredictability. He thrived on doing insane things because, deep down, he was insane. His friends could never anticipate his next move, and honestly, neither could he. That uncertainty kept them at a safe distance. But his next move had to be calculated—sneaky, like a dagger in the night. He was fast and strong, but if he was hit with one well-placed hit, he'd be finished. He couldn't afford an open fight—not until he was fixed.

As he walked downtown the Los Angeles streets with Frank, Theo followed his map.

"Are we there yet?" Frank asked, swinging from a streetlight.

"Not yet," Theo muttered, rubbing his map.

Frank's gaze landed on a young pizza boy. "We may need a disguise," he said, tugging Theo's head toward the delivery guy.

A few blocks later, the pizza boy stopped at a shady basement apartment. Theo and Frank watched him park his car before Theo darted out from the shadows.

"Is someone there?" Theo called out.

The young man hesitated, then replied, "Yes, are you okay?"

"I think I broke my ankle! Can you help me?" Theo pleaded.

"I'll get help," the man said, pulling out his phone.

"No!" Theo shouted. "Just help me out of here."

The young man leaned down, his hand reaching for Theo, who grabbed it with unnatural speed.

A few moments later, Theo emerged, dressed in the pizza boy's uniform, spinning the pizza box in his hand.

"Perfect," Frank said, jumping from behind a trash bin.

"Thanks." Theo grinned.

"We still need the right equipment," Frank added, nodding toward a cop who had just parked.

A cop heard the pizza boy's cries and followed Theo down the alley. As the cop shone his light, he found the real pizza boy unconscious with a bloody head wound. Before he could react, Theo overpowered him, securing the officer's gun and handcuffs.

"Nice job," Frank said, twirling a baton.

Theo glanced at the unconscious bodies, a pang of guilt stabbing him. He knew the moral lines were blurred, but this was about survival, nothing more. He thought about the afterlife, wondering if he'd go to hell. Maybe everyone did. He pushed the thoughts away.

His phone buzzed. Seven missed calls from 'Tabz.'

"Looks like the gang's on the case," Frank smirked. "You should ditch that thing. They might track you."

Theo sighed, tossing his phone into a nearby trash bin. He didn't want them hurt because of him.

Frank cheered. "Good boy! Now, how good a driver are you?"

Theo grinned, syncing the cop's gun into his belt, beneath his shirt, before jumping into the car, his hands tightening on the wheel. Moments later, they roared down the street, sirens blaring, heading for their endgame.

Looking like they'd just escaped from a pajama party, the gang traipsed along the city sidewalk, clutching their coats around them as Tabitha's nails tapped away like woodpeckers on a tree against the 'Find my friend' app she was using. JJ looked over her shoulder in frustration.

"Come on, Tabz, what's taking so long?" he asked impatiently.

"It's not me, it's this damn app!" she snapped. "It's taking ages to find him."

Steve's pendant weighed him down as he walked. He turned to JJ, walking beside him, wanting to understand. "What happened, J? Theo couldn't have just gone crazy?"

"I got back after … getting incriminating stuff on the doctor I was planning to use to blackmail him into helping Theo—"

Amber gasped. "J!"

"Yes, I know it's awful, I get it," he said, before continuing. "But I bumped into Theo and, at first, he seemed fine, but then he wanted the folder and started acting weird. I tried talking to him, telling him I only wanted to help and then he strangled me and threw me in that cupboard."

"B-but why?" Ishaan asked, clutching Chen's hand firmly as he pulled her along. "I don't g-get it. This isn't Theo."

"See, but that's the thing," JJ said. "It is."

Steve frowned. "I'm not following."

"He's sick!"

"Well, duh, he's got a tumour, J," Tabitha said, still holding up her phone trying to get a better signal.

"Not sick in that way. He's insane."

The words echoed through the gang.

Licking his lips, Steve hesitated. "Yeah, but isn't that because of the tumour, making him see things, do things?"

"No, this has been going on for much longer than any of you know, as I said to you and Tabitha at the hospital."

"J, what have you not told us?" Steve asked. "Just say it so we are all on the same wavelength here."

Looking down, JJ breathed heavily. "A few years back, his mom told me how worried she was about him, so she asked me to keep an eye on him. She told me Theo was becoming depressed and isolated and didn't want him to start falling back into doing things, bad things." He paused, looking at them. "She told me that when he was just a kid, before any of us knew him at school, he did things."

"Like what?" Amber questioned.

"Like killing anything he could find: mice, cats, birds. He would give them to her as gifts, and she and his dad used to bury them under the rose bushes in their garden."

Steve swallowed hard, trying to come to terms with this new information.

"Eventually, they sent him to see a doctor. Theo said his imaginary friend, Frank, told him to do it, to kill the animals."

Steve shuddered. "You're bullshitting, right?"

"No, I'm not, I've never been more serious about anything." JJ pushed his hands deeper in his pockets. "With the right treatment and pills, Theo started to forget what he did, and Frank soon went away, until now apparently."

"So, wait, what's Frank?" Tabitha asked.

"His conscience?" Steve said.

"A s-split personality?"

"I don't know," JJ replied. "The doctors couldn't figure it out either, according to his mom. All they could do was help him to get rid of Frank, but clearly, he found a way back." He turned away, his posture tight. "He was there; I could tell. When Theo was choking me, I could see it in his eyes. Theo was listening to something else, telling him what to do. But the one thing I could tell was that he enjoyed it." JJ's face soured. "I've seen his real face, the one he's been hiding all this time."

Steve recoiled. "I'm sure that's not true—"

"Oh, he enjoyed it. I know that look, better than most."

Steve guessed JJ was referring to his father.

Amber gulped. "But surely Theo will come to his senses."

"Like I said, he's insane."

"But he's Theo, our Theo," Steve remarked.

"How do you know this Theo hasn't been the real Theo all along?" JJ asked.

"I've got him." Tabitha jumped up. "He's not far away." She ran on ahead.

"You guys follow, I'm going to the doctor's place," JJ said, spinning around to storm off in another direction.

"I'm coming with you!" Steve shouted.

"Me too!" Amber added, running along with them both.

Steve blocked her way. "Amber, this could be dangerous."

"It could be dangerous either way. I'm coming with you two and nothing you can say or do will stop me."

That left Tabitha with Chen and Ishaan. "Great, so I get left with Minnie and Mickey here."

"You'll be fine," JJ said, following Steve and Amber, as the gang split up.

Theo and Frank came to a halt outside Doctor Locke's luxurious apartment building. Frank, chewing on RED liquorice, lowered his shades to eye the building.

"Sure, this is it?" he asked.

"This is it."

Frank tossed his candy and wiped his hands on his jacket. "Show time."

Theo hesitated, taking a deep breath. Then he walked into the building, still dressed as a pizza boy with the box in hand. A security guard stopped him. The guard saw the pizza and let him through after a quick, awkward pat-down. Theo stiffened as the guard's hands brushed against the gun hidden on his back. At a sharp gulp from the guard, Theo's façade dropped.

"Fuck's sake." Theo shoved the guard into the wall, knocking him out cold. He dragged the unconscious man into a nearby cupboard and duct-taped him inside, locking it with the guard's keys.

Whistling, Theo strolled over to the security desk, turned off the cameras, erased all footage, and poured hot coffee over the hard drive, frying the system.

Theo smiled, feeling a brief surge of satisfaction. He entered the elevator and pressed the button for the 34th floor. As the doors dinged open, a lavish hallway stretched before him, leading to four penthouses.

Marching forward, Theo approached number #3404. An electrifying impulse energized him from the inside. Empowered and ready, he faced the door, sniggering as he raised his pizza box, raised his fist, and began to bang on the door with unyielding might.

On the other side of the door, in his office, Doctor Locke heard the assault. He put aside his paperwork and lifted his glasses, listening. Choosing to ignore it, he went back to his research until another series of loud slams came from the door. In his frustration, he got up to investigate. Locking the office door quietly, he crept towards the entrance, looking through his spy hole to see the name-tagged, innocent-looking pizza boy, smiling widely.

"Wrong number! I didn't order pizza!" Doctor Locke shouted through the door.

"Free pizza delivery!"

Locke's face creased in irritation as he turned to walk back to his work. "Please leave!" he insisted. "I have had enough dealings with greasy urchins for one day, thank you."

Suddenly, the hinges came clean off the door as it fell to the floor, revealing a leg reclining back from a firm kick. The pizza boy entered the apartment, throwing the pizza box and the name tag to the floor. He then removed his jacket and hat, ruffing his golden hair before approaching the taken aback, petrified surgeon.

"Doctor Locke." The young man said firmly. "You and I have some … unfinished business."

Taking public transport, Steve and Amber followed JJ to the doctor's apartment. Making their way to the streets, they ran but soon fell out of breath. Gripping her side, Amber fell back, causing Steve to soon follow and check on her as she breathed heavily. "How much further?" she gasped.

"Not that far, come on." JJ gestured for them to continue as Steve's phone rang.

Amber rose from her hunched-over position. "Who is it?"

Looking at his screen, Steve felt a ripple of apprehension. "Tabz!" he replied, answering the videocall. "What's up?"

On the other end of the phone, Tabitha stood in an alley. "We have an update."

"What kind of update?"

Tabitha turned to look at Chen and Ishaan, who were trying to wake up the unconscious cop and pizza boy. "The bad kind."

CHAPTER TWENTY-SIX

THE ELEVENTH HOUR

Theo sauntered into the doctor's home, now flooded with bright light.

Locke backed away. "How-how did you do that?" he asked, pointing to his broken door.

"That?" Theo indicated with his thumb. "Well, I just gave it a good kick, kept the shoulders loose—"

"I mean, how is that possible … physically?" the doctor asked, clearly astounded by the feat. "Are you on steroids or drugs of any kind?"

"No."

"Get to the point!"

"Yeah, stupid!"

Theo twitched, hearing the whispers. "Shh!" he mumbled to himself.

"I'm sorry?"

"No, it's not you, it's just …"

Doctor Locke studied Theo with professional analytical detachment. "Interesting." "So who are you? Another of Theo Gray's friends?"

"Nope. Theo Gray himself, in the flesh."

A deep-throated chuckle emitted from the L.A. miracle worker. "Very interesting. Have you always possessed such unique strength?"

"Only lately."

'With HIS help!"

The doctor peered at Theo through full moon spectacles. "What specifically is 'lately,' may I ask?"

"A week or more, I dunno."

"You're wasting time!"

Theo felt the rhythmic drumbeat of the broken watch in his pocket.

Locke took a step back. "How does a weakened tumour patient manage to kick down a door with such strength?"

"Who knows? Just one of life's mysteries, I guess."

"He's playing for time!"

"Quiet!"

"A mystery that should be solved." The doctor interlaced his fingers as he began to pace around the room. "Tell me, Theo, are you by any chance schizophrenic? Or do any of your relatives suffer from mental illness?" His tone was neutral, rational.

Theo scowled, and he revealed the pistol holstered beneath his shirt. "Are you calling me crazy?"

"No, not at all—"

"I'm not crazy." Theo stormed towards the slight, scared man who now refused to meet his eyes.

"Like I said, I don't think you're crazy, but have you been hearing voices since you've had your tumour?"

"Maybe …" Theo replied, turning away slightly before shamefully admitting, "Yes."

Locke pushed his shoulders back. "How fascinating. Please do go on, it will help me to understand the degree of your … condition."

Theo flinched slightly. "I just hear voices, that's it."

"And this started after being diagnosed with the tumour, correct?"

Theo paused. "Yes," he lied.

"Honestly, the rate your tumour has been growing, I'm surprised you're still standing." Cautiously taking steps across to his phone, Theo mirrored his every move, ready to spring. "You are marvellous, truly marvellous."

"Always have been, always will be. Now, as much as I'd love to stand here and talk about how great I am, we have business to get to."

"Yes. So, I assume you have the money, plus a bit extra to replace my door?"

"Sock him!"

Theo smiled, replying with a blunt, "No."

Theo clicked the lock and watched the doctor look down to see the handcuff securing him to the warm radiator a mere foot away.

"I don't need money to get you to do what I want," Theo explained, stepping away, hearing the gentle rattling of the chain, savouring the moment. "You're going to fix me, doc, understand?" His face stiffened. "And then the whole world will be at my feet."

"But I can't 'fix' you."

"You are renowned for your skill across the globe, which makes you the ideal person to fix me. And you will."

"Get him!"

"Make it hurt!"

"Shut up!" Theo screamed, ordering the voices to retreat.

The doctor cringed back against the wall. "I might be able to remove the tumour—"

"Yes?"

"But that doesn't necessarily mean I can … fix you," Locke said.

A landline began to ring, again and again, to the annoyance of Theo as he tried to think. Then he heard a familiar voice on the answering machine. "Theo, Theo, I know you're there," Steve said. "It's me, please pick up the phone, Theo …"

As the message waffled on, Theo hissed at the inconvenience. "Crap!" he spat, turning to the doctor. "You have a few minutes to rethink your answer. I suggest you do."

Locke lay back, trapped, the cuff clanking.

Theo went to the phone and answered it. "Yes."

"Theo, thank God," Steve said. "Are you okay?"

"I'm doing fine. How are you? Is J okay?"

"Good, we're all okay, just worried about you. J too, he's angry but otherwise fine."

Theo breathed heavily down the phone, his head hurting.

"Listen! Whatever you're doing, Theo, please stop."

"I can't."

"Of course you can, just stop, think about what you're doing—"

"No, Steve, I can't … I can't help it. Maybe it's survival instincts kicking in or … I don't know, something else?"

"Theo—"

"Don't come after me, or try to stop me, please don't, please," Theo pleaded. "I don't want any of you getting hurt."

"Theo, wait … remember what you told me? What your dad told you about the wolves. Please, stop, just think."

Theo paused. "I'm sorry—"

And then came his answer.

Steve's phone beeped to indicate the call had ended. Steve fought the urge to scream.

Amber was beside him, listening in. "Well, that didn't sound good."

"We need to go and stop him."

She rested a hand on his hyperventilating chest. "Together."

"Together."

"The apartment is about ten minutes away. Come on, let's move," JJ said, running on ahead.

"This is not gonna be easy," Steve said, sprinting beside Amber.

"No, but nothing ever is with us, is it?"

Theo stood in front of Locke.

"Even if I can remove your tumour, the side effects, the brain damage may be too great, you could wind up becoming … I don't know what."

"Well, what's the alternative?"

The doctor merely raised a single brow in reply, suggesting he should give up and accept a respectful, dignified end. This only threw gasoline on Theo's angry fire. A figure emerged from the edge of Theo's vision, dressed in a white satin shirt and midnight black pants.

"Ah, can you get this guy?" Frank gestured with his thumb. "I mean, wow, what a douche. Time to bring out the leverage, my boy." He winked dark lashes.

Frank clapped in excitement as Theo took out the fake images JJ had managed to falsify of Doctor Locke, passing them to him for inspection.

He rotated the unclear pictures, frowning. "What's this?"

"Photos, incriminating photos, of you."

Gazing down at the images once more, a burst of laughter escaped Locke. He raised his free hand to cover it. Theo shook with surprised rage.

"These are fake," Locke stated, throwing them to the floor.

"Maybe, but the press won't know that."

Shaking his head, the doctor said, "Mr. Gray, I have some very powerful friends who control the media; they won't report on those ridiculously edited pictures."

"He's bluffing," Frank said.

"You're bluffing."

"No, I'm not." Locke relaxed a little, sitting back.

Theo walked towards the office door.

"What are you doing now?" the doctor questioned.

"Finding something else." Theo rattled the locked door. "Something else to blackmail you with."

"You won't find anything, I can guarantee that."

With a swift kick, Theo took down the office door with a smirk. "I'll take my chances," he said, disappearing into the doctor's study.

The room contained many degrees and diplomas, awards and embellishments that helped to tickle the man of science's academic ego. Everything had its place. Pens, papers, a laptop, and an open folder were splayed out on a leather chair awaiting their master. Theo picked up the folder and glanced at the words written on the front, his interest piqued.

TOP SECRET.
GOVERNMENT MATERIALS: WORMWOOD.

After skimming past endless detail, Theo gasped then shuddered, feeling his nerves sizzle and fry. He had heard the rumours of the infamous Area 51, but this "Wormwood" was something different entirely. Photos were attached, evidence of horrific, vile experiments. Pictures of creatures, monstrosities. For a moment, Theo held back a gag, then felt like he was looking at the script for a horror movie, but no, this was true; it added up. Of course, someone like Doctor Locke, someone of his skill, worked for these people, the powerful, the ones in charge, doing these awful things. The images were gruesome and the notes beside them cold and cynical in their use of numbers and the constant use of the word 'failure.' It made Theo feel sick to his core. He marched out to confront the scientist, folder in hand.

"This is sick!"

Doctor Locke looked away.

"How can you be involved in this shit?" He slapped the pages. "How can you live with yourself?" The irony of his words and past actions was not lost on him, but this was different. This wasn't out of necessity; this was … well, Theo didn't even know what these cruel games were for.

Doctor Locke remained silent, pursing his lips.

"You won't even admit it, will you? Let me guess, your 'powerful friends' are involved in this, too. And they pay you big money to do this shit, yeah?"

Locke finally spoke up. "History is written by those who strive for a better tomorrow."

"Is that what you tell yourself, huh?"

"It's for the greater cause."

"What cause?"

"A better world."

Theo scoffed, causing Locke to bristle.

"People are living out there in the world, healthy and happy because of my work."

"If people are living healthy and happy because of shit like this, then life is worthless!"

"Who are you to decide that?"

"I'm Theo Gray, you little bitch, and now that I know this, I can blackmail you into silence long after our business is done."

"With what proof? That file? If you play this game, you will die, I can assure you. Just walk away, while you can."

"No."

Frank leaned against the wall and rolled his eyes. "Enough talking, time for some screeching." Blood lust rose within Theo.

"Let me talk to him," Frank insisted, looking the doctor up and down like a cat with a canary.

"No, Frank."

"Who's Frank?" the doctor asked.

"Come on, don't be a party pooper!" Frank nudged Theo's elbow playfully.

"I said no!"

Theo placed both of his hands around the doctor's neck.

Looking deep into Theo's pupils, hot with adrenaline-fueled rage, Locke noted the raw, primal, animalistic energy radiating out of the young man. The strength he possessed was incredible; he could feel it now, crushing his larynx. It was terrifying and yet fascinating. What wonders his biology must be hiding, the scientist wondered as he rasped for air, scratching and clawing with his one good hand as Theo was taken over entirely by something else.

By Theo's side, Frank watched with an open hand, his expression impressed, ready to take over. That's it," he said.

"I-I'm not sure I can do this, Frank." Theo shuddered, trying to pull his hand away from the man's neck.

"Nonsense," said his guardian angel. "Oh, I know it's hard,

kid, but hey, let me help you. Just one little twinge of a finger and I'll finish the job, whoosh! Over before you blink. Just one little twinge, Theo, one … little … twinge."

Theo jumped back, releasing the doctor, who choked and hacked.

He didn't want to do that—he didn't want to *be* that. No, he would not be that. Retaining the dignity and fear he had just earned, Theo lifted a strong finger to the gasping doctor's face. "You are going to fix me," he insisted. "Or I swear to God that I will make you pray for a quick death."

Ten minutes later, the doctor found himself shuffling outside, wrapped up in his finest trench coat, with Theo's gun at his back and his surgical tools in hand. He was then forced to sit at the wheel of the police car Theo had stolen earlier. Locke wondered what kind of night Theo must have had to get the vehicle.

Snapping the cuffs on Locke's wrist once more, Theo tethered him to the wheel as he pointed the gun at him. He perched on the passenger seat with the files and tools on his lap. "Drive," he ordered.

"Where are we going?" Locke asked.

"Just drive." Locke started up the engine and drove along the busy road as Theo watched him closely, not wanting any funny business.

Frank sat in the back, giggling and gnawing on his licorice. "Ah, man, what a night this is shaping up to be!"

Theo glanced back and forth between the doctor and Frank in the rear mirror. For a brief second, Theo thought he saw the ghoulish Hollow Man, but he turned back to see Frank, still chewing on his candy, waving like a naughty child.

Locke looked into the rearview mirror. "Are we being followed?" he asked hopefully.

"No, it's nothing. Just keep driving," Theo said, rubbing his tired eyes with one hand. "Just do what I say, and you won't get hurt."

"Is that a promise or a threat?"

"Both."

Sometime later, JJ, Steve, and Amber arrived at Doctor Locke's apartment with relative ease, as there was no security guard left to stop them at the front desk, just a dent in the marble wall.

"Shit!" JJ shouted upon entering through the broken apartment door.

Steve stomped around, looking. "Theo! Theo!"

"Quit it, he's not here," JJ said.

"Then where is he?"

"Anywhere he knew we wouldn't be," Amber cut in. "He knew we were coming." She looked around the room for a clue. "So, what now? Do we call the police?"

"No!" JJ frowned. "We can't rat him out like that."

"It's not ratting out, J," said Amber. "He's a danger to everyone, including himself."

"No, no police, not yet," Steve commented, standing between his friends. "Let's regroup with the others and think. Okay?"

"Fine," Amber said, leaving the apartment with Steve following. Neither of them noticed JJ looking at the fake photos Theo had left carelessly on the floor. If they were no good, then what else did he have up his sleeve? What did he have to incriminate the doctor? "Theo, you sick son of a bitch, what the hell are you up to?"

CHAPTER TWENTY-SEVEN
A WAR FROM WITHIN

Still skimming over the notes and photos contained in the Wormwood file, Theo fidgeted in his seat as the car continued down a long, lonely road on the outskirts of Los Angeles. Looking up, he saw an abandoned warehouse, set back from the narrow mountain country roads.

"Stop the car," Theo ordered. Locke's foot stomped on the brake, bringing the car to a halt beside the dark, rundown building. Theo undid the Doctor's handcuffs from the car's wheel. Pointing his gun, Theo signalled to the doctor to get out. Locke held up his hands as he slowly began to exit the vehicle. Theo followed, shutting the door, bringing the folder, cuffs, and keys. Crossing the rough terrain, Theo heard a twig snap. Turning around quickly, he saw a corpse, swinging from a tree, hanging by a noose: himself.

"What is it?" Locke asked, clearly not seeing anything himself.

"Nothing, just keep moving." Ignoring the hallucination, Theo focused on the chained-up door that Locke had stopped in front of, preventing them from entering. With one mighty punch, Theo broke the steel chain, pushing the doors back to reveal an ample open space that clearly had not been used in years. Flicking a switch, dust-covered bulbs hummed and sparked into life. Water leaked through the roof, forming puddles on the floor, which was covered with rat droppings, staining the foul air. Theo felt his head growing fuzzy, sensing a blackout coming.

"Are you okay?" Locke asked.

"I'm fine!" Theo directed Locke to a corner with a table and railing. Cuffing the doctor's ankle to the latter, he threw the gun and keys on the other side of the warehouse, well out of reach of Locke. There was no way he was getting out without Theo now. Theo passed the doctor his personal tools and equipment, for whatever reason. Theo didn't want to ask why he kept a bag of surgical tools in his own home. After seeing those images in the case file, he dreaded the thought of why he would need them in his penthouse or on the go. Theo sat at the table, lit by a pale, yellow glow above. "This will do."

Locke frowned. "What here? You're joking. It's not sterile and I don't have the right equipment. Nurses, back-up …"

"I'm not joking." Theo lay down flat on the table with a sigh of pain as he felt the mush within his temple move more aggressively than before. "Get to work. And you better hurry in getting this thing out of my head, I don't think it's happy."

"What makes you say that?" the doctor said, reluctantly laying out his tools.

"I can sense it. Feels like it's trying to claw its way out of me."

Locke couldn't help but admire the boy. "You get curiouser by the minute, Theo Gray."

"Hmm … so how does this work?" Theo asked, panic rising in him at the thought he was actually undergoing surgery.

"Well, when I pull, you push!"

"What the hell does that me—?"

Locke covered his mouth and nose as he pulled out a small vial of something, which he sprayed in Theo's face, causing him to fall into a deep sleep.

Theo's mind swirled in velvet darkness, free from the impending pain of his body. A flicker of light pierced the void, followed by the sudden appearance of a projector screen. TV screens all around then emitted memories—glimpses of his life—unfolded.

A baby, cooing in his cot with a Binky. A toddler stumbling as he learned to walk, then run. The warm, guiding hands of his father as he taught Theo to ride a bike. Laughing with friends, wild adventures in the fields, hide and seek, treehouses, comic books. A life so full, so alive.

Theo saw himself at the dinner table, his mother's grilled cheese sandwich in front of him, her hand ruffling his hair. He saw the science project with JJ, erupting foam everywhere in class. The bar job with JJ, the late-night talks with his father. A lifetime in snapshots—moments of love, friendship, and joy.

But then, the screens froze. Static. A mocking, slow clap echoed from the shadows.

"Not bad, kid! Not bad at all!" Frank's voice rang out, dripping with amusement. Theo's stomach churned. He knew now. Frank had been behind it all: the manipulator, the poisoner, the parasite.

"You," Theo growled. "It's always been you. You're the parasite!"

Frank chuckled. "Where's this coming from? I'm your Frankie. Your best friend."

"My cancer," Theo said, voice sharp.

Frank stumbled. "What do you mean?"

"I see you now!" Theo spat. "A lie. A monster in my nightmares."

"We're connected, kid," Frank snarled. "Together, we could have it all."

"No," Theo said, turning away. "Not like this. I won't be you."

Frank's grin faltered. "You're meant for greatness. We're going to burn it all down, kid. A new world. You'll see."

Theo shook his head. "I don't want it."

Frank's features began to distort.

"Your mask seems to be slipping, Frank!"

"Oh, I've got other faces." He now appeared as Binky, a giant papier-mâché version of the rabbit toy. Theo blinked and it disappeared, now that he knew it was Frank all along.

"Stop."

"You're nothing without me," Frank said, his voice turning venomous.

"No. I'm nothing *because* of you."

The scene shifted to Theo's childhood—a sweet baby boy, innocent, before the nightmare began. Frank's voice, now like a serpent, whispered in his ear, tainting his thoughts.

"I've always been here," Frank purred, his black, slimy tongue slithering into Theo's ear, the smell of death and decay filling his senses. “And I’m not going anywhere.”

Theo jerked back, snapping out of the memory, but Frank’s grip on him tightened. The suffocating pressure of the past, the manipulation, the lies—it hit him at once. Theo’s muscles seized in memory upon hearing the off-note trumpet sound, recalling the repressed images of dead animals and himself as a small child, lit up on all the TV screens, seeing himself as a child sitting with the dead animals in his hand. He snapped back to the present as the clips, once again, turned to static. Frank was there, holding his cheeks with a drunken grin. “I’m trying to help you, kid, come on. That’s all I’ve ever done.”

Theo slapped the cold digits off his cheeks. “What I’m saying is, once this is over and this thing is out of my head, I want you to go too.”

“Kid, you’re breaking my heart.”

“I mean it, Frank, we’re done after this. I appreciate all you’ve done to get me here, but I don’t want the life you keep talking about. I don’t want power. I don’t care about any of that. I want a fresh start, a future.”

“You won’t survive on your own out there.”

“I can try.”

“If it’s any consolation, you’re much … more than I ever expected you to be. I mean, back in the day, I figured I would get you to go out with a bang, but when I realized your full potential, I was like … hell, why not let this kid run his own show. Let him give those other loons out there a run for their money. But then you started getting involved in all that love-and-friendship bullshit. Maybe I should take over.”

“Huh?”

“As I said, I never wanted it to come to this, but if you’re gonna force my hand then …”

Theo’s heart skipped a beat. “What are you talking about?”

“I’ll shove you to the nothing place of your mind. Put you somewhere you can’t be seen or heard, like you did to me, only you won’t be able to get away. Not ever.”

“No, this is my mind, my body.”

“For now. Ah, I can’t wait now to be behind the wheel of that body out there. Just think of the fun we're gonna have. We're gonna set this world ablaze. And the best part, you'll be with me every step of the way, watching from the passenger seat. I don't know about you, kid, but I for one can't wait for my long reign of chaos, terror, and madness."

"No, no, no—"

"Ah, shut up!" Frank growled. Theo stood completely paralyzed as Frank's hands caressed him up and down like he was an animal at a petting zoo. "I tried making you happy, I let you have your family, your friends, but the fact is it's all just too much work and, honestly, all I need from you is your little body and your mind. Well, I couldn't give a damn what happens to your mind."

Theo broke the spell, lifting his arm. "No. You talk a good game, Frank, but we both know you can't do anything. You're nothing but a voice in my head."

"I'm much more than that." A twisted, cruel, devilish grin cracked across his face as hands rose from nowhere to choke the life from Theo. The screens emitted a RED glow. His vision became blurry. Theo could only make out Frank's vague skeletal silhouette. Infecting his brain like a computer virus, Frank had been in Theo's head for years, learning his systems, bypassing his defences, and now he was ready to override the original program. Erasing Theo permanently. He could feel it, he was doing it, and with ease. Theo was gasping for air, losing sight, as the curtain fell to blackout.

But then, a voice. His father's. "You're not alone."

The room flickered, warm orange light filling the space. Theo turned to see Carl standing there, smiling, holding a beer.

"Dad?" Theo gasped, his voice breaking.

Carl chuckled. "How's my right-hand man doing?"

Tears filled Theo's eyes. "You're here … but you're … dead."

Carl patted his son's back. "Nothing's ever really gone for good. And I'm still working off your mom's lasagne," he joked.

Theo sobbed, crumbling into his father's embrace. "I've messed up. I don't want to die. Please don't let me die."

"Hey, hey. Breathe. You're not alone in this, Theo." Carl's

voice softened. "You've been led astray, but that's not who you are."

"But I … I think I'm a bad person," Theo whispered.

"No, you're not. You're a good person. You're just lost. But you still have time." Carl's hand rested on Theo's shoulder.

Theo shook his head, his chest tight. "I just wanted to be normal. I never asked for any of this."

"You're not normal, son, you're you. And there's nothing wrong with that," Carl said. The floor rumbled, dust falling from the ceiling. "Listen, we don't have much time. Do you really think that thing up there is the tumour?" Theo thought for a moment, then shook his head. "No, it's something worse, much worse. But don't let that intimidate you. What have I always taught you?"

"Never use a Ouija board?"

"Not that!"

"Erm … never criticize Mom's cooking?"

"Try again."

"I-I don't know—"

"From the horror movies we used to watch, remember?"

Theo paused in confusion.

"Never run away from your fears. Face your monsters."

"I don't know how," Theo choked out, his voice desperate.

Carl's smile was warm. "By being the badass you are. Do it for me. Do it for you. You're a Gray. You're my son. My beautiful boy."

"What would you do, Dad?"

"Doesn't matter what I would do, you're not me, you're you, so be you, son."

"But-but I'm not strong like you, I'm not like you," Theo said with a deflated sigh.

Carl chuckled a little. "No, you're better than me. *Be* better than me, Theo. Do better." A soft, encouraging hand patted Theo on his back, lifting his hopes and spirits.

"I-I will try."

Carl ruffled the boy's hair and took a sip of his beer.

The room shook again. Carl turned away, his voice soft. "I'll always love you, Theo. Remember, you are not alone."

And then the TV glow brightened, the light harsh and searing, pulling Theo back into darkness.

The pressure on Theo's neck was crushing. Frank's distorted face loomed above him, a grotesque version of the monster from his nightmares. The giant, horrific form was unrecognizable—its teeth gleamed like jagged needles, its eyes empty black pits.

The voices within hissed.

"This is it!"

Theo gasped for breath, trapped. But then, his father's words rang in his head, *'You are not alone.'*

Realization hit. His sickness wasn't just a curse—it was a strength, a key. The doors to his mind creaked open. He could feel it. He wasn't alone.

With a deep breath, Theo focused. He wasn't just one. He was many. The doors exploded open, revealing countless versions of himself. The fractured selves—each with their own minds, their own will, and their shared hatred for Frank, who was vastly outnumbered.

"Franky!" one called.

"Frank!" hummed another.

"Franky boy!"

"Spanky!"

"Frank!"

"Frank!" they shouted in unison, a chorus of voices.

"We're not alone, Frank. You are," Theo snarled as the others charged.

Weapons materialized: swords, maces, guns, flame throwers—anything they could think of to destroy the parasite.

Frank roared, his massive form shifting, contorting, spitting out claws, tentacles, and jaws. But it was no use. The army of Theos swarmed, slashing, stabbing, and tearing through Frank's enormous, monstrous body. Tentacles were severed, claws were broken, and Frank's grotesque form splintered and dissolved only to regenerate—repeatedly. He zapped multiple Theos with RED sizzling lightning.

But the Theos didn't stop. They kept pushing forward, fighting in waves, relentless in their assault, as Frank screamed in frustration.

And then, finally, with a blinding flash of light, everything went white.

Theo woke up, the glow of the bulb above blinding him as he came to. There was a metallic, coppery taste in his mouth as he tried to rise, like Frankenstein's monster. His head felt tighter, the skin anyway, and his head lighter. He lifted a hand to touch his bruised scalp and felt a bandage wrapped tightly around his temple. Was he alive?

"The surgery was a complete success, despite the poor operating conditions and limitations," Doctor Locke said. He shook his leg to reveal that he was still chained up.

"It-it was?"

"Yes, take a look over there." Locke pointed to a fleshy RED mass on the wet floor.

Theo recoiled. "Wha-what's that?"

"Your tumour, Mr Gray."

Theo shook with emotion and disgust, resisting the urge to vomit. "That thing was in my head?"

"Indeed, and it seems like you have suffered no brain damage. Your head will be sore and tender for a good few weeks but, apart from that, you should be fine. My work is done."

"Thank-thank you."

Holding a bottle of pills in his hand, no doubt from his surgical bag, the doctor rattled them, placing them into Theo's sweating hand. "Take two of these a day for the next ten days to help ward off any degree of serious infection."

"Will do."

Locke then presented his cuffed ankle still linked to the railing. "Now, if you would be so kind."

Theo lifted himself upright and stood uneasily on his feet.

Taking a moment, he wobbled, reloading his coordination, then managed to uneasily walk across the room slowly to retrieve the keys, gun, and Wormwood folder.

Locke caressed the pink lines created by the cuffs on his ankle as he was unchained from them. "That's better. Can I go now?"

Theo paused in slight dizziness. "Go on, get out of here."

The doctor went to grasp the folder, but Theo pulled it back. "I'll be keeping hold of this though, for security reasons, in case you ever feel the need to report me."

"Mr Gray, they will come for you if you keep that, believe me. Please, just give me the files, and we can forget this ever happened."

Unsure whether to trust the man or not, Theo finally handed over the thick folder, believing the doctor would honour his word.

"Aren't you afraid that I will tell my … friends about this?" Locke asked.

"No, I don't think you will. Something tells me they won't be too pleased with you if they found out. Don't think you're the type to risk his own skin for the sake of having me killed, a little nobody."

"I'll give you this, you've got gumption."

"Thank you. Goodbye, Doctor Locke."

And with that, Doctor Locke escaped, running down the road, away from the young man whose life he had just saved, leaving Theo alone.

Looking down at the tumour, Theo wondered, *Is that Frank? Was that him all along?* The uncertainty made him shiver until he concluded that it must be. That mound pressing on his brain, making him see things that he otherwise wouldn't be seeing. Yes, Frank was the tumour, he concluded. He marched unsteadily towards it to stomp on it again and again.

He looked at the car waiting for him and coughed up a laugh as he left the warehouse with his gun, pausing to gaze up into the star-filled sky. It was all his for the taking now. His future. What he chose to do with that future, however, was entirely up to him …

CHAPTER TWENTY-EIGHT
THE LOST CHILD

The gang sat in silence in the cramped taxi, rethinking their next move. They had no idea where Theo would strike next.

Back in the alley, after helping the pizza boy and cop, Steve, Amber, and JJ had met up with Tabitha, Chen, and Ishaan just as an ambulance arrived. The friends had played dumb in their statements to the police, pretending they had no idea who was responsible. Then they overheard a policeman get a description over his radio: "An American Caucasian, blond hair, blue eyes." Theo. He'd kidnapped Doctor Locke and stolen a police car.

Steve leaned his head against the window, his breath fogging the glass. The city sped by, the glowing billboards flashing, showing a news report. They all squinted at the teletext below, catching the description: "Highly dangerous." A sketch of Theo flashed on screen, followed by a reporter standing beside the pizza boy and the injured cop.

Steve felt the weight of it. Society loves a villain. Theo was becoming that villain, and Steve couldn't help but sympathize. Theo was just a guy who'd been broken by life, just like all of them. The world made Theo, and now it would punish him for it.

Amber, knees bouncing, spoke first. "We should've seen this coming. We've failed him."

"We can't save him from himself," Tabitha said.

"We can't just wait for the police to catch him," Ishaan added, his voice trembling.

"We need to find him," JJ said, leaning forward. "We can't let him hurt anyone else."

Steve nodded. "We need to get him help. The right kind of

help."

JJ snorted. "People don't change, Steve."

"They can," Steve said, his voice firm.

"No," JJ murmured. "It's not a choice. He's sick. He's insane."

Tabitha frowned. "He's diseased?"

JJ nodded, grim. "He's been twisted by something inside him—he's dangerous."

The tension thickened. Steve met JJ's eyes, his voice softer now. "He has a tumour. It's messing with his head."

JJ's eyes flared. "No, Steve. He's playing us all. He's using us."

"Stop," Amber whispered, looking between them. "We can't just let him go down this path."

"I love him," JJ said, his voice breaking. "But he needs to be stopped before it's too late."

Steve's chest tightened, his thoughts churning. JJ was right, in a way. Theo was sick, but there was still a part of him that could be saved. They had to try.

Meanwhile, Theo raced back to the apartment, gripping the wheel. His palms were slick with sweat. His phone was gone, but he hoped his friends might still trust him. He just had to lie low, keep cool.

As he entered the building, he spotted the little boy, Will, whom he'd briefly met by the pool the day before. Theo smiled at him and the boy smiled back.

A TV in the lobby flashed the news: Theo Gray, wanted for kidnapping and assault. Theo's heart skipped. Will's face fell. Theo saw the panic in the boy's eyes. Theo lifted a finger to his lips, shushing him. Will nodded, as if understanding.

Theo stepped into the elevator, grateful for the boy's silence. But as the doors closed, he felt the weight of the world pressing down.

Doctor Locke stood at a payphone, his heart racing.

The phone rang, and a cold, female voice answered. "Explain yourself, Doctor Locke."

Locke hesitated. "The boy is a threat. He knows about Wormwood."

A long silence followed. "He must be eliminated. Do you know where he is?"

Locke paused, then nodded. "He'll be with his friends."

"Very well," the voice said. "We'll take care of it. And you, Doctor Locke? We'll send a car for you. Wait for our call."

The line went dead, and Locke slammed the receiver down, the weight of his choices sinking in. He was trapped, just like Theo. He'd worked miracles, but now he was a pawn, scared to make the wrong move. Just like everyone else in this mess, he was expendable.

Theo took a deep breath as he entered the apartment, his mind spinning with fear and uncertainty. He had to survive this. He couldn't let his past, or the tumour, or the world's expectations define him. Not yet. Not when there was still a chance to make things right.

CHAPTER TWENTY-NINE
BEAUTIFUL BOY

Theo sat at the kitchen stool, his thoughts racing. The weight of everything—his past mistakes, the darkness he'd carried—pressed down on him. He was almost there. Almost free.

He felt the ticking beat in his pocket from his father's watch. "Enough," he commanded himself, going to his bedroom to fetch his laptop. He sat down on a stool in the kitchen, opened it, and began typing, feeling a need to fill the time with something productive, something he could lose himself in. His work. The secret project he had been preparing.

Collecting the images he had downloaded from the trip on his camera, as well as old photos he had found, Theo began editing and compiling them into a folder. A folder called 'A LIFE.'

Theo looked through the old and new photos of himself with his friends and his parents. He was happy with his collection, his work. Maybe this was something he could show the gang to remind them of their friendship.

"Think I could use a touch of redemption," Theo whispered.

Theo pulled up his email account and sent the folder to each of them in a group message. Holding his finger over the button, Theo paused, feeling the tingle of something else at play. He felt fulfilled, and for no reason he could necessarily tell. Maybe they would see it before him; perhaps it would soften the blow. Either way, it had been sent. He could do no more and no less.

The hairs on the back of his neck stood up as a sharp wail pierced the silence, reverberating off the walls, the off-note trumpet sound making Theo's heart race.

He spun around, and there it was—Frank.

The Hollow Man. Frank.

The figure staggered toward him, his body contorting as if stitched together from rotting flesh. His eyes glowed a sickly red, his teeth clenched, and his voice was guttural. "You can't be rid of me. I'm not going anywhere."

An eerie calm washed over him. Theo could see Frank for what he was: a desperate, sad vulture.

"That's you, isn't it?" Theo said. "It's always been you."

Clearly, Frank wasn't the tumour. Theo felt he should be more curious about what Frank was specifically, but, truly, honestly, he didn't care. He was bored with the gimmicks, the bravado, the performance, the overall act. Theo no longer cared what Frank was; he didn't matter anymore.

"You can't be rid of me. I'm not going anywhere!" Frank roared, catching Theo with a sharp, back-handed slap. He fell to the floor, his cheek stinging.

Frank seemed to stretch, moving once more. He gazed down on the boy with disgust. "Look at you. Pathetic. You're so weak."

"I'm not weak," Theo muttered, trying to pick himself up.

Frank waved his hand, hitting him again. "Coulda' fooled me."

Theo began to laugh. "You don't get it, do you?"

"I get that you're a pathetic shell of what you were, and what you were meant to be. But don't worry, kid, soon you'll be just a faded memory, and I will be the Theo Gray the world remembers."

Theo nodded, understanding. "No, you're just a weak coward. And that won't be the Theo Gray the world remembers."

"So, what's the plan then? Ya gonna talk me to death?"

"I'm not afraid, not anymore, but you are."

Frank's face pixelated slightly before restoring itself. "Ha, kid, listen to yourself, you're not making any sense."

"Nothing makes sense until it does."

"You think you're strong because you've filled that nasty little hole inside of you with love? With friendship? Hope? Well, you haven't, you've been fooling yourself. I'm what's inside you, I will always be what's inside you!"

"Maybe, but I can live with that. And for the record, the love

I have for my friends, my mom, my … dad. That is real, and you can never take that away from me."

Frank sneered. "We'll see about that—" He leaped across the room towards Theo, but Theo remained unfazed. He lifted his hand to push back his nemesis, holding his demon with sheer will.

"You are a part of me, Frank, that's true. But you have no power over me, not anymore. I see you for what you are, my worst self, my dark side, and I reject you. Goodbye, Frank."

Frank's form began to disintegrate, his body unravelling like a frayed thread. His face twisted in disbelief. "No …" he whispered, as if to himself, fading into nothing. "But … I don't want to go …"

With a final, desperate wail, Frank shattered into dust, carried away by the wind through the open balcony doors where he had stood.

Theo exhaled deeply, feeling the weight of the moment lift from him. He was free.

But then, in the distance, he heard the faintest sound—a hum, then a sharp crack.

A searing pain exploded in his chest.

Theo gasped, looking down in shock as blood soaked through his shirt. His hand instinctively reached for the wound, but it was too late. The bullet had pierced him cleanly.

"Shit, Locke," he muttered, feeling his legs go weak beneath him. The room spun, his breath shallow and ragged.

His friends burst into the room, their faces a mix of relief and anger as they saw him stagger.

"Theo!" Steve shouted, his voice cracking with both joy and terror. "You—are you—"

But before Steve could finish, Theo dropped to his knees, a pained laugh escaping his lips. "I … I think I fixed myself … no more tumour. No more voices."

His vision blurred. He was fading, and there was no fight left in him.

"Stay with us, Theo! Please!" Steve shouted, rushing to him.

But Theo barely heard him now, his hand clutching at the

wound as blood pooled beneath him. His breath came in shallow gasps.

"I'm okay," Theo whispered, his voice barely a breath. "I'm okay … I've found peace."

His hand trembled as it reached into his pocket. He pulled out the fob watch and handed it to Steve, his smile faint but genuine. "I—didn't get the ending I thought I would, but … it's okay."

Steve's eyes filled with terror as he gripped the watch. "Theo, don't—please—"

Theo's lips moved, but the words were fading. "I spent so long fighting to stay alive … but I forgot why I was fighting." His chest heaved, his life slipping away in front of his friends. "It's bigger than us … always was."

Steve shook him, desperate. "Theo, please, don't leave us. Stay with us!"

Theo's gaze softened as he looked up at his friends. He could see them, really see them, and despite everything, he was at peace. "I'm sorry … for everything," he whispered, tears streaking down his face. "But … I'm glad I had the chance to know you. I'm glad you're here with me."

JJ knelt beside him, holding his hand. "We know, Theo. It's okay."

His vision grew dimmer, his grip weakening. "You're gonna be okay. All of you … you'll be okay." His last breath rattled through his chest, a peaceful sigh escaping him.

Theo closed his eyes, accepting the inevitable. Life had its winners and losers. He'd played, he'd lost, and now he could rest. Deep in his heart, he knew his friends would be okay, and his mother would be too. That thought brought him peace. He had never liked bedtime—his mind had always been too restless—but now, at the end, he welcomed the quiet.

Through the pain, there was a final kindness: memories. His life flashed before him—laughter, love, the joy of being with his friends, his family. He smiled, feeling a profound sense of happiness, as if reliving it all again, only the good parts.

"Theo." The voices of his loved ones called to him, distant

yet familiar, as if from the future.

His mother's voice echoed in his mind. "Theo, make good choices. Be a good boy."

The ticking of the watch slowed, and Theo's spirit lightened. He drifted into a calm, BLUE tranquillity. Then, in the mist, he saw where he truly belonged: a child again, sitting beside his father, Carl Gray, who ruffled his hair with pride.

"My beautiful boy."

The nightmares were finally over.

Theo whispered, "I'm home," and allowed himself to drift into peaceful sleep, knowing he was free at last.

Steve's voice cracked as he cried out, shaking his best friend. "Theo! Don't go! Stay with us!"

But Theo was already gone, his body going limp in Steve's arms.

As his spirit left his body, a profound silence filled the room.

The fob watch in Steve's hand, ticking, was the only noise in the whole room.

CHAPTER THIRTY

HE WHO KNEW TOO MUCH

Two Weeks Later

Theo's grave lay beside his father's, the marker reading: 'Theo Gray—friend and son—taken too soon.'

The rain fell hard, as if the sky itself mourned the loss, and the wind blew from the east, a sharp, mournful gust. Those gathered stood in their finest attire, umbrellas dripping in rhythm with the steady flow of tears. The priest's voice echoed in the air, soft but steady, as heads bowed in sorrow. To the side, Theo's photo sat in a sea of flowers, picked by his aunt, each petal a silent tribute. Amber and Tabitha squeezed hands, their bracelets clinking quietly as the coffin was lowered into the ground.

JJ stood stiff, a quiet rage brewing beneath the grief. He felt empty, as if part of him were dying with Theo. The anger he couldn't voice twisted in his chest, the loss of his friend, and the frustration of having no one to direct it towards.

Steve stood beside him, fighting the suffocating sadness that weighed him down. Theo never deserved what happened, never deserved to die the way he did. The world was cruel, full of violence and greed, and lately the darkness had once more taken hold of Steve. The depressive thoughts returned, just like before, and the whisper of ending it all lingered at the edge of his mind. But then he remembered Theo's words: 'Feed the Good Wolf.'

He clutched the pendant around his neck, a small spark of clarity igniting inside him. For Theo, he would carry on. He would find his way back to the light, just as Theo had taught him. As the last words of the priest rang out, a sunbeam broke through the clouds, shining down on Theo's grave—a moment of peace amid the storm.

"Ashes to ashes, dust to dust."

Minutes later, after the crowd had begun to disperse, Julie Gray made her rounds of thanks, accepting condolences with a sad smile. As she approached the group, Steve called out softly, not wanting to startle her.

"Mrs. Gray," he said gently.

She looked up, her face a mixture of grief and strength. "Oh, hello," she replied, trying to smile through the tears.

"How … how are you holding up?" Tabitha asked, her voice a little tight.

"Better," Julie answered, but the effort was apparent. "It feels like a bad dream. First Carl, now Theo …" She broke down, her voice faltering. "I don't know what to do without him."

Amber gently wrapped her arm around her, offering comfort. "I'm so sorry," she whispered, handing her a tissue.

Julie dabbed her eyes and blew her nose, her sadness deepening. "He didn't tell me. He kept it all inside, and now …" Her voice cracked. "Why didn't he tell me?"

JJ spoke up softly. "He didn't tell any of us."

Julie sniffed and nodded. "I just wish he had. He deserved more time … he deserved better." She broke down again, her shoulders shaking with the weight of it all. "That damn tumour had to go kill him."

Steve frowned in confusion. "Tumour?" he muttered, caught off guard by the mention. He'd forgotten they had all agreed to tell the lie—that the tumour had killed Theo, not the real cause. JJ shot Steve a look, a sharp, warning glance, but Steve nodded quietly. "Yes, the tumour," he echoed.

Julie wiped her eyes, her grief not diminished by the lie. "I've been getting so many calls from reporters," she continued, her voice rising with frustration. "It's awful. How can they be so callous?"

"They're vultures," Steve muttered, anger flaring in him again.

Ishaan, trying to change the subject, nervously asked, "D-did Theo, by any chance, send you that project he worked on while he was a-away?"

Julie looked confused. "What project?"

"The one with his photos," Steve said, trying to jog her memory. "He collected them over the years … called it 'MY LIFE.'"

Julie's eyes softened at the memory. "He loved photography. I remember the first camera Carl and I bought him. He never stopped taking pictures."

"I'll send it to you," Ishaan promised, pulling out his phone.

Julie smiled faintly, her sadness lifting just slightly. "Thank you. Theo cared about all of you so much," she said quietly, looking over the group with a deep, aching love for her son. "Take care of yourselves."

The group nodded solemnly, watching as Julie walked toward her sister's car, the photo of Theo still fresh in her mind. As she got in, she began flicking through the images on her phone, each one another piece of her son, capturing the moments he had left behind.

Back at home, JJ slammed the door shut behind him. His suit was soaked, his hair damp and wild. He stood for a moment, staring at the photo of his mother, beside which now sat a picture of Theo. He picked them both up, pressing a kiss to their frames before setting them down gently. The house was empty, silent—no note, no sign of his father. JJ had been prepared for a confrontation, but his father had left, taking nothing but his shame. JJ wasn't sure if he hated him more for leaving or for how little it hurt.

As he walked deeper into the house, his eyes landed on a stack of magazines, and he smiled at the sight of the *Decanten Times*—there was a man with highlights in his quiff. An idea began to form. *Time for a change*, he thought, flipping through the pages. He grabbed his phone and selected Tabitha's number.

When she picked up, he asked, "What are you doing later?"

Hours later, JJ stood before the mirror, turning his head to admire the streaks of ruby red now in his hair. "Damn, Tabz, you're a genius."

She smiled proudly. "Yeah, well, you sure made a good canvas."

"Red was Theo's idea," JJ said, a grin tugging at his lips. "He always said red was my colour."

Later, in the familiar booth at Deeny's Diner, the group sat in a quiet circle. The jukebox hummed softly, the mood sombre but at ease now that they were together. Steve had arranged this gathering in the group chat, a chance to drink, eat, and remember Theo.

"To Theo," JJ toasted, his glass raised high.

"To Theo," they all echoed, clinking their glasses together. The burn of the alcohol filled Steve's throat, but he barely noticed.

"Whoa, that stuff burns," he gasped, coughing.

"Burns good," JJ replied, a grin playing at the corner of his lips.

Steve eyed his new look. "Your hair … it's a statement."

JJ chuckled. "Theo would've loved it."

Steve turned. "Yes! Was gonna say … I love it!"

"It has a certain … flare," Steve continued, as if an art critic, studying a piece. "Very you. It completes your unique look."

Amber caught sight of Steve, looking rather glum suddenly. "What's wrong?" she asked, across the table.

"Huh?" Steve looked up, fiddling with his pendant. "Oh, nothing."

JJ tutted. "Either say what's wrinkling your ball sack or quit pouting. It's not a good look on you."

"It's just, doesn't it bother you, the sniper? Like why? Who would wanna kill Theo?"

"Shut up!" JJ snapped, holding his hand over Steve's mouth as the others looked around to see if anyone had noticed.

"Yeah, you wanna get us killed or something?" Tabitha whispered urgently.

Steve pushed JJ off. "I'm just asking."

Tabitha stiffened. "We said we'd never bring this up again.

Remember, we all agreed."

"Asking that kinda shit gets you killed," JJ pointed out.

Steve shrugged. "Well, it was obviously something to do with Locke."

JJ leaned in. "Doesn't matter, trust me."

Steve's forehead creased. "What do you mean?"

"Locke told me himself; he had powerful friends. Clearly, Theo pissed them off doing what he did or … whatever."

Steve felt flustered. "But don't you think he deserves justice?"

"Course I do," JJ said. "Don't you think I, of all people, would get it for him if I thought it was possible?"

Steve reclined in his seat, fiddling with his pendant.

Lowering his defensive stance, JJ added, "Listen, there are some people you just don't go after. Just drop it. Theo died from the tumour, and that's all we ever say."

"To who? The press?" Amber asked.

"To anyone. Just stick to the story, don't ruffle any feathers."

"Let's talk about something else," Amber said.

The conversation shifted to plans for the future. Ishaan had news: he might be leaving for Decanten City for a job with his now girlfriend, Chen. Tabitha was considering starting her own business. Amber, in her usual style, dropped a bombshell—she was heading to South Africa for nine months to work at an animal sanctuary.

"We'll miss you, Ambz," JJ said softly.

Steve was quiet, thinking about how much had changed and how fast. Then the television caught his eye, and he turned to see the news story about Theo's funeral. The voice of the reporter filled the room, detailing Theo's tragic end, glossing over the truth in favour of a safer, sanitized narrative.

"That's it?" JJ said bitterly. "He gets thirty seconds?"

Steve watched, his mind swirling with anger and disbelief. "That's more than any of us will ever get."

The group fell into silence, their thoughts heavy, and then Amber said softly, "I hope Mrs. Gray finds some peace in the pictures."

Steve nodded, his fingers curling around the pendant he still wore. "I hope she can do something with them. He deserves to be remembered."

As the night wore on, the conversation drifted from one topic to the next, and the feeling of finality began to settle in. Amber was leaving. Ishaan was moving. Tabitha had her future ahead of her. And Steve?

He didn't know. He hadn't figured it out yet.

Later, as the group said their goodbyes, Steve watched them walk away, each heading toward their separate futures. There was a quiet moment of tension when he turned to Amber, feeling something unspoken between them. He wanted to say something, tried to tell her how he felt. But when he opened his mouth, the words just didn't come.

He watched her leave, his chest heavy with what he couldn't express. *Maybe next time*, he thought, *maybe next time.*

JJ was the last to leave, walking past Steve, who quickly followed.

"Hey, J!" Steve called.

"What's up?"

"I was wondering what's next. Maybe we could team up?"

JJ hesitated. "I'm leaving too."

"Where to?"

"Decanten City."

"Oh, well, good for you," Steve said, sensing JJ's mood shift.

"I didn't say anything back at the diner because I don't want anyone to make a big deal of it."

"I get it. Seems like everyone's leaving."

"I just need a fresh start."

Steve smiled. "Just don't waste it. What's your plan?"

"Not sure yet. Maybe knock some things off my list." JJ winked.

"That's not enough. You need purpose."

"I think I already found it."

"Not revenge. That's petty."

"Maybe it's what I need."

"You'll find your purpose," Steve said, patting his back. "I believe in you."

"Thanks."

"And you? What will you do?" JJ asked.

"Write my own story. Maybe others?"

"Well, I hope you find what you're looking for."

Steve smiled, moved. "You too."

They hugged, JJ's chest pushing Steve's pendant against him.

"Be good," Steve said, his voice thick with emotion.

"Always."

As JJ walked away, thunder rumbled. He was ready.

As Steve walked home alone into the cool night air, a thought lingered in his mind. He turned his gaze down, seeing a single daisy growing on the sidewalk—a small, unexpected sign. He smiled, taking it as a reminder that it wasn't over, not yet.

He turned around, running as fast as he could. Through endless roads, to her.

"Amber!" he called, running after her.

She stopped, turning in surprise. "Steve? What's wrong?"

"Nothing," he panted, standing in front of her, heart pounding. "I just—" He hesitated. For a moment, everything else faded into the background. It was just the two of them, standing in the rain.

Without another word, he pulled her close and kissed her.

The world shifted. Time slowed. Her lips were warm against his, and for a moment, the weight of everything else—of Theo, of the loss, of the confusion—seemed to melt away.

When they broke apart, their breaths mingling, Steve whispered, "I just wanted you to know. Before you go."

She smiled softly, holding him for a second longer. Then, with a final kiss, she turned and walked away, leaving Steve standing in the rain, wondering what would come next.

Steve didn't know if it was the beginning of something new or just another goodbye. But as he stood there, watching Amber disappear into the distance, the night felt less lonely.

Maybe, just maybe, he would find his way.

CHAPTER THIRTY-ONE

ONE OF A KIND

Three Years Later

Julie Gray had always understood how cruel time could be. The years had left their marks—wrinkles, grey roots, liver spots—but she didn't feel old. In fact, she had never felt better. The fortune she'd made from selling her memoir of *Theo Gray: Tumour Patient* had made her very rich and opened doors to amazing networks. She'd even heard whispers of a movie in the works. It was all for Theo, she told herself. He would have wanted her to be happy—and rich. Of course, he would.

Tonight, she wandered through the art gallery, hosting Theo's final exhibition. 'MY LIFE,' his masterpiece, his legacy. His photographs, each one an intimate snapshot of a boy too misunderstood, too tragic, and too extraordinary. The media had swarmed, eager to get a glimpse of the young man who had captivated the world. The walls were lined with his memories, some framed, some displayed behind glass—his toys, his comic books, his camera, even the apple tree his father had planted in his room.

Julie scanned the room, a smile touching her lips as she greeted guests. She spotted two new arrivals—Tabitha and Amber—entering through the glass doors. Tabitha wore a purple satin dress and a fur jacket, her braids artfully pinned up, while Amber shimmered in a scarlet dress. Amber grabbed a glass of champagne from a passing waiter.

"No champagne for you?" Amber asked, eyeing Tabitha's empty hand.

Tabitha paused, mouth full of canapés. "New diet," she said, swallowing.

Amber raised an eyebrow. "You're glowing. I'd say someone's pregnant."

Tabitha laughed, though a hint of surprise lingered. "Okay, Sherlock, you got me. Just seven weeks along. You and Jerome are the only ones who know, so don't tell my mom. She'll be insufferable."

Amber chuckled. "Your secret's safe with me."

Tabitha's gaze lingered on her bracelet. "Funny. I just remembered … you remember Mistress Solara from L.A?"

Amber smirked. "Yeah, I remember her saying my life would be full of great romance."

Tabitha's voice trailed off. "She said I'd be a mother … but I can't remember the rest."

"Strange how that fades," Amber mused. "Do you think we're just getting old?"

Tabitha shrugged. "Probably."

Just then, a man in a sharp-looking designer suit and sporting a dark beard approached.

"Steve!" Amber exclaimed.

"In the flesh," he replied, grinning as he pulled them both into a hug.

"You look amazing!" Tabitha said, laughing.

Steve waved it off. "Thanks, you two look incredible too. So, where's JJ and Ishaan?"

"Ishaan couldn't make it—work stuff," Amber explained. "JJ … who knows?"

"Same here," Steve said, grabbing a glass of champagne.

They spent the next few minutes catching up. Tabitha proudly mentioned her boutique, and Steve congratulated her on its success. Amber spoke of her travels to Africa with Komari Sebs, prompting Steve to get excited. "Komari Sebs! That's amazing."

The conversation turned awkward when they found themselves alone. Steve and Amber hadn't spoken, not since that one night, that one kiss.

"So … how's life been?" Steve asked, glancing at the art.

"Good," Amber replied, though the weight of the unspoken words lingered between them. "Theo's exhibition is amazing, though I feel a little out of place here."

Steve smirked. "Because you're the most stunning piece in the room?"

Amber blushed, running a hand through her hair. Then, she revealed a new diamond ring. "Laurence got it for me."

Steve froze. "Laurence?"

"My fiancé," she said, keeping her voice soft.

Steve's smile faltered. "Oh … congratulations."

Amber noticed his expression but smiled through it. "Thanks. To be honest, I thought Tabz would have noticed first."

Across the room, Tabitha was still arguing with a waiter over canapés. Steve winced. "I think she has other things on her mind."

"What about you? Surely you have … someone." Amber asked, drawing his attention back to her.

"No, not me. Lone wolf."

"Surely not."

"Yup. So busy writing and editing now, liaising with my agent, that I kinda forget about all that stuff. I just focus on my book."

"Well, maybe you should try writing your own story."

Downing his glass, Steve placed it on a tray. "Maybe."

"Ah, so Mr. Fancy author, what's the next book about?"

"Oh, you know, same old recycled stuff in a different format about the age-old story of good versus evil, oh, and does the guy get the girl?"

"Ooh! Tell me who wins, good or evil?"

"Oh good, of course, I like to inspire people to feed the good wolf." He held up his necklace.

"And does he?" Amber asked hesitantly. "Does the boy get the girl, I mean? In your story?"

Leaning in, Steve whispered, "No. But, you know, that's okay. Sometimes that's just not how the story goes."

"Fair enough," Amber said, her eyes drifting back to the photos on the wall. "What do you think of all this?"

"It's perfect. Theo finally gets his moment," Steve said. He paused. "It's just a shame he couldn't be here to see it."

Amber nodded quietly. "Yeah."

Steve turned to her. "But maybe he did. Maybe in some way, this is exactly what he wanted—to be remembered, to be seen for who he truly was."

"Yeah," Amber said, smiling faintly. "So, I guess he got his happy ending, after all."

Steve met her gaze. "Seems that way … but not all of us get that, do we?"

Amber's smile wavered. She knew where Steve was coming from. Her own heart pulled in different directions. "No, I suppose not."

Steve took a long breath, then turned back to the photos, watching as they flickered between memories—happy, painful, frozen in time. Theo had lived, truly lived. And in the end, that was enough.

They stood there, side by side, as the crowd mingled around them. Amber noticed the old newspaper article on the wall, the one from the night of Theo's death. It painted him as a villain—a destroyer—but that wasn't Theo. He was a builder. He had built a life, a story, and left behind pieces of it for the world to see.

"You know," Steve said quietly, tapping his glass, "in a way, I think Theo did what he came here to do. His story … it triggered something in all of us. It helped us become who we were meant to be."

Amber held back a tear, her voice thick with emotion. "I like that."

Steve smiled, his heart swelling with quiet pride. "Here's to Theo Gray. One of the greatest men I'll ever know."

Amber nodded, her eyes glistening. "Here's to him."

"And here's to you," Steve said, looking down at his wolf necklace.

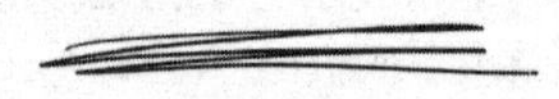

Steve stood beside Amber. Though she was in love with another man, Steve knew that the world was big enough for both to find what they needed. And as for him? He was content. He had friends, purpose, and the truth that time, for all its cruelty, was something that could still be filled with meaning.

EPILOGUE

A NEW FRIEND

The London apartment was quiet. Fresh blood stained the white kitchen floor. A small shadow loomed over two bodies, two parents, their throats slit from ear to ear. Their skin was devoid of colour as their life spilled out. The murderer quivered, a small boy, holding a bloodied knife. Sinking to his knees, the boy, who, according to his soccer shirt, was called 'Will,' felt scared yet free. He was unsure of what came over him, a rage he had never quite felt before, so powerful that he had managed to overpower and kill his parents swiftly.

Weeping with regret, with no one to turn to, he dropped the blade. Through the dark doorway ahead, a RED soccer ball rolled over to Will, who looked up in confusion. In hypnotic wonder, he picked it up, wiping away his tears, to see who had sent it his way. A pair of glowing, cat-like, emerald eyes emerged. Will jumped back a little before an ageless, young-looking boy appeared, a pale, grinning, dark-haired imp, with a name labelled across his colourful dungarees: 'Frank.' He seemed pleasantly surprised by the dead bodies in front of him, as if they were gifts. Nightmares, much like him, wrapped in pretty bows. Slowly, he crept toward the whimpering boy with a kind, nurturing smile as he lifted a cold, skeletal finger to wipe away a spot of blood from his cheek. Will looked deep into the intruder's dark, soulless gaze, at ease suddenly, as he felt a wave of comfort, like a paralyzing snake's venom.

"Now what should I do with you?" Frank asked his new best friend, giggling.

Acknowledgments

Thank you to my amazing Agent Erik McManus and my publishers/editors Tina Beier and Alexandria Brown who all had faith in this story and me.

Also many thanks to the amazing art work of Tiffany Baxter and Kaitlin Thatcher.

About the Author

George Morris De'Ath is a British author who writes thriller and horror books that explore the darker aspects of the human psyche. He is a London West End playwright, actor, and model, as well as a gin drinker. He lives in London where he allows his creative flare to shine. *Something on Your Mind* is his third book.